EMPIRE'S DAUGHTER

Marian L Thorpe

Arboretum Press

Copyright © 2015 Marian L Thorpe
Fourth Edition © 2020

Arboretum Press
Guelph, ON
Canada

ALL RIGHTS RESERVED

This book contains material protected under International and Federal Copyright Laws and Treaties. Any unauthorized reprint or use of this material is prohibited. No part of this book may be reproduced or transmitted in any form or by any means, electronic or mechanical, including photocopying, recording, or by any information storage and retrieval system without express written permission from the author.

ISBN: 978-1-7771783-4-5

A catalogue record for this book is available from Libraries and Archives Canada

Cover Design by Anthony O'Brien

Cover Image: Taiga/Shutterstock
Used under License

Map by Marian L Thorpe

All quoted works are in the public domain.

In memory of my mother

Enid (Buckby) Thorpe

1919-2012

Royal Corps of Signals 1940-1945

loyal daughter of her empire

ACKNOWLEDGMENTS

Profound thanks to my editors, Amanda Barnes and Marla Wick, for showing me how to transform a draft manuscript into a novel.

Thanks to my writing friends, both those of you I've met only in cyberspace and those I've met in person, for reading, suggesting, listening, supporting.

My sister Katie Thorpe and my husband Brian Rennie accompanied me, at different times, in various and extended wanderings around England and Scotland, so necessary for the setting of this book. Their critical readings of the manuscript were invaluable.
Brian, the wet buzzard is for you.

THE CHARACTERS OF EMPIRE'S DAUGHTER

Character	Pronunciation	Allegiance	Role
Aasta	Ah-stah	Inns	Innkeeper
Alda	All-dah	Inns	Ostler
Aline	A-**leen**	Tirvan	Lena's cohort
Alis	Alice	Berge	Exile
Alister	Al-is-terr	Retirement farm	Servant
Anwyl	Ann-will	Empire	Crewmember *Skua*
Anya	Ann-yah	Karst	Council-leader
Ava	Ay-vah	Inns	Apprentice
Binne	Binn-eh	Tirvan	Fisherwoman, cohort-leader
Birel	Bir-ell	Empire	Soldier-servant
Blaine	Blayn	Empire	Traitor
Bren	Brenn	Empire	Major
Cael	Kay-ell	Leste	Soldier
Callan	Kall-ann	Empire	Emperor
Camy	Kamm-ee	Tirvan	Lena's cohort
Casse	Kass	Tirvan	Retired council-leader
Casyn	Cas-inn	Empire	General, brother to the Emperor Callan
Cate	Kate	Tirvan	Weaver
Colm	Collm	Empire	Callan's twin and advisor
Danel	**Dann**-ell	Empire	Crewmember *Skua*
Dann	Dahnn	Leste	Soldier
Darel	Dar-ell	Empire	Cadet, Turlo's son
Dari	Dahr-ee	Tirvan	Kyan's partner, cohort-leader
Daria	Dah-ree-ah	Karst	Trader
Dern	Dern	Empire	Captain of *Skua*
Dessa	Dess-ah	Tirvan	Boatbuilder, Siane's partner
Dian	Dee-**ahn**	Han	Horse warrior
Dorys	Dorr-iss	Inns	Ostler

Character	Pronunciation	Allegiance	Role
Elon	E-lonn	Leste	Deposed king
Ferhar	Ferr-harr	Empire	Crewmember *Skua*
Finn	Finn	Empire	Lieutenant
Freya	Fray-ah	Tirvan	Dessa's apprentice
Fryth	Frith	Inns	Innkeeper
Galdor	Gal-dorr	Empire	Lieutenant
Galen	Gay-lenn	Empire	Lena's father
Garth	Garth	Empire	Maya's brother
Gille	Jill	Tirvan	Council leader, herdswoman
Grainne	**Grann**-yah	Tirvan	Horsebreeder
Guilian	Julian	Empire	Lieutenant
Gwen	Gwenn	Tirvan	Lena's mother. Council leader
Halle	Hall-eh	Karst	Village woman
Hilar	Hill-arr	Karst	Winemaker
Ianthe	I-**an**-thee	Karst	Tice's sister
Ilene	I-lee-nee	Karst	Cooper
Ione	I-**own**-ee	Karst	Tice's great-aunt
Jedd	Jedd	Empire	Retired general
Joce	Joe-ss	Karst	Tice's sister
Josan	Joe-sann	Empire	Lieutenant
Karlii	Kar-lee	Ballin	Cheesemaker
Keavy	Kee-vee	Inns	Innkeeper
Kinley	Kin-lee	Karst	Tevian's son
Kira	Keer-ah	Tirvan	Lena's sister, apprentice midwife
Kirthe	Kurr-thee	Torrey	Exile
Kolmas	Kol-mass	Leste	Ship captain
Kyan	Kie-ahnn	Tirvan	Woodworker, cohort-leader
Lara	Lah-rah	Tirvan	Siane's daughter
Largen	Larr-genn	Empire	Crewmember *Skua*
Lena	Lee-na	Tirvan	Fisherwoman
Livia	Li-**vee**-ah	Inns	Innkeeper

Character	Pronunciation	Allegiance	Role
Mar	Marr	Empire	Maya and Garth's father, deceased
Mari	Mahr-ee	Inns	innkeeper
Martin	Martin	Empire	Captain
Maya	Mai – ah	Tirvan	Fisherwoman, Lena's partner
Mella	Mell-ah	Tirvan	Village woman, pregnant
Mikelle	Mick-ell	Karst	Council leader
Minna	Minnah	Tirvan	Retired potter
Nessa	Ness-ah	Tirvan	Village woman
Nevin	Nev-inn	Empire	Traitor
Pel	Pell	Tirvan	Maya's brother
Rai	Rye	Tirvan	Lena's cohort
Ranni	Rahn-nee	Tirvan	Village woman
Rasa	Rah-sah	Han	Horse warrior
Roxine	Rocks-een	Karst	Council leader
Salle	Sahl	Tirvan	Lena's cohort
Sara	Sah-rah	Tirvan	Council leader, Lena's aunt
Sari	Sah-ree	Inns	Apprentice
Sarr	Sarr	Tirvan	Village boy
Satordi	Sa-**torr**-dee	Empire	Crewmember *Skua*
Sherron	Sher-onn	Ballin	Cheesemaker
Siane	Shanna	Tirvan	Record keeper, Dessa's partner
Tali	Tah-li	Tirvan	Maya's mother, Lena's aunt
Tamar	Tam-**arr**	Karst	Tice's mother
Tevian	Tev-ee-an	Karst	Tevra's sister
Tevra	Tev-rah	Karst	Tice's ex-partner
Tice	Tie-ss	Tirvan	Potter, Lena's cohort-second
Tiernay	Teer-nay	Empire	Crewmember *Skua*
Turlo	Turr-low	Empire	General
Valle	Vahll	Karst	Tice's son
Xani	Zahnni	Tirvan	Casyn's mother,

Character	Pronunciation	Allegiance	Role
Zilda	Zill-dah	Inns	deceased Innkeeper

THE WORLD OF *EMPIRE'S DAUGHTER*

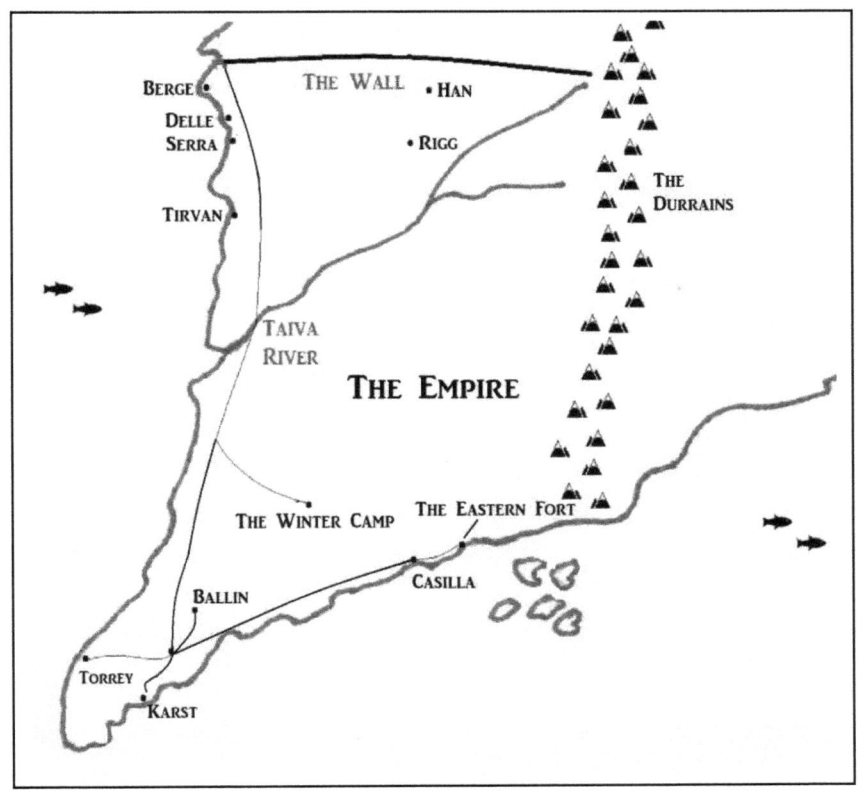

The swallows gather, summer passes,
The grapes hang dark and sweet;
Heavy are the vines,
Heavy is my heart,
Endless is the road beneath my feet.

The sun is setting, the moon is rising,
The night is long and sweet;
I am gone at dawn.
I am gone at day,
Endless is the road beneath my feet.

The cold is deeper, the winters longer,
Summer is short but sweet;
I will remember,
I'll not forget you,
Endless is the road beneath my feet.

Tice's song

PART I

I do perceive here a divided duty. Shakespeare.

CHAPTER ONE

I WAS SEVENTEEN THE SPRING Casyn came home. He rode quietly into the village late one morning, a few weeks after Festival, with his tools and a few personal possessions. I—along with my cousin and partner, Maya, and her young brother, Pel—had sailed out in the still dawn that morning to check crab traps around the south side of the rocky headland. In the warmth of the spring sun, we hauled traps, took the catch, and reset the lines.

At my insistence, we sailed a bit further along the headland, into coves we hadn't fished before, setting a few traps to see what these waters might yield. The late sun shone on a golden ocean before we moored back at the harbour, tired but with work still to do. My aunt Tali had come down to the harbour to collect fresh crab for supper. She helped us unload the catch, sort the damaged traps onto the jetty, and sluice down the deck of *Dovekie* before she mentioned the arrival.

"There'll be a meeting tonight, Lena," she said, sorting through the catch for the largest crabs.

I looked up from the trap I was examining. "A meeting? All of us?" I frowned. Only a major event would justify a full meeting outside of the usual schedule. If something minor but urgent needed attention, the council leaders—my mother, our Aunt Sara, and Gille the herdswoman—met to mediate or decide.

"What's happened?" Maya asked.

Tali stood, her basket full of crabs. "Take this, Pel, and go home. I'll be there soon." Pel, tall and strong for his six years, took the heavy basket and started up the hill to the village. Women's business held no interest for him. Tali watched him for a minute before turning back to us.

"What's happened?" Maya repeated.

"We have a prospective tenant for the forge," Tali said.

I looked at her in puzzlement. This was expected. After burying Xani, our metalworker, in the cold of last midwinter, we had heard of a young smith looking for work at Delle village, several day's ride to the north. She had just finished her apprenticeship and their forge had no place for her. We had sent a message north in the saddlebags of a returning soldier; her arrival was expected any day.

"Of course," said Maya. "What's her name?"

"Is there a problem?" I asked.

Tali grinned, her teeth white against her tanned face. "Oh, there's a problem," she said. "Our prospective new metalworker is neither from Delle, nor newly-qualified. As a guess, I'd say our new smith brings thirty years of experience—military experience. And his name is Casyn."

I stared at my aunt, my hands tightening on the crab trap. Maya gasped. All men left the villages at seven to enter the Empire's military schools, spending their adult years serving in the army. In retirement, they raised horses or grew grapes or taught in the schools, finishing out their days with whatever part of their regiment had survived. Twice a year, war and distance allowing, they came to the villages for Festival, to be provisioned, to gather food and cloth and wine, to make love and father children, to give and carry messages. Festival lasted a week, and then they left. This pattern had shaped our lives for generations. I shook my head. "But he can't."

Tali shrugged her narrow shoulders. "That's to be decided at meeting. He was born here—he's Xani's son, actually, so that may give him double claim." She bent to pick up a broken crab trap. "Are these to go to Siane? Let's get the catch into the holding pools and take these up. If we stand here talking much longer, you won't have time to clean up or eat properly before meeting, and I want to get those crabs into boiling water." We finished our work quickly, and together walked up the short hill to the village, leaving the broken traps stacked outside Siane's workshop. The traps carried *Dovekie*'s mark. Siane would notify us when she finished the repairs.

We walked in silence, tired from our long day on the water. At Tali's house, where Maya and I shared the big front room upstairs, we stopped on the porch. Maya leaned into me, her slight form light against me. Her head just reached my shoulder. I gave my partner a brief hug. "I'll see you at the baths in half an hour," I told her. "I'm going to see my mother for a few minutes."

"Don't let her feed you," Tali said. "In fact, tell her to come here to eat. We'll have more than enough crab chowder."

I turned to go.

"Lena?" Tali called after me. "If Gwen has some extra bread, we could use that at supper."

I nodded. The smell of freshly baked bread always filled my mother's house, except during the twice-yearly periods when the offspring of Festival alliances are born. My mother is the village midwife.

I stepped off the porch onto the path before I realized my hands were empty. "Maya!" I called. The shutters to our room opened. She leaned out. "Bring my towel and clothes, will you?"

She laughed. "Maybe."

I chuckled, continuing on. I probably hadn't needed to ask. As I walked up the path to my mother's house, I remembered her teaching me how to bake bread when I was eight or nine. I had kneaded the dough with all the strength in my young arms, while Maya, learning with me, did the measuring and supervised the baking. She liked order, even then, never forgetting a step.

The smell of crab rose off my hands and clothes. Daughters sometimes followed their mother's craft, or an aunt's, but just as often they chose to apprentice outside the immediate family. My choice at twelve to go to the boats had met with no argument: I belonged in the open air. When Maya had announced six months earlier that she wanted to fish as well, I hadn't been surprised. For six years, we'd done just about everything together. Breaking with usual practice, the council had let her wait so we could begin our apprenticeships together.

We'd served our five years, and this spring, we'd outfitted *Dovekie* and passed from apprentices into craftswomen. Fully adult now, part of the village council, we addressed all women as equals, could form Festival alliances and bear children, or just slip *Dovekie's* moorings some morning to sail away into adventure. All this could happen in the secure village world we had grown up in and had taken for granted would continue forever. Tali's news had shaken the foundations of my assumptions. Adult or not, I wanted my mother's counsel.

My mother's house stood in the centre of the forty houses or so that made up Tirvan village. Like most village houses, it was built of wood, two storeys high, with gabled ends. Salt air is hard on paint, so the wood of the house had been allowed to weather to a soft silvery-grey, matching the shingles of the roof. The shutters were painted blue, as was the front door, which stood open to admit the cooling breezes of late afternoon. My sister Kira, three years my junior and apprenticed to my mother, sat outside in deep conversation with a young woman. They looked up as I approached.

"Lena, you stink of crab." Kira looked like my mother, compact and curved, and liked to wear her hair up. With my darker hair and eyes and long limbs, I take after my father. Or so I'm told. His name is Galen. He serves on the northern Wall. I've never met him.

"I know. I'm on my way to the baths." I looked at the other woman. "Hello, Cate." Six months older than I, trained as a weaver by my aunt Sara, Cate had helped make *Dovekie*'s sail. Festival had concluded six weeks ago, so I suspected that she had come to confirm pregnancy. But that was for her to tell when she chose. "Is Mother inside?"

"Writing records," Kira answered. The midwives must record all alliances that result in pregnancy, so we know who our fathers are, and our brothers. Inside, the seabreeze had chased out most of the day's heat. My mother sat at her desk in the workroom, her record book open on the long pine surface. Neat lines of her writing covered half the page. She looked up, the fine lines around her blue eyes creasing in pleasure.

"Six babies to be born in the new year, all being well," she said. "How was the catch today, Lena?"

"Good. We found some new coves. Tali's making crab chowder for supper. She asked for you to come and bring bread if there is any." I paused. "Mother, what's going on? Tali says Xani's son has come to take over the forge. We won't let him, will we? Why would he want to live here and not with the men?"

Mother closed her record book, standing. "I'll come to the baths with you," she said. "I'll give you what answers I may when we've soaked out the day. Or at least this half of it. We may be in for a long night." She glanced at me. "Did you bring clean clothes? Or a towel?"

I shook my head absently. "Maya's bringing them."

Mother smiled. "She takes good care of you. Give me a moment to collect my things, and we'll go."

As we climbed up the hill, the forty or so houses that make up Tirvan, clustered together along the paths, came into full view. The village had grown according to need, with no real pattern. The oldest houses surrounded the harbour or sheltered under the hill pastures; newer houses filled the spaces between. Only the forge sat alone, halfway up the hillside, isolated to protect against fire.

At the very top of the village, hot springs bubbled out of the hillside. The very highest, the sacred one, provided us with water for the rituals of birth and fertility and death. The bracken that surrounded it sheltered small offerings brought by women asking the goddess for intervention or bringing thanks. Another group of springs fed the stream that ran down to the harbour on the far side of the village. At the lowest springs, our foremothers built the bath-house. Here, the channelled water flowed into two large pools, tiled and stepped to allow us to sit partially or completely submerged, sheltered by the walls and roof of the structure. The steaming water rushed in from the springs and out again through pipes to form a stream that then flowed west, tumbling down a cliff to the ocean. After a day on the boats or in the fields, the water—clear, sulphurous, and very hot—felt wonderful.

Maya was waiting for me, clean clothes in hand. The three of us washed quickly, settling into the hot pool to soak. I stretched my legs out, worked my sore shoulders, and sighed.

My mother repinned her knot of greying hair tighter on her head, a sure sign she was thinking out what she wished to say. "Casyn is Xani's son," she said. "He is here as an Emperor's Messenger, but part of his request was that he stay here to take over the forge, to be our metalworker. The Council told him that we alone could not make such a decision. The village must hear his reasons."

"What did he say?" Maya asked. "Was he angry?"

"Not at all. We offered him Xani's cottage to use until we make a decision. He is there now. I took him bread, cheese, and apples this afternoon." She paused. "He is a quiet man, grave, I would say. I don't remember him. The records show that Xani bore him forty-eight years ago."

"Will he be at the meeting tonight?" I asked.

"Yes, at first. He asked for that, too, when Sara and Gille and I spoke with him this morning. He said he knew there would be debate, and that he shouldn't be present for that, but he has something to say that needs to be heard by us all before we make our decision. And that, my dears, is all I can tell you." She sat up. "Enough? This has been a busy day, even with Kira taking most of the new pregnancies off my hands. I'm hungry."

Reluctantly, we dried off. Maya combed out her hair. I kept my own hair short, which was better for working on the boat, but I loved Maya's hair. Most of the time, she wore it braided and tied back. Loose, it reached past her shoulder blades. In our bedroom, later, I would brush it for her.

Walking back from the baths, we passed the forge. A roan horse grazed in the paddock, but other than smoke rising from the chimney, there was no sign of Casyn. At home, the rich smell of crab chowder greeted us. Tali put bread and salad on the table. I followed Maya up to our room. The warm evening sun brightened the braided rug on the floor and the blue of the coverlet. Maya sat on the bed. "I don't like this, Lena."

I looked at her in surprise. Maya was so practical, the organizer and record-keeper of our working partnership. I was the dreamer, the one given to mood swings and doubts. "What don't you like, love?"

"This man. Casyn. Something doesn't feel right." She shrugged. "I'm scared. I feel like I did when I was six and Garth was leaving." Garth, her older brother, following custom, had gone with the men after the Festival following his seventh birthday. Born only fifteen months apart and sharing a father, Garth and Maya looked almost like twins. We had all played together as children. I'd liked him, in the uncomplicated way of small children, but Maya had adored her brother, grieving for months when he left. Maya swore she would bear no children, and I thought this was why.

"I'm scared, too," I said slowly. I wondered if I spoke truly. I sat beside Maya, putting my arms around her. She rested her head on my shoulder. I kissed the top of her head. We sat like that for a few minutes, each lost in her own thoughts, until Tali called us for supper.

Tali had simmered the crab in milk with root vegetables and onions. Freshly churned butter filled another bowl. I spread some on the bread, eating with an appetite honed by a long day on the water. Maya ate very little. I caught my mother and Tali sharing a concerned glance. Tali shook her head, slightly. I said nothing.

After the meal, I washed the dishes while Maya made tea. We spoke only of trivial things: a cracked mug, the need for more firewood. Siane's daughter Lara arrived to stay with Pel; she was eleven, too young to attend the meeting. My mother slipped out, and a few minutes later, the bell rang, calling us to the meeting hall.

The hall sat on a slight rise on the right-hand side of the village, looking up from the harbour. Wooden, like all village buildings, the octagonal shape of the hall allowed us to sit in a circle, more or less. Whoever spoke, stood, to be easily heard by all. The three senior councillors: my mother, my aunt Sara, and Gille, sat last, never together, and always at random. The rest of us sat where we pleased.

Some meeting nights, people straggled in for a good half hour after the bell rang. Not so tonight. Word of Casyn's arrival had spread quickly. Tirvan has an adult population of about eighty, and everyone was seated not ten minutes after the last peal had faded. I looked around. Someone had lit a fire against the cool of the evening. The wood crackled loudly. The faces of the women in the room showed differing emotions: curiosity, anger, worry. I looked for my mother. She stood, speaking to Sara in soft tones. I could not see Gille.

My mother walked across the hall to sit between Siane and Dessa. Maya and I had bought *Dovekie* from Dessa, a soft spoken, level-headed boatbuilder. Sara remained standing but moved into the circle.

"Women of Tirvan." Sara's voice, never loud, commanded immediate attention. "Thank you for coming to this meeting, so promptly and on such short notice. Most of you know why we are here, of today's extraordinary arrival of Xani's son, Casyn. Most of you will have heard of his request to take over the forge, to stay in Tirvan. He would be the first man to live in a woman's village in ten generations." Sara raised her hand to quell the rising murmurs. "This in itself will need much debate. But there is more. Before we say yea or nay to Casyn, he has asked to speak to you as the Emperor's Messenger."

I glanced at my mother, but Sara had her attention. Men came, occasionally, emissaries from the Empire, to ask for more food or more trade goods, but I remembered no talk at Spring Festival, six weeks past, of new or increased trade. *If Casyn wanted to stay at Tirvan, how then could he be an Emperor's Messenger?*

"Women of Tirvan," Sara spoke again, "will we hear Casyn speak in the name of the Empire?" While we had the right to turn down such a request, in practice they were always granted, making the question essentially a formality. We voted with raised hands, unanimous in our decision to hear Casyn speak.

At once, a middle-aged man, not tall, his dark hair streaked with grey, entered from the north-facing door of the hall. Gille walked beside him. If eighty pairs of women's eyes made him uncomfortable, he did not show it. At the ring of benches, he paused, turning to Gille. She gestured him on. He strode into the centre of the circle, where he turned slowly on his heel, taking us in. His eyes met my mother's. He inclined his head to her, looked around once more, and began to speak.

"Women of Tirvan." His deep voice and measured speech conveyed a sense of authority. My mother had described him as a grave man. Now I could see why.

"I thank you for allowing me to speak. I would ask one further thing: that you hear me out. The message I bring you tonight will not be welcome, and I am afraid your first reaction will be to reject the messenger." Maya inched closer to me. I found her hand and held it briefly.

Casyn hesitated, then turned to Gille. "Forgive me," he said, "but I am unused to speaking in such an arrangement. May I join the circle, so that my back is to no one, or speak from outside it?"

"From outside the circle, I think," Sara said from her seat. "We can turn to face you." He nodded, moving past the benches; we shifted ourselves, and he continued.

"Forty-eight years ago, I was born in this village to Xani, your smith. For seven years, I played in the fields and at the harbour and called Tirvan home. And then I left, as all boys do, and learned another life. This is how things are, and have been, for many generations. For all those generations, there has been peace in the Empire, or if not peace then small wars, wars in which we have been victorious. We have policed our borders and administered our lands, with little disturbing our way of life." His eyes moved over us as he spoke. "But the world changes. In all the women's villages of the Empire, this week or next, a soldier like myself will arrive to ask to live in the village, to take up a trade." Casyn paused, for a breath, a heartbeat. "And to teach you and your daughters to fight."

No one spoke. Casyn watched us in silence. In some small part of my mind, I felt myself measured, judged; the rest of my thoughts scattered like grouse from a harrier. I gripped Maya's hand, looking up. In the firelit room, I could see my own confusion reflected on every face. *Teach us to fight?* I struggled for clarity, to make the words mean something. I heard Dessa speaking, her voice very low, and strained to hear.

"Do you know what you ask of us?"

Casyn met her eyes. "Yes," he answered. "Are not all boys taught, at our mother's knees, why we must go with the men when we turn seven? Why women's comfort and love and the laughter of our children are ours for but one brief week, twice a year? Why we live apart and die apart? You teach us first, and then the Empire yet again, to remember that decision, made two hundred years ago, to divide our lives." He spoke evenly, but with an undertone of resignation, or regret. His gaze widened to take in the room as his voice rose. "You all know the facts: At that assembly, two centuries past, after a ten-day of passionate debate, our forbearers chose Partition as the compromise, to save an empire divided. For our forefathers wanted a strong army, to war on the frontier against the northern folk, and defend against incursions from the sea. But our foremothers wished only for peace to fish and farm. And so came the assembly, and the vote, and Partition there has been for these long years." His voice softened. "For the most part, it has worked and satisfied both sides, though we both have paid a price." He fell silent.

He knows our history, I thought, *but he does not truly understand.* All those long years ago, the women's council voted for more than Partition. They voted to turn their backs on war and weapons, to make them only the province of men. Women did not fight. We learned, in our youth, enough hunting skills to protect our herd animals or add to the cooking pot. I could shoot a bow to take down a hare or a deer, and if need required, throw a spear with reasonable force and accuracy, but that was all. More went against our teachings and our skill. How could Casyn, not taught this way, and with thirty years of military life behind him, even begin to comprehend? I looked toward Gille and my mother impatiently. *Tell him,* I thought. *Tell him we cannot do this thing. Tell him to go away.*

"Why, then, do you ask this of us?"

Casyn met Dessa's gaze. "Because," he said simply, "there is need."

"What need?"

"Great need," he replied. Again, his focus seemed to widen, to encompass the room. "There is, a week's sail to the west and south, another country, Leste—an island both large and rich, warmer than our lands. You will have heard rumours and stories of this land, of their jewelled hands and green eyes, and their boats, each with a leopard's head on the prow. They may even have come here, to trade their spices and fruit for your cloth and grain. But their island grows crowded, and food is short. Trading is no longer enough. We have spies among them who report that in the autumn, just at harvest, Leste will attack us. They will first come here, to Tirvan and Delle and the other villages, to the unprotected source of food."

My mother spoke for the first time. "Could you not send part of the army to all the villages, to lie in wait?"

"We could," Casyn said. "It was, in truth, our first plan. But it would be only a stopgap at the beginning of many years of raids and counter raids. Better, we thought, to finish things once and for all. So, women of Tirvan, women of the Empire, this is what we ask of you. Learn, against your inclinations and beliefs, to fight. Defend your villages against the raiders. And while you do so, the men of the Empire will have sailed to an island depleted of its fighting force. There will be no one to mount a defence against us. We will take the island in a matter of days, and the thing will be done. The choice is yours: fight once and then go back to your peaceful way of life, or live with years of uncertainty and battle."

"Can you not defend us and still send an army to take the island?" Sara asked from the position she had taken beside Gille and my mother.

"No," Casyn said. "There are not enough of us. We cannot leave the northern wall undefended. We can leave you the veterans, and the youngest men, but in the end, they will not be enough. The men of Leste would take the villages, growing strong on our food while we grew weak and hungry in their land. Come spring, they would sail home to defeat us. I think you can imagine what they would do to you over that winter."

Above the sudden din in the room, I heard Gille calling for order. Women stood, clattering benches, speaking urgently to partners or family members. Maya called my name. I turned to her.

"We can't fight," she said. "We can't. We don't. Men fight. They must protect us. They have to. That's what was decided at the Partition assembly. We feed them; they protect us. Isn't that right, Lena?"

"Yes, love," I said slowly. I heard the fear in her voice. Maya needed order and predictability. In our business partnership, her need for stability balanced my impulsiveness. In our personal relationship, it had always cast a small shadow. I searched for words, wanting to reassure her, but knowing in my gut that our world had just changed. I pushed away something else, something I could not let Maya sense. While Casyn answered my mother's last question, I had named what churned inside me: not fear, but excitement.

I took a deep breath. "Maya," I said finally, hugging her close. "They'll protect us. That's why they want to take Leste, to subdue it and protect us. They're just asking us to help."

She pulled away from me. "No," she said, her panicked voice rising. "I won't fight. I won't, Lena."

"Hush, Maya," I said. "Gille wants to speak."

Slowly, the room quieted. Gille waited until the last murmurs died away. "Casyn," she said, her voice clear and strong, "we thank you for your honesty. I will ask you now to leave us, so we can debate this matter with no hesitancy." He bowed his head to her, glanced at my mother and Sara, and left. I heard his footsteps crunching on the path outside. A log cracked in the fire. Someone gasped. Gille waited until the sound of Casyn's steps had faded before she spoke again.

"Women of Tirvan," she said formally. "What we have been asked to do tonight is beyond easy understanding. We are being asked to put aside the decisions made by our foremothers, decisions that have shaped our lives for ten generations. We cannot do this in haste. All of us must give this much thought. We will make no decision tonight. Tomorrow morning, the council leaders will speak again with Casyn, and then we will all meet here, to debate and to decide. We will adjourn this meeting until one o'clock tomorrow. But," she added, her tone changing from formal to her normal way of speaking, "the hall will remain open tonight, as long as the firewood lasts. There is tea in the kettle. Please remember that Gwen and Sara and I know no more than you."

I wanted to talk to my mother, but I felt Maya trembling. I rose to fetch tea from the pot, adding more honey than usual. She drank it in silence, not meeting my eyes. Around us swirled voices—angry, soothing, unbelieving. I sat with my arm around her shoulders, wondering a bit at her shock. No decision had been made; we were only going to talk, to debate. We could vote no.

Eventually she spoke. "I'm going home," she said. "I know how I'll vote, and nothing will make me change my mind. Are you coming?"

"No," I said. "I want to talk to my mother. Maya, don't—"

"Don't what?" she snapped. "Don't make up my mind so soon? I know how I feel, Lena. What Casyn is asking, what the Empire is asking, is wrong. I know that, and so do you. Women don't fight. We don't kill or harm others." Her voice held conviction now, certainty.

"Except in self-defence," I reminded her. She shook her head.

"Maybe that's true, further north, near the wall," she said. "But who have we ever needed to defend ourselves against?" She pulled away from my encircling arm. "You think this is an adventure, Lena?" she said fiercely. "Something new? Something different? You always want to sail a little further, find another cove, even though the ones we know provide us with all the fish we need. But this isn't the same; we can't just sail out into this for a day or two, and then turn around and come back to our safe harbour. If we sail into this storm, Lena, we won't come out."

Tears stood in her hazel eyes. She knew me so well. I put my hand on the cloud of her black hair.

"But if we don't sail into it, Maya," I said gently, "it will find us anyway. It will batter our boats at their moorings until there is nothing left. Our safe harbour will become a prison."

CHAPTER TWO

I SLEPT LITTLE THAT NIGHT. I sat in a chair by our bedroom window, watching the moon set over the boats in the harbour. Maya lay in the bed, sleeping or pretending to. No words passed between us.

I had spoken with my mother as I walked her home from the meeting. Even in the moonlight, I could see the lines of strain around her eyes. I told her what had been said between Maya and myself.

"Maya has always looked for certainties," she said wearily. "But you know that, Lena. When Garth left, she could only find peace by putting her faith in tradition. I warned Tali that to have two so close together, and with the same man, was a mistake. But she loved Mar and didn't listen. Like her mother, Maya can be stubborn when she believes she's right. I think, in this, she is wrong." She stopped on the path to face me. "Until tomorrow, Lena, these words are for you only. I see no choice for us but to accept this."

I shivered in the night air. Somewhere an owl called. "Will the village agree?"

"In the end, I think they will." We resumed walking. "To not fight, but to passively wait for whatever happens, is the greater violation of the spirit of the Partition assembly. Tradition then would have dictated that we support the men in their empire-building."

"But we do support them," I argued. "We feed them, make saddles and stirrups, and weave cloth for them."

My mother smiled wearily. "You forget your lessons, Lena," she said. "We do now. But not at first, not in the first years following Partition. Then, there was only Festival, and sons for the Empire."

I had forgotten. I had endured my schooling, not enjoyed it. "Then we have changed the rules once, and we can do it again."

"We can," my mother agreed. "And I think we will, but it won't be easy, for any of us." We paused outside her house. "Maya is right. At the end of this, even if we are victorious, the world will have changed." She opened the front door. "I am very tired, Lena. Try to rest."

But I could not. At the first light of dawn, I slipped down to the kitchen, brewed tea, found some bread left over from dinner, and went to the boats. I was scrubbing the hold, brush in hand, when Maya joined me several hours later.

"Did you sleep?" I sat back on my haunches.

"A bit," she said. She re-tied her hair, not looking at me. "Did you?"

"No. I got back fairly late and couldn't stop thinking."

She met my eyes. "Can we just work and not talk about it?"

I sighed. "If you like." I knew from experience that when Maya did not want to talk, insisting on it would just irritate her more. "Can you see if any of the ropes needs splicing? I thought one was fraying yesterday." She nodded, turning away. I held my tongue, channelling my frustrations into my scrubbing.

We worked until the noon bell rang, talking only of the boat and the fishing, calmly but distantly. The routine of the work eased my irritation. Around us, other fisherwomen went about their daily chores. To an outside eye, the life of the village would have appeared to go on as normal. When the bell rang, I gave the hold one last swipe. I dumped the dirty water overside and put the bucket and brush away. Maya, on the dock, coiled the rope in her hands, stowing it neatly. We walked back up the hill with a half-dozen other women and apprentices. The illusion of normalcy had vanished. The tension crackled like summer lightening, and few of us spoke in more than brief murmurs or sharp retorts as we returned to our houses. Tali had put bread, cheese, and fresh radishes on the table. My stomach growled at the sight.

"Maya?" I asked. "Do you want some food?"

"No." She turned away to climb the stairs.

"Tali?"

She leaned against the sink, drinking tea. She shook her head. "I don't think I can eat," she admitted.

I sliced the radishes thinly onto the bread, layered cheese on top, and sat outside on the steps in the noon sun to eat. I wanted space, not walls. Maya came back down the stairs, her footsteps resonating on the pine planks. I ate half the food, and suddenly, I had had enough. I took the remainder back to the kitchen, wrapped it in a cloth, putting it on a shelf. Tali hadn't moved. She had lighted a candle in the small shrine by the hearth, an offering to the goddess. She looked at me, and in her eyes I saw both fear and resolve.

"Time to go," she said quietly. I nodded. Maya emerged from another room. She had pulled her hair back and braided it tightly, accentuating the pale planes of her face. Without a word, she walked past us and out the door.

"Maya," Tali's voice was almost pleading and so quiet I did not think Maya could have heard. I looked at my aunt. Tears gleamed in her eyes.

"Tali?" I said. "What is it?"

She brushed a hand across her eyes. "I'm so afraid for her," she said. "Of what she might do."

"So am I," I said slowly. "But even if we vote to defend Tirvan, she won't need to fight. Someone will have to take care of the babies and cook."

"Maybe," Tali said. "Maybe."

Maya waited for us on the porch, standing apart from the other women who had gathered there. When we entered the hall, she walked beside her mother. We stopped just inside the door, letting our eyes adjust to the dimness. Women sat on the benches or stood in small groups around the walls, talking in low tones. Tali saw my mother across the room and went to join her. Maya slipped onto a bench. When I sat beside her, she slid an inch or so over. I reached over to take her hand. She shot me a cold look, giving a tiny shake of her head. I felt a spurt of anger. We'd had arguments before, of course, but usually she accepted my gestures of reconciliation. I shrugged, and increased the distance between us on the bench, bumping into Kyan. I murmured an apology. Kyan made space for me, sliding closer to her partner, Dari.

Gille rose to speak. "We meet here this afternoon under the rules of the council," she said formally. "You were all here last night. You know what Casyn, in the name of the Emperor, has asked. Gwen and Sara and I have met with Casyn for much of the morning, but there is little I can add to what he told us yesterday. There is good reason to believe that Leste is planning to attack the women's villages in the autumn, after harvest, to take food for their land. We are being asked to defend ourselves, to allow the men to subdue Leste and, at the same time, keep the northern Wall manned. This afternoon, we need to debate and discuss this, and then vote." I heard a few whispers as Gille spoke, but mostly we kept to the rules and did not interrupt. I looked at Maya. Her face was grim, and a muscle worked in her cheek. "That is our task," Gille reiterated. "Who wishes to speak?"

A dozen women stood, scraping benches. Sara scanned the room. In council, we speak from youngest to oldest. Maya did not stand. Sara nodded. "Cate," she acknowledged.

"The men were here so recently." She frowned. "Why did we hear nothing from them? Even rumours? All the talk was of the Wall. How do we know this is true?"

"Aye!" The agreement came from several places in the circle. *A good question*, I thought. At Festival, the men had many stories, told publicly and, no doubt, I assumed, privately. I knew only the songs and the tales told in the public gatherings, but Cate spoke truly. The Wall loomed large in those. Occasionally stories of Casilla, the only true city of the Empire, down on the Edanan Sea, took centre stage, but I remembered nothing about Leste.

"Casyn spoke as an Emperor's Messenger," Sara reminded us. "They are bound to speak the truth. As to why we heard nothing from the men, it is simply that they did not know. Only the Emperor and some men of rank were fully aware."

"That's what he says, is it?" I turned to see who had spoken out of turn: Minna.

"Mother!" her daughter hissed. Minna muttered something, then subsided. I turned away. Minna's mind wandered, we all knew; she could not be held responsible for the lapse of council etiquette. The murmurs of assent audible in the room, though, told me many shared her doubt. I turned to Maya again, hoping to see some reaction, but she stared at the floorboards, not looking up.

Ranni spoke next. Six months into a difficult pregnancy, she leaned on her partner's shoulder for support. "If it is food they need," she asked, "why can't they just trade for it? Or we could just give it to them." A louder wave of murmurs swept the room. Gille raised her hand, requesting silence. Feet shuffled, bodies shifted. Gille waited for the room to calm.

"They have little to trade, or little that we want," Gille answered. "Even the military needs only so much dried fruit, or spices, or wine. And we have only so much extra without going short ourselves."

Ranni nodded and sat. Her partner put her arm around her. Sweat beaded on my forehead and neck. Again, Gille waited for silence. "Mella," she indicated, nodding to another pregnant woman.

"Does an Emperor's Messenger have the right to ask this of us?" she said simply. "Does even the Emperor have the right to ask us to break the precepts of Partition?" She cradled her unborn child with both hands, looking down at her swollen stomach. "How would I explain that, to her?"

"You can't," someone called.

"Quiet!"

"There's reasons!"

"It's not right!"

The hall resounded with voices. I'd never seen us break order before. Startled, I turned again to Maya, but she seemed unaware, still locked inside herself. When I put my hand on her rigid shoulder, she pulled away again without looking at me. I felt tears threaten, tears of fear and sudden loneliness. I scanned the room, searching for Tali, or my mother, and met the eyes of Tice, our new potter, sitting alone across the circle. Her face showed no emotion, but she cocked her head slightly to acknowledge me. She gazed back at me steadily. I looked away, embarrassed that she might have seen the tears glinting in my eyes.

The clang of the meeting bell reverberated through the room. When the last vibrations had stilled, and with them the voices, my mother spoke, quietly and firmly.

"All of you," she reminded, "learned the rules of Partition in your school days. Siane," she addressed a seated woman, "your Lara is still a student. Have you helped her learn the rules, as they were written at the Partition assembly?"

"Yes," Siane replied.

"Would you remind us what it said, regarding food?"

Siane did not rise. She had been a herdswoman before a berserk bull smashed her left leg to pieces, and now stood and walked with difficulty. She kept the village accounts and breeding records, and had a prodigious memory.

"Whatever foodstuffs a village produces, whether meat or grain, fruit or vegetable, is theirs to keep and trade among the villages. No tithe will be given to nor expected by the Empire's armies, fleets, or messengers, or by the Emperor himself," she recited. She looked questioningly at my mother, who nodded. "This was superseded some fifty years later, as a benefit to both the villages and the men. Many villages produced much more food than they needed, and the men fighting the northern peoples and building the Wall could not farm as well. But," she paused, "I do not know how that change was made."

Several of the women waiting to speak sat down again, relinquishing their opportunity to be heard. Casse, nearly eighty, leaned on her stick. Once a council leader, her thoughts bore weight among us.

"Casse," my mother said.

"When we move the herds to the hills, in the spring," she began, "we send the apprentices with them, to guard them against the eagles and the wildcats that prey on the newly-born lambs and calves." Casse spoke in a strong voice that belied her years. "We give those apprentices weapons: slings and sometimes staves. Those are enough, even in the hands of a twelve-year-old, to keep those hunters off. But nearly seventy years ago, when I was first apprenticed to the herds and the hunt, they were not enough, because wolves, packs of wolves, still roamed the hills and took even fully-grown sheep and cattle. Shepherding then needed an adult woman, or several, who had skill with spear and knife and bow. We defended our animals, and ourselves, with weapons." She thumped her staff on the floor. "I have killed a wolf or two in my time, and I would again. Why is this any different, except this time the wolves have two legs?" She gave a sharp nod and sat down.

No one else remained standing. My mother looked around. I followed her gaze. Around the room, women leaned forward, tense and focused, or huddled with their eyes downcast. Some grasped hands, others hugged. Some sat alone. I could smell the tang of sweat and fear in the room.

"You have questioned Casyn's veracity, and his right to ask this of us," she said. "You have suggested that food be traded, or given, to turn aside the threat of invasion. You have been reminded that the rules of Partition are not fixed but have been changed before when there was benefit perceived for both the villages and the men. And that, sometimes, killing is necessary for survival." Beside me, Maya flinched. I reached for her hand again, and this time, she let me take it. I slid a little closer to her.

"I speak on behalf of your council leaders." She glanced at Sara and Gille.

"Our thoughts, as always in a council vote, are only to guide you, not to direct you. We recommend that Tirvan accede to the Emperor's request, that we learn the skills and tactics needed to defend our village against invasion, even though this goes against the precepts of the Partition agreement. If we do not, if we refuse to defend ourselves, and the invaders are victorious, we will have no voice and no choice in what happens to us after that. If the Empire wins, we can write a new agreement. So say I, Gwen of Tirvan, Council Leader," she ended in the formal words.

"And I, Sara of Tirvan, Council Leader."

"And I, Gille of Tirvan, Council Leader."

The formal recommendation of the council leaders signalled the preparation for the vote. Gille and my mother walked the circle. Gille handed each of us a dark pebble for no, my mother a light one for yes. The stones felt cold against my palms. Sara unlocked the two voting boxes, one for the vote, one for the discarded pebble, showing the room that both were empty. Then she locked them again, standing them on a table. Sixty light pebbles in the voting box meant no further debate, no second vote.

Separating the pebbles meant letting go of Maya's hand. She did look at me then. Her eyes were anguished, but dry. I reached out to hold her, but she shook her head. "No," she said quietly. "Not now."

"Maya," I pleaded. "Don't be angry."

"I'm not angry. Not at you. I just can't—" She broke off, took a breath. We walked toward the boxes, pebbles hidden in our hands. Maya's knuckles were white. Mine were, too. My pebble dropped into the voting box, where it clicked against the others already there. I dropped the dark one into the discard box. I watched Maya flatten her palm against the hole and heard her pebble drop. Then we sat again to watch the others vote. Finally, the council leaders opened the boxes, pouring the pebbles onto a cloth. Maya moaned. I could hear my heart beating out the seconds. It took less than a minute of those beats to count, one by one, the sixty-three white pebbles.

Sara stood. "All women of age in Tirvan have witnessed the count. Tirvan votes to accede to the request of the Emperor." The required words spoken, she hesitated. "We have voted to change the rules of Partition, for only the second time in two hundred years," she said. "Whether this was wisdom, or no, only the future will tell us. But it is our choice."

"Not all of us," Siane reminded her. Tears glistened on her cheeks, but she spoke clearly. "Seventeen of us voted no. What of us?"

Gille stepped forward. "Siane, must we do this now?"

"Yes!" Maya said defiantly. "We need to know. I need to know."

Gille sighed, and turned away, speaking softly to Sara and Gwen.

"Maya," I cajoled, "can't this wait? Let's see what Casyn wants us to do."

"No," she said, her voice high. She wrapped her arms around herself, pulling her knees up, rocking slightly on the bench. "It's not what Casyn wants, Lena, it's what the village wants. What the rest of you, who voted to fight, want of me, and Siane, and whoever else said no. That's our choice, not his, not the Emperor's. Ours," she repeated. Her eyes glittered. She looked feverish. At the table, the council leaders' talk ended. They turned towards us.

"Siane," Gille said. "You will lead the group who decides this. For the women of age who voted no, and for the apprentices who hold the same views, what will we ask? Casyn told us last night he believes we should train all girls over the age of thirteen. What you, Siane, and seven more must decide is how we handle this. Do we excuse some from the training, and if so on what grounds? Do we make training compulsory, and if so, what are the consequences for refusing? It will not be easy, nor will whatever you choose be accepted easily by all."

Siane nodded in acceptance. "I will do this," she confirmed. She pushed her stocky body up and bent to hold Dessa, murmuring something. Then she took her stick, limping out to the porch to await, by our customs, the rest of the chosen group. I looked around. In theory, I knew how this worked, how we chose the women who now would decide the question given them. In practice, I'd never seen it happen. Four of the eight walls of the hall had doors. The chosen leader sat outside the north door, away from the village; one council leader standing at each of the others. Which door we exited from depended on where we sat in the hall.

"We go east from here, don't we?" I asked.

"That's right," Kyan said beside me, stretching. "You remember the rest?"

"Two hands," I murmured. Each of us offered a hand to the council leader as we left the hall. If she grasped it with one hand, we continued on. But if both her hands covered the offered hand, we did not leave.

"Right again," Kyan said. She ran a hand through her cropped, fox-red hair. "Difficult one, this." She worked in wood, building boxes or barns with equal skill, and on long winter nights made our hunting bows. Slight, dark-haired Dari worked with her.

In joining the line, Dari had moved forward to speak to Maya, and now both she and Kyan stood between us. I could just see Sara take Maya's hand with her right, touching her gently on the shoulder with her left. Just perceptibly—to me, at least—Maya relaxed. She glanced back at me, but protocol said she could not wait near the porch.

"Maya," I heard Dari call. "Come for tea." *Good,* I thought. *I can catch up with them on the path.* Kyan blocked the light for a moment, then went on her way. I held out my hand to Sara. She took it in both of hers. I froze.

"Sara," I said, "I can't do this."

"Yes, you can," she replied quietly. "I know Maya is one of the seventeen. That is, in part, why we chose you." Unexpectedly, she touched my cheek. "You are very much like your mother, Lena. The mix of pragmatism and compassion that makes her both an excellent midwife and an excellent council leader is in you, too. Find Siane and begin what you have to do."

Someone had arranged chairs in a circle on the porch. Six other women were with Siane, Casse and Mella among them. I was the eighth. The porch held the warmth of the day. Someone brought out a jug of water and cups. I poured myself a cup and sat. My mouth was dry.

"You are the last of our group," Siane said. She held her injured leg out in front of her. I could see the twist in it, where the bones had knitted wrongly. Her partner, Dessa, a woman of strong views, would almost certainly have voted to fight. Maya and I were not the only partnership in the village to be divided in this matter. Somehow, that thought made me feel less alone. "You all know our task?" Siane asked, glancing around the group. We nodded. "There are several issues here," she continued. "Casyn expects the attack to come in late September. At that point, we will have three women, Mella among them, with new babies, and several more, I assume, who will be nearly six months pregnant. Lena, do you know how many?"

"Six."

"That many?" Siane said. "Well, those six, barring complications, should be able to participate in the training."

"We always work during pregnancy," someone said. "This should be no different."

"I'm willing to learn what I can for the next five or six weeks," Mella said, "but I can't deny that I am getting clumsy." She smiled ruefully, her blue eyes crinkling, "Of the others who became pregnant last autumn, Ranni's is a first pregnancy, and she nearly lost the baby a few weeks back, and Nessa is carrying twins and is even more awkward than I am. But there must be work in planning and carrying out a defence that isn't dependent on being able to shoot a bow or throw a spear."

"A tactical role, I think Mella means," Casse said, "which is where I think I might be able to help a bit." Casse had led hunting parties for many years and had spent hours out in the fields.

"For you, yes, and I can see Nessa in that role," Mella said. "But for myself and Ranni, I was thinking more of giving support, supplying arrows or new spears. Something like that."

"But," I found myself saying, "you'll still need to defend yourselves, if it comes to that. At the very least, all of us will need to be able to use a knife."

"Lena has a point," Siane said. She shifted, grimacing as she bent her leg. "If we are willing to participate, a role will be found regardless of physical limitations. That isn't really what we're here to decide. But what about those of us who don't wish to fight? I'll assume for the moment that all of us who voted that way did so for the same reason: we find the taking human life abhorrent. What is to be expected of us? You know that I do not hold that belief lightly." We all knew Siane found the concept of taking life repellent. She ate no meat or fish, and even the man she had chosen to father her daughter held a medic's post, not a soldier's. Sara had chosen wisely, I realized, in appointing Siane to lead this group. Whatever our decision, it would be respected by all because Siane had led us.

"Perhaps," Casse said gently, her wrinkled face compassionate, "you should tell us what to expect of you."

"A fair request," Siane acknowledged. "I spent most of last night wrestling with this. I don't believe I can kill a man."

"Not even," I asked, "if he were trying to kill you?"

"Not even then."

"What if it meant life or death for Dessa? Or for Lara?" The woman who spoke was my senior by a decade. I did not know her well, but her son had played with Pel until Festival this spring. He had ridden away with the soldiers only six weeks ago.

Siane said nothing. We could see the struggle of her conscience reflected on her face. We waited. When she finally spoke, her voice choked with emotion. "I thought of that, too. Truly, I thought of little else. For Lara," she said, "I would kill."

Casse reached out to squeeze her hand. "Do not judge yourself harshly. We all would, for our children." Her gaze turned to me. "Lena, would you endanger yourself to protect Maya?"

"Of course," I said.

Casse held Siane's eyes. "You see?" she asked softly. Siane nodded.

"Individual convictions must be acknowledged and respected," Casse said firmly, "but not to the point at which they endanger others. I propose this: all able-bodied women in Tirvan must, regardless of how they voted or of personal belief, learn to defend themselves with a knife. More than that will be up to each woman and her conscience."

I thought of Maya, of her passionate conviction that women did not fight, did not kill. I wondered if she would see the necessity of this ruling, or if she would think only that we had betrayed her beliefs.

"What if a woman refuses?" I asked, though I knew the answer. We all did.

Casse, once a council leader, answered anyway. "Then she is free to leave Tirvan," she said. I held her calm gaze for a moment. I saw compassion in her eyes. Compassion and pragmatism, my aunt had said. I tried for pragmatism. *Using a knife? Maya could do that.* We gutted fish and killed the occasional seal. She could agree to that, for self-defence only.

"I second the proposal," I whispered.

The clang of the meeting bell called the village back. Gille pulled the bellrope steadily as the women filed in. From where our group sat together, as required, I saw Kyan and Dari come in. Maya was not with them, nor did she accompany her mother. Then I spotted her with Dessa. Terror filled me. *What had we done? How could we make her fight when she so passionately believed it wrong? Who gave us that power?* I leaned forward, gulping air. A cold sweat broke out on my forehead. A hand gripped my shoulder. "Courage," Casse said quietly. "Find it. You have it in you." *No, I don't,* I thought, but my breathing steadied under her strong fingers. After the last women hurried in, Gille let the bell swing to silence.

My mother spoke in a clear voice. "Women of Tirvan, we have called you to hear a binding decision. Eight women, one tenth of the council, have debated this question. Seventeen of us voted not to fight. What will be asked of those seventeen, in the weeks of preparation to come, and when the fighting begins?" She turned. "Siane, you led the debate. Have you reached a decision?"

"We have," Siane answered.

"Tell us, please, so we may know the ruling."

Siane stood, leaning against a chair to support her bad leg. No one moved. "I was one of the seventeen," she said. "You all know my views. This is our ruling: We will all learn to fight to the point that we can defend ourselves. All of us, without exception."

A buzz of voices rose in the hall. Casse's grip on my shoulder had not lessened. When I saw Maya rise from her seat beside Dessa, I tried to rise, too, but Casse held firm. The voices stilled. When Maya's eyes found mine, they held an expression I could not read. Then she looked straight at Gille. "I dissent," she said, in the ritual words. Even from across the room, I could see she was shaking, but her voice barely wavered. "I know what I say and what I do. I dissent. I will not fight."

Sara and Gwen moved to stand beside Gille. "Maya," my mother began, "do not do this." She turned to me, anguish on her face and in her voice. "Lena, can't you stop her?" But even as Casse released me, and I stood to go to her, Maya spoke again, the third and final and binding time. "I will chance exile," she said. "I dissent."

CHAPTER THREE

I TRIED TO RUN TO HER, but hands caught me. I twisted and kicked helplessly. The bell tolled once. Gille spoke the answering words—words we had all learned, but I had never heard spoken.

"Maya, daughter of Tali," she said with grief coursing through her voice. "You stand against the will of the Tirvan council. Go you now from this hall, and by tomorrow at sunset, go you from Tirvan. All doors and gates and harbours are closed to you, Maya, for three years and a day. You are exiled, and no longer welcome here. Go you now."

I heard Tali sob.

I watched Maya go to her mother. Tali bent to hold her daughter, rocking her. After a minute, Maya pulled away. She said something, very quietly. Tali shook her head, and Maya repeated it. Then she turned. Even from across the room, I could see the determination in her eyes. I was struggling again to pull away from the many arms that held me when I saw Maya mouth the word "No." I stopped. Maya turned back to Gille.

"Tomorrow morning, I will be gone. I go on foot and alone," she said. Her voice echoed in the silent hall. "I will go now, to prepare. I will sleep tonight at my mother's house." She paused. "Alone." She did not look at me again. "Farewell, women of Tirvan." She turned on her heel and walked out.

My aunt Sara held Tali by the upper arms, speaking low and urgently. Dessa still restrained me, but my strength was suddenly gone. I slumped against her. Dessa guided me to a bench. I let her sit me down. Nothing made sense. I heard Dessa speak, but her words had no meaning.

Distantly, I realized others were leaving. Women stopped to speak to me and to Tali, but I heard only noise. Someone brought me tea. I held the cup, registering the warmth. Finally, only my family remained: my mother, Sara and Tali, and Gille, in her role as headwoman.

My mother put the mug of tea to my lips. I swallowed obediently. The warm liquid suffused my throat, and the fog in my head cleared a little. I sipped again, then took the mug from my mother.

"Oh, Lena, I am so sorry," she said, sitting beside me. She put her arm around me. "I didn't think it would come to this."

"She said," Tali said, her voice flat, "she would go to look for Garth."

Sara and my mother exchanged looks. "I'm not surprised," Sara said.

"But," I said, finding my voice, "Maya isn't brave. How could she do this? How could she walk away from Tirvan and all she knows?" *And from me.* Tears pricked my eyes.

"Lena," my mother said, "this isn't bravery. In Maya's mind, Tirvan is deserting her. There are some things that perhaps you don't know, that Maya has never told you. Did she ever talk of Garth's leaving?"

I shook my head. "She would never speak of it."

"Then I will," my mother said. "Unless, Tali...?"

"No," my aunt said. "Better from you, Gwen. It's not a good memory." My mother straightened, letting me go. She stood, her hands automatically retying her hair.

"You know," my mother said after a moment's thought, "that Maya was just a few months short of her sixth birthday when the time came for Garth to go with his father. What you don't know is that he did not want to go. Most boys are happy to join the men. Pel, as you know, is already talking of little else. Garth was different. He liked the sea and the woods and was happiest herding the sheep and watching the gulls. He threatened to run away, and Maya swore to go with him if he went."

"In the end," Tali interrupted, her voice low, "we had to drug him. Mar took him, a day early, from his bed, so heavily dosed with poppy that he wouldn't wake until they were far from Tirvan. We drugged Maya, too, a lesser dose, but enough to keep her from realizing what was happening." I could see the strain in her face as she spoke.

"And then," Sara sighed, "we convinced her that tradition said Garth had to go, and that tradition ruled us all. We had many long arguments when I would take her with me to gather herbs for dyeing. Somehow, over that long summer, we won her over."

"Now," my mother added, "we are seeing the fruits of what we did all those years ago. She missed Garth so terribly, Lena. You must remember." I nodded, thinking back. I, too, had been only five, but I remembered Maya crying, endlessly, inconsolably. I had tried, even then, to entice her into games, but she would not be distracted. Finally, the tears had stopped, leaving a solemn, quiet child.

"When we apprenticed together," I said, remembering, "she always wanted to know why things were done the way they were. The answer that seemed to satisfy her the most was 'it has always been done that way'."

Tali continued. "That summer, she prayed endlessly. If we couldn't find her, we only had to look at the holy spring. But when her offerings failed and her prayers weren't answered, she turned her back on the goddess and turned to tradition as a source of meaning and consistency."

"Maya would say," my aunt Sara added gently, "that she isn't rebelling. That it's we who have rebelled, gone against tradition. In her mind, she's doing the only thing she can to maintain the old ways."

"Could she find Garth?" I asked.

Tali shrugged. "If Garth is alive, she might find him by asking every patrol she meets. She knows their father's name and the number of his company. But the seventh were posted to the far reaches of the Wall the year after Garth left, and Mar was killed ten months later. When the message finally reached me, it contained no mention of Garth. I did nothing. Garth belonged to the Empire by then, and I was afraid to unbalance Maya again."

"And if she does find him?"

"I don't know," Tali said. "Maybe she thinks they'll run away together, as they promised when they were children. She may think that Garth will honour that oath over his oath to the Empire, if he lived to make it. I do not know, Lena."

I nodded. Regardless of our love for her, there were places in Maya that neither Tali nor I knew. "May I go to her now, to say farewell?" I asked.

"No, Lena," Gille said. I had opened my mouth to protest when she cut me off. "Not because I forbid it, but because she did." I frowned.

"Maya knows the ritual words as well as any of us," Gille reminded me, gently. "She knew exactly what she said when she commanded that you stay with Gwen. It is her right, as an exiled woman, to protect you, her partner, from blame. She will go without seeing you again."

"No," I said, "no," and then the tears started. My mother held me. When nothing remained but desolation, they took me to the baths. The heat of the pool stopped my shivering, and they gave me wine and poppy. They must have carried me to my mother's house, but I do not remember. I slept, dreaming the dreams grief and the poppy bring. In the morning I woke, as Maya had eleven short years before, to an empty world.

I heard the meeting bell through the waning effect of the drug. In my dreams, the bell had rung first as a warning and then become the tolling-bell for a funeral. My head ached when I finally woke. I closed my eyes against the light of the room. Maya would have left at sunrise. I lay on my back, trying to think through the pain and noise in my head. I could tell from the sun's position that perhaps four hours had passed since dawn. Maya would have climbed the track up into the hills to find the military road. If I got up now, packed some food and clothes, I could catch her. But the road ran north to south, and footprints would not show on its cobbles. *How would I know which way to go? Maybe she left a sign.*

No. I opened my eyes. My head throbbed. We had never spoken of the world beyond Tirvan, never travelled in thought to Berge, or Casilla. I had no idea where she would go. Besides, she had told me to stay, and in that command absolved me of what she knew I would choose. For all my wishing, for adventure, for something new, at the end of the day, I always turned for home. I would not follow her.

Shamed, I wept again, tears of anger and self-loathing, deep, racking sobs. I slid off the bed and wrapped my arms around my knees, my body shaking. When the sobs ended, I sank onto my side and lay still, my mind empty.

Eventually, the need to relieve myself forced me to get up. I used the chamberpot. Then, reluctantly, I washed and dressed and went downstairs. I drank some water, feeling it cold against my raw throat. I stepped outside into the late morning sun, and with nothing else I could think to do, turned towards the meeting hall.

I hesitated at the door, but Siane beckoned me in. The plans for the defence of Tirvan had begun. Casyn had organized us into planning teams—food, supplies, fortifications, secure penning of our herd animals. Every detail mattered. Casyn himself sat with a group of women.

"They're talking about weapons—spears and knives, how many we'll need, and what metal there is at the forge," Siane explained, when she saw me looking their way. I nodded, not really caring. I wondered where to go. My head throbbed dully. I felt as if I moved against a tide.

"Where are the other fisherwomen?" I asked, looking around.

"Over by the south wall," Siane answered. I thanked her, turning to thread my way through the groups to join them.

"Lena," Casyn approached me, his face grave. "I regret I have brought sorrow to you so soon." He touched my shoulder lightly in what seemed a formal gesture. I murmured thanks. Part of my mind registered surprise that he knew my name. He nodded. Not knowing what else to do, I nodded too, and went on to join my group. They made room for me, speaking quiet words of sympathy and concern. Dessa reached over to squeeze my hand.

"We're talking of how we can catch as many fish as possible," she explained. "Casyn thinks we may be besieged, or the fields burned and cattle slaughtered. If either of those happens, we might need to rely on smoked fish over the winter."

I tried to concentrate. I didn't think I really cared, but the planning gave my mind something to do.

"We could start the pilcod fishing early," I suggested. The pilcod were the small, schooling fish of the cold waters to the north.

"Will they be there?" someone asked. "We'd be six weeks early. They won't have moved south yet."

"We can sail further," I said.

"It's rough further north, dangerous."

"They'll be feeding where the waters change," Binne countered. "We can fish just inside the chop line, stay in sight of each other. Should be safe enough." Some fifteen years older than I, Binne fished from *Petrel* with her partner. She had let Maya and me sail *Petrel* a time or two when we were trying to decide what to buy for ourselves. *Dovekie* had been built to the same plans.

"And we'd be out longer."

I shrugged. "I don't mind."

"Is anyone else willing to sail out to catch pilcod?" Dessa asked. "I think there should be at least three boats, maybe five, to be safe. I'll go. Anyone else?"

Several fisherwomen shook their heads. Others conferred with their fishing partners. "We'll go," Binne spoke up, "I won't take my apprentice though," she said. "Can someone else take her on for this?"

"I'll put her on *Curlew*," Dessa said. "I had a mind to send Freya with Lena, anyhow, so that'll make space." Dessa's boat, large and graceful, needed a crew of six. Maya and I had apprenticed on *Curlew*.

"We'll go, too," another pair confirmed.

Everything we spoke of made Maya's absence palpable. These women had trained us and worked alongside us every day. I clenched my jaw against the scream that wanted to burst out. My head started pounding again, and I lost the thread of the talk.

The group planned for another hour. I said very little. Food had been placed on tables against the west wall. We took a break to eat. I nibbled a piece of bread and some cheese without appetite. My mother came over to me, her look questioning. She handed me a mug of sweetened tea. "You need to drink," she said, "and eat a bit. But drinking is more important." She studied me. "I'm glad you're here," she said. She was beginning to say something else when someone interrupted us. I nodded, and she moved away. Others spoke to me, and I answered but did not encourage further talk.

After lunch, Gille asked us to sit again as a large group, so Casyn could address us. We settled, and he began speaking, I noticed, from inside the circle.

"Thank you," he said. "You have worked hard this morning, truly, and I know that your decisions have been made wisely. My job here is only to teach and to advise. I am not here to lead. You already have leaders, and they are admirable." He inclined his head to the council leaders. "You have some skills with the tools of war, with bows, spears, and knives, but they belong to the hunt and to husbandry, not to combat. You must all train for part of every day to learn to use the weapons of war, for war. My job is to teach you to do that."

Gille raised a hand to still the chatter. "To allow time for this instruction," she said, "you will work only half-days unless the immediacy of a task demands otherwise. Half of you will train in the mornings, half in the afternoons, until there are women among us who are skilled enough to teach. We begin tomorrow."

Before dawn the next morning, I untied *Dovekie's* ropes and began to row away from the dock. I took Freya with me, as Dessa had suggested. Quiet and competent, Freya had eighteen months left in her apprenticeship. We sailed north to the edge of the waters where the pilcod schooled, accompanied by the little boats *Petrel* and *Dunlin*, and Dessa, fishing from her second boat *Avocet*. A light fog hung at the chopline. We maneuvered the boats along the line where the cold waves of the north broke on the warmer southern waters and dropped sail.

Quickly, we moved to the stern and picked up the first of the fine, weighted nets. "We're shallower than *Curlew*," I explained to Freya, "so you'll need to throw upward a bit, so it goes far enough out and doesn't foul." I considered. Freya stood half a head taller than me, and her shoulders carried muscle. With Maya, I held my arms lower, to compensate for our height difference. "Drop your arms a bit," I instructed. She nodded, and we threw. The first net landed and sank, well out from the boat.

"Nicely done," I offered. Freya simply nodded again. We stood in silence on the rolling deck. I noticed her glancing at me a time or two, but she didn't speak. After ten minutes, we drew in the ropes that ran through the metal rings at the edge of the net, pulling it tight. "Tie those off," I said. Freya wrapped the ropes around the cleats with no wasted effort.

When Freya picked up one of the boathooks, I grabbed the other, and we hooked them into the net. "Pull!" I yelled. Together, we hauled the heavy pursenet close to the boat. "Hold it," I said, and Freya kept her boathook in place. I attached the winch rope and untied the rope from the cleats. Immediately Freya dropped her boathook to run to the winch, winding up the rope to bring the dripping catch over the side and onto the deck. "Wait," I called, pushing the net away from the gunwales with my boathook. The little boat rocked, but Freya stood steady, and we brought the catch up without incident.

"Not bad," Freya said, looking at the catch.

"About half of what we would get in another month or two," I estimated. "But I agree, not bad. We'll keep fishing." We dumped the catch into the hold and refolded the net to throw it out again. After that, the routine took over: throw, draw, haul, dump, fold. We had two nets going: hard, slogging work, and not without danger, but the hold filled steadily. The work focused me. A lack of concentration could mean a full net fouling and a boat capsizing. I had long ago learned to ignore physical pain or emotional turmoil. The world shrank to sea and net and fish, the shriek of gulls, and the burning in my muscles.

In early afternoon, we returned from the northern banks, leaving the catch and the care of the boat to women who had spent the morning in training. At the house, I stripped off my scale-smeared fishing gear and found bread and cheese to eat. Then, as instructed, I found my hunting bow and its quiver of arrows and climbed up to meet the others at the flat field behind the meeting hall. No one had washed. Collectively, we smelled of fish and byre and sweat.

Casyn waited with a sword held loosely in one hand. "Welcome," he said. "If you have brought a bow, please put it to one side, then sit. You will be watching for some time and sitting will give you some rest after your morning's work." I lowered myself to the dusty ground and crossed my legs. Across the circle, I saw Tice drop gracefully into a similar position in one move.

"The first thing you must do," Casyn said without preamble, "is hold your sword, or your knife, firmly but not too tightly." He took his sword with both hands, holding it out from his body, pointing down, the tip just brushing the ground. "Look at my hands," he directed, as he turned slowly through the circle. His right hand gripped the sword just below the crosspiece, his left, just below the pommel. "If I hold tightly, if I clench my hand," he demonstrated "there are two results. My wrists and forearms become less supple, which means I have less control of the sword, and, my hands and arms will tire more quickly. You know this," he added, "from the tools you use every day. You must learn to handle a sword the same way."

"Now," he said. "Look how I stand, at the position of my feet and legs." Casyn's left leg extended forward, his knee bent slightly and his left foot directly under his hands; his right leg angled back with the foot turned away from his body. I nodded in recognition: the stance provided balance and stability. I stood the same way, hauling nets on a rocking boat, or rod-fishing for big sea-fish.

"How I stand, and how I hold the sword," Casyn continued, "is called a guard. You protect yourself while judging what your opponent might do. There are five major guard positions and five minor. Additionally, there are five major strikes, which are used to counter the cuts and thrusts from your opponent. Watch."

He held the sword up, in front of his right shoulder. "Eagle's Guard," he called, swinging the sword down and to the front, keeping the point upward. "Scythe strike, into the Horn Guard." The sword thrust forward, twisted upward, "Thrust and cut," Casyn called, pausing with the hilt at his left shoulder and the point slightly down. "Bull's Guard."

He kept going, turning slowly through the circle, calling the guards and strikes. Gradually he swung faster, and faster again, until the swordblade blurred against the sky. I saw the power and control from his years of discipline, but like the stoop of a peregrine or the leap of a wildcat, beauty and grace lived in this lethal dance. I realized I was holding my breath. When he finally slowed and stopped, sweat matted his hair and stained his shirt. *I'll never be able to do that. Never. And if Leste fights like this, what chance will we have?*

Tice spoke suddenly. "It's a dance," she said. "Just a dance."

Casyn considered. "Not just. Dancing and sword fighting do have many things in common, but your partner may not take your lead. Also," he added dryly, "he is trying to kill you. Never forget that." A few women laughed. He wiped the sweat from his eyes with the back of his hand. "Under the tree are the wooden practice swords I made in the past few days. Find one that is the height of your waist and hold it the way I showed you. Try the Snake's Guard—like this." He held his sword out in front of him as he had when he first demonstrated the placement of the hands.

We went to the practice swords, neatly ranged in order of height. I held one beside me: too tall. The second one I tried seemed right, the crown of the pommel reaching to just below my hip. I moved away from the women still testing swords for size, holding it as I thought Casyn had. The sword, with a blade the width of my closed hand, had a cross-piece a bit more than two hands-widths down from the curved pommel. Tightly wrapped leather covered the grip. I hefted it, surprised to find it heavier than I had expected.

He came over to where I stood. "Move your left hand back," he instructed. "Good, now turn your upper hand just a bit. Now grip more with your littlest fingers, and let each finger after relax just a bit, until your forefingers and thumbs are the loosest, but not loose." I tried.

"Like holding a rod," I observed, "when fishing for braidan."

"Is it?" he asked. "I've never sea-fished. Now, let's see how you're standing." He looked at my legs and feet. "Good. Bring the sword up to the Eagle's Guard." He moved my arms up to the correct position with the sword at shoulder height, pointing slightly down. "Now bring it down like a scythe to the middle of your body, or just beyond, with the point just upward, like a bull with its head down." I tried the move. It had similarities to rod casting, but as I brought the greater weight of the sword down, I stumbled, embedding the point into the ground. I grunted, feeling the shock of impact through my body.

"You bent too far forward," Casyn said calmly. "Stay straight. Keep working on it." He moved away to work with another woman. I walked a bit further away from the group to try again.

I stumbled several more times. On the next stroke, I brought my hips forward and leaned back as I did when playing a sea-fish on the line, and on the scything downstroke I fell backward. I sat for a moment where I had landed, flushed with humiliation. I glanced over at the others. Casyn moved among the women, correcting a stance or a hand hold. I saw Freya stumble, falling forward, and Dessa drop her sword on the sidestroke. Tice, though, turned as she swung and thrust, already graceful, in control of her body and the sword. I set my jaw, wiped the sweat from my hands, and stood to try again.

After an hour, Casyn called a halt. "You've done well," he said. "Wipe the grips, and then oil the blade and pommel and leave them propped up to dry. The oil and cloths are under the tree. After you have had some water, we will start on archery."

I found a rag to wipe the leather, then poured oil on the cloth, rubbing it in into the wood. Dessa came over to work beside me. "I'm sore," she said. "I feel like I've been fighting a king braidan for hours. I'll need the baths, tonight."

I flexed my shoulders. "I'm not too bad."

She snorted. "You're less than half my age."

"Do you think we'll ever learn this?"

"Yes," she replied. "We will. Some of us faster than others, and to different levels of skill. But we must, and so we will." She wiped the pommel, propping the sword against the trunk of the nearest tree. "Let's give Casyn a hand setting up the butts. You won't have much to learn, here."

The butts—the frames that held the targets for archery—belonged to the village. Many of us knew how to use a hunting bow. Herds-and-hunt apprentices, of course, had to, but others of us, me included, had learned for the pleasure of the hunt. We placed the withy-and-straw stands at the eastern end of the field, with the sun behind us, and hung the painted targets, woven of straw, on the butts.

"Who can shoot?" Casyn asked. Several hands went up, mine and Casse's among them. "Show me." Those who had no skill in archery settled down at the edge of the field to watch.

Casse shot first, using a light bird bow. Three arrows, short-shafted and tipped with a fine, single bone point, flew from her bow. All landed in the central ring of the target. Casyn nodded in approval. She walked forward to pull out her arrows. "I can't see to fletch them properly anymore," she said, "but the target is as clear as it has always been."

"Can you handle a hunting bow?" Casyn asked.

"No," Casse admitted. Casyn had excused her from learning the sword, I knew, beyond the basic holds and thrusts. "The big bow is too heavy for me now. But I can teach its use still, as I always have."

"And you will," Casyn said. "Lena?"

I stepped forward. I had strung the bow as Casse and Casyn talked, bending the curved frame back to loop the gut string over the ends. I strapped the quiver on my back and pulled an arrow out. Meant for killing deer, my arrows had a thicker, longer shaft, and a wider point; a groove ran down the shaft to create a blood-trail if an animal did not fall immediately. The deer hunt occurred in the fall, although we would take animals throughout the winter and even later if the food supplies ran low. I hadn't shot for half a year.

I raised the bow and nocked the arrow, feeling my muscles remember the task. I pulled back the bowstring, sighted along the arrow, and released. I felt the arrow speed by my cheek, flying true to the target. With pleasure, I saw it hit the centre. I nocked and released two more in quick succession. The second one hit the target just outside the centre ring. The third landed beside the first.

"Can you use a bird bow as well?" Casyn asked as I retrieved my arrows. I shook my head.

"Not as well," I said, "and better on rabbits than birds."

"We'll need both. Practice with the light bow, but you will teach with the hunting bow."

I watched as several others shot, using a mix of light and heavy bows. Almost all hit the centre at least two times out of three. This pleased me. I wanted Casyn to see our skill with the bow. He spoke briefly to each archer as she finished, and when all had shot, he gave us our instructions.

"As yet we do not have enough bows for everyone, but Kyan tells me she and her apprentice will soon rectify that. For now, each teacher will work with a small group who are close to her in height, so that you can share the bows. Today, you will only string and unstring, and learn the fingering on the bowstring. That will be enough."

Mella joined me along with two others. Mella's breasts had swollen with her pregnancy, and the others too had large breasts. "You'll need to see Kyan to be fitted for breast straps. Otherwise, the breast on your shooting side interferes with the shot. And it hurts, too, I'm told." I held out my bow. "This is a deer bow. It's made of hazel. Kyan made it, of course. Pass it around. Feel its weight."

"It's light," one of the women said.

"To string it," I explained, "you loop the bowstring around the notch at the lower tip, steady the bow with your foot, then push down on the upper limb and loop the bowstring over and into the upper notch." I demonstrated. "Mella, you try."

I unstrung it, handing her the bow and cord. Awkwardly, she looped the string into the lower notch, stood the bow upright, and rested her foot on the curve of the limb. Then she pushed on the bow, hard.

"Stop!" I cried. I took the bow from her to examine it. It appeared undamaged. "Push gently, but steadily," I explained. "Otherwise, you can break the bow."

"You didn't say that," she said angrily. "How was I to know?"

"I'm sorry. Try again?" She took the bow from me, looking unhappy, and repeated the actions, this time pushing much more gently. She nearly had the string into the upper notch when it slipped from under her foot. The rebounding bow hit her hip.

"Ahhh!" she cried, rubbing her hip. "Lena, you didn't warn me that could happen. What if it had hit my belly and hurt the baby?" Her eyes filled with tears of pain and fright.

"I'm sorry," I said again. *Why did Casyn think I could teach? Just because I could shoot a bow?* "I've never shown anyone how to do this before. Maybe if we do it together?"

She shook her head. "No. Let me watch someone else. I'll try again later, maybe."

I asked another woman. This time, I stood beside her, steadying the bow myself, and guided her in pushing down to loop the string. We strung and unstrung the bow three times in that manner, and when she tried it alone, she got it on the first attempt. By the time the other two had also strung the bow successfully, Mella had overcome her fright, and using the same guided motions, strung the bow without mishap.

Once everyone had strung the bow two or three times, I took it back, holding it in the shooting position. "I'm right-handed, so my left hand grips the bow here." I indicated the grip, the wood shaped for a hand and cross-hatched to make it less slippery. "I use the first two fingers on my right hand to draw the string back." I drew, bringing the bowstring back to just below my ear where I held it for a moment before releasing. "Mella?"

She hesitated, then took the bow.

This time I stood behind her. I helped her discover how to hold the bow, showing her where to put her fingers. Then I stepped back. "Pull now," I said, and she did, the bow wobbling a bit in her inexperienced grip. "Keep pulling," I urged when she stopped with the bowstring still in front of her head.

"It's hard," she said, pulling further and biting her lip in concentration.

"Release," I ordered, once she had got the position right and held it briefly. She let her fingers slip off the string too slowly. Had she nocked an arrow, it would have tumbled harmlessly to the ground a foot or two in front of her.

I asked her to repeat the action several times. By the last attempt, the bow shook noticeably. "You're tired. That's enough."

"Oh, thank you," she said, breathing hard. As she handed me the bow, I considered: Mella spun wool and kept bees, for honey and for candlewax. Neither resulted in the type of strength she needed for the hunting bow, regardless of her pregnancy.

"I think you would be better learning the small bow."

"So do I," she agreed. "But so many went to Casse, and the others with small bows are shorter than I am. So I came to you."

"I'll speak to Casse. Someone can switch." I said, wondering who.

"Thank you," Mella said. "I'm sorry I spoke angrily earlier, Lena. But I thought I would only be learning the knife because I am so clumsy in this pregnancy. Then Gille told me to try all the weapons because I might need to know how to use them. I am trying," she spread her hands, "but I'm not doing very well."

"I fell over my sword at least a half-dozen times, earlier."

"Did you?" she said in surprise. "Really?" I nodded. "That makes me feel better," she said, smiling.

"Stop, now," Casyn called after some time. I unstrung the bow and wiped down the wood, coiling the string to tuck in the quiver. After we stowed the bows, I drank some water, then joined the semicircle of women sitting in the dusty grass. I sat beside Tice, who glanced at me, smiled slightly, but said nothing.

When he had our attention, Casyn bent slightly to pull a short knife from his deerskin boot. He tossed it into the air. It tumbled, point over hilt, shining in the afternoon sun. He caught it effortlessly.

"This is the secca, the throwing knife," he said. "You saw how it spun when I tossed it. It is balanced to do that." He threw the knife at a butt. It turned in the air, flying straight and true to the target, embedding itself to the hilt.

"You will learn to do this," he said bluntly. "The knife is the thing that can save your life, either from a distance, in the throw, or in hand to hand fighting. This is the one weapon that you all, all," he emphasised, "even Casse, even Mella and Ranni, must learn."

I gazed at the secca with bile rising in my throat. A handspan of metal—the size of the knives we used to debone a fish or to cut line—and Maya chose exile over it. Anger rushed through me. I took a deep breath to keep myself from screaming. Tice glanced at me, raising an eyebrow in question. I shook my head, re-focusing on Casyn's lesson.

He sheathed the secca and brought out a wooden knife, banded with metal. "Like the swords," he explained, "these are for practice. They are weighted so as to spin and fly like a secca, but are less dangerous. When we learn close combat, the points will be guarded, but we will first learn to throw them."

He divided us into groups of five. Each group had one practice knife. It was all he had time to make, Casyn explained. "Now," he said, "this is what you will do, for the rest of this hour. Hold the knife with the tip pointing into your palm, grasping the blade from the top, and flick it upward. As it tumbles back down, catch it by the hilt." He tossed the wooden secca and caught it. I saw a hint of a grin on his face. "The first group to have all its members catch the knife correctly five times in succession wins the first lesson at the target tomorrow."

Someone whooped, and suddenly the seriousness of the afternoon disappeared. The lesson had turned into play. We spread out. Laughter and curses rang over the field as we tossed and dropped the knives, scratching ourselves before we began to catch them properly. Groups began to shout their scores. As I threw and caught the knife for the fourth time in a row, my group chanting encouragement, the pain inside me receded, just a bit.

We lost to Dessa's group, but we threw second the next day, and I fell over my sword less. Gradually, as spring gave way to summer and we spent our afternoons with sword and bow and knife, my muscles and nerves learned the skills, and my swordplay went from clumsy to competent. I learned the guards and the strikes; I could hold my own when we moved on to practice fighting. All around me on the field, I could see similar transformations taking place. Mella, her belly huge now, could, with a bird bow, hit the red centre on the target nine times out of ten from a hundred paces. Casse learned to throw the secca with deadly precision, delighting in learning something new at her advanced age. Casyn watched, corrected, sometimes chastised, and with his grave good humour kept us working through the long summer afternoons.

I slept well at night from sheer physical exhaustion, but when Freya and I sailed to and from the fishing grounds, I rarely thought of anything but Maya. In calm seas, I could sail without thinking, while my mind replayed the events of that evening, inventing scenarios in which I stopped her from leaving, or, alternately, went with her. Freya's natural quietness, combined with, I suppose, her reticence to interrupt my reverie, meant that mostly my thoughts had free rein. Inevitably, this led to remembering the insights of that first, terrible morning, but I shied away from too deep a re-examination. When I forced my mind away from that fruitless course, by trying to think about the finer points of swordplay, or teaching archery, it always led me back to Maya, alone somewhere in the outside world, with no skills to defend herself. I feared for her, but more intensely, I missed her. Only the relentless focus of the practice field could distract me from the physical ache of her absence.

†††††

Two weeks after Maya left I had moved back to Tali's house. "Are you sure?" my mother had asked gently. "You know you're welcome to stay."

I shook my head. "Tali is alone, too," I said. "It'll be better for us both. We can be company for each other." I didn't know if that was true. When Tali and I had spoken, she had said little about Maya, but at my mother's, I found myself reverting to the familiar roles of childhood, arguing over little chores, squabbling with Kira. I wanted to grieve as an adult. At my mother's house, I could not acknowledge the emptiness of my arms and my body's need for Maya's warmth. I cried into my pillow, but I needed to howl. My mother considered, twisting her hair.

"I do worry about her," she acknowledged. "But please come here, to eat, or to talk."

"I will," I promised.

Once a week, we had a day with no training after our morning's work. Casyn insisted on this, saying our minds and bodies needed rest. On the next free afternoon, I packed my few clothes, slung the bag over my shoulder, and walked down the path toward the harbour and our house. Empty rooms greeted me. I climbed the wooden stairs to our room, hesitating before the closed door. Then I stepped forward, opening it.

Tali had changed the bedclothes, and an unfamiliar blanket covered the bed. *Why?* I wondered, then realized Maya must have taken the other one. With that thought, all the grief and anger resurfaced.

I began to cry. Pulling the wardrobe doors open, I dragged a shirt she had left behind out to hold it to my face, smelling her on it. "Maya." I wailed. I collapsed across the bed, sobbing, despairing of comfort. I could find no hope in my mind for Maya, or for me. When I could cry no more, I simply lay on the bed, staring at nothing, hugging the shirt. Tali found me there when she returned from the fields. I blinked up at her.

"I slept with Mar's tunic for a year," she said gently. "I think you were right to come home. Pel misses you, both of you, and it will help him to have you here. Supper's ready. Wash your face and come down."

Pel chattered happily to me, and I made the effort to respond with interest. We ate chicken and dumplings while he told us about shepherding on the hills, where he spent much of his time with the young apprentices guarding the sheep and lambs.

"Is Maya coming home, too?" he asked suddenly.

Tali raised her eyebrows, signalling me to answer him. I swallowed, hoping my voice wouldn't betray me. "Not yet," I answered. "Maya's gone to another village. She won't be home for a long time."

He thought about this. "Will I have gone with the men before she gets back?"

"Yes," Tali said. "You will have. I told you she said goodbye, and told you to be good, too. You remember?"

He nodded. "I remember, but I miss her. Do you miss her, Lena?"

I smiled, blinking rapidly. "I do, Pel. I do."

CHAPTER FOUR

IN HIGH SUMMER, ANOTHER messenger came. He arrived in the morning, spending the day with Casyn and the council leaders. None of us expressed surprise the next day when we heard that afternoon training would be replaced by a meeting on the following day. It seemed a luxury to return from the fishing and have time to soak in the baths and eat a leisurely meal twice in one week. Generally, I disliked rest days, as nothing distracted me from thoughts of Maya, but today, with the expectation of something new happening, I welcomed the change.

After a meal of fish and early root vegetables, we walked up the hill to the meeting hall. Heat radiated off the ground, and a fine layer of dust covered everything. The world seemed baked and hard, and around me, the women seemed the same, skin burned brown from the sun, muscles taut in hard bodies. We had been fit before, but not like this. We settled in the circle. I sat with Siane. I had taken to visiting with her when I could find the time.

Casyn and the messenger spoke quietly to my mother and Gille. The new man, slightly built and about my height, appeared not more than some half-dozen years my elder. His hands were callused like mine, or Dessa's, hands that worked with ropes in salt water.

Gille called the meeting to order. "This is Dern," she said simply, after the formal words of opening had been spoken. "He has come to tell us what the Empire requires of us now. We—Casyn, Gwen, Sara, and I—went over the plans with him this afternoon." She paused for a moment, then continued. "In a week or two, a ship will arrive at Tirvan, a fighting vessel from the Empire's navy. The ship is called *Skua*. Dern is her captain, and she has a crew of forty men. While she is here, *Skua* must be provisioned and made ready for the invasion of Leste. Also, and perhaps more importantly, *Skua*'s crew are fighting men, who will test our readiness to defend Tirvan. Over the weeks they are here, they will hone their skills, and ours. They will attack our defences, to find our weak points. And they will help us correct them." Gille paused. "I find this reassuring. We will not go into battle untried."

From the reaction of the women around me, I gathered that most of us felt the same. If nothing else, this new challenge would provide a diversion from the rote practice on the field. Gille called us to order.

"With fair winds, *Skua* should arrive in ten days," Casyn said. "In those ten days, we will continue to practice with sword and spear and bow, but we must also give thought and time to organization. I will not be here when the attack comes. I will be leaving aboard *Skua*."

Several women gasped. We had assumed Casyn would be staying with us. He continued. "Gille will command, with Gwen and Sara as deputies. They know the strategies and the plans. We need now to divide you into cohorts, with one woman designated to command each cohort. I have watched you for ten weeks, on the field and about your work, and I have met with the council leaders. In battle, there can be no democracy, so I—we—have chosen the cohort leaders, and the cohorts." He paused. "I know this is not your usual way of doing things, but these are not usual times. Shall Dern and I leave you for a while, so you may debate this?"

He watched us, grave and courteous as ever. I wondered if the soldiers sent to the other women's villages had the same qualities. I had thought soldiers brusque, rough in manners and speech, from what I had seen at Festival. Casyn's boundless patience, his courtesy towards our customs and traditions, his gentleness seemed at odds with this. *Did it have to do with the skills needed to command?*

"Do we need time for debate?" Sara asked the assembly.

"I'll abide by your decision," said Kyan, the bowyer, from the other side of the hall. "We've all had ample time to see that Casyn knows his business. If he and the councillors have chosen our leaders, I trust they will have chosen well."

A chorus of "ayes" followed this statement.

"Does any woman here request debate?" Sara asked again. Silence pervaded the hall.

She glanced over at Gwen and Gille. "We will proceed. Casyn, if you would?"

He nodded, stepping forward, a list in his hand. "There will be seven cohorts, twelve women and apprentices each. Your council leaders, and a few of the oldest women, are not included in any cohort. I will address their roles later. Some cohorts will be specialists in one skill; for example, we have put the best archers together. Others will have a mix of skills. Each cohort will be assigned a specific role in the defence of Tirvan. I will tell you, first, who the cohort leaders are and then who is in each cohort."

Women leaned forward in their seats, waiting.

"These are the cohort leaders. Please stay in your seats for now," Casyn said, "but I will want to meet with you briefly, after all the assignments are made. Kyan, Tali, Dessa, Dari, Binne, Lena, and Grainne. Do you all accept?"

Kyan, I thought, *would lead the archers, and do it well. Tali had proven herself expert with a sword, endlessly patient in correcting the parries and thrusts of others. But the others...* I realised Siane was clapping me on the back. "Lena," she said urgently, "Lena! Casyn is waiting for your answer."

"What?" I said stupidly.

"You have been chosen as a cohort leader. You must formally accept."

"But I'm only just eighteen." My birthday was a few days after midsummer.

"You are an adult and more than competent." Siane said firmly. "Do you doubt Casyn's judgement, and your mother's? Give him your answer."

I thought of Casyn watching me on the field, his rare words of praise. A week ago, we had spoken at the end of training.

"Tell me, Casyn," I remembered saying. "We haven't learned anything new for a week or two. I know we need to keep practicing, but won't there come a point at which we think we know it all, get bored, and start making mistakes?"

He had looked at me gravely. "Complacent, I think you mean."

"Yes," I had agreed. "Complacent. That would be dangerous, wouldn't it?"

"It would be. You have good instincts, Lena. You would make a good soldier. Be patient just a little while longer. Changes will be coming soon."

The changes had come. I met Casyn's gaze. "I accept."

The cohort I would lead consisted of younger women and several apprentices.

"You will need to become highly skilled with the secca," Casyn explained. "I told you once before that it is the knife, above all other weapons, that may be the difference between life and death. Your skill with it may also mean the difference between winning the battle here, or losing."

I glanced around the cohort. Their eyes flicked from Casyn to me, and I realized they were waiting for me, their leader, to respond.

"How so?" I asked, thinking as I spoke that the question lacked insight.

"When the invasion comes," Casyn answered, "this cohort will not fight openly. Your job will be to lay hidden, to be the last line of defence. You will need to know every loft and winter store and stable in the village—all the places you can hide. You must be able to move between them silently in the dark, and to kill, silently, in that dark."

I swallowed. "Why were we chosen?"

"Youth," he answered, "and the speed and reflexes you have all shown in the training. You all handle the secca well, too, but you also have something more: fearlessness, perhaps, although that does not quite describe it. A willingness to take chances, when chances are required."

Take chances? If I took chances, wouldn't I be with Maya now? How could Casyn think me not just fearless, but capable of leading such a group and such a task? To command women older than I, if only by a few years, disconcerted me. I marshalled my thoughts.

"What must we do first?"

"Choose a second-in-command and begin your work together."

The twelve of us sat in a circle at one side of the council hall. Four apprentices, including Freya, and eight women, including myself, under thirty. Looking around the circle, I saw no hostility, no obvious challenge to my leadership. I knew I had to show decisiveness in this, my first task as leader. My eyes travelled round the circle again to rest on Tice. I knew her only slightly better than I had at the beginning of the summer. At spring Festival one night, she had danced in the southern style, graceful and precise and silent. I thought of that, of her grace with the sword, and of her calm, assessing gaze. "Tice, you are cohort-second."

Her dark eyes met mine, and she nodded. The other women said nothing, but I saw Freya nod in approval. I glanced out the window. A good hour of daylight remained. "Fetch your knives," I said, "and meet in the upper corner of the training ground in ten minutes. Tice, stay back, please."

"I need you," I said when we were alone, "to teach the others to move silently. And to teach me, too. I've always envied the way you dance."

Tice chuckled. "What a reason to be chosen cohort-second," she said. "Because of the way I dance!" Her chuckle became a deep, full-throated laugh.

I blinked, spluttered, and then found myself laughing with her. The tension drained out of me. I couldn't remember when I had last laughed.

"Can you think of a better reason?"

Tice shook her head, still laughing. I realised we had piqued the curiosity of other cohorts still in the hall. "We'd better go out to the training ground."

She nodded, solemnly, then burst out into gales of laughter again. "Yes, commander."

"Don't call me that!" I protested. "It makes me feel about six again, playing soldier with the boys in the hills."

She stopped laughing. "Isn't that exactly what we're doing? Except now, the boys have grown up, and the game is deadly serious. I will teach them, and you, silence, as best I can in such a brief time, and you will improve their knife skills and show us all how to think. Casyn did not choose you as cohort-leader because of your skills with secca and bow, Lena. You are good, but so are others. He chose you because you think differently. You see what could happen and plan for it. That's your strength. Teach us to think like that, a bit, and you may keep us alive, more so than silence in the night."

"She's right," a voice said from behind me. I turned to face Dern. His eyes—blue, with fine lines radiating out from the corners—met mine.

"Casyn said as much to me, and Casyn is a fine judge of men. Of soldiers," he amended. "He was my cadet-officer, once. I am Dern, captain of *Skua*. You are Lena, and this is—?"

"Tice," I said. "She'll be our cohort-second."

He inclined his head to her. "From Karst?" he asked. She nodded. "I have served with men from Karst. They are like cats, all stealth and grace and silence. You have chosen well, Lena."

"We were just going to watch some knife play." Dern's casual judgement of both myself and Tice annoyed me. *How could he know anything about us?*

"May I come?" he asked. He must have seen the look on my face, for before I could answer, he spoke again. "I wish only to observe and to hear your recommendations afterwards. I will start to teach tomorrow, but the cohort is yours to lead. I would not usurp that leadership, but I would like to see what your cohort can do. With your permission."

I shrugged. "If you like."

"I will meet you on the field." He turned gracefully, striding across the hall to where Casyn stood with Kyan. Tice looked at me, one eyebrow cocked, but said nothing.

"They're waiting," I said.

On the field, we divided the women into more-or-less evenly matched pairs, based on height and weight. Each woman had her own wooden secca now. Casyn had been hard at work, forging real ones in the evenings. Dern stood back, under the trees, watching.

Freya and Rai had lost the draw. They walked onto the field to face off, each holding her secca close to her body. They circled each other. I watched them, conscious of Dern's gaze, wondering what I should focus on. Freya had strong shoulders and arms from fishing. Rai, ten years her elder, stood half a head shorter but carried more muscle. I judged she outweighed the younger girl by twenty pounds.

Freya feinted first, and Rai stepped sideways, turning her body so that Freya had less of a target, moving backwards at the same time. Freya's cut went wide. She turned quickly, but Rai had swung too and had her knife up, aimed for Freya's unprotected left side. Freya twisted, not away from Rai, but towards her, bringing her secca up to catch Rai's knife arm. The blade struck Rai's forearm. A metal secca would have cut deeply. The wooden practice knife only bruised, but Freya struck with enough strength to force a grimace of pain from Rai. She did not drop the knife, but forced her arm down against the secca to push Freya off-balance. In the same motion, she tossed her knife sideways, caught it with her other hand, and had it up against Freya's throat in an instant.

"Enough," I said. They stepped apart, panting.

Rai rubbed her arm. "That hurt," she said. She shook the arm to loosen the muscles. "But I've had worse from an angry ram," she added, grinning at Freya.

"It would have hurt more had Freya held a real secca," I said. I wanted to glance at Dern, to see what I could read in his face after this first demonstration, but I kept my eyes on Rai. I wondered if he could hear all we said. "You wouldn't have been able to push back against her without driving it deeper into your arm. So while that was a good move now, you shouldn't rely on it. Freya, what did you misjudge?"

"I didn't expect her to push back," she replied, pushing her hair back from her face. "But I suppose if the enemy wear leather, or have arm-guards, they just might. Although then I might not have gone for the arm."

"Right," I said. "Who is next?"

"Wait," Tice said. "I have some things to add."

"Of course," I said hastily.

"Freya, your stance needs work," she said bluntly. "If your left foot had been further back, you could have withstood the pressure without losing your balance so early. We can work on it."

Freya blinked, then glanced at me. I kept my face impassive.

"Yes, all right," she said after a moment, her voice flat. I knew her well enough now to know she took criticism too personally.

"I imagine many of us will need to perfect our stances," I said. "A good observation, Tice. Who is next?"

Aline and Camy, both apprentices, took the field. Slight and wiry, neither had the advantage after three minutes of thrust and parry, and neither had landed a blow. I called a halt. They stopped with some reluctance.

"You're fast," I said, "both with the knife and on your feet. I think you've practiced together quite a bit?"

They looked at each other. "Every day," Camy said.

"So you know what each other will do," Tice said. "Are you practicing, or playing?"

"We're practicing," Aline protested. "Sometimes one of us adds a new move, something we've learned or want to try. We're not children."

"How you will do paired against someone taller or heavier will prove interesting."

"That will be fun!" Aline said. "I bet we're faster." As she turned to leave the field, she made a move towards me with her knife. I jumped back.

"Aline!" I shouted. Tice moved forward, ready to take the secca, but I held up a hand. "Never do that again, to me or anyone," I said, my voice still raised, "or I will take your secca and have you reassigned to another cohort. You say you're not a child. Don't act like one."

She hung her head.

As they walked off the field, deflated, I turned to Tice. "Your comments are accurate," I said very quietly, "but somewhat blunt. Perhaps you could be a bit gentler?"

"Their lives may depend on their knife skills. I see no point in being gentle. And they need to learn that you and I are in command. I would argue that blunt and calm is better than shouting, as you just did."

I bit back an angry retort. Aline had startled me, and I had reacted. I thought of Dern watching. "You may be right. Shall we watch the next pair?" She nodded, turning away from me in a fluid motion, returning her focus to the field where two more women prepared to fight. Solid women, both of them, with the agility required to move up and down rocky hillsides or to maintain balance on a rocking boat. *Tice moves so gracefully,* I thought. *She controls even the tiniest move of her body. Telling a story through dance requires such control. The rest of us have balance, strength, and speed, but our skills come from countering forces—waves or winds or the pull of the earth. Our enemies will have the same skills. Tice can teach us how the move of a thumb, the slightest turn of wrist, can change the odds and the outcome when we fight.*

I signalled for the fighters to begin. With my new insight, I saw where a turn of a foot, or the angle of a thrust, needed not correction, but refinement. "Her balance is too far back. She needs to bring it forward, to the balls of her feet," I murmured to Tice, pointing at one of the women.

"You're right," she said, surprised.

"I was thinking about why you move differently." Just then, one woman stumbled backward, and the other had her pinned, knife at her throat, in a second. "Stop now," I said to them. "Tice, tell them what you saw."

We had little light left. I stole a look at Dern but could not read his expression. "We better do two pairs at once," I said when Tice had finished her critique. "Tice, will you watch the next two? I'll take Salle and Kelle."

When we completed the round of pairings, I divided the women again, this time with as much disparity in size as I could find, then we watched and critiqued again. Tice tempered her comments a bit, and I tried to keep my voice calm.

By the end of the day, we had a rough evaluation of each woman's skills. Dern had moved closer as the light faded but had said nothing.

Finally, in the deepening dusk, Tice and I both took a knife. As we circled, I again marvelled at her grace. Dern had likened her people to cats; I thought it an apt comparison.

I focused on Tice's eyes and the muscles in her knife arm. When I saw her tense to strike, I slid sideways. I twisted up, striking at her, but she danced backwards, then pivoted and thrust at me again. Her secca brushed my arm. I stepped away from the thrust, my eyes on her face. For a heartbeat, neither of us moved, then I feinted left. As she turned just slightly, I changed direction, knifing upward towards her left side. She ducked, falling forward onto her hands, then springing up again. She moved so fast that by the time I had rebalanced and turned, she had her knife against my stomach. I held up my hands and dropped my secca, grinning. The cohort applauded.

I glanced over at Dern.

"Well done, both of you," he said. "May I speak with you both, for a while?"

"Tonight?"

"I would prefer it."

"Yes," I said. "We can go to my mother's house. When should we meet in the morning?"

"Three hours after sunrise?"

I nodded then turned to the waiting women. "Meet here two-and-a-half hours after sunrise. Bring your knives. If you're sore now, go soak it out in the baths. Sleep well tonight." The women drifted away in pairs and small groups.

"They'll all go to the baths," I said to Tice. "I hope it doesn't turn into a late evening, with lots of wine, or they'll be useless in the morning."

"You're thinking like a leader already. I was just envying them the baths and the wine."

"There is wine at my mother's," I said, "if you want it."

"I would be glad of some," Dern said.

My mother's door, as usual, stood open to let in the evening breeze off the sea. When we arrived, my mother, Sara, Gille, and Casyn sat around the kitchen table. The lamp glowed softly, attracting moths to its flame.

"Mother," I greeted her, "Dern and Tice and I need somewhere to talk. May we use your workroom? And may we have some wine, and some cheese and bread?"

"Yes, to all of that," she said. "Tice, Dern, you are very welcome. You'll need to bring in a third chair from the porch." Dern went out to get the chair. Tice followed me to the kitchen cupboards. I handed her the wine flask and cups, pointing the way to the workroom. I put bread and cheese on a plate. In the workroom, I opened the shutters to let in the air and lit the lamp. Dern came in with the chair and closed the door. Tice poured wine for all of us. She held up one cup, its deep red glaze reflecting the lamplight. "I made these."

"With great skill," Dern observed. Tice inclined her head, acknowledging the compliment. "You are both women of many skills," he said, looking steadily at me. The comment made me uncomfortable, and the confidence I had felt after he had praised us slipped away. I picked up my cup without meeting his eyes.

We sat sipping wine in silence. Dern leaned forward, helping himself to bread and cheese. In the flicker of the lamp, he looked older than I had first judged him to be, and very tired. Finally, he spoke. "Savour the wine, and remember it. This is Lestian wine. If we are not victorious when the battle comes, you may never taste it again."

"What did you want to talk about?"

"Lena, you were chosen to lead these women for several reasons: for your ability in the practice ring; for your family connections—the women of Tirvan are accustomed to having your mother and your aunts as their leaders; for your depth of thought." He paused. "But we also chose you to lead this cohort because you have shown that you can make a difficult decision, even when it affects you personally." He held up his hand to prevent me from speaking. "You may need to do that again. You may need to send someone from the cohort—Freya, perhaps, or even Tice—into extreme danger, alone and to certain death. A single death might mean the saving of Tirvan, or of the Empire. I am not exaggerating."

A chill ran through me. I stared at the wine-cup in my hands, my mind in turmoil. I thought of all the hours I had spent on *Dovekie*, reliving that evening. *On the basis of that day, those decisions, Casyn appointed me to this task? What could he know of the recriminations, the fears that had haunted me since?* "What if," I said angrily, "I made that decision from cowardice? What if I did not go with Maya simply because I was too scared? What sort of leader would I be then?"

Dern leaned forward. "Is that true? Look me in the eye, now, here in this room with only the three of us and tell the truth." He spoke gently, but with an undertone of command. I swallowed, looking at the floor. I didn't want to answer him.

"Tell us," he said, firmly.

I looked up and met his eyes. "No," I whispered in a voice barely loudly enough to hear. I cleared my throat to try again. "It is a night thought, or a thought for the empty sea, nothing more."

His gaze did not release me. "Then why did you let Maya go?"

"Because," I hesitated, "all of us, in the village…" *How could I say what I knew inside me?* "We have been here so long…our history, what our foremothers built here…it matters. It matters more than one person. Or two people."

Dern smiled slightly. I realised I had just passed a test. I could hear Tice breathing in the silent room. "Drink your wine," he said gently. "We did not misjudge you."

Tice put down her cup. "May I go? I understand why you wanted me here, but I think there are things you would say to Lena alone."

I opened my mouth to object, but Dern nodded. "Sleep well, Tice."

"Can we speak, tomorrow, before practice?" I asked, remembering my earlier idea and wanting to delay her departure.

"At the field?" she asked. I nodded. She said goodnight, closing the door carefully behind her.

"A perceptive woman," Dern said, leaning back in his chair. As he reached for his wine cup, the lamplight accentuated the lines of fatigue around his eyes. "I am twenty-six. I chose the sea at twelve. Like you, I am from a fishing village—Serra, in the north. When I was sixteen my captain called me to him and told me he was sending me back to land. He sent me to Casyn, to learn to do what you must learn to do." He took a drink of the wine. "I know what it is to send a friend to die. You can do it, Lena. Even now, when I first told you, your thoughts were not that you could not do this, but only that perhaps you would do it for the wrong reasons. When the doubts begin, come to me, Lena."

Not likely, I thought.

"You need to talk them out, not to your cohort or your cohort-second or even your mother. I am here to teach your cohort, but I am also here to teach you, as Casyn taught me."

As I pondered this, something that had been puzzling me at the edges of my consciousness came into focus. "Casyn doesn't seem to be an average soldier. He taught you this…craft of secrecy…and now you are here to teach us. Why could Casyn not have taught us? Why is there such a concentration of expertise here in Tirvan? Is the Empire spending talent this generously on other villages?"

Dern smiled again. "Always thinking," he said. "You are right, of course. I am primarily here to plan tactics with Casyn. We have learned things about the invasion plan in the past few months, and they need to be considered. Casyn is a master of this craft of secrecy, as you call it. The Emperor was loathe to let him come to Tirvan, but he argued that he needed to have first-hand experience of what a woman's village was capable of before he could make his final plans against Leste. I'm here to make him privy to our newest information, and to take him back, in a few weeks, to our command post."

"What does he think us capable of, after his months here?"

"He believes you to be physically capable of as much as a group of men would have been, after only a few months training. But he believes you will fight much harder, and with more tenacity, because you'll be defending your houses, your village, and your way of life. You said, a few minutes ago, that you belong here, that Tirvan is something more than the sum of its parts. Almost all of you feel the same way, in different degrees. You will fight for that feeling of place and belonging." In his voice, I heard the same faint echo of regret that I had heard in Casyn's voice, the night he first came to Tirvan.

"For what do you fight, Dern?" I asked softly.

"For the Empire, and for brotherhood, and because it is what we are trained for from the minute we leave our villages." We sat in silence, sipping our wine. The lamp flickered in the night breeze.

I broke the silence. "What happens to boys, to men, who don't make good soldiers? Who just want to farm or fish?"

"They can be medics, or cooks, or teach the little ones. If they insist, we let them go at sixteen. They work with horses or go to the farms and villas of the retired officers, to pick grapes and make hay. But they can't come back to the women's villages."

"Not at all?"

"No. Not that they would likely want to. They pay a price for choosing not to serve the Empire. This village farms as well as fishes. You must know a bit about breeding horses, or cattle. What does your herdswoman do with colts that are weak around the quarters or ewe-necked? The empire needs men to be soldiers, not farmers. We need our sons to be strong, so we make sure that only those who serve the Empire father sons."

Shaken, I drank the dregs of my wine. From our earliest childhood, we knew how our lives were structured and where the duty of both men and women lay. I had not considered, until tonight, that sacrifice underpinned that structure, that each of us paid some inestimable price for our calm and ordered existence. Until tonight, I had thought only of Maya, and of myself.

Dern stared upward at nothing, his lips tight, exhaustion or worry webbing his face. "I said too much." He sounded apologetic. "Blame the wine."

"It's late," I said. "And the Lestian wine is strong. I won't repeat what was said here tonight."

He nodded. "Thank you." He gazed at me steadily for a minute before standing. "I sleep at Casyn's cottage until my ship is in harbour. Would you point the way?" I took the lamp from the wall and opened the door. Darkness shadowed the outer room. We walked out onto the porch. A light still burned at the forge cottage: Casyn, bent over papers and maps, planning. Dern bade me a soft goodnight and set off, silent, on the gravel path. I blew out the lamp, setting it on a bench before turning in the opposite direction, downhill, to Tali's house and bed.

CHAPTER FIVE

THE DAY DAWNED HOT, the air still and humid. As I washed in the morning light, at the open window of my room, I could hear Tali in the kitchen below me, talking to Pel. I brushed my hair back off my face, strapped my knife onto my belt, and went down for breakfast.

"Dessa was here last night," Tali said. "She wants to borrow *Dovekie* while you're not fishing. She said she would sail her herself and let her senior apprentices sail *Curlew*."

I poured myself a mug of tea, considering. Both Freya and I now trained all day with Dern, and the village needed all the food it could stockpile. Reasonably, I could not refuse. "Can Pel go down to the harbour to tell her yes?"

Pel looked unhappy. "I wanted to watch the knife play."

"It won't start for another hour," I said. "Go to the harbour now to tell Dessa that I said she may use Dovekie for as long as she needs her. If you're quick and don't linger at the boats, I'll teach you a move or two with the knives before we start practice this morning." Pel brightened and jumped up. He glanced at his mother for permission, running out the door almost before Tali had finished saying "Go." I cut a slice of bread, spreading honey on it.

"Don't let him become a nuisance."

I shrugged. "There's always a gaggle of them about, the small boys and some of the girls. It won't hurt them to learn a bit." I finished my bread and took a sip of my tea. It had cooled, so I drank it down. "Would you send him to the practice field when he gets back? I want to speak with Tice before the others arrive." I rinsed my mug and plate, setting them to drain on the wooden rack over the sink. From a basket on the table, I took an apple and a pear. Tali filled a water bottle. "What are you doing today?" I asked.

"Picking more apples," she said. "They're a bit green, but they should dry well." She grinned. "If a big storm blows up and drowns all the invaders, we're going to be sick of smoked fish and dried apples this winter."

I laughed and went out into the sunlight. From long habit, I turned to look out to sea. A haze hung over the horizon, but the white sails of fishing boats dotted the bay. I walked up the hill to the empty practice field, my sandaled feet kicking up small clouds of dust. I stopped in a shaded corner and began the stretching exercises Casyn had taught us. Methodically, I counted my way through the routine, one-two-three, one-two-three. My skin gleamed with sweat when I sensed rather than heard someone approaching. I looked up.

"Good morning," Tice said.

"And to you. Did you sleep well?"

"Yes," she said. "The wine helped. Did you stay with Dern long?"

"We talked for a while longer," I said. "Tice, I want you to teach us to dance."

"To dance!" she exclaimed.

"Will you?"

"I can try," she said, "but we don't have much time. I don't know if what I can teach in a few weeks can make much difference."

"In a few weeks, we have learned the sword and the secca, and the bow, for some."

"True," she said. "I'll do my best, cohort-leader."

I grinned. She pulled her dark hair back off her face and tied it, then joined me in the stretches. When our muscles felt loose and supple, we switched to knife play, and then to wrestling. When Pel arrived with his friend Salle, we taught them the simpler moves with the wooden knives. They went off to the far corner of the field to practice. Tice and I sat in the shade of the tree. I gave her the pear, and we sat in silence, savouring the crisp tartness of the fruit.

I tossed my apple core aside. "Show me how to move more quietly, before the others get here."

"I can show you some things," she said. "But unless you have danced the dances of Karst since you were a babe newly on your feet, you—or any of the cohort—will never be truly silent."

"Anything would be an improvement. I couldn't sneak up on a hibernating bear."

Tice laughed. "You're quieter than you think," she said. "Your body has learned some grace from the knife-play, and the beginnings a different sort of balance than you needed on the boats. But come," she said, on her feet in one swift move, extending a hand to help me up, "I'll show you what I can."

Patiently, she explained how to roll my weight along my foot and push off lightly from the ball of my feet and from my toes. I practised this for a while. My movements felt exaggerated and artificial, but I did make less noise. We had moved on to the steps of the first dance learned by Karst children when Dern arrived. I stopped, suddenly self-conscious.

"Taran taught me that dance, too, when we served together," he observed. "Come, Lena," he said, grasping my hands. "Dance with me." I stopped myself from stepping back. His hands felt cool and dry against my moist palms. Our heights matched. "To the left, to begin," he said, sliding his left leg sideways in the first move of the simple dance. I looked at my feet and followed.

After two or three steps, I looked up to find Dern also watching his feet. Tice slowly chanted the moves, and I relaxed. We managed a dozen steps or so before our feet collided. Dern stumbled, and I stopped. We looked at each other, his hands still holding mine. For a handful of heartbeats, we stood, his eyes travelling from mine, down to my lips, and back again to meet my gaze. I flushed, pulling my hands away. "I was never a dancer," I said.

"And I am out of practice. Apologies for my awkwardness. Shall we return to the knives, where we know the moves?" He turned away to begin his warm-up exercises. Tice caught my eye, grinning. I felt myself flushing again and busied myself with my knife.

The cohort began to arrive a few minutes later. After the stretching exercises and basic moves, I sent half the women to work with Dern, and Tice and I began the remedial work with the other half. We worked on grip and angles, on wrist actions and on movement. By the end of two hours, I could see a marked improvement in the entire group. Lara arrived with water. We took turns drinking before stretching out in the shade for a well-earned rest.

After the break, Tice took over. As a group, we kicked off our sandals, to learn how to walk in a new fashion. Dern excused himself and went back down the hill towards the forge. The cohort practised silence—foot-silence, anyhow. Laughter and muffled curses punctuated the activity, especially when the time came to judge each woman individually. Freya topped us all.

With about an hour left in the morning's training, I called a halt. The cohort settled into a rough half-circle on the grass.

"You've all worked hard this morning," I said. "But we're going to introduce something new now. I think you've all noticed how graceful Tice is, how smoothly she moves?" Several heads nodded. "I'd like us all to move our bodies like that, and to help us learn, I've asked Tice to teach us to dance."

"To dance?" Aline said, unknowingly echoing Tice's reaction of the previous night. "I'm not going to learn to dance. We were chosen to learn knife skills, not to dance." She sounded disgusted. I almost laughed, remembering how black and white the world seemed at fourteen. "You're not my apprentice-master," she continued. "Casyn chose me, not you."

"As he chose me to lead this cohort," I said quietly. "So you will do as I say, and as Tice says, and you will learn to dance. Not for pleasure, but for the precision of step and balance and movement it teaches. I will be learning right beside you. It is Tice who is the master in this. Do you understand?"

"Yes," she muttered, but she did not meet my eye. *Had I misjudged my response?* I thought of Casyn's words: *In battle, there is no democracy.*

"All right," I said. "Let's get started."

I went to my mother's to eat. Neither she nor Kira answered my call. They were out in the village, I surmised, checking on Nessa's newborn or one of the other soon-to-deliver women. I took some cheese and bread and sat on the porch, where breezes from the sea cooled the air a little. I watched the gulls over the sea, and the sails of the boats out on the fishing banks, the blue-and-white of *Dovekie* among them. There was a line of clouds on the horizon, building up from the heat. Rain later, with a bit of luck. *Will Maya have shelter, if it rains wherever she is? Does she have food?* My chest tightened. I blinked back tears. *No, I* thought. *Think about something else. Think about correcting Gayl's balance.*

A while later, I saw my mother walking up the path, looking tired. I got up to bring her water. She sat on the porch, drinking thirstily. "Ranni's labour started. I've left Kira with her for a bit. She's capable of handling the early stages, now."

"Will it be all right?" I asked. Nessa had lost one of her twins at birth a few days earlier, after a long and difficult labour.

"Everything seems normal, but she's scared, with it being her first baby. And with the times. I shouldn't stay away long." She poured herself another drink. "I will be calling meeting tonight, or tomorrow—tonight if the rain comes early."

"Why?"

"*Skua* will arrive soon," she said. "Her crew of men will be going into battle soon, chancing death. We are a village of women facing the same truth for the first time. I won't deny either group comfort, but neither can we risk new pregnancies. All of us, apprentice to elder, who are of childbearing years must begin to drink anash tea as soon as possible."

Anash tea, if drunk before and after Festival for a few days, and each day during, prevented pregnancy. A poor harvest or a bad winter meant general use at Festival, but an individual woman drank it whenever she did not wish a Festival liaison to result in pregnancy. I thought of Dern and forced the thought away.

"Apprentices?" I asked. "But we don't allow apprentices liaisons."

"No," my mother agreed, her voice tired, "in usual times, we do not. But we feel, Gille and Sarah and I, that we cannot deny that these are not usual times. In the coming raids, some of us will die or be raped. These are not Empire's men. Providing the council agrees with us, we won't stop liaisons between *Skua*'s crew and our girls and women, regardless of status. And all of us will drink anash tea until the war is over, both against wanted encounters, and unwanted."

"I see," I said slowly. I did see, but I didn't want to drink anash. I fetched my mother some food, and we sat on the porch and ate and drank cool water. After another half hour, I went back to the practice field.

Dern did not come back in the afternoon. I wondered where he was, and with whom. The cohort worked and danced for another two hours, until the thunderheads building in the western sky rumbled, and the fishing boats ran back into harbour ahead of the storm. I went down to the docks to help unload and prepare the boats.

Lightening flashed, and the first fat drops of rain splashed into the water when we finished. The air smelled of wet dust and the sharp tang that followed lightening. I stood on the dock, holding my face up to the rain. Maya loved thunderstorms, loved the feel of the rain and the play of light and shadow in the clouds. She would sit in the window of our room on summer evenings, watching the storms out over the sea and the seabirds playing on the storm winds, laughing in pure delight. A wave of loneliness poured over me.

I closed my eyes. Behind me, I could hear someone moving around on the boats—Dessa, probably, inspecting for storm-readiness. Work provided the antidote. I opened my eyes and went to help her, checking ropes and hatches while the rain grew stronger.

By the time we finished, my hair and clothes were dripping. I walked up the hill, grabbed a change of clothes and a towel, and went to the baths. Someone had tacked an announcement of meeting tonight to the door. I went in, rinsed my feet and hands, and sank into the hot pool. For a while, I just floated, letting the warmth ease my tired muscles. The gentle movement of the water against my skin comforted me. Maya had excelled at back rubs, working the kinks out of neck and shoulders, aching from hauling nets. I missed her touch, missed not the pleasure but the solace of lovemaking, the basic human need for connection. If I wanted, I knew, Dern would meet that need, both mine and his.

I considered. Maya and I had paired before puberty, her sadness evoking some instinct for protection in me. We had become lovers as adolescents, and in the eyes of the village had partnered in all senses. Liaisons with men had little effect on most partnerships between women, although some women, like my aunt Tali, who had truly and deeply loved the man who fathered her elder children, chose to live partnerless. We'd talked about this: Maya had wanted no children to give up to the Empire. I remained ambivalent, but childbearing had nothing to do with how I felt. Loneliness did. I wanted, simply, arms around me, the scent and warmth and feel of another body against mine.

The sound of the door opening startled me out of my reverie. Dessa, I guessed, correctly, and Siane with her. They joined me in the hot pool, Dessa supporting Siane carefully as she edged into the pool. "Ranni's doing well," Siane said, once she had settled. "We stopped on the way up. Gwen thinks it'll be another five or six hours."

"Good," I said. Dessa moved forward and began to rub Siane's bad leg. Siane sighed, leaning back. I had seen this a hundred times, but in my current state of mind this casual, accepted support of each other rankled. I wanted the same, and Maya had taken it away.

I left the baths, saying goodbye to Dessa and Siane. I dried and dressed, going out into the early evening. I walked along the gravel path, passing the forge and Casyn's cottage. Through open windows, I could hear the murmur of voices: Casyn and Dern, I surmised, planning tactics. The storm had cooled the day and an evening breeze, gentle now, blew off the sea. I felt a sudden urge to be out on the water. *Why not?*

I readied *Dovekie*, rowing her out beyond the shelter of the harbour, to where the winds would fill her sail. The sun westered in a clear sky, only a few wisps of cloud trailing eastward behind the storm. I shipped the oars and set *Dovekie's* sail, tacking northward along the coast. Seabirds soared and plunged around me, hoping for fish. The breeze blew more stiffly here. I became lost in the familiar, the feel of the tiller under my hand and the smell of the sea around me, the rush of water against *Dovekie's* side and the cries of the gulls overhead. I sailed north, until the land curved out to meet me. Beyond that promontory, the bay gave way to the open Lantanan Sea, wilder and crueller: no place for a lone sailor even on a calm summer's evening. I brought *Dovekie* about, heading home.

"How do we know anash is safe to use for weeks on end?" Kyan asked, after my mother had explained both the council's reasoning and decision on the subject. "Or for young girls?"

"To answer the first," my mother said, "let me tell you that I read what books I have carefully. While I cannot say with certainty that anash is safe for long use, it is clear that, before Partition, most women drank it regularly to space their pregnancies and to limit them. I wish I had more books, but I could find nothing to suggest there was any danger attached to the practice."

"Fair enough," Kyan said. "But for the girls?"

"I truly do not know. It was first used against the Eastern fever, so it would have been given to girls, surely. I gather our foremothers learned of its other properties accidentally. I doubt its use is a greater risk than pregnancy for girls of twelve or fourteen. If a girl is capable of conceiving, she needs to use the means to prevent it."

"But a twelve-year-old?" Siane said, her voice wavering with fear. "Or even younger?" Siane's daughter Lara, only eleven, had remained home tonight, but when she brought water up to the practice field, I had noticed how her shirt pulled against her developing breasts. Her menses could begin at any time.

"Rape," Sara said, "especially in wartime, has little or nothing to do with normal desire. Rather it is an act of domination and aggression. Age will not matter, if it comes to that."

Casse stood to speak. "I doubt anyone here but Gwen knows my mother was not Tirvan-born, but came from Berge to be the smith here a hundred years ago," she said. "I was born when she was thirty, so these memories are very old. When she was a girl in Berge, raids from across the border were not uncommon, and rape happened. Do not think it cannot, here." She sat down again.

Siane buried her face in her hands. I shuddered.

Sara continued. "For girls below apprentice age, the use of anash is a decision for the girl and her mother. The council will not interfere. But for girls of apprentice age, we deem the use necessary."

"What do I say to her?" Siane said, clearly not expecting an answer. Sara chose to answer regardless.

"That is between you and Dessa and Lara, Siane," she said. "You have some time. We see no need for the younger girls to begin drinking anash more than a week or two before the autumn equinox.

"Perhaps," my mother added, "I can be of help." Several women assented eagerly. "We can talk after meeting is done," my mother offered. "But now we need to speak of the older apprentices. We are proposing that those sixteen this year and above be allowed liaisons with *Skua*'s crew, if desired."

Freya's mother, Binne, stood. "I asked my daughter," she said. Freya sat with the other senior apprentices. This age group came to meeting at the invitation of council leaders, to hear debate and to learn the protocols, but they had no right to speak. "Freya would like the right to choose a liaison this summer. If we lose, she knows that may mean no choice at all, and she would prefer her first experience with a man to be something she wants, with a man of her choosing. I cannot find fault with her argument."

"Except," another woman said, "that we could make the same argument for those younger than sixteen."

"How old are the ship's crew?' Marna asked.

"I asked Dern that," Gille said. "There are no cadets; the youngest will be about eighteen."

"Fifteen is just too young," Kelle said. "We structure our apprenticeships so that we have little experience in making decisions until we reach sixteen; we observe, and do what we are told. I couldn't have made a good choice about this at fifteen."

"Nor I," said her sister Salle. "I agree with Kelle."

"Shall we vote?" my mother asked. Hearing agreement from the women of voting age, she continued. "Two votes, then. First, in the red boxes, we vote on the requirement of all apprentices under sixteen to drink anash, beginning shortly before the equinox. Second, in the black boxes, we vote on whether to allow apprentices sixteen this year and older the opportunity for liaisons with men from *Skua*'s crew."

The council leaders distributed the pebbles, and we voted. Both proposals passed, although fewer women voted for the first proposal than the second.

"Now," Sara said, "for practicalities. Does anyone need anash? There is plenty of time yet this summer to harvest and dry it." Every house had an anash bush, or two, in the garden, but they needed to be either harvested or pruned yearly to maintain the growth of the young leaves. The midwife's house, not surprisingly, had several bushes, and I had picked leaves since earliest childhood as one of my chores. I knew my mother would have a lot put by, but I doubted the supply would serve the entire village.

A few hands went up. "See me," my mother said. "Please remember to teach your daughters to steep it for at least three minutes and to drink it at the same time every day."

"And to add honey," Tali said, grimacing. "I can't stand the stuff without honey."

The meeting dispersed. Tice fell into step beside me on the path. "How about some wine? I've got a flask, not from Leste, but good southern stuff, and some food to go with it."

I hadn't eaten, and Tice's invitation meant I would not have to go back to my solitary room. "Thank you," I said. Where the path divided, we went left, uphill to Tice's cottage. I hadn't entered this cottage since old Minna had given up the wheel and kiln entirely to move in with her daughter, some eighteen months before. Tice had whitewashed the walls and softened the wide boards of the floor with intricately woven rugs in bright colours. On shelves, scattered around the room, stood examples of Tice's craft—vases and pots in deep reds and rich cobalt blue. A tortoiseshell cat stretched itself awake from the windowsill, mewing a welcome.

"Have a seat," Tice said.

I sat cross-legged on one of the rugs, holding out a hand to the cat. It approached warily, sniffed my fingertips, and immediately broke into an ecstasy of purring. I scratched its ears. It collapsed on the rug, rolling over. "Don't!" Tice said, as I reached over to rub the cat's stomach. I looked up. She handed me a wine goblet and a flask. "It's a ruse. Rub her belly, and she'll tear your hand to pieces with her hind claws." She picked the cat up before sinking gracefully to the floor a few feet away.

I poured two glasses of wine. The cat curled up on Tice's lap, purring. I held up my wine glass. "Health and luck," I said.

"Health and luck," Tice replied. "Although in the south we have a saying: choice is better than chance. "She sipped her wine. "Hence the anash."

"Tell me about the south. I've never been more than a day's sail from Tirvan." The wine was spicy, tasting of blackberries.

Tice rubbed the cat's ears, reflectively. "The land in the south is flat, with long fields running down to the sea. Karst isn't really a village, not like Tirvan. No one wanted to waste land on a village, so each farm has its house and outbuildings, scattered over the district. There is a hall, at a central crossroads, for meetings. Above the meeting hall is a belfry. In an emergency, the bell is rung. It can be heard for miles across the fields."

"It sounds lonely."

"Do you find it lonely on the sea, in a small boat, all day?"

"No," I answered, "but we come back to the village, and the baths, and the people."

She nodded. "In the south, we reverse this. We tend to work communally, at harvest or in the spring when the grapes need tying. Each farm is slightly different: the grapes grow faster or slower depending on the soils and how close the farm lies to the sea. So, we're together a lot, and there are many dances and celebrations and meals, but we go home to our own farms, and the open space above us, and the long views down to the water."

I thought about this and my need today for space, and the wind and seaspray against my face. "Why did you leave?"

"Karst had no need of another potter, so I saddled my pony and brought my skills north, seeking a village that did."

I hesitated, conscious of the warning in her voice. "Was it hard, on the road?"

"Hard enough," she said. "You're thinking of Maya?" I nodded. "She should be all right, if she thought to take warm clothes, and if she finds a place to stay before winter. The inns always need help. North, south or east, she will be able to find work and food and a roof over her head, if she wants it." I knew very little of the world beyond Tirvan. A single dirt track, dusty or muddy according to the season, lay between Tirvan and a pass in the hills. I had never wondered, until now, what lay beyond those hills, where that track met the broader, paved roads of the Empire.

The cat meowed, a demanding, plaintive sound. "She's hungry," Tice said. "Let's all eat." She stood, holding the cat against one shoulder. I put my wine on a low table. Tice led the way into the small kitchen. She put the cat down on the stone floor, pouring milk from a blue jug into a bowl glazed to match the tortoiseshell of the cat's fur. Tice caught me looking at the bowl. "That way I know it's hers and don't eat my soup out of it," she said. She took a covered crock down from a shelf, handing to me. "Olives," she said. "Put some on a plate. There are pickled onions in the red bowl." I scooped olives and onions onto a plate while Tice cut a loaf of barley bread. The cat lapped at the milk. Tice handed me the basket of bread. "It's getting dark. Take the food back into the other room. I'll light the lamp."

We sat on the rug again, the lamp on the table and the food between us. The cat jumped onto the windowsill to wash. I bit into an olive, relishing its rich saltiness.

"Has Dern said anything about when *Skua* will arrive?"

I shook my head, my mouth full. "Nothing more than what was said in meeting. Why?"

"Just wondering," she said. "It'll be a bit like Festival, won't it?" The lamp gave enough light to eat by, but I could not read her eyes.

"I suppose," I said. "Are you thinking of a liaison?" I wondered if I presumed too much in asking this, but Tice just smiled.

"No," she said, "no liaisons for me. And you?" She took a piece of bread from the plate, dipping it into the olive bowl to sop up the oil.

"I don't know," I said. She cocked an eyebrow in the quizzical expression I was beginning to know well.

"Dern will ask."

"I know." I took a mouthful of the wine. "Tice, have you—?"

"Have I been with a man? Yes. And you haven't?"

"No." I admitted. "I've only been old enough for one Festival, and Maya and I...well, we had each other. But now...I'm confused, Tice." I was suddenly glad of the low light in the room.

"Do you want him?"

"Yes, I do." I had said it.

She smiled, a slow and somehow sad smile. "He is an honourable man, I think," she said, "and you are well matched. But only you can decide, Lena. Choice is better than chance."

Through the open window, I could see stars in the night sky, and the rising full moon, the last of summer. We sat in silence for a while. The lamplight flickered in the night breeze. Tice began to sing, unexpectedly, a slow, sorrowful song.

The swallows gather, summer passes,
The grapes hang dark and sweet;
Heavy are the vines,
Heavy is my heart,
Endless is the road beneath my feet.

The sun is setting, the moon is rising,
The night is long and sweet;
I am gone at dawn,
I am gone with day,
Endless is the road beneath my feet.

The cold is deeper, the winters longer,
Summer is short but sweet,
I will remember,
I'll not forget you,
Endless is the road beneath my feet.

"Is that a song of your people?" I asked, after the last bittersweet note had faded.

"No," she replied. "It is a song from Casilla, which is many miles east of Karst. I learned it from an old soldier, a general, who had his retirement farm half a day from our vineyard. He grew grapes and raised horses and collected songs. Jedd, his name was."

"A general?" I said, surprised. "But, then, there were men around? I mean, not just at Festival?"

Tice laughed. "Not every day, no. But, Lena, the retirement farms have to be somewhere! And Jedd and his household were old, as old, nearly, as Casse. We traded with him, a bit, for new varieties of grapes, or we would buy casks or corks from a trading ship and then he would buy some from us."

"If Jedd was that old, who worked the farm?"

Tice looked uncomfortable. "He mostly hired women from Karst, to prune and tie the grapes in the spring, and for autumn harvest. But there were some men, young men, I mean, who worked with the horses. Some of them were slaves, from the northern peoples." She hesitated. "And some were not. But they never came to Festival."

Nor would they, I thought, remembering what Dern had told me.

"I knew there were retirement farms, but somehow I thought they were far, far away, not near the women's villages at all. Although I suppose there are villages throughout the Empire, too."

Tice nodded in agreement. "Jedd showed me a map, once. Some of the villages are on the coast, but most are inland. But in the far north and east there are none, not near the Wall or the mountains. After all those years serving in the north, the men want warmth and sunshine." She grinned. "And if they live to retirement, they are too old to want anything else, so they are not, shall we say, disruptive, to the villages."

"There's so much I don't know," I said, feeling both frustrated and foolish.

Tice shrugged. "Why would you? I didn't know of the world beyond Karst, either, until I left, except what Jedd told me. And even now I can't claim to know much more, except of the road between here and Karst, and the inns I stayed at."

Tice filled my wine glass. After the lamp flame flickered and guttered, we sat in the moonlight, listening to the night sounds. The cat made a soft sound and jumped off the windowsill, heading out to her night's hunting. I stood, stretching.

"Thank you, Tice. I enjoyed the evening."

I let myself out. I could tell by the stars that it was near midnight. I looked east, into the night, toward the road I knew lay beyond the hills, the road Tice had ridden, the road Maya had chosen to take, and I had not.

CHAPTER SIX

I SPOONED HONEY INTO MY MUG of anash tea, stirring it vigorously. After eight days, I had nearly grown used to its smoky, slightly bitter taste. I covered the teapot to keep it warm for Tali. I could hear her moving about upstairs. The day had dawned cloudy, with a band of sea fog about half a mile off shore. I could hear voices down at the harbour, but they would wait for the fog to lift before setting out. Already the sun showed weakly through the cloud. When it rose higher, in an hour or two, the day would heat up. The autumn equinox was approaching. Soon the fog would last all morning, and then all day. On many days not fogbound the wind would blow too strongly to safely sail, and the boats would stay in the harbour, sails furled, or be hauled up on the beach for repair.

Last night, Tice and Dern and I had eaten together at Tice's cottage. Tice had cooked a spicy bean stew, and I had begged a loaf of fresh bread from my mother. We did not eat together every night, but I had suggested we needed to review the cohort's progress.

"Little Aline is deadly with that secca," Dern said. "She can throw accurately with either hand when she's standing, and even crouched, she's hitting the target most of the time."

"She's still resentful of me," I said. "Not overtly, but there's just a bit of sullenness there when I give her an order." I sipped my wine.

"She wants you to notice her," Tice said. "She's very young. She needs your praise."

"Which she gets," I pointed out, "when she earns it." The cat appeared from somewhere to wind around my legs. I put a hand down to pet her.

"Praise her privately," Dern said unexpectedly. I raised an eyebrow. "I've worked with cadets like this, too. Praise on the field is good, but impersonal. I agree with Tice."

"I'll try. We need to begin working on the hiding places in the village." I said, changing the subject. "Tice won't know most of them,"

"Or even any," she interjected, "saving the loft and cellar of my own cottage."

"Do we give the cohort a day off, and the three of us investigate where we can hide, and how we can move across the village without being seen? Or do you, Dern, take the cohort, and Tice and I do it together?" I looked from one to the other.

"We don't give them the day off," Tice said immediately. "Aline and probably Camy would only follow us. I'll take the cohort. You and Dern work together."

I saw her logic. Dern had experience and training. I needed him with me to analyse the possibilities. "You're right," I said, after a pause.

"When do you want to do this?" Dern pushed his chair back to stretch his legs. His fingers played with the stem of his wine goblet. I wondered what they would feel like on my skin.

"Tomorrow?" I suggested. He nodded.

"Tomorrow, then, at our usual morning start." He stood. "And now I should find Casyn. Goodnight, Lena. Goodnight, Tice. Thank you for the meal and the wine." He smiled at us both, bent to stroke the cat, and left.

"You should find lots of possibilities, tomorrow," Tice said, when his footsteps had faded. She grinned.

I blushed. "We're working."

"All day?" she inquired, eyebrow cocked. "I see the way you look at him. And the way he looks at you. Probably half the cohort is betting on it. Freya would like to use her secca on you, she's so jealous."

"Really?" I said, startled. "Freya?"

"Freya," she confirmed. "Cohort-leader, you're good with tactics and planning, but you need to think about your cohort as individuals. You've known them all so long, I think you just don't notice things." She shrugged. "I'm still an outsider, so they don't have that gloss of familiarity for me. I'm trying to understand them. Maybe I see more."

"Maybe you do," I said slowly.

Dern was waiting for me at the forge, so I finished my tea, called a goodbye to Tali, and walked up the hill. I walked as Tice had shown me, rolling my weight along my feet. It no longer felt as awkward or as artificial as it had a week ago, and I thought I moved more quietly.

Dern stood in the paddock, currying his horse, and I reached the fence before he looked up.

"Lena," he said, surprised. "Did you come up the path?"

I grinned. "Yes. I could have put a knife into you ten paces back."

"You could have," he agreed. "Well done."

"The waterfall masks a lot of sound up here. Are you ready?"

As he removed his horse's headcollar, it nuzzled him, blowing through its nostrils, looking for a carrot or a piece of bread. "Nothing this morning, boy," he said, slapping its shoulder. He took the headcollar and the brush to the stable, pausing to rinse his hands in the water trough. I looked up at the cottage.

"What exactly are we looking for?"

"A few things," Dern said. "Places where a woman can hide, armed with a secca, and take a man by surprise. Ways to move through the village without being seen, to reposition part or all your cohort, or to send a messenger. Secret places, secret routes." He looked up at the forge cottage. "There is a tiny loft above the rooms," Dern said. I followed his gaze. "The door is in the ceiling of the west bedroom. It's not much. You can only crouch. But there are ventilation windows, with sliding panels to cover them in winter."

"Likely, no one would think of it being there," I said. "It's clear there is an attic of some sort over my mother's house, and Tali's, but here, and I think at Tice's, you wouldn't think of it."

He nodded. "Exactly," he said. "They will look for the forge immediately, to repair weapons or to make more. There would be no easy escape for a person hidden in the loft here."

"Down the waterfall," I said, without hesitation. "It's dangerous. Some of the boulders are far apart, and you must jump from one to another. They're also very slippery, and some of them move, but I'd guess almost every eleven or twelve-year-old here can do it. It's strictly forbidden, of course."

"Of course," Dern said, with a hint of a grin. He considered for a moment. "Did you ever climb up it?"

"I did," I said. "It's difficult. You have to jump up. I made it, but I never tried again. Freya has climbed up, too," I remembered. "We talked about it, once, when we were fishing." In unspoken agreement, we walked the short distance uphill to where the stream channelled out from the bathhouse pools to begin its westerly descent down the rocky cliff face. On either side of the watercourse, thick thorn bushes grew. In the spring, the thorn blossom hummed with bees from the hives kept nearby. "Where is the hardest part?" Dern asked. "Climbing up, I mean?"

I paused, remembering. "About two-thirds of the way up, there's a spot where the cliffside has fallen away, leaving a sheer wall with just slight depressions in the wet rock for your hands and feet. Freya and I both made it because we're tall and could reach the handholds, and because we'd already fished for a season and had strong arms."

"If we fastened a knotted rope there, would it help?"

"Yes, I think so. But it would still be a dangerous climb."

"These are dangerous times," Dern said. He walked over to where the water began its descent. Green algae grew on the rocks, and a faint sulphur smell rose from the stream. He squatted to put his hand in the water. "Warm," he said. "Does it freeze?"

"No," I replied, following his train of thought. "But some of the pools form ice at the edges, further down. And the rocks ice over. I wouldn't want to climb it, up or down, past the first snowfall."

"Climb it soon, Lena. You and as many of your cohort as can manage it. Up and down, until you can do it in the night, if need be. If Leste takes the village, or even just the forge, this might be the only way up from the harbour. Add ropes or even ladders where they're needed. Casyn will help you fasten bolts into the rock. Leste is a flat isle. Lestian men have no skill in rock-climbing."

He straightened. "Lena," he said quietly, "what is your father's name?" The first question of courtship.

I flushed. I could tell him he did not need to know, the usual, gentle refusal. "Galen," I said, "of the third regiment, born at Skeld."

Dern nodded. "My father is Valder. He sails on *Albatross*," he said, holding my gaze.

I looked away, up to the hills, confused. The heather made waves of purple between the rocks. Sheep dotted the lower hillsides, and a golden eagle soared far above them. "There are caves, up on the heights. We played in them as children. They're not large. I think streams like this one made them. One or two of them still have a trickle of water running through them. They could hide a woman or two, and weapons."

"Can you find them again?"

I shrugged. "Some of them, yes. The children will know better, the older ones. Lara will remember, or we can ask the shepherd apprentices. They shelter in them, sometimes, when it rains."

"We could send the children there if we have is sufficient warning."

"We could," I said doubtfully. "But food cannot be stored in the caves. Wildcats take it, or the foxes."

Dern grinned. "Not even a fox can take ship's biscuit from inside a metal box, and there is a good supply of such on *Skua*. If there is water, as you remember, then we can equip the caves for survival, if not for comfort. No one," he added ruefully, "would call ship's biscuit comforting."

I laughed. "We can look over the caves," I said. "We'll take Pel. He spends a good deal of time up there with Sarr, whose sister is apprenticed to Gille. The girls stay with the flocks, but the boys wander, playing soldier. Sarr and Pel will know the caves."

"As I did, once," said a voice from behind us. We turned to see Casyn approaching. "Good morning to you both," he added. "I am going to shoe Siannon. Dern, is your horse in need of reshoeing?"

Dern considered. "Yes," he said. "It's been some weeks. My thanks, Casyn."

Casyn nodded. "I heard you speaking of the caves," he said. "If memory serves, there is one, quite large, where a stream runs across the back and into a pool of some size. I remember it as being big enough to live in, comfortably, but those are the memories of a child of six. If you can find it, it should be equipped with food, blankets, and a store of firewood. And weapons. It was a good thought, Lena. I had forgotten the caves."

I flushed again. I found being praised in front of Dern by this man, once his teacher, now his superior officer, discomfiting. I felt Casyn's eyes on my face, but he said nothing, turning instead to Dern. "Does Tasque stand easy to be shod?"

Dern nodded. "He'll give you no trouble." He paused. "Did you ever climb the waterfall, Casyn, up or down?"

Casyn looked surprised. "No," he said. "I was too small. Oh, I clambered on the rocks and in the little pools on a hot day, but no more. I remember falling, once, on a slippery rock at the base and truly scaring myself. We thought, the little boys, I mean—" He glanced at me. "My pardon, Lena, if I trespass here. We thought it a ritual, a rite of womanhood, I suppose, because only the girls who were of an age to be apprenticed climbed down it. I did not know anyone ever climbed up it."

I grinned. "The only rite it was, was one of defiance. When Cate fell and broke her arm, we carried her along the shore until we came to the shellfish pools and then told her mother she had slipped there." I stopped, thinking of what Casyn had said. "I had never considered," I said slowly, "that my mother, and her sisters and their mother before them, had climbed down that waterfall, too. It's never spoken of. I've climbed up it, and Freya too, but no one else that I know." Half to myself, I added, "I will have to ask Tali."

"You are thinking of it as an escape route?" Casyn asked.

"Possibly," Dern said. "But more as a way up to the top of the village, if needed." Casyn cocked his head. "If the fight goes badly," Dern continued, "there could be several reasons to have Lena's cohort able to climb up the waterfall: to coordinate an attack from the heights, to send a messenger out from the village, to reach the caves if we use them. And an equal number of reasons to climb down: to reach their boats, to fire the Lestian ship, to kill."

Casyn nodded. "Sound thinking," he agreed. "But a last resort, I hope. We will talk tonight. Can you eat with us this evening, Lena?"

"Me?" I said.

Casyn laughed. "You are a cohort leader, and you have proven again this morning that you know more about this village than either Dern or myself. We need you there if we are to plan tactics. Bring Tice. You will both need to know the plans and the reasons behind them and be able to explain them to your cohort. Those plans, and your cohort, may be Tirvan's saving." His tone had become serious, with his last words.

"And now I am going to heat the forge and shoe horses," he said, cheerful again. He turned away, moving back toward the forge.

I looked at Dern. "We have forty cottages to look at and nearly as many outbuildings."

"Do you know how many might have lofts or cellars?"

I shook my head. "No. Most cottages will have a cellar of some sort, if only to store root vegetables and apples. Both my mother's cottage and Tali's have cellars and lofts. But there is something else, too,"

He cocked his head.

"Some of the older cottages have tunnels between the house and the barn."

"Tunnels," Dern said, thoughtfully. "Yes, Serra had these, too. I can just remember one between my grandmother's house and her barn. She showed me, once. The blackness and the cobwebs scared me." He shook his head in wonder. "I had completely forgotten the tunnels. They were built because of the snows, many generations ago. Is that right?"

"So we were taught," I said. "But they're long unused and may have collapsed. I only remembered them in the night." I had lain sleepless, thinking about Dern. "Perhaps we should start by speaking with Casse."

"The snows," Casse said. "I remember my mother speaking of them from her own mother's memories. But yes, I think I remember where all the tunnels are."

"What about the forge?" I asked.

"No. There is a cellar, of course, where ore and wood are stored, and the unwrought bars of metal, but the stable isn't connected."

"Thank you, Casse," Dern said. "Tirvan is lucky to have you."

She smiled. "You flatter as well as any young man ever did, but I am glad to be useful, and even gladder I still have my mind. Now, go to work. You should start with my loft and cellar."

After we examined Casse's home, we moved on to her neighbours. When women could not be found at home—the case more often than not—we investigated anyway. Our etiquette required knocking, and checking the garden and byre or stable for the owner before entering an apparently empty house during the day. Word of what we did would travel quickly.

After the first five houses, we stopped. All had lofts, and three of the five had cellars. None had tunnels. We stood looking at the village. Casse's house, and the four nearest, lay on the northern, rockier side of the wide, curving bowl of flatter land where Tirvan had grown. The northern side of the valley rose more steeply to the headland and the deep valley of the waterfall. Large boulders embedded in the ground meant suitable building space for only a few houses, with small yards that ran upward to the edge of the cliff. Between these five, and Tali's house below them, a ridge of reddish rock ran parallel to the shore. Above them, a deeply eroded gully blocked easy access to Tice's cottage. "Perhaps," Dern said, turning to look northward, "we could find a route up to the forge behind these houses, along the cliff edge. It might be safer than the waterfall."

"It may look that way," I said, "but it isn't. The rock here is soft and the cliff edge dangerous. And we would have to bridge the gully, somehow."

"It can't be that soft."

"It is. A foot or more of the cliff edge falls into the sea every year, either after heavy rain or after the winter. That's why there are so few houses on this side."

He walked nearer the edge of the cliff. "See?" I said, following. I pointed out the cracks feathering the rock. "And look at the waterfall. It's washed out all the softer rock, leaving only the big grey boulders, like the ones in the ground on this side."

He nodded, turning back to look southward, to the far side of the valley where most of Tirvan's houses stood. Here, the land sloped slowly up to the hillfields and the headland; the stream on this side of the village flowed gently down to meet the ocean behind Siane's workshop and the docks. "Then we need to concentrate on that side."

"I think so," I said. "All the tunnels are over there, at the oldest houses."

We crossed the central common of the village to where three more cottages stood in a loose cluster. I knocked at the first. From inside, a voice bid us enter. The door opened into a large, low-ceiling room, windowed on two sides. Cate sat at her loom. She turned on her stool, her pregnancy just beginning to show in the curve of her belly. "Lena," she said, surprised. "Dern. How can I help you?"

"We're planning defences," I said. "Remind me, Cate, does this cottage have a loft?" She nodded. "Is there a cellar? Or a tunnel to the byre?"

"Why, yes," she said. "There is a tunnel, but no real cellar, only a space dug out under the kitchen floor for vegetables in the winter. No one has used the tunnel in years and years."

"May we see it?" Dern asked. Cate pushed her stool back, indicating we should follow. She walked through the kitchen, out into the lean-to at the back of the cottage. Firewood lined two walls in neat stacks, and a large vat held spun wool soaking in a dye bath.

"We'll have to move the wool," she said. Dern stepped forward and took one handle. I took the other, and we managed to move it without slopping. Behind where the vat had stood a door lay, flush to the floor at the bottom but angled up by stone walls to about my waist at the top, where it abutted the shed wall. Dern pulled its handle. Nothing happened. He tried again, and this time the hinges gave just a bit. A smell of dank and damp rose from behind the door.

"Try this on the hinges," Cate said, taking a crock down from a shelf and handing it to me. I opened it. I knew from the distinctive smell that it was fleecefat, the natural oils that make the fleece of sheep repel water. I dipped my hand in, rubbing the hinges with the oily substance, doing my best to work the fat into the mechanism. Cate handed me a rag for my hands. Dern pulled at the door again, and this time it opened with a shriek of metal.

Stone steps angled downward into cobwebs and darkness. "We'll need a lantern," I said, and Cate disappeared into the kitchen. I looked at Dern. "Shouldn't we see if the door in the byre isn't blocked before we explore the tunnel?"

"A good idea," he agreed. Cate returned with the lantern. "What about the other end?" Dern asked her. "Is the door blocked there, too?"

She shook her head. "No," she said. "We store the turnips there, the ones we feed the goats in winter. So I know the steps and the first part of the tunnel are good. It's empty, now, but the door opens easily."

Dern held the lantern up as we descended the steps. We could just stand upright. In the lantern's glow, I could see the beams and crossbars that supported the earth. White fungus grew on several of them, gleaming damply in the light. Roots curled downward between some of the beams, and cobwebs furred the walls. I shuddered.

"Come," Dern said. When I hesitated, he reached out a hand.

"I'm all right," I said. We moved forward, slowly, Dern holding the lantern up so we could inspect the beams. He took his secca from his boot to pry at a beam where the fungus grew in profusion. The tip penetrated the wood, breaking a chunk off.

"Rot," Dern said.

A short distance further, one of the roof beams had collapsed, partially blocking the tunnel. Enough space remained in the gap between the fallen beam and the roof of the tunnel to allow a slim and agile person to pass.

Dern raised the lantern to light the space beyond the fall. "It looks clear," he said. I eyed the gap.

"Do you want me to try to go through?"

"No," he said. "We can investigate from the other side. If this is all that has collapsed, we should be able to shore it up and dig it out. The rotten beams will need to be replaced."

I nodded. I waited for him to precede me with the lantern, but he didn't move. Slowly he put the lantern on the floor, his eyes, wide and dark in the low light, never left mine. He took a step closer. "Lena," he said, his voice deep. I swallowed. He put out a hand to touch my face, then pulled me to him. He kissed me, gently, tentatively, and then more deeply. I felt the response in my body, low and deep. I pulled away.

"I don't know," I said. "I don't know if I can. I...." I hesitated. "I want to, Dern, but...not yet. I need to think."

"Thinking hasn't got much to do with this," he said. He watched me for a moment. "I won't stop asking, you know."

"I know," I said. "And I will tell you, yes or no, soon."

He smiled. "I'll try to be patient." He picked up the lantern.

The other end of the tunnel proved to be cleaner and drier, probably due to its use as a turnip store. The fall that blocked the passage could be easily cleared. We climbed out, closing. Outside, we breathed fresh air gratefully.

Dern looked around. "This is the only house Casse thought had a tunnel, of this group?" he asked.

"Yes," I answered. I measured the distance from this cluster of cottages to the next with my eyes. "Not a lot of use, if we're trying to move any distance through the village."

"True," he agreed, "but potentially useful as a hiding place. Look," he said, squatting in the swept earth of the yard. He sketched the harbour with his finger, placing small pebbles to represent the houses. I squatted beside him. "If I were commanding this raid, I would divide my men into four. One squadron I would send up the main path, one up the right side of the village, and one up the left." He drew the routes in the dust.

"And the last group?"

"Would stay at the harbour to guard the boat."

I looked at the sketch. "So these cottages could provide shelter for an attack on either the left group, or the centre."

"Exactly. But an attack from archers, maybe swordswomen. One or two of your cohort can hide in this tunnel until need brings them out. If need brings them out," he amended.

I studied the rough map. "Or," I said, "we could fence the common, at least on the harbour side. That would force the left squadron over to the cliff edge. It's rough going through those rocks, and with a bit of luck, the cliff will collapse and take a few with it."

"Very good," Dern said. He grinned. "And a knife or two in the back, thrown from the loft of Tali's house, might encourage them to move closer to the cliff edge." He straightened. "Those tactics we can repeat, from any of the lofts or tunnels throughout the village. But you also need to be able to move about the village, up and down, and maybe across, without being seen. We haven't found those routes, yet."

"The oldest houses are over there," I said, indicating the southern cluster of houses. "They have more tunnels and less space among the houses." We—Maya and Garth, Cate and the other boys and girls under seven—had played hide-and-seek among those houses and barns in the long summer evenings, with bats hunting insects around us and the first stars gleaming in the deepening blue of the sky. I thought I still remembered some of our hiding places and the spots where hedges could be wiggled through. Whether or not they would be useful remained to be seen. "Let's start at the harbour."

Investigating the oldest houses took most of the rest of the day. One or two of the tunnels needed digging out and shoring up, and several lofts needed knotted ropes to provide quick egress. When we finished in mid-afternoon, I poured water for Dern on the porch of my mother's house. Chaff and cobwebs clung to our clothes and hair. I could hear Tali calling the guards with the sword cohort and the clang of metal as they struck and parried. The heat of the day had not yet begun to recede. I glanced at the man beside me, who drank deeply of the water.

"This evening," I said on impulse, "do we have to talk of tactics?"

"What did you have in mind?" Dern asked, putting his empty mug down.

"Practice," I said. "I think I can move from the docks to the forge without Casyn seeing me. At dusk."

"Only unseen by Casyn? Not by me?"

"You know where the routes are."

"True," he agreed. "But perhaps you can prove too evasive for me, too."

"Perhaps. Even better, if I can."

"I think Casyn will agree to this," he said. "I'll leave a lantern at the forge. When you get there, light it. We'll watch from the meeting hall, on the hillside."

Just before moonrise, I crouched in Siane's dockside workshop. I eased open the shutters that covered the storeroom's window, slipping out into the shelter of the bushes. The shutters moved silently; we had greased them earlier. I wore dull green and grey and had darkened my face and hands with ashes. On my feet, I wore soft deerskin boots. From the hedge, I picked a careful route up the hill, keeping behind bushes and boulders, moving slowly. Haste here would be a mistake. I could move faster on the flatter ground of the village. I gained the first building: Kyan's woodshop. The woodshop's big doors, which were tall enough to allow long timbers to be passed up directly to the second floor, opened onto the village street. On the other side, a rough shed abutted the back of the workshop. This shed sheltered oddments and enclosed a privy, with doors at both ends as well as into the workshop. Regardless of the ventilation, it stank. I passed through the shed, holding my breath. The next building, a stable, lay about thirty feet away, and the cottage's goats kept the space between close-cropped.

At the door, I paused, watching the shadows. A bat quartered the goat's field, hunting insects, and then suddenly changed direction to disappear over the cottage roof. I dropped to my stomach to crawl across the space, moving a foot or two and then stopping, keeping my breathing steady and quiet. Goat droppings covered the area, and I could feel them squash beneath my weight. I thought wryly that I might cause less commotion in stable and byre if I smelt like goat and not human. At the stable, I pulled the door open just enough to slip inside. Three goats munching hay looked up at me in the dim light and then went back to their haybags. I edged my way to the corner of the stable to a trapdoor. As I bent to raise it, an animal jumped, snarling. I froze, my arm raised over my face in instinctive defence. The creature crouched and spat. I could hear mewling: the straw-filled corner beyond the trapdoor held a nest of kittens. I moved forward to open the trap. The tabby growled low in her throat but made no move toward me.

Dense blackness filled the tunnel. I pulled a candle from my pocket and lit the wick. This tunnel, I knew from the afternoon's exploration, needed no repair. It led to the pantry of Rette's cottage, where a woven rug covered the other trapdoor. The pantry and kitchen of the cottage stood at the back of the main building to help isolate them in case of fire. Most of the village houses had the same plan, with a separate entrance in the kitchen opening onto the kitchen garden and well. At Ranni's cottage, I knew I could cover the space between the trapdoor and the door to the garden in four paces. With enough stealth, no one in the living areas of the cottage would know I had passed through.

The candlelight showed me the outline of the trapdoor above me. It opened easily, and I held it open with one arm while I licked my thumb and forefinger to douse the wick. Then I waited, letting my eyes adjust again to the dark, listening. I could hear voices in the cottage, but they sounded stationary, as if whoever spoke remained in one place. I pushed the trapdoor open, hearing a faint slither from the rug, and slid out onto the floor. I let the trap down again, easing it closed with only the tiniest sound, and slowly stood. The voices in the cottage did not change. I stepped forward, rolling my weight along my feet as Tice had taught me. The garden door had two halves that opened separately to allow light and air in but to keep the goats out, and the faint light seeping in at the join gave me my bearings.

I had just reached the door when I heard a scrape of a chair on wooden floorboards. I froze, rapidly trying to remember what in the pantry might provide cover for me, but footsteps did not approach. I felt along the lower door to find its latch, slid it upwards, and slipped out.

The rising moon lay low in the east, giving me almost full dark for cover. A fence edged Rette's kitchen garden against the goats, but a stile led into the field beyond. I kept to the fence, pausing once to clean off my shoes as best I could.

Barley had grown in the field until last week. The stubble crunched sharp and noisy underfoot. The breeze brought the spicy smell of thyme to my nostrils. I froze. *Someone gathering herbs?* I moved to the edge of the field, where a footpath ran beside the south stream. Willows grew between the two bridges used to cross the stream to the fields and fruit trees, and the footpath ran beneath their overhanging branches. I followed the path for about a hundred yards before I turned off the path, jumped to grab an overhead branch, and pulled myself up into the tree.

I waited, tucked up against the trunk behind the screen of leaves. I saw movement at the stile. Slowly, I crept out onto the thick branch overhanging the stream. With relief, I found the half-remembered route, where the limbs of a willow leaning from the other bank intertwined with the tree I had climbed. I slid over into the other tree, and then down its rough trunk to the ground, pausing to catch my breath, grinning with enjoyment of the task.

I used the willows for concealment as I moved. The bubbling of the stream down its rocky bed masked the noise of my movement. At the upper footbridge, I dropped to my hands and knees to crawl across.

Another footpath ran along this bank behind the outbuildings of a half-dozen houses, my mother's among them. I headed upstream for a few hundred yards before turning left across a stile, moving in and out of two byres. At the last byre, I stopped. The meeting hall lay opposite me now, with open ground between where I stood and the forge. I planned to move across the hillfields, where the natural unevenness of the land and the deep heather would provide camouflage, but I had to do that without coming too close to the sheepcote. The herd dogs would raise the alarm if they caught my scent or heard me move. I also had to cross the stream again.

No trees or structures bridged the stream this high up, but generations of children, not wanting to go around by the bridges, had dragged rocks to create stepping stones across the flow. I had added to them myself, carrying chunks of frost-sheared rock down from the hills to repair the crossing after the damage of the first spring spate. I slid down the bank to pick my way along the stream until I found them. I crossed quickly.

I used a stone wall for cover until I reached the first of the rough hillfields. A sheepdog yipped once, but when the other dogs remained silent, she did not bark again. I turned left, from the shelter of the wall, and in a half-crouch moved through the heather, going from boulder to gorsebush to boulder, keeping to the low ground. The moon gave just enough light to keep me from tripping over rocks or splashing in puddles, but even so I had wet feet and scratches on my face and arms from unseen branches when I reached the forge.

In the shelter of some bushes above the forge I paused, listening, for a good five minutes. I could hear Siannon snuffling and moving in his stable, and faint voices from the village. When a passing cloud darkened the moonlight, I crawled the last few yards to the forge, eased open the door, and stepped in.

I listened. Nothing. I lit the lantern, then reached for the bucket and dipper and took a long drink.

"Well done," Dern said as he came in the door. "I saw you once, or rather, I had a sense of movement, for just a moment. If I hadn't been watching for you, I might have thought I had seen a fox, or another night creature. I wasn't expecting you for at least another quarter-hour, or perhaps a half. How were you so quick?"

"I crossed the south stream below my mother's house," I said. He looked at me quizzically. "The willows lean into each other there. I climbed one on the north bank and came down another on the south. I did it all the time as a girl. It's much faster than going up or down stream to the bridges. You can climb and go from branch to branch along the stream, too." I added. I paused. "When did Casyn decide to follow me?"

"You saw him?" Dern exclaimed.

"Only barely," I admitted. "Like you, just movement. I guessed it was one of you, and as you are here and he isn't, it had to be him."

Without answering, Dern moved to the door and whistled, a piercing sound. "Our signal," he explained.

"You thought I might elude him?" I asked, pleased by this thought.

"We debated the possibility," Dern said. I heard footsteps outside. Casyn came in, breathing deeply as if he had run up the hill.

"You did well, Lena," he said, with a brief smile. "You climbed the willows, I assume?"

"I did."

"By the time I made the bridge, I had lost you."

"That's not all you lost," Dern said, chuckling. "You owe me a flask of wine, Casyn."

"You bet on me?"

Dern laughed. "Soldiers wager on almost anything, Lena. It provides diversion. Casyn bet he would catch you. I bet he would not. You should be pleased. We can share the wine."

Casyn spoke before I could. "What was the hardest part, Lena?"

I considered. "The hillfields. On a darker night, I could well have fallen or blundered into a pool. But I don't see an alternative. If I had gone higher, into the rocks, the sheepdogs would certainly have barked."

"There will always be risk," Casyn said. "The higher route might be safer, if time is not of the essence. But you did well tonight. Now, take yourself to the baths. Change your clothes, collect Tice, and join us here for dinner in an hour."

I could smell goat rising from my clothes. Dern put his hand on my shoulder, a comrade's gesture. "You did well."

I smiled and slipped out. Walking down to the baths, I could still feel the touch of his hand, warm and gentle, resting on my back.

I left my clothes soaking in a tub of hot water and soap, bathed myself, and tended to my scratches. Tice met me outside the baths, and we walked up the hill together to the forge cottage. The door stood open to the evening, but I knocked. From inside, Dern called to us to enter. Casyn had a pot of soup simmering on the stove, smelling richly of fish, and bread and greens to go with the chowder. We sat around the plain pine table to eat, talking of what we had learned today, and the work needed with the cohort.

"Do we tell the rest of the village what we are about?" Tice asked.

"I think we have to," I answered. "Many women helped us inspect the lofts and tunnels today. In some cases, we had to ask for furniture to be moved, doors to be unlocked, or to be shown the location of the trapdoors. We were asked if we were looking for hiding places for valuables, for the children, for ambush. Rumour will be rife, and the sooner it's ended the better. Also, if we don't explain our plans, we risk finding a door blocked against us."

"But if the others know our plans, they could reveal them under threat of death or torture," Tice countered.

"That is true of all the plans. I don't want secrets," I finished, more sharply than I had intended.

Casyn nodded, then spoke gently. "I agree with Lena. We cannot afford to divide the village against itself, and things kept secret have a way of doing that. The risk is one we will have to take."

Tice looked thoughtful, but did not argue. We spoke some more of assigning the necessary work, and of how to train our cohort. We agreed that I would show Tice the routes and hiding places tomorrow, and then she and I would take the rest of the cohort through the training. We would practice in the evenings until all of us could move through Tirvan unseen and unheard.

When we left the men an hour or so before midnight, the moon rode high. The breeze, still on-shore, had freshened, holding a hint of dampness.

"Rain tomorrow," Tice said.

"Likely," I agreed. "We'll meet at the training ground after breakfast, rain or no." We came to the point where our paths diverged. Tice took a step up the path to her cottage.

"Goodnight, Lena," she said quietly.

"Goodnight, Tice," I answered, before a thought struck me. "Can you climb trees?"

She stopped, chuckling. "There weren't many in the grape fields, but I can shimmy up a rope and walk the timbers of a barn twenty feet up. Will that do?"

CHAPTER SEVEN

THE NEXT EVENING, I SPOKE to the village as a whole for the first time. "Women of Tirvan." My voice sounded high to my ears. I cleared my throat, beginning again. "Women of Tirvan. Yesterday, Dern, commander of *Skua*, and I explored your houses and your barns." I saw heads nod. "Many of you have been wondering why." I glanced at my mother, who smiled back. "We were looking for hiding places. Hiding places and routes to allow my cohort to move through the village unseen."

"Why?" someone called.

"My cohort's job is to use our knives, to kill those who get by our swordswomen and our archers," I explained, forgetting my apprehension. "For that, we need surprise and stealth. We need your lofts and cellars, and your tunnels. We need hinges to be greased, and doors unblocked. We'll need to repair tunnels and hang ropes. My cohort will do the work, but we need you to give us access. Are there any objections?"

Heads shook. I looked around the hall. "We'll start in a day or two. I—or Tice—will let you know what exactly we need." I started to step away, then stopped. "Thank you. If you have questions, I'll be glad to answer them."

"Well done, cohort-leader," Tice said, after the few women with questions had dispersed. "You made us proud."

Aline bounced up to me. "Did you find the tunnel from the sheepcote to the big barn?"

"No, I didn't. Casse must have forgotten about it. Will you show me tomorrow?" She grinned and nodded before running off to find Camy. "That could be useful," I said to Tice, "if we can teach the dogs to be silent."

"I wonder what else we might have missed."

Over the next few days, we tested routes in daylight, added ropes, and planed down a door or two. The more difficult work of rebuilding the two collapsed tunnels we left to the women of the village with experience in building. Aline showed us the tunnel, luckily undamaged, between the hillcote and the barn, and contributed the inspired suggestion of making the ropes we hung into swings, so that they would appear to be only children's playthings. I praised her both publicly and privately for this; she blushed and beamed.

A few days later, in the early afternoon, we gathered at the top of the waterfall.

"Has anyone here not climbed down the waterfall?" I asked.

The youngest girls looked up with surprise on their faces as they heard me, an adult, speak casually of something so forbidden.

Tice spoke. "I haven't."

"Why," Salle demanded, "are we climbing down the waterfall?"

"Because we may need to," I said simply. "What if it is the only unguarded route down to the harbour, or by doing so it gives us the chance to fire the catboat?"

"I thought that's what the tunnels were for?"

"In part, yes," I replied, "but what if we can't use them?"

I watched as my cohort glanced at each other. "I suppose," Salle said finally.

"It is dangerous, but it may give us an advantage of surprise or speed, which is why we need to practice. Now, who will show Tice the way?"

"I will," Freya offered. She slipped off her shoes, tying them on her belt, behind her back. Tice did the same. Freya walked to the top of the waterfall and jumped down to the first of the boulders. Tice followed. I could hear Freya instructing Tice for a moment or two, and then the sound of the water drowned their voices. We waited. It took, I remembered, about ten or fifteen minutes to clamber down, and no one else should begin the descent until Tice and Freya reached the bottom. If a climber higher up on the rocks fell, she endangered one immediately below.

One by one, we climbed, jumped, and slid down. I went last. The initial descent was easier than I remembered, but, I reflected, my body had changed since I had last done this, three or four summers back. At one point, the cliff face had broken off, leaving a vertical drop of about seven feet. I hung from the rocks at the top by my fingers, feeling the strain in my arms, then dropped down onto the boulder below, remembering to lean into the rockface. Even so, I fell hard on one knee. I stood on the wet rock, rubbing my knee, looking up. I could see the irregularities that I had used as hand-and-foot holds when climbing up. They looked horribly shallow. I judged it next to impossible for the cohort's shorter members, and absolutely impossible for any of us at night. A ladder, bolted into the rockface, would provide the safest answer, if we had the time. *Otherwise*, I thought, *a rope, looped and knotted, would work.*

I finished the descent, joining the others shivering in the cool breeze off the sea. No one had had serious problems in the descent, but we all had scratches and bruises, and wet clothes. "Now," I said to the waiting cohort, "who has climbed up, other than Freya and myself?" Silence. "No one?"

"I tried, once." Salle said. "But there's a place where I couldn't reach anywhere to hold on to. I had to come down again."

No one else had tried the climb. I looked at the cohort. Freya and I had strong arms from hauling nets, and the height needed. Tice, taller than either of us, could not climb with me. As cohort-second, she would need to take command if I fell. "Freya," I said, "you and I will climb up, again. The rest of you, go back to the top of the waterfall to wait for us. Practice knife-play to keep warm. Tice, a moment, please." She waited as the rest of the women began to pick their way along the rocky pools at the edge of the sea, back to the harbour. Freya waited at the base of the waterfall, where the rush of water would obscure our words.

"If I fall—" I began.

Tice shook her head impatiently. "You won't. But, yes, I know. I will be in command. I pray I know the plans by now. But you won't fall. Go, before you get cold and your muscles cramp. I'll see you at the top."

I insisted Freya follow me. If I could reach the handholds, so could she. The first part of the climb passed easily. The cliff sloped gradually and the boulders clustered close together. But as we climbed, the rocks grew further apart, requiring us to pull ourselves up half our height in some cases. Water drenched us. After each particularly difficult piece, we stopped briefly to study the rocks, to determine where ropes or iron bars set into the boulders might help.

At the rockface, we stopped. "Watch where I put my hands and feet. If you see a better choice, call up to me." I stood about eighteen inches out from the wall, bent my knees, and jumped, reaching up to a small ledge. My fingers grabbed the wet rock; at the same time, I brought my right foot up to a knob of protruding rock about half an arm's length above the boulder where I had stood. My left foot swung free for a minute, and then found a crevice about a handspan's above and to the left of the protrusion. I pushed up with my bent knees, reaching my right hand up to another crevice about a foot above the ledge. I pulled my body upward. I could hear my heart pounding. Above me was another small ledge. I brought my left hand up, grabbed it, hanging for a moment, my bare toes searching for grip on the rockface. I looked up. The falling water hit my face. I blinked, shook my head to clear the water from my eyes. I felt my left hand slip slightly. A bolt of fear shot through me. I scrabbled with my feet, seeking purchase.

"Bring your right foot up a bit further," Freya called from below me. "To the left, there," she shouted, as I found the grip. "Now push up. The top of the rockface is an arm's length above you." I heaved myself up, reaching blindly with my right arm. I found the ledge, pulling myself up onto it. I lay panting for a moment. The pounding of my heart slowed. I rolled to my stomach, looked over the edge, and talked Freya up.

"How did either of us do that as kids?" I said to Freya, when both of us rested safely on the ledge. She grinned. "Blind luck," she said, still panting. "And dry summers. The water makes it difficult to see. It's not really that hard a climb."

"We're not done yet," I said, but I knew she was right. The rest of the climb repeated the lower part, jumping upward from boulder to boulder, still dangerous enough but not really difficult. When we reached the top, the cohort gave us a round of applause. Eager to try it for themselves, they moaned, arguing when I vetoed the idea.

"None of you is tall enough except for Tice. We will have to put ropes in place. Then," I said, "you will climb it, up and down, and so often you'll know every rock intimately." I looked at the sun. "Go to the baths. It's early, but we are all wet and starting to chill."

Dern and I explored the caves the next day, leaving Tice with the cohort. Pel and his friend Sarr came with us. We climbed up the hillside through the sheep meadows, crossing stone walls and wading small streams.

Gille's apprentice spent some of her day up on these hillsides, but today there were only the younger girls. They watched the sheep with half an eye each while playing the ring-game on a flattish space, cropped flat by the sheep. They had fallen to the ground, giggling, when one of them spotted us. They sprang up. Dern spoke to the girls—two of them nine, and one eleven—respectfully, and they responded in kind.

"The largest cave would be up there," the older girl said, pointing higher on the hillside, "The big rock, there, in the heather—looks like a lobster pot? The opening's just to the right. Sarr knows," she added. I remembered he was her cousin.

"I'll show you," Sarr said. "Pel hasn't been there." He looked doubtful, suddenly. "I don't think," he added. Pel shook his head.

"Let's go," he said, impatiently, wanting the adventure. We thanked the girls, leaving them to their games and their sheep. There was a faint track climbing up beyond the pastures, into the rougher ground. The boys ran ahead. Far above us, a buzzard screamed. Behind me, I could hear Dern's breathing.

The boys waited for us at the mouth of the cave. From the opening, which was maybe as wide as I was tall, we could see the rock walls and floor sloping down and then turning. The boys hung back. I pulled the lantern from my pack, lit it, and entered.

The floor sloped gently downward. At the sharp left-hand turn, where the natural light ended, a small lantern sat in a niche in the wall along with a metal box of flint and some tinder. I lit the second lantern, giving it to Dern. In the flickering light, we could see where the tunnel turned again, to the right. The air smelled damp. Beyond the second bend, the walls and roof opened up into a room perhaps fifteen feet wide and twice as long. Water seeped down the furthest wall, to collect in a small rock pool before trickling away. The roof curved maybe two feet over our heads. "Is this natural?" Dern asked. I shook my head. I remembered being here, with Maya, and Garth, playing at being borders scouts.

"I don't know," I said. "Enhanced, maybe? Dug out a bit, the seep water captured? If so, it was done before Tirvan kept records, or no one thought to write it down. The shepherds use it, always have. That's all I know." Dern raised his lantern, taking a few steps more into the cave. He looked around.

"Have you gone through there?" he asked, speaking to Sarr, indicating the narrowing fissure where the walls converged again.

"It just peters out," Sarr answered. "Gets too narrow even for me. But," he added, "there's something beyond, because a candle flame gets pulled toward the back, and you can feel a breeze."

"Good lad," Dern said. "That means there's airflow," he said to me, "so if we had to mostly block up the entrance, the air won't go stale. What's in the boxes?" he asked, indicating the two wooden boxes against the closest wall.

"Hay," Sarr answered again, "and some old blankets. In case the shepherds get caught in a storm," he added. "The hay's for sleeping on, and for feeding the lambs."

"The cave's dry," Dern said, "enough to store ship's biscuit and maybe some dried fish in metal boxes to keep out the vermin." Pel, bored by conversation he could take no part in, had wandered off to explore. Suddenly I heard his voice calling me, though the sound was faint. Dern pointed up the entranceway. Urgency made Pel's voice shrill, but the words were clear.

"A boat, Lena!" he cried. "A big boat!" A frisson of fear ran through me. I looked at Dern. He saw the alarm on my face and grinned.

"*Skua.*"

CHAPTER EIGHT

IN THE MORNING, LISE, who had been working at the forge with Casyn, brought me a dozen knives and the leather belt sheaths to go with them. Neither knives nor sheaths were handsome things, but they were made well, and with care. I held one. It had the weight of our wooden practice knives, but not the feel, or the sound as it passed through air. The handle was wrapped in thin leather and bound tightly. I thanked Lise, gathered the knives into my shoulder bag, and walked up the hill toward the practice field. Light cloud webbed the sky this morning, creating a haze over the sea. Tice joined me where the paths met. She looked tired.

"So they're here."

"Lise brought them this morning," I answered.

She shook her head. "I meant the men."

"Oh," I said, feeling stupid. "Yes. The boat's here. Nobody knows anything else."

"A bit of time will fix that," she said. "Let me see the seccas." I gave her a knife. She feinted with it. "It's different," she said. "It weighs the same, but the blade cuts the air—how? Faster? Everything will happen more quickly."

"I felt the difference," I said, "but I couldn't put words to it."

She shrugged. "It's like clay," she said. "My fingers, hands, know the smallest difference in the clay itself or how wet it is. I'd imagine you can tell, from the play of a line, what fish is on the other end."

"Usually," I admitted. Suddenly I wanted the feel of a line in my hands, the smell of the sea, and the simplicity of wind and tide. I pushed the thought away.

At the practice grounds, the cohort waited. They should have paired off to practice or to wrestle—the morning warm-up exercises. Instead, they stood talking in tight clusters, their voices edged with excitement.

Skua had reached our cove in the early afternoon. Dern had excused himself immediately after Pel brought her to our attention, striding off down the hillside. I had stayed in the hills, investigating other caves, studying the hollows and outcroppings, thinking about cover. When I saw *Skua* anchor in the cove, and the first of the small boats being lowered, I abandoned the task to return to the village. But the small boat had held only one man; it had been sent to ferry Dern and Casyn to *Skua*, where they had remained.

The conversations quieted as Tice and I approached. Aline looked ready to jump out of her skin, and even Freya's eyes shone.

"I don't know anything," I said without preamble, once everyone had moved into the shade of the oak. "Nobody yet does, not even the council leaders. And we won't know anything until Dern and Casyn return."

"When will that be?" Aline asked.

"No one knows. Now, I have the real seccas, but I won't give them to you until I think you are all ready to concentrate. These are dangerous weapons." I held one up, but most of the women looked only briefly before flicking their gazes back to the water. I bit back a sharp command.

"Into the meeting hall," I said firmly. "Clear the benches to the sides, and close the shutters on the seaward walls." The cohort hesitated.

"Do it now!" I snapped. Freya moved first, and the others followed, Aline and Camy trailing after. I stole one last glance at *Skua* before I followed them.

The hall, lit only from the west windows, had just enough light to allow us to practice. The cohort moved the benches against the walls. I handed out the knives and sheaths.

"Space yourselves well apart," Tice instructed, "and try some moves. You'll feel a difference. And be careful!" As she finished speaking, Aline yelped. I looked over to see blood dripping from the first finger of her left hand. She stuck the finger in her mouth, speaking around it.

"I was just feeling the edge," she mumbled. I dug in my bag for a bandage. Even the wooden seccas had drawn blood. I had learned quickly to have supplies available. I smeared the shallow cut with a concoction of fleecefat and herbs and tied a strip of linen around it.

"At least it's your left hand," I said to Aline. "Keep it clean."

The cohort practiced individually for a quarter of an hour with no further injuries. When I thought they had grown used to the different feel, I called a halt. Along with the sheaths, Lise had given me a leather bag with a couple of dozen balls shaped from the corks of wine flasks—Tice's idea. We showed the cohort how to ease one onto the tip of the secca, deeply enough to keep the ball in place, but not so deeply that the knife tip protruded. "We'll use these for a while," I explained. "We can't afford to injure each other. Try not to lose it, and always check it's in place before you begin practice."

The women put the tip guards in place, dividing up to begin one-on-one practice. Their first hesitancy with the real knives had just begun to subside when Freya slipped on the wooden floor and fell. The knife clattered harmlessly away, but everyone stopped.

Freya sat up and rubbed her knee. "I'm fine," she said. She reached for her secca, but I held up a hand.

"I hadn't thought about the floor being slippery. You're all used to being outside, on the field, and I don't want you having to think about both your footing and the new knives. We'd better go back out." Tice nodded.

We trooped back outdoors into dazzling sunlight. A moment passed before I saw the group of six men climbing up the path with Dern leading them. He raised a hand in greeting.

"Cohort-leader, cohort-second, good morning," Dern said formally, when they reached us.

"Captain," I replied, following his lead. I met his eyes. His gaze was direct, business-like, soldierly.

"These are men of *Skua*," he said, "those with the best knife skills. I wondered if we might practice together over the next weeks." I noted how he had worded the request, establishing that he did not command here. I looked at the men. They ranged in age, I guessed, from about eighteen to well into their thirties, perhaps older. The youngest among them looked the most apprehensive.

"We might," I answered, "but not today. My cohort just received their seccas, newly forged, and we haven't yet grown used to them. But let me introduce my cohort, and perhaps we can know who our opponents will be?"

"Of course," Dern said.

I had the cohort give their names, which they did with differing levels of confidence. Camy spoke her name, but stared at the ground. The men seemed surprised when she and Aline stepped forward. They must not have expected girls quite so young.

The oldest of the men spoke first. "Anwyl," he said, in a relaxed manner. He would have been in and out of women's villages for Festival for many years. The other men followed suit, oldest to youngest: Ferhar, Largen, Tiernay, Danel, Satordi. I doubted I would remember who was who, at least at first.

Men and women eyed each other. Aline and Camy giggled. None of us, I realized, knew how to proceed: This was not Festival, and we had no other customs to guide us. I needed to say something, to establish my authority, and set the tone.

"Cohort," I said. "Shall we show the men how we fight? Find your practice knives. We won't use the new seccas for this. Tice, pair them, please." I turned back to Dern. "Captain, would your men be more comfortable watching from the shade of the trees?"

"I want each man to watch one pair, and to do that, we need to be around the edge of the field, if we may, not grouped in the shade," he said. I nodded. "Men," he said, his tone relaxed but unmistakably still that of command, "watch a pair practice, and look for what is different. Not for mistakes, but for moves you would not have used, holds that are unfamiliar. Understood?" The men murmured their assent. As the cohort took their places on the field, the men spread around the periphery. Dern remained beside me.

Tice had paired the women by size for this first round. They fought confidently, used to their partners and their tactics. Camy and Aline showed off a little, but behaved after I took them aside briefly. The men watched, some squatting, others standing, speaking quietly among themselves. The oldest, Anwyl, watched with a sceptical look on his face.

After ten minutes, Tice stopped the demonstration to pair the women again, this time by disparity of size. At the end of this round, Freya had a welt on her arm from a fast strike from Camy, and I had heard much more discussion among the men.

"Our turn," Dern said. He turned to me. "May we borrow your practice knives?" I agreed, and six of the cohort handed their wooden seccas over. As Tice had done, he paired the men by size for their first round.

We watched as they circled on the field. The sun, high in the sky now, could not be used to advantage. The two youngest—Danel and Satordi—moved lightly, their mode of fighting not dissimilar from ours. The two oldest fought quite differently, using their strength and weight of muscle, striking less often but with more force. Tice focused on the youngest pair; I watched the oldest two.

Dern re-divided them after a quarter of an hour, again following Tice's lead to pair them by the greatest difference in size and body weight. This time Satordi fought against Anwyl. The younger man danced around the older, not landing many blows but not being hit, either. About ten minutes into the bout, Satordi landed a blow on Anwyl's upper arm. Anwyl lunged forward, aiming for Satordi's chest, but he stepped back and sideways. Anwyl tried to check his momentum, turning towards the younger man, but he fell, unbalanced. He tried to roll into the fall, but his left shoulder hit the ground hard. He lay still for a moment, then pulled himself up. He put a hand to his shoulder.

"Let me see it," Dern said.

"It's nothing," the soldier said. "Just a bruise."

"Let me see it," Dern said again. Anwyl grimaced but pulled his tunic off. Dern probed the shoulder. I saw Anwyl wince.

"More than a bruise, but not a sprain," Dern concluded. "Keep it moving, but don't overdo it." He looked up at the sun. "Enough for today."

"We're needed in the fields," I said. "Can we eat together this evening, all of us, to talk over the morning?" We made the arrangements, sent the injured to the baths to soak, and went to find food.

Harvest-time would not wait, even for an invasion. Now that *Skua* and her men had joined us, the council leaders had decided that practice and defence work occupied the mornings, the harvest the afternoon, and a review of the morning's work in the evenings. I ate bread and pickled fish quickly, found an apple and my hat, and went back out, this time to the grain fields. I found Tali teaching *Skua*'s crew how to scythe.

"Hold the top handle in your left hand, and grasp the middle grip with your right," she instructed. Each man did as she said, their movements awkward. I was surprised to see Anwyl holding a scythe. Perhaps his shoulder injury had been slighter than Dern had thought. "Now," Tali continued, picking up her own scythe. "Watch."

Holding the mowing tool with her body twisted to the right, she positioned the blade, curved and very sharp, and as long as her arm, less than a handspan above the ground. Then, with a smooth turn to the left, she moved the scythe in an arc, keeping the blade parallel to the ground. The cut wheat fell neatly beside her.

The men did their best to duplicate her movements. One or two made a decent job of it, but others hacked at the cereal, chopping rather than cutting.

"Stop," Tali said. "Watch me again. Hacking at it wastes energy, and it's more dangerous. Dern, you weren't bad, but keep the blade higher: you'll need to sharpen it every stroke if you hit soil and rocks."

They tried again. Inwardly, I grinned. They'd all be needing the baths tonight. Scything, for someone new to it, took a lot of effort, and left the reaper sore and aching, especially on the first day. Anwyl misjudged his sweep, digging his blade into the soil, jarring his already sore shoulder. He dropped the scythe.

"Pah!" he spat. "This is work for women and slaves, not soldiers." Before Tali could speak, Dern had dropped his own scythe to round on Anwyl.

"Pick up that scythe, soldier," he said, his voice calm and low and cold. "You asked to do this, against my recommendation. So now you will do it, until I tell you otherwise." For a moment Anwyl stared at him. A muscle in his cheek twitched. Then he dropped his eyes.

"Yes, Captain," he muttered. He bent to pick up the scythe, turning back to the work.

After ten minutes more of instruction and observation, Tali pulled two of the men—Ferhar and Danel—out of the scythe line. "We don't have time to let you learn," she said matter-of-factly. "Lena, show them how to tie and stook." I looked up from my work to beckon them over.

I straightened, taking the opportunity to press my hands against my lower back. I hated tying and stooking, but I had never learned to scythe well. "This is fairly simple," I said to the two men, "but you have to get it right. First you gather up a cut," I demonstrated, pulling a neat pile of cut wheat up into my left arm, "then wrap the ties around the sheaf, top and bottom, and tie it off firmly. It has to be tight enough to keep the stalks together. Use a reef knot, and tuck the ends under."

They tried it, making sheaves ranging from neat to ragged, but they would do. We bent to the dusty, prickly work, gathering and tying. Every twelve sheaves made a stook, a circle of sheaves leaning into each other, the heads a shaggy ring at the top. This allowed the sun and wind to dry the wheat, and if it rained before we took them into the threshing floor, the grain would not rot.

All the village worked. The children twisted ties or carried water. Lise went from one scythe team to the next, sharpening the hammered leading edge of the blades with a whetstone. Scythe blades dulled easily, needing to be sharpened several times an hour. Other women gleaned, picking up the heads that had broken off. From a perch, a yellowhammer whistled his "oh see-me see-me see-me please" over and over.

Halfway through the afternoon, the women's scythe line began to sing. They had moved faster than the men, and their swath of cut grain was neater, not that the cattle would care. The song had a rhythm that matched the swing of the scythe. Danel stopped, listening.

"I remember that song," he said. "The women sang it at harvest in my home village, too. As a child, I carried water and twisted ties, like these boys." He indicated Pel and Sarr.

"Where is your home village?" I asked.

"Torrey," he said. "In the south."

"Near Karst?"

He considered. "Not too near. North and west of it. Lena," he added shyly, "tell me, if you would, who is the woman in the scythe line, two from the right? I do not remember her name."

I looked up the field to where the scythe line moved rhythmically through the grain. I smiled. "Her name is Freya."

He flashed me a quick smile that lit his face. "Thank you."

When Casse and Siane arrived a bit later with freshly baked cakes and tea, Tali called a halt. We sat or sprawled in the cut swathes and ate and drank. The cakes, dense with dried fruit, renewed my flagging energy, and the tea, sweet with honey, soothed my throat, dry with the dust of the harvest. I surveyed the field. We had eight days until the autumn equinox. Another two afternoons would finish this field, but another two wheat fields, and three of oats, awaited. We had finished the barley harvest before the men arrived.

Casse, I noted, had brought her bow and arrows. As the scythe teams moved closer to the centre of the field, rabbits and hares, and possibly game birds, would break from the diminishing cover. We ate a lot of rabbit during harvest. I finished my tea and had just stood to return the mug to Siane when Dern's voice—his command voice—rang in the warm air.

"Stop scything now, Anwyl," he said. "If you continue, you will damage that shoulder beyond what heat and a night's rest can heal, and you will be useless to us. You have made your point. Go and stook grain." I watched as Anwyl thrust the scythe at Dern and turned away, not looking at his crewmates. He started towards us.

"Soldier," Casse called out. "Yes, you," she added, when Anwyl looked at her questioningly. "Please come here." Anwyl changed course to walk over to Casse, who had her birdbow in her hand. She said something to him I could not hear. He nodded. After a moment or two of further talk, he took his secca out of his bootsheath to show her. They spoke a minute longer. I saw him indicate his left shoulder, shaking his head. "Captain," Casse called. "I am going to try for rabbit and quail for the pot tonight. I would like this man's help. May I borrow him?"

"Certainly," Dern called back. "There is no danger to his left shoulder in hunting rabbits. Throw true, Anwyl," he added. "I like rabbit stew." The two men I was working with glanced at each other. Was that relief on their faces?

The long rays of the westering sun had turned the heather on the hillside a brilliant purple before we stopped, aching and exhausted. Far overhead, a golden eagle cried as it hunted on the last of the warm updrafts over the hills. Smells of stew and fresh bread drifted up from the village.

The scythers stopped first, making their way to the forge to leave their tools. Lise, and Casyn, I supposed, would work into the night, rehammering and sharpening the edges. The rest of us finished stooking the last sheaves before we left the field. For the first part of the evening, only women could use the baths. The men could soak later. Twenty minutes later, I sank into the hot pool with a deep sigh. I soaked for half an hour, letting the heat penetrate, just floating. All around me, women did the same. Almost no one spoke. After some time, I started thinking about the morning, the women and men fighting, how they differed. I sat up. Across the pool, Tice saw me move, and she too sat up, cocking an eyebrow. We climbed out and dried off. "My cohort," I said to the soaking women, "meet us at the council hall in twenty minutes."

During harvest, the oldest women cooked, and we ate communally at the hall. With bowls of stew and chunks of bread in hand, I claimed the west-facing porch for our meeting spot, sitting on the step to eat. The cohort drifted out, followed by Dern and his men. Danel slid into a spot near Freya. When we had eaten the stew, Camy and Aline brought out a tray of fruitcake and tarts.

"I would like to talk about what we saw this morning," I began. "What is different, about the way we use the knives, and how you do. And what that might mean when we fight."

"You're not as strong," Anwyl said bluntly. He sat slightly apart from the others, leaning against one of the posts that supported the roof of the porch. "I could take the knife away from any of you, easily."

"Not easily," another man said. "Satordi is not as strong as you either, but you've never bested him in practice because he's faster. Strength isn't everything, Anwyl."

"There is something else, though," Satordi spoke. *He could be no more than eighteen*, I thought. "I can't explain it, but you move differently. It's like seeing an animal from a distance: you can tell whether it's a dog or a fox, just by its movement."

"He's right," Tice said. "The men move differently than we do. They carry more muscle on their upper bodies, and their centre is higher. They move from their chests. We have more strength and more movement lower down on the body, from the hips."

Dern reached for a tart. "What does this mean?"

"We tend to aim low, or at arms, not chests or backs," Freya answered. "We can duck away easily and move out of range, but stabbing at the body takes more arm strength. We do it, but not as much as the men."

"So we should expect more attacks directed at our upper bodies," I said. "Think about that and prepare for it. Tomorrow we will pair off with the men, with our practice knives, to begin to learn what it is to fight a man. Is there anything else?" No one spoke. "My cohort, to bed, then." They stood, gathering bowls and mugs. I picked up one of the trays and piled dishes onto it. Danel said something to Freya. She smiled, bidding him good night.

I heard Dern order his men to the baths. He followed me into the meeting hall, carrying one of the trays. We deposited them on a table. "May I walk with you?" he said quietly.

I shook my head. "Go to the baths with your men. I'm tired. I need to sleep."

He nodded. "I suppose you do," he said without inflection. "Good night, then, Lena. I'll see you in the morning."

I called a goodnight to Casse and her helpers and walked out into the night. I didn't want to think about Dern. Watching Freya and Danel tonight, their budding awareness of each other, had changed something. However I felt about Dern, it didn't have the same delight as what I saw between Danel and Freya. I wanted him. But was that enough?

The next morning dawned on another cloudless harvest day. We gathered at the practice field, the men climbing up from harbour and the boats where they slept. I saw another group of men with bows, heading for the butts, and others joining in the work of the cohort building the fences above the tideline that we hoped would funnel the invaders along defended paths. Dern and his men brought their own wooden seccas.

We conferred on how to pair them off, deciding on height to begin with. I named six women. "You six fight first. The rest will watch."

"Go slowly, at first. We want no injuries from carelessness or pride," Dern added.

Wooden knives in hand, the combatants moved out onto the packed dirt of the practice ground. They paired off, and at a nod from me, the practice began. Tice and Dern and I watched the pairs. At first, they hesitated. The men, I supposed, not comfortable with the idea of fighting women; the women unsure of the strength and expertise they faced. In almost all cases, the fighting only began in earnest after a skilful blow from one of my cohort. I moved over to Dern to tell him what I saw. "We can't let this continue, or we will come to expect it, and the advantage it gives. The Lestian men won't hesitate."

"You're right," Dern said, "but neither will they attack with full force. They won't be expecting any sort of skilled resistance." He hesitated. "From what I know of Leste, they won't attack to kill, not at first. They'll attack to overpower, and then use you for their pleasure."

"Casyn warned us," I said, keeping my voice calm. "Can we begin again?"

We stopped the practice, and while Dern spoke to his men, Tice and I talked with the cohort. I told them what I had seen, and what it meant. When we began again, with different pairs, it looked better. It looked real.

We practiced, in different pairs, until late morning. I pulled Tice aside at one point to tell her of the attraction between Freya and Danel, advising her to watch them closely when they paired.

"They're unlikely to be the only ones, but I'll pay attention. If they are too gentle with each other, I'll step in." While she watched, I fought several men, trying to note the differences, predict the moves. Anwyl kept me completely at bay: I could only defend myself. Finally, I turned, ran, and then threw my knife. I hit his shoulder—the left one—and he roared in pain and surprise. His pride had let him think I had panicked and run, and he had not thrown his own knife. By the end, bruised and dusty, I thought I had the beginnings of an understanding of what fighting against the invaders might entail.

For the next five days, we practiced in the mornings and went to the grain fields in the afternoons. The weather held. No rain soaked the grain or replenished the streams. On the fifth morning, I left the cohort with Tice, and went with Anwyl and Tiernay to build a trail up the waterfall.

Dern and I had spoken of it two nights before, at dinner. I had kept him at arm's length all week, which he had seemed to accept, but we still needed to plan. We sat on the west porch of the meeting hall after the others left. I sipped tea as he outlined what he believed needed to be done at the waterfall.

"I want you to take Anwyl and Tiernay," he said. I started to protest, but he held up a hand. "Casyn has made half a dozen iron rings that can be hammered into the rocks where needed, to tie ropes to. And before you object to Anwyl, hear me out. Anwyl has skills you need. He was born in a tiny village east of Casilla where the mountains come down to the sea. He grew up scrambling up and down cliffs, taking seabird eggs and nestlings even before he was six. A dozen years ago, he was sent into the Durrains as part of a scouting group because of his skill with climbing. He's not the easiest of men to deal with, but there is little about climbing rockfaces safely he doesn't know."

"All right," I answered slowly. "And Tiernay?"

"Tiernay is strong and careful, and Anwyl likes him. And he has a head for heights." Dern said. "Who will you take from the women?"

"I was going to say Freya," I said, "but that's not right. She's as tall as I am. Kelle, I think. She's strong, but she's a lot shorter. If she can climb the trail we build, everyone else should be able to as well."

He nodded, reaching out to cover my hand in his own. I felt the tug of desire, but I turned my hand up to squeeze his, then withdrew it. He looked at me quizzically.

"Dern, I think the answer is no."

"Are you sure?"

I exhaled. I owed him the truth. "Not quite. Part of me wants to—very much. But part of me says whatever I'm feeling—it's not enough. Can you understand that?"

"Not really," he said. "But perhaps the difference is that you have loved someone, and I haven't. But I certainly want you, and perhaps there could be more." Crickets chirped in the night. I looked up at the stars. He shifted slightly. "I'll ask one more time, Lena. But no more."

"I understand," I said. "I don't want to mislead you, Dern."

"I'll survive," he said. "Sleep well."

I stood at the base of the waterfall, with Kelle, Tiernay, and Anwyl, and the tools—picks and shovels, a bag of iron rings, drills and hammers and rope—that we needed.

Anwyl studied the waterfall for some minutes while we waited. I had told Kelle of his expertise, and that I would defer to his advice. "Wait here," he said finally. Taking off his overtunic—the morning had not yet warmed—he began to climb.

Nearly half an hour passed before he returned. "Down is easy," he said briefly. "You climbed up it?"

"I did. Twice. So has Freya." He raised his eyebrows. I thought I saw new respect in his eyes.

"You were lucky not to fall," he said. "She couldn't, though," he indicated Kelle.

"No," I agreed. "Kelle is too short. We need to make it possible for Kelle and the rest of the cohort to climb it. Not easy, but possible."

He nodded. "Let me take Tiernay up, to start getting those rings in place. That's going to take some time, and then we'll start stabilizing some of the rocks that wobble." He handed Tiernay tools, and the bag of rings. "Meanwhile, start looking for flattish rocks, about this big"—he indicated with his hands— "that we can wedge under boulders."

Kelle and I had a fair pile of flattish stones when Anwyl joined us. He nodded with approval at the pile. "We'll need a lot more."

"Kelle, see if you can round up some of the children. If not, get Camy and Aline." She nodded, turning towards the village.

"Get some bags, or baskets, too," Anwyl called. "For carrying them up."

Anwyl showed me how to hammer the flat rocks under a midsized boulder that rocked. Once he saw I understood, he left me to it, scooping up some of the pile, climbing higher to begin on the next unstable rock. I could hear the chink of hammer and chisel on the rocks higher up, where Tiernay worked. Occasionally, a chip bounced down to join the pebbles on the foreshore.

When Kelle returned with Camy, Aline, Lara, and Sarr, we toiled through the morning, wedging and digging, carrying rock higher and higher up the waterfall. As it grew warmer, we welcomed the splashing water for its cooling qualities. Anwyl came down several times to check our work. "Good," he said briefly. He was not a man of many words.

At midday, Lara left to bring us food. When she returned, we sat at the base of the waterfall to eat. Tiernay had climbed down, reporting that he had one ring in and a second well on its way. "After we eat," Anwyl said, through a mouthful of pickled fish and bread, "Kelle will test our work."

Kelle looked at me. I swallowed my own mouthful. "Anwyl," I said, as calmly as I could muster, "it is up to me to tell Kelle what to do. I appreciate your expertise in rock-climbing, and I'm glad you are here to direct what needs to be done, but my cohort is under my command." I waited. Anwyl stared at me for a moment before dropping his eyes.

"As you say."

"Thank you." I wondered what Dern had said to him. "I'd prefer it if you would show us both and let us practice with you watching. Climbing is your skill, and we'd be glad to learn from you."

He chewed. "When you're ready, cohort-leader."

We finished our food, and after a brief rest, started up the waterfall. The first part of the climb went easily. Anwyl had indicated we should climb ahead of him. Tiernay had gone up first to attach the rope. I climbed first of our group, with Kelle following. From just behind us, Anwyl gave instructions whenever I or Kelle hesitated, sometimes pointing out a better choice of hand or foot placement. After ten minutes, we reached the first place where frost and water had sheared off a section of the cliff. Where Freya and I had hung on with fingertips to the upper ledge while we scrabbled for toeholds, Tiernay had drilled and hammered an iron ring into the cliff-face above the ledge, and chiselled out a smooth half-circle in the rock to let the rope pass through without fraying. The rope itself, a thick mooring line, had been knotted to provide hand and foot grips.

"Not much to it," Anwyl said. "Climb up the rope. When you get to the ledge, put your elbows on it and pull yourself up until you can roll on. Who's going first?"

"I am," I said. I grabbed the rope at a knot to pull myself up, then cursed, dropping down again. I took off my shoes, tied them through my belt at my back, and began again, grasping the rope with my feet. The falling water had soaked it, but the knots provided purchase. Slowly I worked my way up the rope to the ledge, and, tightening my toegrip, slid my elbows up onto the ledge, found places my hands could grip, and pulled myself up. *Much easier*, I thought, *than when I'd climbed it earlier this summer.* I sat up. The knotted rope continued for some distance above my head. I swung my body back out onto the rope and descended.

Anwyl nodded. "Good," he said. "You could have been quicker, but that will come with practice. Better to be safe."

"Kelle?" I said. She swallowed hard but nodded. She had already taken off her shoes.

Two thirds of the way up, she froze. I started to speak, but Anwyl stopped me. "Move your right hand up," he instructed. "Just your right hand." Slowly she complied. "Now your left," he said. He gave her firm instructors until she lay on the ledge. He gave her a minute. "Now come down. You saw what Lena did. Grab the knot."

She came down without freezing, to stand, panting slightly, on the boulder. "Well done," Anwyl said.

"Very well done," I echoed.

"You'll do it again in a minute," Anwyl said. He glanced at me. "Providing your cohort leader agrees, of course. First I want to check the rope." He climbed rapidly, reaching the ledge in only a few seconds. There he examined the rope where it brushed against the ledge, looked up at the metal ring, then dropped back down to the boulder faster than he had climbed. "No fraying," he said. "Do you want Kelle to climb again?"

"I do," I said. "Kelle?" She nodded, beginning to climb, not hesitating this time. She rolled onto the ledge and did not pause for breath before coming back down.

"It's not bad," she said, "once you're used to it. Thank you, Anwyl."

We spent another couple of hours stabilizing the last of the boulders, by which time Tiernay had the next ring in place and the rope knotted and hung. With Anwyl guiding us we both climbed to the top, and back down again without mishap. At the bottom, as we gathered our tools, I stopped to speak to him.

"Thank you," I said. "You gave us both confidence. If I embarrassed you earlier, I apologize."

"You didn't." he said after a minute. "I was out of line. Although…" He hesitated.

"Although?"

"You could take it as a compliment, I suppose," he said. "When this was all first told to us, I thought, women, what can they do? I mean," he flushed slightly, "I know you farm, and fish, and do all the things that need doing in a village, without men, but when it comes to fighting, that's men's work. But what I've seen, here, this week—I'm impressed. So when I told Kelle to climb, instead of asking you, it's because I was treating you both like cadets. I did forget you were in command, but I didn't mean to be disrespectful. I was just teaching you like I usually do."

"And will keep doing, I hope. Will you come back with us, when I bring the whole cohort to climb, tomorrow morning?"

"If the Captain says I can," he said.

The next morning, Dern took the rest of the men off to assist elsewhere in the village, and my cohort and Anwyl spent the morning at the waterfall. By noon, we could all climb up and down with reasonable speed and confidence.

The last of the oat fields fell to the scythes that afternoon. From the lower wheat fields, I could hear the shouts to the oxteam as the wagon filled with dried sheaves, heading to the barn for threshing. That night, the temperature fell suddenly. We woke to a thick rime of frost on the grass and clear blue skies. As I stood at my window looking out, I heard the sound I had subconsciously been waiting for: the peal of the hunting horn. The first heavy frost of autumn marked the start of the deer cull. I dressed, took my hunting bow from the corner where I had propped it, and went downstairs.

Tali had made tea, and the smell of bacon frying made my stomach rumble. Eggs sat in a bowl, waiting to be fried in the bacon fat. The pace of a hunt frequently left no time to eat again until late in the day, so we ate well at breakfast. I sliced bread and set the table.

Siane and Lara joined us, Siane eating only the bread and eggs. Too lame for the hunt, Siane oversaw the preparation of the smokehouse and kept the hunt records. Tali and I left the clean-up for later and walked up to the stableyard.

Only a few women would ride. We had, as a village, very few hill ponies. Horses, expensive in terms of feed, served few purposes that could not be met by oxen. The riders, with the help of the dogs which spent most of the year herding sheep and cattle, moved the small, delicate, red-coated deer off the hilltops and down into the lower slopes. There we chose a few young males to cull each year. After last year's mild winter and the fine summer, we might take half-a-dozen this year.

I took my orders from Gille, who acted as hunt leader. For the first half of the day, my job would be to walk the hillsides, flushing deer from small coombs and copses. In a friendly rivalry—soldiers, did, after all, need to be competent hunters of fresh meat—we divided the range of hills between *Skua*'s crew and the villagers. I had Lara with me. At eleven, she was old enough to participate in the first half of the day.

We walked up the path into the hills, skirting the springs and the burial ground, going higher even than the caves. As we walked, a thought occurred to me.

"Lara, does your mother mind you participating in the hunt?"

"No," she said, surprised. "Why would she?"

"She doesn't eat meat, and she disapproves of killing."

"But she didn't always. She was a farmer, remember?"

"Yes. And she still keeps the herd and hunt records, I know."

"Long ago, before I was born, she had a liaison with a soldier who told her all about the soldier's god, the bull they worship. She had forgotten about it, but on the day the bull attacked her, she suddenly remembered. She prayed to it. She promised that if it spared her life, she'd never kill again. She says the bull turned away at the last minute, and its horn only hit her in the leg. So she keeps that promise. She says she owes the soldier's god her life."

"I see," I said slowly.

We had reached the high moorland. The heath shone with dew. "Shhh, now," I whispered. "Feel the breeze. It's coming down over the hills, so we're upwind of the deer." Early frosts always resulted from clear nights and a wind off the hills. Wind from the sea carried too much warmth to allow frost to form. "We need to move very quietly through the heather, down towards groups of boulders, or the little coombs, where the deer spend the night. As we approach, stay quiet, but hold your arms out like this"—I demonstrated—"to make yourself look as big as possible. We want them to move down."

"What if they go up?" she whispered.

"Then the riders and the dogs will force them back down."

As we approached the first group of boulders, I could see the antlers of a seated stag poking up from the heather. I pointed them out to Lara. With hand signals, I indicated she should approach from one side of the boulders, I from the other. She waited while I made my way to the far side of the boulders, and then, arms outstretched, we approached the deer.

When the stag saw us, he bolted up, snorting, to bound down the hillside, followed by three others that I hadn't seen. I gave Lara a signal of approval, and she smiled. We continued to work along the ridge. Slowly, through the morning, we drew the noose of people and dogs tighter, driving the deer down to the lower meadow.

As we approached, I saw Gille conferring with Siane and Gwen. I picked up my bow, and Gille motioned me over. "We will take six," she said, "four for us, one for *Skua*, and one for the Empire's provisions." She paused. "Do you see the young stag with the malformed left antler? The first shot is yours."

I nodded. If I missed, or only wounded, someone else would let a second arrow fly before I could re-nock. This policy kept the kill swift, reducing the time we held the deer.

I positioned myself and waited for the first signal. When it came, I sighted, drew, and on the second signal, released. The arrow hit the stag in the neck, as I had intended. He leapt forward, took three or four steps, and fell.

We killed our six animals with eight arrows—four from the hands of *Skua*'s crew, four from women's bows. It was a good, clean, cull. Cleaning and butchering took the rest of the day. Much of the meat went for smoking, but tonight we feasted.

The smell of fresh liver frying over the fires brought us all to the council hall by early evening. Tice waved to me from across the hall. I worked my way through the bodies to her. She was in high spirits. "A good shot, cohort-leader," she said. "So why the boats and not the herds, then?"

"Simple," I replied, picking up a plate and spearing a slice of liver from the platter of roasted meat. "The hunt is once a year, but herds-and-hunt apprentices—and masters—look after the sheep and cattle, too. And I hate sheep."

Tice laughed. "Fair enough." We added vegetables and bread to our plates, moving outside where the cooking fires, now banked to heat water for tea, acted as focal points for groups of women and men. Freya saw us, waving us over to where she sat with Danel and a group of men and women. Freya and Danel sat close enough that their legs touched. Pastries, fruit, and quite a bit of wine followed the meat, making the meal leisurely and prolonged. Sitting around the fire, the night felt celebratory, a mood, I suddenly realized, of Festival.

"That was a good shot, Lena," Tiernay said suddenly.

"Thanks."

"Do you ever stalk deer in the hills?"

"Yes," I said, "sometimes, in the winter, if food is running low. I've taken one or two like that."

"It's harder, yes?" he said. "The wind can change suddenly, and they smell you, or you misjudge the arrow flight."

"Yes," I agreed. I sipped my wine, listening to Tiernay describe a winter hunt where they had taken three deer in the end, saving the camp from starvation. "And better for the deer, too," he ended. "There was so much snow, they couldn't find food."

"Where was this?" a man from across the fire said.

"Under the Durrains," Tiernay said, "some four or five years back."

"Winters are vicious over there," the man agreed. "Like being north of the Wall."

"By the god, yes," someone else said. "We did a winter sortie a few years back, with dogs, chasing after northerners who had tried to raid a guardpost for food. We had to turn back. I think they go underground."

"I heard they can walk on the snow," Largen said.

"On the snow!" Salle said.

"Yes," Largen answered. "They strap frames of hide and wood to their feet."

"It's true," the man across the fire said. "I've seen these frames. But I don't think you can move very fast."

"Faster than we could," the second man said. "I've never been so cold." The woman beside him—Lise—slipped her arms around him.

"You're warm now," she said. He nuzzled her hair.

"I am," he said.

As the conversations became more private, I sat quietly. Tice had excused herself some time earlier. Freya and Danel slipped away, hand in hand. Casyn and Gille were at the next fire. I watched as he put his hand on her shoulder and she leaned into him. Voices murmured, laughed. String and wind instruments played.

Dern approached, crouching beside me. "Walk with me, Lena," he said. He stood and held out a hand. I took it, letting him pull me up. We walked away from the fire, uphill, towards the sound of the waterfall. Beyond the ring of light from the fires, he stopped. "Last time, Lena," he murmured, putting a hand on the back of my neck, kissing me, hard and insistent. I felt the expected shock of physical desire, and beyond that, a deep regret.

Dern stepped back, running a hand gently down my upper arm.

I shook my head. "I can't. I'm sorry, Dern," I said. Tears pricked my eyes. "But Maya believed—believes—that she had been betrayed by everything she trusted. To go with you, when there is nothing more between us than physical desire, would be to betray that trust one more time."

A half-smile crossed his face. "I guessed as much. But I had to ask one last time." He looked back, toward the music, and the fires.

"Go," I said. "Enjoy the night." He looked at me steadily for a moment, then nodded. Beyond us, in the hills, an owl called. I could see a light in Tice's cottage window. I waited. Dern turned to walk back to the others. *He would find comfort somewhere*, I thought. I watched him for a moment, then took the uphill path to Tice's cottage.

She sat on the doorstep, a flask of wine and a cup beside her, looking out at the night. She must have seen—or heard—me coming but said nothing until I was only a few feet away.

"Said no to Dern, did you?" she said softly.

"I had to. For Maya. I only wanted physical comfort from him, Tice. There is no love between us."

She nodded, a half-smile playing around her lips. "You're still very young, cohort-leader. I hope you can keep to your ideals in what is coming."

I wanted to protest, but what could I say? Tice gestured. "Get a cup from the kitchen and join me." She edged over on the doorstone. I walked past her into the lantern-lit cottage, found a cup, and sat beside her. Tice reached for the wine to fill my cup. We drank in silence.

Tice spoke first. "Have you ever wondered why I left Karst?"

"Yes," I said. "Was it not by choice?"

"No," she said, so quietly I had to strain to hear her. "I was banished, sent away by the council. Do you want to know why?" I heard a challenge in her voice.

"Do you want to tell me?" I answered softly.

"Yes," she said, in a normal tone. "You're my friend, I hope, Lena, and my leader in these strange times. You deserve to know." She paused. "I had a child. A son. Out of season, conceived between festivals by a Lestian trader."

"Why?" I blurted.

"Why?" She laughed. "Because I was young and rebellious, and because the woman I loved had conceived a child the year before, and I was jealous, and angry."

"But, Tice, liaisons produce children."

"I wasn't jealous of the liaison. I am not proud of this, Lena. I was jealous of the child. Once she knew she was pregnant, all her attention was given to the unborn baby. And I was angry because she had gone against my wishes. I didn't want a child in our household, but Tevra did."

"She didn't come with you into exile?"

She shook her head. "She left before that, even before the babe was born. I had made our life together unbearable, so she went to Casilla to live with an aunt."

"Does she know what has happened to you since then?"

"No," she said. "Not even my mother or sisters know where I am."

"And your son? Where is he?"

"Being raised in the slave quarters at Jedd's retirement farm. The council arranged that. What else would there have been for him? No father to claim him, no regiment to house him. He will never know. They let me bear him and name him—Valle, I called him—and then they took him. They sent me away a month later." She fell silent. The cat appeared from somewhere to rub against Tice's legs. She stroked it absentmindedly. After a while, she spoke again. "I had gone to the farm to see the accountsman—something about payment for some grapes. But he was chambered with Jedd and the captain of the Lestian ship, and my errand was not important enough to disturb him. I decided to wait. I wandered around a bit, looked at the horses. And met Kirthan. He was a junior member of the Lestian entourage, bored by all the waiting. He had a flask of wine, and I was just an afternoon's distraction." She shrugged. "He was too young, probably, to even know the taboos we were breaking."

"Does the council know?"

"Yes," she answered. "I was exiled, and so must tell. Maya chose exile: she need not tell her reasons. You know that," she added. I remembered it, vaguely, from schoolgirl lessons. It had seemed very unimportant, then.

"Tice," I said, "what if—"

"Kirthan is aboard this raiding ship? We shared next to nothing, Lena, and I have paid all the price. I and Valle. Kirthan is nothing to me. If my knife finds his heart, I will feel no regret. You need not worry, cohort-leader." Something in her voice told me the moment had passed and the subject was closed. I poured some more wine.

"Tomorrow, will we practice one-on-one combat with the men, or should we test our routes again?"

"Practice, I think."

We spoke of tactics for a while before I bade her goodnight and walked back to my room. The house was dark. I could hear music and laughter. It did not touch me. Too much betrayal, done or revealed, this night. I let the tears come. I wept for the pain Tice had caused and carried, for my own fears for Maya and for myself, and for the comfort I could not give, or take.

CHAPTER NINE

SIX DAYS LATER, ON A FOGGY, wet morning, *Skua* sailed on the tide. For the last few days, Dern had not accompanied his men to the practice field but had spent his days with Casyn. I had seen him only from a distance. While he always waved and shouted a greeting, he did not come to me privately. Nor did I go in search of him.

The day before, I had met Casyn at the lower footbridge. I was carrying a basket of carrots and small turnips on my way to Tali's from the fields.

"Lena," he said, in his measured way, "I hoped to find you."

"Casyn," I greeted him, putting my basket down. "Do you need something?"

"No," he said. "Only to tell you we sail tomorrow, on the morning tide."

"Tomorrow! Then you think the invasion is very soon."

"A week, give or take. We need to be well away, out beyond the quickest routes from Leste, so that we are not seen. We will approach the island from the west, as they sail east."

I glanced at the sky. The breeze blew from off the hills, and only a few clouds lined the western horizon: good weather to sail west.

"Are we ready?"

"You are," he said. "Trust your training, Lena, but also your instincts."

"I wish you were staying."

"You have to do this yourselves," he said. "Were I here, you would defer to my experience and not take true leadership. This way, you must." He held out a hand. "Fare you well, Lena. I will see you again."

I too held out my right hand. He took my arm in the soldier's grasp, his hand at my elbow. I returned the grasp, feeling the muscles of his arm, hard against my hand. "Farewell, Casyn. We will have tales to tell, when we meet again."

The entire village came out to see them leave. The men rowed aboard in small boats until only Dern and Casyn stood on the jetty. They saluted us, and we them, and then they boarded the last boat to begin their short, measured trip back to the ship.

We watched, singly and in small groups, until the sea fog obscured the last glimpse of *Skua*. I wished suddenly I had spoken to Dern before they sailed, if only to thank him for what he had taught me. But I had missed my chance.

As women began to walk away, up the hill to the meeting house, cohorts fell in behind their leaders. I saw Freya watching me. I nodded, joining the exodus from the shore. We walked up the hill without much talk. My cohort sat together at the meeting house, Tice taking her usual place beside me. Gille, with Sara and my mother, stood in their familiar place in the centre of the circle. When all had gathered, Gille raised her hand for silence.

"Women of Tirvan," she began, "we are once again a village of women. Four months ago, our lives consisted of farming and fishing, and our thoughts and our skills were given to these pursuits. We are something more now: a military unit, trained to fight. And we have paid a price, both personal and collective."

I listened, puzzled.

"We have changed our traditions. We have learned to fight. We have lived beside men, abandoning the role of Festival in our personal relationships with them. After the invasion, we will resume our normal lives, but we will not be as we were before this summer. But in this time before the invasion, we must maintain the structures of authority in the village. Much of our autumn work awaits completion. In the fields and on the boats, authority still belongs to the masters of those trades, regardless of their position in our defensive cohorts. When this is finished, when the invasion is quashed, and the Empire is safe again, we will need to think about the future, and what it will look like. But not until then. Are there questions?"

No one stood. Tice met my eyes, cocking an eyebrow in her usual unspoken question. I shook my head slightly. Had Gille meant to raise speculation?

Sara stepped forward. She spoke of the tasks still needing to be done, the familiar autumn work: root vegetables to be dug, boats to be cleaned and repaired, cider apples to be pressed. The bulk of the harvest was done, thanks to the work of *Skua*'s crew. We would accomplish these remaining tasks in the afternoons and continue to drill in the mornings.

Gille spoke again. "Casyn and I, with Dessa's help," she nodded toward the cohort-leader and master fisher, seated to her left, "have studied the tides, and the moon. We believe that the most likely time for the attack is between six and eight days from now, at dawn. The tide will be high and the moon set." She paused. "We will use against them what they believe they are using against us: darkness and surprise. We will be waiting, armed and hidden. With luck and skill, they will never get past the beach."

I considered what Dern had told me about the catboats of Leste—keeled longboats, driven by oars and a single sail, that floated in less than three feet of water. At high tide, they could gain our harbour, which meant they would attack at full force. They would have no reason to send an advance party. Lestian catboats had come occasionally to trade with Tirvan, so they would know the harbour and expect no defence. Forty men against eighty women, skilled with bow and knife and with the advantage of surprise. I felt suddenly confident.

Gille continued. "Cohort-leaders and seconds, please remain. The rest are needed in the fields and at the boats, but before you go, I would say one last thing. Women of Tirvan, we have a job to do. We have much at stake. We cannot slacken. The patrols and exercises must continue. We fight for our lives." She paused, then continued in a voice softened by fatigue and sorrow. "You have done well, my friends. We will come through this, but not unscathed. Some of us will die. We will win our lives, but we will pay yet another, grievous price. Be brave, my friends, and strong." She stepped back, her face drawn. I thought of what these weeks must have cost her. She had found brief solace with Casyn, both sharing the strains of leadership, and now he was gone.

The hall emptied of everyone but the leaders and their seconds. I moved forward, to the inner ring of seats, with Tice beside me. When only the cohort-leaders remained, Gille began.

"We have gone through the records for the last twenty years. Leste has sent boats thrice in that time, the last six years ago." Heads nodded among the women. I remembered the boat, the graceful curved sides of the longboat and the carved leopard's head on the prow. At eleven, I had found that of far more interest than the men who had sailed on her. "Casyn believes that it will be that boat's captain who will steer his ship into our harbour, both for his knowledge of our waters and his memories of the village. They were here five days, and we took him and some of his men around the village to see fleeces and cloth and grain stores. Xani did some small repairs for them, so they'll know where the forge is. The men traded freely for small items, pottery and jewellery and the like."

I saw the logic. The Lestians would leave a few men to defend the boat, moving the rest, under cover of darkness, up to the top of the village. They would then drive us down through the village to the harbour at first light, catch us between the invading force and the sea, giving us no choice but to surrender.

"We'll let them get themselves into position above the village," Gille went on. "At that moment, the mounted cohort, who will be hidden and waiting by the shellfish ponds, will attack the men who stayed with the boat. Archers lying in wait in the net sheds will defend the riders. The men above the village will, we believe, rush back toward their boat through the centre of the village. The main path from the baths will be visible and clearly the fastest way to the harbour. We hope they will run that way, to be trapped on the path, with archers and mounted swordswomen below them, and the rest of us above, on foot and in the second floor of houses with bows and knives."

I nodded. Dern and I had spoken of this plan. The wattle fences around the path would not hold them for long, but in the confusion and surprise of those first few minutes, under an unanticipated attack, we would have the advantage. I shivered. I saw my cohort slipping through tunnel and loft, solitary and swift, to kill those who had escaped the battle. Assassins. I looked at Tice. All the laughter had gone from her. She sat still and hard and cold.

"I'm not going to live in a cave!" Minna shouted. "I want my own bed and my chair."

"You must, Mother." Her daughter tried to soothe her. "It's for your safety, and it's only for a few days."

"You must," Gille echoed, her voice firm.

"I won't," Minna said.

Casse stood. "Let me try," she said, looking to Gille for permission. Gille nodded, and Casse moved to stand in front of Minna. "Look at me, Minna," she said. Minna obeyed. "Who am I?" Casse asked.

"Casse," Minna mumbled. "Council Leader."

"When we give the word, Minna, you will go to the caves," Casse repeated calmly. "You are needed there, to help care for the babes and the new mothers. Do you understand?"

Minna dropped her eyes. "Yes, Council Leader."

"You will not argue?"

"I won't," Minna said. "I will go where I'm needed."

"Thank you, Minna."

"Thank you, Casse," Gille murmured as Casse returned to her seat. "As I was saying, there is food aplenty in the caves, and straw and blankets and water. We cannot risk a fire, so you must huddle together for warmth and wrap the little ones well."

"I worry we can't keep the children quiet," Nessa said, jiggling her grizzling baby.

"There is poppy, dissolved in wine. It can be given in sips, or rubbed on the gums for the littlest ones, just enough to keep them sleepy," my mother said. "And Casyn warned the boys that any reports of disobedience would become part of their cadet records. I think they believed him."

"Pel certainly did," Tali said. "Is there any fencing left to do or work on the tunnels?"

"Nothing," I said. The wattle panels already fenced the common and the path. We had dismantled the hunt enclosures, and some of the sheep pens, to do this, so that fresh wattle did not warn of recent change.

"All the boats not fishing daily are anchored in the hidden cove," Dessa reported. "There will only be a few left at the jetty, just enough not to look odd."

The meeting over, I had stood to leave when my mother called my name. Tice was waiting for me on the porch, so I signalled to her to wait before turning to my mother. She looked very tired, and spoke quietly. "Lena, there may be no other time to say this. Much has been asked of you this summer, losing Maya, being called to command so young and in such a role. I am proud of you. But I think you will soon have to make some terrible choices, with no one to advise you. You must always consider what course of action benefits the most. The village comes before the individual."

I found my voice. "Do you think I do not know my job, Mother? When have you had to make such a decision?" I heard my own words with an odd sense of detachment.

"Many times, and your sister is learning, too." Her voice was soft, but I saw a flash of anger in her eyes. "When we had to choose, this summer, between saving both of Nessa's twins and losing Nessa, or letting the second child die to keep Nessa and the first one safe, were we not making the same decision? For the village, a mother who will live to raise her child, and to work and to contribute and to bear more children if she wishes, is worth more than two babies. If the decision had been Nessa's, she would have died to let both twins live."

I flushed. "Forgive me, Mother. I should not have said what I did."

"Kira cried for two days after that birthing, but you won't have that luxury. Nor do I think you have properly grieved for Maya. You will do what you need to do, but when this is over—and it will be over, soon—you need to grieve. For Maya, for our changed life, for the lives you will have taken and lost. If you do not grieve, Lena, you will break."

I could feel the tears threatening. I looked away. "Do your job," my mother said.

"I will," I said softly, turning away.

We rehearsed the attack, pulling two women from each cohort—different women, each day—to be the invaders. We practiced being still and keeping the ponies quiet. We practiced with sword and bow in the half-light of dawn and at dusk. We timed how long it took the mounted cohort to reach the harbour. We perfected signals—night bird calls, the bark of a fox. My cohort hid in lofts and tunnels and crawled and leapt and perfected landing on the balls of our feet, knives out, ready.

On the third morning, just as the sun crested the ridge above the sheep pastures, a shout came from high in the hills. Horses, silhouetted against the sky: two with riders, the rest riderless but saddled and carrying packs. Gille, with her eyesight honed by years of herding and hunting, spoke. "The riders are women."

They clattered into the village, pulling up outside the hall where we had, by habit, gathered. The riders were not much older than I. They wore their long hair tied back, carrying swords in scabbards on the saddles, shields on their backs, and spears in their hands. The horses they sat on were muscled, conditioned, and disciplined. Warriors. I tried not to stare.

Gille stepped forward. "Welcome to Tirvan."

The riders dismounted. The shorter of the two women spoke. "I am Dian, and this is Rasa. We come from Han village, in the grasslands. Four weeks ago, the three grasslands villages met in joint council to determine our role in fighting Leste. We decided that half of us would go to the coastal villages to add to the defence. The others would stay to act as a rearguard against any Lestians who might slip through the coastal defences. We brought what horses we could."

The grasslands villages bred and trained the majority of the horses for the army. The villages raised cattle, too, making, from the tanned hides, the saddles and bridles for the Empire. Horses, beef, and harness. For everything else, they traded.

"Thank you," Gille said. "We welcome your assistance. I am Gille, council leader; Sara and Gwen make the three. And this is Grainne. She leads the mounted cohort. We expect attack within three days."

Dian nodded. "We had hoped to be on time."

"Grainne, your cohort is excused from field duty," Gille said. "For the rest of us, to work!"

As we dug root vegetables that afternoon, the women of the mounted cohort learned to control the warhorses in the lower pasture. Han had sent six horses, plus the two Dian and Rasa rode. That meant we now had ten horses trained to war, as Casyn and Dern had left their horses with us when they sailed. The hunt ponies would now, I surmised, be ridden only by the smallest women.

In the late afternoon, we called a halt to the harvest, ate a quick snack, and, as the evening deepened, took our places once again to rehearse the defence of Tirvan. I slipped into the loft above the forge, sliding open the ventilation window. From here, I had an almost unobstructed view of the village. I settled down on my heels to wait.

The night call of a thrush, repeated twice, sang through the dusk. From the harbour, I could see the group who represented the Lestians moving up to the top of the village. I waited. When they gathered above the houses, I barked twice, and then twice again, the sharp sound of a fox on its evening hunt. The horses erupted from the scrub that hid the shellfish ponds, their riders shouting, spears held high. The group of women above the village drew their weapons as they ran toward the harbour.

All but one. She turned away from the group, beginning to run toward the forge and the waterfall. I dropped silently through the trap door onto the bedroom floor below, creeping out the door to the small porch. As she passed the corner of the cottage, I leapt, knife in hand, and brought her down. I felt the resistance and strength in her muscled body, but when my knife found her throat, she capitulated. Dian.

I squatted beside her as she caught her breath. "Well done," she said, sitting up and pushing her black hair back. "I thought I would test your defences. I wouldn't be sure that all the men will immediately return to the boat. One or two may realize it's a trap and do what I did. You're well prepared," she said ruefully, brushing the dust from her hands. "Now what do you do?"

"Move down through the village, to help where I'm needed."

"Then do it," she said. "I'm dead. Take my knife and go."

I hesitated, then took the knife from her belt, slipping it into mine. I moved away, using bushes and boulders as cover, heading for the stream and the willows.

An hour later, we met in the council hall to discuss the evening over tea. I found Dian and returned her knife. "Would you eat with me?"

"Surely," she said, "after I have seen to the horses and bathed. Rasa has much to talk about with Grainne, so I'll be glad of the company."

I told her how to find Tali's house and left for the baths myself. Twenty minutes later, I walked down to Tali's. I had slept at the forge cottage for the past few nights but didn't bother to cook for myself. Tali had stew simmering, and there was bread on the table.

"I asked Dian to eat with me."

"There's plenty," Tali said. "I've eaten, and I'm going to help Rette string herbs for drying. There's cider if you want it."

I found the cider, poured a small amount, taking it out on the porch to wait for Dian. She came about forty minutes later, her hair newly braided and clean.

"Your baths are wonderful," she said, accepting a mug of cider. "We have nothing like them in Han."

I ladled bowls of stew and cut bread. We sat at the kitchen table to eat. The stew was venison, the last of the fresh meat from the hunt, redolent of herbs, with a rich, thick gravy.

"Dian," I said, "I really could have killed you this afternoon."

She nodded, her mouth full of stew. A moment later, she spoke. "I know. I could see it in your eyes. For a moment, I was actually frightened."

"I didn't realize...the training takes over. It's all reflex, and no thought, except to stay alive. It's so—cold."

"If it wasn't, I doubt we could do it. If one of our horses breaks a leg, we cut its throat immediately, or we will have second thoughts. We would try to save it and just extend its suffering. And that too feels cold. All killing must."

I nodded. "Are your horses all right?" I asked, changing the subject.

"Fine. The barn is clean and airy, and we brought extra grain with us. Tell me, what did you think of Casyn?"

I looked up from my stew, surprised. "How did you know he was here?"

"His horse. We bred him at Han. The mare I ride is from the same dam. Casyn visits Han every few years to buy horses, and he has two daughters there. He wanted to buy my mare last time—she was still a foal then—but she had been promised to me as my coming-of-age gift."

"Casyn was born here," I said. "He was the right man to send to Tirvan." A thought struck me. "Is that what was done, all over?"

"I think so," Dian said. "The man who came to work with us is my uncle, my mother's brother." She looked at me steadily for a minute. "It was easier for us, I think. We are half-trained in warfare already, to prepare the horses."

"You look like warriors. We only hunt," I added, "but we have learned."

"You have," she said. "I am impressed. And your mounted cohort ride well. They have good balance, which isn't surprising, being used to hunting in these hills." She sipped her cider.

"How long did it take you to reach us?"

"Three weeks. But we didn't come directly here. When we left the grasslands, there were eighteen of us and seventy-two horses. We stayed together on the road, with smaller groups breaking off on the byways to the villages. We left the last two, heading north to Delle, four days ago."

"Did you stop at the inns?"

"Sometimes," Dian said. "Although we made camp more often, and picketed the horses. The inns can't cope with large numbers. But we stopped for water or to buy cheese or bread." She looked at me curiously. "Why do you ask?"

I hesitated. "My partner, Maya, chose exile, rather than learn to fight. She is out there, somewhere, alone. I was hoping you had seen her. She's about your height, with long dark hair and hazel eyes."

Dian remained silent for a minute. "Not I," she said finally, "but Rasa is the best bargainer amongst us, so she went most often to the inns. I'll ask her. Maya is unlikely to be alone, Lena. In almost every village, one or two women made that choice. No one did from Han, but from Rigg, the village just to our north, three went. They will find each other on the road." She put down her cup. "Thank you for the food. I sleep at Grainne's cottage."

I said goodnight, watching her walk up the path. *They will find each other on the road.* A certainty settled inside me about what I would do after the invasion. I stayed outside in the warm night for a long time, looking west, up to the hills, and the road that ran beneath the glittering stars.

CHAPTER TEN

THE DEEP PEAL OF THE MEETING BELL reverberated through the village in mid-afternoon. I looked up from the knife I was sharpening, muscles tensing. Dessa stood watch this afternoon. I slipped the knife into its sheath and ran to the meeting hall. Other cohort-leaders did the same as the cohorts gathered in their appointed places.

The council leaders waited. Longsighted, accustomed to searching the sea for the movement of birds or water that told of fish, Dessa spoke with authority. "I saw something on the horizon," she reported. "It could be no more than a flight of seabirds, far out, or a breaching whale, but I think not."

My heart skipped as my mind raced through our preparations. The leaders ordered the children and new mothers to the caves while I counted weapons in my head. No one panicked. No one argued. Freya would be in Ranni's byre, and Camy in a loft.

"Cohort-leaders," Gille said. "Check your weapons and your gear one last time, then command your cohorts to rest." Her voice did not waver. "They will wait till night." Her gaze quartered the room. "Eat lightly, but enough. I doubt there will be another chance for food for some time. Carry water if it will not hinder you." She paused. "We are ready," she continued, her voice gentler. "Remember that."

My cohort had gathered under the trees at the training ground. No one spoke as I approached. They had gathered their weapons.

"Cohort-leader," Tice said formally. "What is the news?"

"Dessa has seen a sail," I said. "Or, something she believes to be a sail. I doubt she is wrong."

"She won't be wrong," Freya confirmed. "They are very far out, then?"

"Yes," I said. "It will be very late when they land. We will review our posts and our tactics and check our weapons. Then you all must try to rest and take some food and water. You should be in your places two hours before midnight. Tice will review with half the cohort, and I'll take the other half." I hoped I sounded calm and in control. The cohort divided. I looked at the girls and women standing in front of me.

"Freya, your orders?"

"Ranni's byre," she said. "I do nothing until I hear the dogfox bark twice. Then I pick off any man who comes within throwing distance or closer. If they do not climb the hill, but attack the buildings, I will use our routes to move up to the hills and wait until our skills are needed." I nodded.

"How many knives do you have?"

"Six."

"Sharp?"

"Yes."

"Good." I had grown to both like and trust her in these last months. I put out a hand to touch her shoulder. "Get some rest. I'll see you at your post." She nodded, moving away, making room for Kelle.

The review took no more than twenty minutes. Each woman knew her orders and posts and answered me calmly. Finally, only Tice remained. She and I would both be high in the village, I at the forge, she at the big barn, places where we thought men might splinter off to, to hide or regroup.

"Aline and Camy are nervous."

"Everyone is nervous. They just can't hide it as well as the older women. Will they hold their posts?"

"I believe so," she said. "But if either thinks the other is in trouble or hurt...I'm not sure."

I nodded. "They are closely bonded." As Maya and I had been at that age. They would be posted in the lofts of adjoining houses on the far side of the village.

"May they be safe," Tice said. "May we all be safe."

Shortly after midnight, I crouched in the loft of the forge. I had done my rounds, checking on each member of my cohort, over the previous hour. A light seafog shrouded the village, and no breeze moved the air. I sat back on my haunches. Listening. An owl called and mice rustled in the roof. Stars wheeled through the sky. I shifted quietly to keep my muscles from cramping. I smelled the sharp musky scent of a fox about its night's hunt. I heard the rhythm of the waves on the shore. Then, above the gentle susurration of the waves, I heard the sweep of oars.

My heart beat faster, and my breathing quickened. I forced myself to relax my grip on my knife. Tired muscles grew clumsy. I waited. I heard them disembark, the noise muffled by the fog. I heard footsteps, and then a thrush called, sleepily, twice. From the barnyard, a cock crowed.

I crouched, staring into darkness as minutes passed. Then I heard them climbing the hill toward the open space above the council hall. We had guessed right. I listened until no more boots sounded on the path. I barked twice, and twice again.

The horses exploded from their hiding place, hooves hitting sharply upon the rocks, riders screaming defiance. The sheepdogs gave tongue from the barns. I heard the scrape of metal on leather as swords came out of scabbards. Voices spoke in surprise. The horses and their shouting riders grew closer. Steel clashed on steel as men and women screamed. Arrows cut the air, whistling. I strained to see through the small window and the dark.

Two shapes broke off, heading towards the barns and the fields. I saw them fall, as Casse calmly rose from behind her sheltering rock to throw a knife, once, twice. Beneath me, in the village, the battle raged in full force. I heard the chop of sword on leather, the whir of bowstrings, screams of pain and challenge. My heart pounded in my ears. A man turned from the melee, running toward the forge. I dropped out of the loft, landing silently, and slipped through the door. He wore no helmet. I grabbed his hair, and his cry of surprise turned to a gurgle as I slit his throat. His hot blood spilled over my hands. I felt my gorge rise. No different than the hunt, I told myself. Don't think about it. I bent, wiped my hands on the grass. I took his knife from his boot.

More followed. I could see at least three pounding up the path. I ran behind the forge and into the longer grasses, working my way toward the barns. I forced myself to stay quiet, to move slowly. I reached Casse. She had taken the knives from the men she had killed and was hefting them in her hands, judging their usefulness for throwing. She looked at me sharply.

"I'm not hurt," I assured her. "I'm going to the barn. Stay here. There are three at the forge, at least."

"None got past me," she said. "Not that I saw." A shout of rage rose from the battle below us. The water of the harbour reflected the flicker and glow of fire: the catboat, burning.

I moved through the field until I reached the barns. I whistled softly, the meadow pipit's call. Tice answered and stepped out from behind a partition.

"They sent two men to burn the barn," she said. "They're both dead, though one killed a sheepdog first."

"Good," I said. "There are three, or more, at the forge. I killed one. Casse remains on guard. Stay here, Tice, and watch this end of the village. I'm going down to assess where we are needed." She nodded, and I moved through the barn and out the far end, into the heather.

I reached the stream and its cover of willows easily. I climbed up, to edge through the branches, keeping parallel to the stream and the footpath. Once I thought I saw movement in the field beyond. I paused to watch, but saw nothing more. A fox, perhaps, or a badger. From the village and the harbour, the sound of battle continued, but women's voices were raised in command more often than men's. The morning grew lighter.

I crossed on the branch, sliding to the ground on the other side of the stream, taking the now-familiar route through byre and tunnel toward the harbour. Freya was gone from her hiding spot in Rette's kitchen, but a dead man lay in the doorway. Fifty feet from Siane's workshop and the net sheds, where the archers had lain in wait, I stopped.

The flames of the burning catboat and the rising sun gave enough light to see well. The fog had lifted with the dawn. A group of six men fought with swords and shields at the base of the dock, surrounded on three sides by the sword cohort. As I watched, one man broke, running along the jetty. I heard the twang of the bowstring, and he fell with an arrow in his back. Further up the hill, a horsewoman swung a sword, and another man dropped.

As the day brightened, I saw the tallest of the fighting men look desperately around. The catboat smouldered, listing on its side in the shallow water at the edge of the jetty. Above, in the village, a few men still fought, but the main path was littered with bodies. He stepped back and dropped his sword. "I surrender," he said, hoarsely, in the accents of Leste.

The men with him did likewise. Tali stepped forward to pick up the swords, passing them back to other cohort members. "Shields," she said. They too, dropped. She bent, taking the knives from the men's boots. "Take off your belts."

They tied the men's hands with their own belts. "Now," Tali said to the leader, her voice calm and deadly. "Call your men to you. Tell them it is over." He stood impassively. She put the point of her sword at his neck. "Tell them." The sun broke over the ridge.

He raised his head and called out, one word, three times.

"How many on the boat? How many men, in total?" Tali demanded.

"Three and forty," he said.

We gathered at the meeting hall. As my eyes adjusted to the dimness, I looked around for my cohort members. I heard quiet sobs from across the room where my mother stood with her hand on Dessa's shoulder. Dessa kneeled beside a covered body. Siane. I approached them, hoping I was wrong. My mother looked up. I saw the flash of relief on her face. Dessa did not move. With a motion of her head, my mother indicated we should move away.

"What happened?" I whispered.

"Her knee gave out," my mother said. I could see the tears in her eyes. Mine remained dry. "She stumbled and fell into a swordstroke meant for someone else. It was quick, at least." She shook her head. "She should have gone to the caves."

"Anyone else?"

"Not yet. But not everyone is back. Is all your cohort here?"

I looked around. Aline and Camy were slumped against a wall with mugs of tea. Freya sat beside them. Kelle spoke to her sister on one of the benches. Casse had gone to Dessa. Everyone but Tice. I had just opened my mouth to tell my mother this when I saw her at the door, her eyes searching the room. She saw my mother, and then me, and beckoned us over.

"Gwen," she said. "You are needed, although I fear it is too late. Lise is near the common with a sword cut to the thigh. She is bleeding badly."

"Is the blood deep red?" my mother asked. "Is it pumping out?"

"No," Tice said. "But she's lost a lot of blood, and she's unconscious."

My mother nodded. "I'll come." She found her basket, following Tice out the door. I was hesitating, wondering if I should go too, when Tali called me.

"Lena! Please join me."

I went to where she stood with Gille and Sara at the side of the hall.

"We can account for thirty-two men—dead, wounded, or surrendered." Tali said. "You said there are three at the forge?"

"That I saw," I said. "Others could have joined them."

"True, but I doubt all eleven are there. We need your cohort, Lena to check everywhere a man could hide. I think we should leave the forge alone for now."

I considered. "Yes," I agreed. "We'll have to plan an attack there. They will have made peepholes in the walls, so we won't be able to take them by surprise. But we should guard it, with horsewomen, perhaps?"

"A good plan," Gille said. "Is your cohort ready?"

"They will do what is needed. But Tice isn't here. She went with my mother to tend Lise, who is badly hurt."

"Send someone down for her," Gille said.

I nodded. "Give us ten minutes." I walked over to Kelle. "We'll need to go out again soon. Can you fetch Tice? She's at the common with my mother."

Kelle nodded and slipped off the bench. I did a circuit of the room, speaking to each of my cohort, ensuring they had eaten and drunk. I had done neither myself, I realized, so I filled a mug with sweet tea and took a hunk of yesterday's bread. I had a mouth full of stale bread when Tice and Kelle came back. I could see the news in their faces.

"We were too late," Tice said.

"I'm sorry. But we have work to do. Mourning must wait." Shock flickered over Kelle's face. Then she nodded, and I saw her body straighten.

"We hunt?"
"We do."
"Good," she said.

I found my first man in Kyan's timber loft. He chose to surrender, eagerly offering up his weapons. I tied his hands and took his boots, and once out in the street, found a member of the sword cohort to take him to the council hall, where the prisoners were being held. As I turned away, I saw Freya slip out of a byre. I whistled. She held up one finger, then drew it across her throat. Thirty-four.

My second man did not surrender. The deep wail of a cat caught my attention; I moved towards the stable behind Ranni's cottage. I heard the tabby growl, then scream in pain. I opened the door. The man sprang up, leaving the bleeding cat on the stable floor, to come at me with his knife out. I sidestepped, but the knife grazed my upper arm. It stung. He turned against his momentum, stumbling. I ducked, letting the knife swing harmlessly above me. I stood, grabbed his arm, and drove my knife up under his ribs.

He did not die easily. In the half-light of the stable, I watched as he moaned and coughed, a froth of blood around his lips. He seemed younger than I, and thin. Blood trickled down his chin, and his eyes held only terror. He tried to speak, but coughed. Blood bubbled up between his lips. He began to choke. I stepped forward, pulled his head back, and cut his throat as if he were a deer at the autumn cull. Then I fell to my knees beside him, vomiting bile until nothing came up. I heaved a few more times, then pushed myself up to a squat, not looking at the body. I found straw, wiped my hands and my mouth, the motions automatic, without thought. I kept my eyes averted, and stepped, shivering, out into the day.

At mid-morning, we gathered at the training ground. Inside the meeting hall, the shackled and bound prisoners sat against the wall. My mother and sister tended the wounded and shocked. Aline had stumbled over the body of Binne, the knife that had killed her still in her chest. We had all heard Aline's screams. Kira gave her wine and poppy, and she slept now

I shook my head to dislodge thoughts of Binne and our other dead. The cohorts reported five men killed or captured. That left six, still, somewhere in the village.

Grainne rode up, on Siannon. "We can find no one in the hills," she reported. "The children and the women with them are fine and have seen nothing. I left Dian and Caryn on patrol."

Similar reports came in from other cohort-leaders. We turned our attention to the forge.

"They have swords and knives, perhaps spears," Gille said.

Kyan knelt to sketch in the sand. "Look," she said. "The forge building has three solid walls. At the front, the large doors are split horizontally to allow the top half to be opened separately from the bottom. At the back, there is a small door meant only for escape from fire."

"What's underneath?" someone asked.

"The metal store, where the ore and charcoal are stored."

"They will have found that, by now." Gille said. "But they have no food, nor a water source."

"There's a little water in the forge, for cooling iron," Kyan said. "But it won't last long."

"Why don't we negotiate surrender?" Sara asked. "Have their captain—Kolmas, his name is—order it, even."

"Do you think he'll do it?" Tali asked.

"We can ask," Sara said.

Gille unlocked the Lestian captain's chains, leaving his hands shackled, bringing him over to where we met.

"We want to negotiate surrender with the men hiding at the forge," she explained. "We need to you to speak to them. Will you do this?"

He grunted. "Do you know names?" he asked, his use of our language passable.

"No," Gille admitted. "Does it matter?"

"Maybe. If Dann is there, he will not listen. But I will try."

We escorted Kolmas to within hailing distance of the forge, under close guard. Tice and I flanked him with knives at the ready. Horsewomen and archers made a semi-circle around us.

Kolmas took a step forward. A tall man, barrel chested and strong, he did not test his shackles. He called to the men inside, in Lestian. I thought I heard his name in the string of sounds.

The doors remained closed, but a voice answered from inside, the derision intelligible, even if the words were not.

Kolmas shrugged. "Dann. He will do as he choose, and others will follow him. I can do no more."

"Does he speak our language?" Gille asked.

"He understands." Kolmas said. "But speak? A few words only."

Gille raised her voice. "I am Gille, headwoman of Tirvan. I give you one more chance: surrender, or die."

Dann laughed. "No, woman," he said, heavily accented, followed by a stream of words, guttural and angry.

"He says that not easy," Kolmas translated. "He is not weak trader, he says, but soldier. If he led battle, you would be dead or in chains. He says he is man, not traitor or coward, like men you breed."

"He has chosen," Gille said calmly.

Later, at the training ground, Gille told us what she had learned from Kolmas. "Leste has a small army. They sent half-a-dozen soldiers with each raiding boat to teach arms and tactics. Dann is the most senior among them, but Kolmas's captaincy, and his knowledge of the village, made him the leader."

"Kolmas is being uncommonly helpful," Tali observed.

"He is hoping for clemency, I suppose," Gille said. "And in the end, he is, as Dann said, only a trader, and half his crew lies dead. He was led to believe this would be a quick and bloodless raid, with glory to those who led the capture. Glory matters to the men of Leste. Their reputations are everything to them."

"Which means," I said, "that Dann would think a glorious death preferable to an ignominious surrender."

"Yes," Gille said.

"So let's give them an inglorious death," I said. "If we burn the forge, they will be forced to choose between death by fire and death at the hands of women."

Gille considered. "The forge won't burn easily. The roof is sod, and the walls are fireproofed with plaster."

"The plastering is on the inside, not the exterior," I said. "If we start the fires on the outside, the boards will catch quickly."

"How will you set the fires?"

"With tinder and kindling, piled along the foundations. Three of us, one for each wall, can do it quickly in the dark of night. When the men run, we will have armed women waiting to pick them off."

"How will you get there without being detected?" Tali asked.

"The waterfall."

"In the dead of night?" my mother exclaimed. "Lena, no. It's too dangerous."

"Gwen," Tali said. "Lena is right. There is no other way."

"There is," my mother said firmly. "We can simply starve them out. They will be forced to surrender, and that will be even more inglorious than death at our hands."

I shook my head slowly. "These men are soldiers. They will be planning tactics, as we are now. They won't wait until they are weakened but will attack soon. I believe we would win, but not without a considerable fight. We have already lost three women. Do we wish to lose more? We can burn the forge tonight."

"I do not want to lose you, Lena," she said sharply.

"Tirvan comes first," I reminded her, as gently as I could. I saw the tears in her eyes, but I could not let them move me. I had a job to do.

"It will work, I think," Gille said, considering. "They may go to the metal store, though."

"Then they'll die of suffocation." Tali said. "The fire will take all the air."

I briefed my cohort on the plan, and we spent some time preparing bundles of fatwood, the resin-soaked interior wood of the pines that made the best kindling. All houses had a supply. We chose the best, shredding the ends well. Then we practiced building and lighting small fires until we could—and did—do it blindfolded.

At mid-afternoon, I called a halt. We finished wrapping our wood in greased leather pouches, with flint and tinder tucked deep inside the packages. We would carry these on our backs to keep them as dry as possible as we climbed. I had chosen Freya and Salle to climb with me. Now I bade them rest, to sleep if possible, and to eat lightly. "We'll meet at the waterfall's base, at dark."

I walked with Tice toward the cottage that Dessa and Siane had shared. My mother and Kira had washed Siane's body, and she lay on the bed. Among several other women gathered there, I found Dessa. As my apprentice-master, she had taught me, disciplined me, and become my friend. She sat at the kitchen table, a cup of tea in her hands. When I put my hand on her shoulder, she reached up to take it. Dessa did not give way to outward expression of emotion, but I could feel her hand trembling. "I will miss her, too," I said.

"I wanted her to go to the caves, but she would not," Dessa said. "She did not want Lara to think her mother a coward."

"Does Lara know?"

"We sent the message with the horsewomen. The children are to stay at the caves until it is completely safe." She looked up at me. "I wish you luck tonight, Lena."

"Thank you."

I stepped away. Tice spoke briefly to Dessa, the formal words of sympathy, and then we left. We made our visits to where the other victims lay. We would bury our dead in the hills tomorrow, or the next day. Outside, women dragged men's bodies down to the rocks beyond the net sheds where we would build their pyre. The tide would take the remains. Blood and vomit dried in the sand of the paths.

We climbed onto the porch of Tali's house. She had guard duty at the meeting hall, so the house stood empty. Inside, I went to the sink to pour water, washing my hands and face and arms. The blood on my tunic had dried, brown and hard.

Tice washed. I found a loaf of day-old bread and some cheese, and gave her half. I poured water. We sat at the table and ate in silence, tasting nothing, the bread dry as ashes. Tice spoke first. "How many did you kill today?"

"Two," I said. "One at the forge, and one at the stable." Saying the words made me even colder inside.

"Two for me also," she said, "but neither was Kirthan."

For what do you fight? I had asked Dern. I had never asked Tice.

At dusk, we gathered at the base of the waterfall. We wore dark clothes and had blackened our faces and hands with charcoal. Soft leather boots gave our feet protection but allowed us to use toes and arches to grip. I would climb first, then Salle, and Freya at the rear. The last report from the women keeping guard around the forge had told us what we expected: the men inside had drilled holes through the walls, on all four sides, to keep watch. Other than that, nothing had changed. Six horsewomen ranged around the forge, and as many archers and swordswomen.

I checked my parcel of fatwood one last time before climbing onto the first boulder. The air temperature had dropped, and the water, initially warm against my skin, felt cold. I moved upward. I could hear Salle behind me, but the sound of the water obscured most of our noise.

At the rockface, I stopped to catch my breath. The weight on my back affected my balance. I found the rope and began to climb the sheer face. My feet slipped on the wet rock. I hung by one arm from the rope, fighting back panic. My searching hand found a protrusion in the rock and grabbed it. I hung on, trying to remember what the rockface looked like as water splashed into my eyes. The knob of rock under my hand felt roughly triangular. In my mind, I saw another piece of rock jutting out, above it and a bit to the right. I reached up to the next knot in the rope and hauled myself up. My foot found the triangular hold. I pushed upward.

I finally hauled myself onto the ledge and lay panting. The sweat of fear and exertion cooled against my skin. My injured arm ached. I counted to ten before tugging on the rope, the signal for Salle to begin climbing. My eyes had fully adjusted to the dark. In the starlight, I could just make out the movement of water. I climbed onto the next boulder.

As I neared the top, I found a dry spot to wait. Salle arrived a few minutes later, then Freya. I felt their parcels of wood—dry. I touched both on the hand and met their eyes. Both nodded. I crawled forward, keeping to the thorn bushes, trying to move and breathe silently.

Over the sound of the water, I could hear the horses moving. The guards rode at a slow walk around the forge, keeping out of range of a surprise attack. Their noise would help muffle ours. We reached the meadow. The forge lay about ten strides away.

I had the right side, as we faced the building, Salle the left. Freya had the back. In open ground, now, we went at our own speeds, waiting until a horsewoman appeared to catch the attention of any watchers. I crawled a body length, stopped, waited, crawled again. It took ten minutes to cover the distance.

Huddled against the side of the building, I unstrapped the parcel of fatwood and unwrapped it. The greased leather fell open silently. I found the flint and tinder, pushing them into the pocket of my leggings. I counted out five sticks of fatwood by feel, and built a pyramid, carefully, quietly, against the boards of the wall.

I did this five times. I could hear movement and voices inside the forge. Whenever the footsteps or voices seemed too near, I lay still. I had no idea how long I was taking. I built the last pyramid, then took the flint and tinder from my pocket.

I moved into a crouching position. I struck a spark, lit the tinder, then held the frayed end of a fatwood stick into the small flame. It crackled, and shrivelled, and caught.

On my feet now, I thrust the burning fatwood stick into each pile of kindling, forcing myself to wait until I saw the flames licking upward in the pyramid. At any second someone inside would notice the flickering light through the spy-holes. As I lit the last one, a shout came from inside. I ran for the waterfall hearing the crackle of the fires behind me.

In the shelter of the bushes, I turned to look back. Through heavy smoke, I saw growing flame. Salle dropped beside me. "Where's Freya?" I hissed.

"Don't know," she gasped, coughing. She had breathed too much smoke. At the forge, the rear door swung open, and men ran out, swords drawn. I heard an arrow fly, but no one fell. The horsewomen closed in. I saw a shape crawling towards us, awkwardly: Freya. I crawled forward, grabbing her shoulders, ignoring her gasp of pain, and pulled her to the bushes. The smell of burned flesh assaulted us. "I waited too long," she murmured. "My arm...." I pulled her to the stream's edge and pushed her arm into the water. She moaned.

"Leave it there," I said.

The crack of timber snapping shot through the night. I looked up to see the forge collapse. It fell slowly, the sod roof breaking through the burned rafters, the flaming walls spreading out. Sparks spiralled upwards. Like fireflies.

Grainne rode over to us. "There were only four. The others may have tried to shelter in the metal store, but we won't know until tomorrow."

My job—our job—was not done, then. "Freya needs help. Her arm is burned." Grainne nodded and rode away. I sat with Salle and Freya, keeping Freya's arm in the water. The heat from the fire had died. Freya began to shiver.

My sister arrived with a torch and two others bearing a stretcher. We moved Freya gently onto the stretcher, covering her with a blanket. "You did well, Lena, keeping her arm in the water," Kira said. She moved the torch closer. "Are you all right? Whose blood is that?"

"Not mine," I said.

"You're shivering. Go and get warm. There is soup at mother's. You too, Salle," she said authoritatively. We did not argue.

We walked down the hill. The cut on my arm from the Lestian soldier pained me, but it would wait till morning. At my mother's, I drank hot soup and found some dry clothes to change into. I gave Salle some of Kira's clothes. Tice came to the door.

"Kira told me you were here," she said.

"We're not finished," I said, trying to muster some energy.

"I know. Grainne told me. Tonight?"

"Later," I said. I needed rest. "After midnight. Tell the cohort to meet me here in four hours." After she left, I sank into a chair, holding my soup mug in both hands. I wanted to sleep, but when I closed my eyes I saw the eyes of the boy I had killed. So young, and so thin, and so scared. Had he thought to gain glory? Would his mother ever know what had befallen him, on what shore the waves had claimed his ashes? I hugged the steaming mug, staring into the night.

At midnight, a wispy seafog gathered. Most of the women would sweep the village from the harbour upward, but Tice and I would be on lookout. We had the best eyes at night.

"I want us in the trees," I said. "Looking over the village and the fields. Look for movement, listen. If they have hidden in the fields, they might choose now to move."

"Can you climb with that arm?"

I shrugged. It throbbed, but I could ignore it. "I climbed the waterfall. I can climb a tree."

She looked at me levelly for a moment then grinned. "Let's go."

Our best vantage points lay about twenty strides apart, close to where the willows bridged the stream. Tice looked toward the village and the harbour while I peered outward, to the fields. Stars glittered in the cold air. Wisps of fog gathered in the lower areas. I waited, flexed my muscles to keep from stiffening, and watched.

I could hear the occasional murmur of conversation from the guards at the meeting hall. The moon, half-full and high, gave a faint light. I heard a fox bark, high in the hills, and saw a barn owl hunting along a hedge.

An hour passed, and another. My arm ached. I moved it, trying to keep it supple. The barn owl rose from its perch on the hedge to fly straight across the field. I could see nothing in its talons. A rustling noise came from the far side of the hedge. I stood, stiffly, and moved along the branches, trying to see beyond the bushes.

I swung clumsily into the next tree, hearing Tice moving towards me across the bridging branch. A small field barn stood at this end of the field, partly shrouded by hanging fog. Tice crouched beside me.

I stiffened. A figure moved toward us, hugging the wall for concealment. The clothes and the long, braided hair told of Leste, yet I hesitated. Something about the way he—or she?—moved, and the planes of the face, that sent a stab of recognition as sharp as a knife-thrust through my gut. Maya? It couldn't be... And then I realized. I touched Tice's arm. She followed my gaze and immediately drew her knife.

He stepped away from the barn into the moonlight. I heard Tice's indrawn breath, and the barely audible name she spat: "Kirthan." She raised her arm to throw. I grabbed frantically at her arm, catching it on the downward arc. The knife veered high into the barn over his head. He froze, looking up. I dropped from the branches, hands open and empty.

"*Garth?*" I said.

Tice dropped beside me.

"Garth?" she said, disbelievingly.

"Garth, son of Tali, brother to Maya?"

"How did you know?" I could see his confusion and fatigue. He seemed, at that moment, very young.

"Your sister is my partner. You move like her, look like her, too. For a moment, I thought you were her."

He stared at me in the faint light.

"I am Lena, Gwen's daughter. Garth, we played together."

"I remember."

"Do you remember me?" Tice said fiercely. "I knew you as Kirthan."

He shook his head. "I have been Kirthan for so long now. Where did we meet?"

"At Jedd's farm. In the barn, one afternoon," she said bluntly. He said nothing for several heartbeats.

"In Karst. I remember," he said. He gestured helplessly. Tice strode forward to pull the knife from the boards of the barn. She did not sheath it.

"Have you a weapon?" I asked. He drew a small knife from his boot, handing it to me. His hand shook. I waited.

"That's all. I had a sword, but I left it back there," he pointed up the hill, "in the caves." I must have looked puzzled. "When we came ashore at dawn, I left the others—it was easy, in all the confusion—and climbed to the caves. I remembered where they were. I've been there ever since. The women hiding in the large one didn't see me." He met my eyes. I remembered the movement I had seen from the branches of the willows yesterday morning.

"Put your hands behind your back," I said. He did so, and I tied them, my fingers trembling. Tice stood silently, her knife still in her hand. "I am taking you to the meeting hall," I said. "You can tell your story there, to the council, and your mother."

"Why not kill him?" Tice asked, coldly. "He has proved thrice a traitor, to the Empire, to Leste, to us. Why should he live?"

"He surrendered," I said, keeping my voice level. "And if there is retribution to be made, for deserting the Empire's armies, that is not for us to demand." I looked at Tice, her face in the moonlight pale, and hard with anger. "Cohort-second, continue with the patrol. There is still a man to be found. I will take Garth to the council. You may speak to them later, and privately, if you wish."

For a moment, I thought she would refuse, but she nodded. "Cohort-leader," she said formally, turning back into the willows, her knife still in her hand. I looked at Garth.

"Come," I said, unsheathing my own knife. "You have a story to tell." In the moonlight, I could see tears in his eyes. He swallowed hard, and at my gesture, began to walk along the path, toward the footbridge. I walked a few steps behind, watching him. We crossed the bridge, following the path uphill, toward the council hall. He stumbled more than once. At the hall, a fire burned, and lanterns lit the porch. A figure rose to meet us.

"Tali, I bring you a prisoner."

CHAPTER ELEVEN

"MOTHER."

"Garth?" Tali stopped, raising her lantern higher. In its flickering light, her face reflected disbelief followed by a joy that was quickly quenched. Her lips trembled. "You look like Mar. Now I understand why Dann said we bred traitors."

Garth shook his head, a barely perceptible movement. He stood a little straighter, goaded by her words. "Are you a council leader, Mother?"

Tali laughed, a short, sharp sound. "Does it matter?"

"Yes," he answered. "I may speak of my role only to the council leaders." He had gained some control over himself. His voice sounded clearer, more assured.

"By whose orders?" Tali asked, her lips thin.

"My orders come from the Empire. I report to Dern, Captain of *Skua*."

"Dern," I scoffed, incredulous. "His orders?"

Garth turned slightly to look at me. "I must speak to the council."

Suddenly I remembered the night—so long ago, it seemed—when I had demanded to know why Dern had really come to Tirvan. He had referred obliquely to new information the Empire had received about the invasion. This must be what he meant. "He tells the truth," I said.

"Gwen is here," Tali said. "Gille and Sara are sleeping. I will send someone for them." She turned to her son. Her face momentarily softened. "If what you say is true, it would be unwise to take you into the hall where you will be seen by the other prisoners. Lena, will you stay with him on the porch for a moment?" She disappeared back into the lit hall. I gestured to Garth, and we climbed the few steps onto the wide porch.

"You may sit, if you wish," I said. He sank down onto a bench, leaning back against one of the pillars that supported the roof of the porch. He closed his eyes. Even in the lantern light, I could see lines of fatigue deeply etched on his face. Such weariness came from a longer struggle than just a day and a night without food or sleep.

Tali reappeared with Gwen, carrying a cup. She held it to Garth's lips, and he drank deeply. "Thank you," he said. Her fingers lingered on his cheek.

My mother knelt beside him. "Are you hurt?"

He blinked at her. "No."

She took his wrist, felt his pulse, then laid the back of her hand on his forehead. Tali watched intensely.

"No fever," my mother finally proclaimed. "He needs sleep, water, and food."

"You are my aunt, I think," he said quietly.

"I am," my mother said. "Gwen. Try to sleep."

We waited in silence as Garth closed his eyes, dozing. Tali sat beside him, not quite touching him. I sheathed my knife, watching him, seeing again the resemblance to his sister. I wanted him, very much, to be telling the truth.

Sara and Gille arrived about twenty minutes later. Garth opened his eyes at their approach, and stood, clumsily, his bound hands hindering him.

"Garth," Tali said, fighting to keep her voice even. "Once of the Empire's seventh regiment. My son. He says he reports to Dern and can speak only to you three." She turned to go back into the hall, but Gille stopped her.

"Stay," she said. "You too, Lena."

"Gille," Tali said. "I can't."

"Come over here," Gille said, walking Tali further down the porch. Snatches of their words reached me.

"I cannot let myself believe him," Tali said. Whatever Gille replied I did not hear, but Tali shook her head.

"...not after Maya," I heard.

"You will witness," Gille said clearly. "I request it, as council leader."

I thought Tali would refuse, but she just nodded, letting Gille lead her back to where we waited. I looked away. I did not want Tali to know I had overheard.

Gille addressed Garth. "I am Gille, and this is Sara. We are the council leaders, along with Gwen. Whatever you have to say to us, Tali, as your mother, should hear, and I think Lena should, too."

He nodded, slowly.

"I was to speak to the council, but also to anyone else you chose to be present." He paused, searching for words. "What my mother said is true. I report to Dern."

"You are a spy?" Gille spoke calmly without a hint of surprise in her voice.

"I am. One of maybe a half-dozen on Leste. How I came to serve the Empire in this way is not a pretty story, but I am to tell you the whole of it." He straightened, looking from Gille to the others. "I was taken from here unwilling, and unwilling I was schooled as a soldier. I had—I have—no talent for fighting. The regiment saw this and offered me training as a medic. But even that was not to my liking. At fourteen, I ran away."

Tali gasped.

"The seventh were on the move along the south coast. There was a trading ship from Leste preparing to sail from one of the retirement farms. I found my way aboard at night. They were happy to take me. Leste does not love the Empire." He cleared his throat. "May I have some more water?"

Sara held the cup to his lips. He drank, then thanked her and went on. "For over three years, I worked on that ship and on the jetties of Leste. I grew to like the sea, and I learned the language. Then, nearly four years ago, while we were trading in a harbour along the south coast, *Skua* arrived. I thought I was safe, dressed as a Lestian, my hair long, and speaking their language. Somehow, Dern recognized me. He had me captured and taken to him. The penalty for desertion is death. He offered me an alternative." He spoke flatly, without emotion. I hugged myself, listening, thinking of what Dern had told me all those weeks before, of the price paid by those boys who could not bring themselves to serve.

"For these last few years, I have spied on Leste for the Empire. We trade frequently with the retirement farms, which made it easy enough to leave messages, and I was privy to much of the planning of the invasion. Kolmas trusts me. Also, I am betrothed to his niece." That startled me. Betrothed? He went on. "Dann was more suspicious and did not want me to be aboard ship, but Kolmas insisted. With my medic's training, I could care for the wounded."

"What did you tell the Lestians about Tirvan?" Tali asked, her voice just barely audible.

"Nothing." Garth shook his head. "They do not know this is my birth village. I claimed to have been born inland, so they were not interested. Kolmas had traded here, before I was part of his crew. The invasion plans were based on his recollections."

"What were your instructions for the invasion?" Gille asked quietly.

"To help the village if I could. I was supposed to stay with the catboat; I was going to burn it, but at the last minute Dann ordered me to go with him. He wanted me where he could watch me, I think. I pretended clumsiness on the path and fell twice. Dann lost patience with me and sent me to Kolmas. I slipped over the wall into the field and worked my way up to the caves. I thought if the battle went against you, I might be able to be of use."

"What were you promised, if the Empire was victorious?" My mother spoke.

"A second chance to serve the Empire, aboard *Skua*," Garth said, quietly.

"And you wanted this, or were you more afraid of death?" Tali asked.

Garth met his mother's eyes. "When Dern first found me, and offered me the choice of spying or court-martial, I agreed to spy because I knew that the alternative was death. But when Leste began to plot against the Empire, I realized where my allegiance truly lay."

"And your betrothed?" I said.

He flushed. "I had to behave like any Lestian man of twenty to remain unsuspected. I regret the betrothal. She is a gentle girl, who does not deserve such deception. I have done many things I am not proud of in these past few years. I will make redress where I can, if I can."

Gille spoke. "The council will confer. Tali, please join us. We will not be long, Lena." As they walked into the night, I could hear the murmur of their voices, but not the words.

"Kirthan," I said, testing the name. He smiled, just a brief movement of his lips.

"That is how 'Garth' is rendered in Lestian. Tice is your friend?"

"And my cohort-second," I said. "I don't know if you can make sufficient redress, there. That is between her and you, and the council."

I leaned back against the wall of the council hall. My reaction to him confused me. He confused me. He is so much like Maya, and yet not. A gentle breeze moved the air. The moon sank closer to the sea. Inside, I could hear movement, and the occasional moan from an injured prisoner.

"Where is Maya?" Garth asked suddenly.

I straightened. "Gone. She chose exile, rather than fight."

"But you stayed?"

"You are not the only one looking for a second chance, Garth," I said angrily. "When this is over, I will find her."

"I missed her so much, those first years. I hoped to see her again."

When the council returned, Gille spoke. "We think it best," Gille said without preamble, "that you are kept in custody, Garth, for two reasons. While we are inclined to believe your story, until we have confirmation from Dern, we cannot be entirely convinced. And secondly, were you to be given your freedom, your role would become immediately apparent to the other prisoners. We would not endanger your life. We will chain your hands and feet, loosely enough to allow you some movement, and confine you to a cottage under guard."

"It is fair."

"No it's not," I said, indignant. "Mother, Gille, he's telling the truth. I know he is."

"Is he?" Gille said sternly. "He admits to a web of lies, Lena, going back many years." She softened. "I said we were inclined to believe him, but you must see we have to be sure."

I looked from her to Garth. "It is fair," he repeated.

The spurt of anger Gille's words had engendered subsided. If Garth thought it fair, why should I argue? I nodded. "Where?" I asked.

"The forge cottage," Gille said. "It's far enough from the hall and easy to guard."

Tali chained his feet, loosely enough to allow him a shuffling walk, her deft fingers finding ways to touch her son briefly. I unbound his wrists and let him eat the bread and cheese and apples Sara brought.

Then Tali loosely shackled his arms again, and we escorted him to the forge cottage, matching our pace to his slow shuffle. He stumbled once, and I put out a hand to steady him. My fingers tingled where I had touched him.

At the cottage, he lay down on the bed, chains clinking, and closed his eyes. Tali covered him with the blanket.

"We'll send someone to keep watch," Gille said. "Tali, Lena, watch him till then."

Do they not trust me alone with him? Then I saw Tali's face, watching Garth, trying for impassivity and failing. "He is so like Maya," I said. She nodded. Did she see the resemblance to Maya, or to Mar, their father and her dead love? Or just her son. In the normal course of events, she would never have seen him again after he was sent, drugged and unknowing, with the men. I left her with him and went out into the night.

When a swordswoman came to take the first watch, I briefed her on the limits of his freedom. Tali joined us outside. The first hint of dawn lightened the eastern sky as we walked down the hill. At the meeting hall, I poured a cup of tea from the ever-present kettle, going back outside to where I could see the training ground from the porch. I sat on the bench, sipping the hot, sweet tea. My arm throbbed, and I could not get warm. I looked at my hands. I had killed two men in the last twenty-four hours, cut both their throats, one in a fair fight, one in pity. I had trained and practiced, yet the last day felt like a dream. Months of training seemed to have more substance than one day of battle.

I should not have refused Dern, I thought. I had wanted love, not realizing that the comfort, and perhaps the pleasure, would have been enough. *I wish I had said yes. When had I last touched someone, except to correct a hold, or to console? Or to kill.*

I sat, struggling to sort out my feelings, as Salle approached from the northern edge of the village. I greeted her and sent her in for tea. One by one, the women of my cohort arrived. When most were present, we moved out to the training ground. The eastern stars had faded quickly. Somewhere a cock crowed. Ten of us stood on the field. Freya, wounded and resting, made eleven.

"Has anyone seen Tice?" I asked. No one had. Somewhere out there, the last man waited, hidden. "Sleep," I ordered. "Half of you until noon, half until tonight."

I sent the cohort to their beds, with much grumbling from Camy and Aline, and waited for Tice. As the sky changed from dawn grey to blue, a knot of apprehension tightened in my gut. I waited another ten minutes, then reported to Gille, to begin a different search.

I walked down under the willows, wondering if Tice had fallen asleep in the branches. Finally, I spotted her leaning against a trunk, not sixty feet from where I had sent her back on patrol. "Tice," I called. "Wake up!"

She did not move. "Tice," I shouted again. A wave of fear washed through me—fear and cold certainty. I grabbed a branch to swing myself up into the tree, climbing quickly. I put out my hand to touch her, feeling the chill of her dead flesh.

"Tice!" I tried to turn her towards me. My hands found the knife, embedded in her back. "Oh, Tice," I moaned. I leaned forward, resting my head on her shoulder. My hand found hers and held it.

I had sent Tice back on patrol when I knew her anger might distract her. Clearly and coldly, I analysed what I had done. I had sent her back when I should have sent her home, and I had done so to prevent a confrontation between her and Garth that I did not want to have to handle. I had failed as a leader. The thought turned my heart to lead. I let go of her hand, placing it so it did not dangle helplessly, and sat up. I pulled the knife from her back. The blade gleamed with blood. A drop fell on my hand. I threw the knife into the earth beneath the tree, wiping my hands on my tunic. I could not move her by myself. I would wake Salle. My cohort alone would handle this.

Salle and I lowered Tice's body carefully down from the willow, placing it on the stretcher. Then we carried her through the village to her cottage. My mother waited. I had gone to tell her, and fetch the stretcher, while Salle dressed. We laid Tice on her bed, and then I sent Salle away. I removed her clothes, and my mother and I washed the body and dressed it again. We worked in silence except for brief words of instruction or direction.

When we finished, we sat at the kitchen table. The cat was nowhere to be seen. "Mother," I said. "Tice told me of her son."

"We will send word to Karst. Do not worry yourself. You are exhausted and need sleep."

"There is more, though. Did Tice speak of the father to the council?"

"Only that he was a Lestian trader," she replied. "We did not need to know more, as he was not of the Empire." She sighed. "Tice was very private, Lena, as you must know."

"Yes, but she told me the father's name. She said he was a young Lestian, called Kirthan. But the boat was Kolmas's, Mother, and Kirthan is the Lestian form of Garth."

My mother looked at me, startled. "Are you sure?"

I nodded, tiredly. "Yes. She told me of it weeks ago, a few days before *Skua* sailed. But when she and I captured Garth, Mother, she called him Kirthan, and he acknowledged her."

"He will have to be told of the child," my mother said, slowly, "but not yet."

"Will you tell Sara and Gille?"

"Yes," she said. "But not Tali, not yet. Nor must you, Lena."

"I won't," I said. There were footsteps outside. Casse came in the door.

"I will sit with her, Lena," she said quietly. "You need to rest."

"Thank you, Casse," my mother said, before I could protest. She touched my shoulder. "Come, Lena. You must sleep."

I let my mother lead me away as if I were a child again. My body, heavy and cold and slow, seemed to take a long time to respond to my thoughts. Outside in the cool morning breeze, I stopped on the path. "I can't sleep," I said, almost petulantly. "We have a hunt to finish."

"You must sleep," my mother said. "You are wounded and exhausted. I am ordering you, Lena, as a council leader. Name a cohort-second." I stared at her, shocked, before the simple practicality of her words sank in.

"I would have chosen Freya, but it will have to be Salle, now."

"Then tell her," my mother said. "Brief her on tactics, if you can think clearly enough. Then I'll treat that arm and give you just enough poppy to let you sleep for a few hours. You can lead the search this evening if it's still needed."

I agreed, reluctantly, and with my mother beside me went to wake Salle for the second time. We found her sitting on the porch of the cottage she shared with her sister, Kelle.

"I need you to be cohort-second, Salle," I said, after she had greeted us. "And I will need you to lead the search this afternoon."

"What would you have me do?" she asked, calmly.

"Concentrate on the edges of the village, the outbuildings and field barns." I struggled to think past the fog in my brain. "He's probably been watching. He'll have seen us searching in the village." She nodded, understanding. "Work in pairs. I want no one on her own." *Too late*, a voice in my mind said.

"Grainne and the horsewomen are patrolling the higher fields," Salle said. "The women preparing graves are guarded by archers. And we'll be searching the village. Our man will feel harried. Perhaps he'll make a wrong move."

"Perhaps." Fatigue closed in on my muscles and my mind. I let my mother lead me away. She took me home, to the room where I slept as a girl, and gave me a small cup of wine, warmed and dosed with poppy and other herbs. I did as she told me, though I felt like a husk, hollow and dry. She undressed me, bathed my arm, and bandaged it. Somewhere during that treatment, I slept.

When I woke, the sun had begun its western descent. In the half-light of the room, a fragment of dream still made disturbing images in my mind: Maya coming home, changed almost beyond recognition. Then I remembered. *Tice.* The hollow inside me widened into an abyss. I sat up quickly. The room swam. I waited until it stopped then stood, stripped off my clothes, and washed.

Dressed again, I went out to the kitchen. A kettle simmered on the stove, and a mug with dried leaves and honey sat ready on the table. I poured in the water, stirred. My arm felt stiff, but less painful. I flexed it tentatively. I sipped the tea. Anash. I reached for the honeypot to spoon in more, to counteract the bitterness.

Outside, the day was cool, with a slight haze and a strong on-shore breeze. I walked up to the meeting hall. Around the inner periphery of the octagonal hall, Lise and Casyn had drilled eyebolts deep into the structural timbers. The prisoners stood or sat, shackled to the eyebolts. The severely injured lay on pallets in the centre of the hall. Six women stood guard, escorting pairs of prisoners, chained at hands and feet, out to use the privy and get some exercise. Casyn had estimated that *Skua* would not return for five or six weeks. We could not keep healthy men constantly chained to the wall for that long a time. These Lestians were no soldiers. Dann and his men would have struggled against the chains, but they had died at the forge. These others, shocked by their defeat and seeing their captain cooperate with Gille, followed his lead.

Gille was studying a list as I came in. "Food stores," she said briefly. "We have twenty-odd extra mouths to feed." Her face softened. "Lena, I am so sorry. Tice found a friend in you, I think, as well as a cohort-leader."

"Thank you," I said, my voice trembling.

She looked at me sharply. "Are you all right?'

"I dreamt Maya came home, but I almost couldn't recognize her. From the poppy, I suppose."

"Probably," Gille agreed. "And not surprising, given how much Garth looks like her."

Garth.

"Lena?' she asked, concern on her face.

"I had forgotten about him." Confusion flooded through me. Yesterday, he had been all I could think of. "How could that happen?"

"You were shocked and exhausted, and we gave you poppy. He became confused with Maya in your sleeping mind. Nothing more, or less, than that, Lena."

"Is he still at the forge cottage?" I could see him in my mind, in the moonlight, with Tice's knife vibrating in the wall of the barn above him. I remembered her anger, and my response.

"We need to call the cohort-leaders together to explain about Garth," she said. "He looks enough like Maya, and like his father, for those who remember, that tongues are already wagging."

"What will you tell them?"

She shrugged. "The truth, as much as we know. We are inclined to believe his story. Casyn told us there were spies, but we are waiting for his story to be confirmed by Dern."

My thoughts had started to clear. "How is Tali?"

"Confused," Gille said. "Angry at him for deserting, proud of him for taking the second chance, if he is telling the truth, that is, and happy that he is alive. She's with him now."

"What guard will you want tomorrow, for the burials?"

If my question surprised her, she did not show it. "If you do not find the last man before then, we will need archers and horsewomen, in a circle around the graves, facing out. And two from your cohort, to guard the dead and their bearers, on their way to the burial ground."

I calculated. "That will mean only two from our cohort can bear Tice's body." Four women usually bore a body to burial. In the absence of family, the cohort would do this instead.

"I realize that," Gille said, "but it will have to be. Half-a-dozen women will have to remain behind, on guard. I have asked for volunteers, and one to guard Garth, as well. Although I think Tali will do that."

I left the hall to walk to Tice's cottage. Casse sat beside the still form. She said my name in greeting, but nothing more. Tice looked peaceful. I touched her cold face.

"I am sorry," I whispered. I said goodbye to Casse, walking up the hill. The forge was now only a pile of ashes and burned timbers, the anvil and stove sitting blackened in their midst. The guard walked back and forth near the cottage, sword in hand. Through its open door I could see Tali and Garth sitting at the table. Two-day old stubble darkened his jaw, blurring his resemblance to Maya. I stopped at the door.

"May I come in?"

"Surely," Tali said. I entered, leaning against the wall. Garth smiled at me. I looked away, and then back.

"Tice is dead," I said bluntly. "She was stabbed in the back, in the willows."

He closed his eyes. "I am sorry."

"There is only one man left at large. Do you have any idea who it is?"

He thought a moment. "How many were with Dann?"

"Four."

"It may be Cael," he said. "He was one of Dann's men, but he always kept apart from the others, somehow. Dann and the other three had served together for some time, but Cael was a stranger to them and did not always seem to take his orders from Dann."

I nodded. "Thank you."

Tali stood. "I have stayed long enough. Lena, I will walk with you."

We left Garth at the table. Outside, the guard came over to speak to me, words of consolation. I responded, somehow.

We walked some distance from the cottage before Tali spoke again. "His first questions were about Maya."

"Do you believe his story?"

She considered. "Yes," she said finally. "Perhaps it is just a mother's blindness, but I do." She did not ask me what I thought.

CHAPTER TWELVE

WE DID NOT FIND OUR MAN that afternoon, or that night. Late in the afternoon, we lit the pyre at the water's edge. Gille escorted Kolmas, shackled like all the other men, to the site, so that he could speak a few words over his dead kinsman and bear witness to the flames. He surveyed the pyre, and the bodies, nodding solemnly.

"This is good," he said. "We burn our dead, or, if death finds a man at sea, we give him to the waters. They will go to our gods this way. I thank you."

He said a few words in his own language, raising his shackled hands up to the sky, as far as he could, then bowing to the ocean. Gille strode forward to push the lighted torch into the wood of the pyre. Drenched in oil, it caught quickly. The wood crackled. Smoke rose, almost straight up. For a while, it smelled only of wood. Then a smell of roasting meat overpowered the clean smell of the woodsmoke, and I could hear the hiss of fat. Around me, women turned away with hands over their mouths. I swallowed the rush of cold saliva but did not move.

The stars shone in the western sky before the pyre had burned to the strand. The incoming tide would wash the beach clean. Tomorrow, we buried our dead.

I slept for a few hours between dawn and mid-morning. When I woke, the first of the heavy autumn fogs hung, grey and cold, over the village. I washed in cold water, shivering, and dressed in clean clothes before walking up to Tice's cottage. Salle met me there, along with Casse and Dari, who had volunteered to be the other two bearers.

"I spoke to Gille and Sara about postponing the burials because of the fog," Casse told us. "They debated it and decided we must go ahead. The fog could last for days, and we need to bring the mothers and children down from the caves. They cannot stay there indefinitely."

"They're guarded," I said, "and Cael does not know the village. The fog will provide protection for us."

"Let us hope so," Casse answered.

We wrapped Tice's body in a woven sheet of deep blues and reds, the colours of her pots, and placed it on the stretcher. Then, each taking one corner, and, guarded by Aline and Camy, we carried her up to the burial ground. We walked carefully and slowly, gauging where we walked by the familiar curves of the path and the shapes of trees and boulders that loomed out of the fog. Focusing on my steps took my mind away from our burden.

As we neared the burial ground, I heard the voices of other women.

"Lena?" I heard my sister ask.

"Here," I answered, stopping. Kira stepped out of the fog.

"Let me guide you," she said, glancing down at the stretcher. "The graves are to your left. Come up higher, this way." We followed her, laying the stretcher where she indicated. The other dead lay in place.

"You're the last," Kira said. "We are all here, now."

"Thank you, Kira." I heard my mother's voice but could not see her. Droplets of water condensed on my hair and ran into my eyes. I put a hand up to brush them away. My mother appeared in front of me. "Lena, will you do the rites for Tice?"

"I will." She handed me a small, stoppered flask containing water from the sacred spring. I would place a few drops on Tice's forehead, eyes, and lips, and then place the flask between her hands before we buried her. I slipped the flask into the pocket of my tunic, wondering as I did what the rites of Karst were, and whether it mattered.

Voices and the sound of hooves and jingling harness floated down from above us as the women from the caves, and their guard, descended the path. A baby cried. Suddenly, a woman shouted, and a child screamed. I heard Grainne snapping commands amidst more screams. I ran, past the dug graves and up the hill path, pulling my knife from its boot sheath.

I found the women not more than fifty paces above the burial ground. They had formed a ring around the children and Minna, and they too had drawn knives. Dian sat her horse just above them on the path.

"What happened?" I asked, panting.

"The Lestian snatched one of the children," Dian said grimly. "Grainne and Rasa have gone in pursuit."

"Which one?"

"Pel," Mella said from the circle. She held her child with one arm, her knife in the other hand. "He was supposed to be in front of Ranni—we were keeping the children between the adults—but someone slipped on a wet rock, jostling him, and he ran out of the circle. Cael grabbed him almost at once."

"How did Cael know we were here?" Kelle asked. Other women from the burial ground had reached the group now.

"He must have been following us," Dian said. "In this fog, we wouldn't have seen him."

Rasa rode up. She shook her head. "Nothing," she said. "I think he's gone into the caves, with Pel as hostage."

"Get the rest of them to the burial ground," Dian said. She turned to me. "Where is Pel's mother?"

"On guard duty at the hall," Gille said. "Take them down to the burial ground. We will bury our dead," she said grimly. "There is little we can do in this fog. He won't harm the boy if he wishes to bargain."

We brought the women and children down to the graves. Lara ran to Dessa, burying her face against Dessa's breast. Dessa rocked her, tears streaming down into Lara's hair. Around them, mothers found their children, comforting the little ones who sobbed with fright and cold. It was some time before we could begin the rituals.

Dessa stepped forward first, holding Lara's hand. She knelt beside Siane's body, uncovering her face. Lara sobbed once, then controlled herself. Dessa handed her the flask, removing the stopper for her. Guiding Lara's hands with her own, together they let a drop or two of sacred water fall onto Siane's forehead. Lara touched it. "Be at peace, mother," she said, her voice barely audible, but not breaking. Dessa, too, touched Siane's forehead. "Be at peace, my love," she said. Then she dropped water onto her own fingers to touch Siane's closed eyes and lips. Then they drew back the covering blanket to tuck the flask into Siane's hands, before covering her again and stepping away.

Other hands lowered the stretcher into the grave. We repeated the ritual three more times. Tice was the last. Carefully, I rolled back the blanket to touch the water to her forehead. "Be at peace, Tice," I said, "my friend, my cohort-second." I touched her eyes and lips with my wetted fingers and placed the flask in her hands.

The council and the cohort-leaders gathered at my mother's house in the early afternoon. The sun, a pale disc, barely showed through the fog. We gathered around the fire in my mother's sitting room. Tali sat with a shawl over her shoulders, staring at the flames.

Gille had ridden with Grainne and Dian into the hills, hoping to find the cave where Cael held Pel. My mother made tea. Subdued by burials and loss, we said little as we sipped the hot, sweet liquid. Finally, Sara spoke.

"Some of you know what I have to tell you already," she began. "Two nights ago, Lena and Tice took a prisoner. This man is not Lestian, though he sailed with them as part of their force." She glanced at Tali before she continued. "This man is Tali's son, Garth."

"What?"

"Are we sure it's Garth?"

"A traitor?"

I felt a wave of anger at this comment. Sara held up her hand, and the group quieted. My mother sat beside Tali, putting an arm around her. "Hear me out," Sara said. "He is Garth, and he claims to be a spy for the Emperor, under Dern's command. This is consistent with information that Casyn told Gille and that Dern told Lena."

"Yes," I confirmed.

"We are inclined to believe him," Sara went on, "but until we hear from Dern or Casyn, we hold him guarded at the forge cottage."

A harness jingled outside announcing Gille's return. She strode in, water droplets condensed on her wool cloak. "Cael is in the large cave," she announced. "Pel is unharmed, but Cael will let him go only if we release our prisoners and give them boats to sail to Leste. He gives us a day before he kills Pel." My mother took her cloak and hung it to dry.

"Could Kolmas reason with him?" someone asked. Gille shook her head.

"We could try," she admitted, "but he is not one of Kolmas's men. Kolmas says he barely accepted Dann's leadership. I don't think it is worth the time it would take."

The cave, defensible from inside, had no other entrance. Cael had Pel for hostage and shield. For all my cohort's skill at stealth and the knife, we faced an opponent at least our equal, and more likely our master. Sara spoke. "Garth is our only chance."

"Explain," Gille said.

"We send Garth to the cave. Cael will think only that he has also eluded capture and will not be on his guard. Garth can kill Cael, or wound him, and let Pel escape."

"Or we will find ourselves up against two holding Pel hostage, not one."

"I think Garth is telling the truth," I said, "but Cael may have seen him captured. We would have to make it look as if he had escaped. I agree with Sara. Garth is our best chance."

We debated for another twenty minutes, but in the end, even the most reluctant agreed. Gille stood. "Who will go with me? Tali? Lena?"

Tali looked up. "No," she said lifelessly. "I can't. Lena, you go."

I found a cloak, and Gille and I walked up the hill to the forge cottage through the fog. Garth sat in the kitchen, playing cards with Salle. "Leave us, please," Gille said to Salle. When she was gone, Gille began. "Cael holds your brother, Pel, captive. He took him this morning at the burials."

"What does he want?" Garth asked.

"He is giving us a day to release the prisoners and give them the means to sail away, or he will kill him," I answered. "We need your help."

"How?"

"If we release you," I said, "and make it look like you escaped, will you go to the cave and set Pel free?"

"Kill Cael, you mean?" He said softly.

"If that is what it takes."

He hesitated for a few heartbeats, looking from me to Gille, and then back to me. He raised his chin.

"I will."

We cut the leg chains, leaving the shackles around each ankle and a small piece of chain trailing. We unlocked the shackles on his arms, tying the hasps with blackened string. He would say that he had overpowered his guard on the way to the privy and fled into the fog.

We could not follow him. The fog shifted as we waited with our questions. Would Cael believe Garth's story? How long would it take Garth to find the cave in the fog? Would be able to overpower Cael? Would he even try?

When it grew dark, we fed the animals and the prisoners. Tali sat in my mother's kitchen, watching her make bread. I stayed for a while, then went out into the night. I could not be still. The breeze had risen, and the fog thinned. I walked up to Tice's cottage, lit a fire in the kitchen stove, and opened the window. I waited.

With a soft chirrup, the tortoiseshell cat jumped onto the windowsill. I put the fish I had brought into her bowl. She jumped down to feed. When she finished, I stroked her gently, my hands smoothing her fur, accustoming her to my touch. I picked her up, feeling her muscled warmth. She struggled a bit. I held her tightly with one arm and bent down to pick up her bowl with the other. "Shhh," I said.

I carried the cat, with some difficulty, down to the house I shared with Tali. I put her in my bedroom, with her bowl, and closed the door. Tomorrow I would bring a rug or two from the cottage. Perhaps the familiar smells, and food, would convince her to stay with me. I realized I did not know what Tice had called her.

At midnight, I went to do guard duty at the hall. My sister tended the wounded, two of whom had died earlier in the day. She looked up as I came in.

"No news," I said. "Will these men live?"

"I think so," she said, brushing her hair back from her eyes. "One or two have a mild fever, but there is no other sign of infection, and they're responding to willow bark tea." The wounded men lay on pallets, bound by chains at their wrists or ankles. Most slept. The other prisoners slept around the outside of the room, huddled in whatever position of comfort their chains allowed. They had a blanket each, and a thin sack of wool for a pillow. Fires burned in the fireplaces. *They would have little to complain of*, I thought, *when we turned them over to the Empire.*

The night passed. When I took one man outside to the privy, the fog was mostly gone and the air was frosty. Inside, I locked his chains again, making a tour of the room before joining the other guards playing a game of chance at a table.

We had played three games when Dari came to the door. "They are back," she said. "Pel is safe and unharmed. Go to them, Lena. I'll take your place, here."

I ran through the night to my mother's house. In the sitting room, Tali held Pel. He crackled with excitement, self-importantly the centre of attention. As I came through the door, he squirmed from his mother's arms to run to me.

"Lena," he said, hugging my legs, his words spilling over, "the enemy captured me and took me to the cave. This man rescued me! He killed the other man. I saw the blood on his knife." Pel looked up at me. "He says he's my brother." I looked over Pel's head to where Garth stood. He smiled, and this time his smile reached his eyes. His eyes, not Maya's. A faint warmth, a barely glowing ember, flickered in the void inside me. I picked up Pel, holding him close, and buried my face in his hair. When I looked up again, Garth was still watching me.

"He is your brother," Tali said. "His name is Garth."

"Who do you serve with, Garth?" Pel asked, always the first question of the boys to the men, spring and fall. Garth hesitated.

"He serves with Dern," Gille said, from behind us. "Welcome him home, Pel."

†††††

Two days later, I stood at the top of the village, waiting for Garth. Below me, women went about their business, save for those on guard in the meeting hall. We had prevailed. Much of what we had feared and made ready for had not happened: no barns had been burnt, no animals slaughtered, no women raped. But we had lost four women to death and one to exile, and we had killed nearly twenty men. Could we go back to tending fields and catching fish, to Festival and raising children, and slowly forget?

Brilliant sunshine washed the village. The last of the heather shone purple on the ridge where Sella and the smaller girls herded the sheep. Garth climbed the path to join me. I had asked him to walk with me, sending Pel to tell his story of capture to Freya. Pel had, not surprisingly, attached himself to Garth. His new brother was a prize to brag about to his friends. Garth took patiently to being followed by a gaggle of small boys, but I had spoken firmly to Pel, and we walked through the fields alone. I had one more duty, apart from the guard rotation, to fulfil.

Tali had cut his hair, which diminished his resemblance to Maya, but I could still see her in the tilt of his cheekbones, and in his eyes. The palpable tension that had marked him during his first few days with us had faded. We walked along the edge of the fields, eating handfuls of berries from the brambles that grew there, climbing higher, away from Sella and the sheep. As the rocks grew steeper, I held out a steadying hand to him. His skin was warm and dry. A buzzard hunted over the ridge, its screams loud in the clear air. At a group of rocks, warm in the sun, I stopped. "Shall we sit?" I asked.

We sat, looking out over the village and the sea beyond. He stretched, and his arm brushed mine. I closed my eyes.

"Garth, we need to talk about Tice."

He pulled away slightly. "I had hoped to make redress, if I could."

"You can," I said, gently.

"How? She died hating me. She would have killed me, that night, had you let her." Overhead, a lark hovered, singing.

"She hated you, Garth," I began, and stopped. "No, she hated Kirthan because he had been the tool with which she shaped a future different than the one she had thought she wanted. But she was a grown woman, Garth, and free to choose. She hated you because she thought you would never have to accept the consequences of an afternoon's pleasure." I picked a dried grass stem from beside the rock, weaving it between my fingers. "That afternoon meant exile for her, and one other. She bore you a son."

I heard his sharp intake of breath. I played with the grass for a moment more before looking up. He stared blindly out to sea, tears on his cheeks. I knelt beside him, holding him while we both wept, for the betrayals, and the lost, and at the cruelty and joy of hope.

Finally, he sat up, brushing the back of his hand over his eyes. "Where is he?"

"His name is Valle. He is being raised in the slave quarters of Jedd's retirement farm. Tice said there was no other choice for a son with no father to claim him."

"I had left the message for Dern high in the rafters of the barn," Garth said, his eyes distant, remembering. "When I found her there, climbing the rafters to amuse herself while she waited to see Jedd's accountsman about some wine business, I was afraid she would find the message. So, I set about distracting her. It went further than either of us meant it to, I suppose. I gave no thought to a child."

"And Valle?"

"I will claim him, as soon as I am able. But who will raise him?"

"Tice's mother, or sister, or aunt—a woman of Karst, anyhow. You will need to speak with the council there." I hesitated. "After *Skua* comes and the prisoners are dealt with, I will leave Tirvan to find Maya. We could ride together for a while."

"I'd like to have some time with you, Lena. But I don't know what Dern will say."

"Nor do I," I said, "but he is a compassionate man." We walked again, in silence, each lost in our own thoughts. A light breeze rippled the grasses. I could hear the distant calling of sheep in the high pasture. I slipped my hand into his. He stopped for a moment, smiling down at me. We followed a path that led into a small grove of trees. In the shade of the branches, I stopped. "Garth," I said softly. He turned toward me. I put my hand up to his face, to the shape of Maya's face under his skin. "I love your sister, and nothing can change that. But she isn't here, and you and I are, and we are both in need of comfort. We could be that for each other, for a while." He smiled, slowly.

"Are you sure?" he whispered. I nodded. He brought his lips to my hand, and I heard his breath catch. I stepped closer. We stood like that, drawing warmth and strength and life from each other, until I felt desire rise and moved my mouth to find his. He tasted of blackberries, of earth and water and sun distilled into sweetness, the taste of harvest and celebration, and of the end of all the summers of childhood.

PART II

If the past is not to bind us, where can duty lie? George Eliot

CHAPTER THIRTEEN

I SLID THE LAST FOLDED SHIRT inside the saddlebag, buckling it closed, my fingers stiff in the morning cold. I checked the bedroll, tied behind the saddle on my sturdy Han mare. Beside me, Garth and Casyn did the same. The horses snorted and stamped, their warm breath steaming in the frosty air.

A crowd had gathered to see us leave. I caught my mother's eye. She smiled back at me. I had said my private good-byes, to her and to my sister, and Tali, earlier. I waved to Freya, and to Pel and Sarr, watching our departure in sulky silence.

I swung up into the saddle. My horse moved restlessly, eager to get warm on this cold morning. Garth mounted, steadying Tasque with hands and voice. Dern and Casyn exchanged some last words and embraced before Casyn turned to mount Siannon. Then he raised his hand, in salute and farewell, and we started up the path.

We rode slowly, letting the horses pick their way up the narrow, stony track. Hoarfrost whitened the ground as we climbed higher. A grouse, already half-moulted into its white winter plumage, rose from the heather beside the track. At the top of the ridge, we stopped. Below us lay the village, the smoke from the hearths hanging over the houses. Ahead of us, still out of sight, ran the paved road. The thought of it brought a tightness to my throat. I looked down at the village. It already looked so small beneath us. I swallowed.

"Come, Lena," Garth said after a minute. "You won't forget." I turned my horse to ride east, further into the hills.

Ten days before, in the early afternoon, I had gone in search of my mother. I found her, alone, hanging herbs from the beams of the kitchen.

"Lena," she greeted me from the top step of a short ladder. "Can you give me a hand? Kira has taken a salve to Ranni for the baby, and this is easier with two."

"Of course," I said. The bundles of fresh herbs lay on the table, already tied. I began to hand them up to her. "I wanted to talk to you."

"What about?" my mother asked, her eyes on the job.

"The men should be back soon, right?"

"I believe so."

"Once they've come, and we no longer need to guard the prisoners, I'm going to look for Maya."

She said nothing immediately, but her hands stopped tying the herbs. Then she looked down. "I thought you might," she said. "Leave those for now," she added, indicating the herbs. She climbed down the ladder to put her arms around me. I leaned into her. She smelled of lavender, as she always had. She held me tight for several heartbeats, then gently stepped back. She put out a hand to stroke my hair. "When I bore you, and Kira afterwards, I remember being thankful you were both girls, so that I wouldn't have to say goodbye," she said. My throat tightened. She smiled. "You will need money and warm clothes, and maps. And what about camping supplies, and food? Have you made a list?"

I laughed, relieved that she wouldn't try to dissuade me. "Not yet. Let's get these herbs hung, and I'll tell you my plans as we work. You hand them up to me. I'm taller than you, anyhow," I said. I climbed up a couple of steps of the ladder, taking the bunch she handed me, tying it to one of the many small hooks that lined the beam. "I will ride," I said. "Dian and Rasa will sell me one of their horses. They have a little mare I like. I can buy her if Dessa will lease *Dovekie* from me for a year." I glanced down to take another bunch of herbs.

"She might," my mother said. "But even if you find Maya, she cannot come back for three years, remember."

"I know." I had my own thoughts on that, but they weren't ones I wished to share yet, not with the council, or even with my mother. "I'll give myself a year to find her. If I don't, I'll come home. If she wants, Freya can fish with me. Her apprenticeship will be done by then." I had lain awake last night, listening to Garth's soft breathing beside me, thinking this out.

"And if you do find her? What then?"

"I don't know," I said. "I can't make those plans now. I can only plan the looking." I tied the next bunch, knotting the string with a sharp tug. I reached down for another bunch.

"That's all of them," my mother said. "There is something else you could do, Lena, on the road."

I climbed down the ladder. "What's that?"

"Ride to Karst," she said gently, "to tell them of Tice's death. Exile or no, she has family there, and they should know. I had thought to send a letter, next Festival, or even to ride out to the first inn to send word from there. But it is news that would be better given by someone who knew her and knew how she died."

I did not want to do this, but I knew my mother spoke the truth. I had a responsibility. "But what if Maya went north, towards the Wall?"

She considered. "You'll only know that by asking at the inns, so ride south first. If at the first inn, they have no news of Maya, leave a letter there, to be taken to Karst. The first inn is no more than a day's ride, or so I am told. But I hope she went south, Lena. It will be winter soon."

An hour later, I walked down to Dessa's workshop. The doors stood open to the afternoon sun, revealing Freya and Dessa planing planks for a new hull. Two of the village boats had burned with the catboat; it would take much of the winter to replace them. The smell of freshly shaven wood made the air pleasantly spicy. The women looked up at my footsteps.

"Hello, Lena," Dessa said quietly. She spoke and moved with less confidence now, and I thought her hair had greyed. But she worked, and directed her apprentices, and came to council. Lara, Siane's daughter, watched from a corner of the workshop.

"Did you want me?" Freya asked, straightening.

I hesitated. "Yes, but if you're busy—"

"I can spare her," Dessa said.

"I came to see if you would like to go sailing with me. Not to fish, just to go out on the water." I wanted to talk to her away from the village and other ears. Beyond that, a general restlessness made me want to take *Dovekie* out.

"I'd like that. Let me get some warmer clothes, and I'll meet you at the wharf."

We sailed south, something I rarely did, keeping the coastline in sight. For a while, we said little. Seabirds followed us, and clouds scudded along the horizon.

"How is your arm?"

"Healing well," Freya said. "It's not bothering me much." She rolled up her sleeve to show me. I saw new skin, pink, shiny, and slightly puckered at the edges. "It's still a bit tender, but I can work. I have to rub salve into it several times a day to keep the new skin from tearing."

"Good."

"Kira says you kept it from being much worse by putting my arm in the stream." Freya said. "I don't believe I've thanked you."

I shrugged. "It seemed the right thing to do. I'm glad it helped."

"Dessa thinks I'll be able to fish without problems in the spring."

"How is she?"

Freya sighed. "She's quiet, as you saw, and subdued. She doesn't talk about Siane much, except to Lara. And she works all the time."

"And Lara?"

"I worry about her," Freya admitted. "She cries often, and she doesn't like to be out of Dessa's sight. I wonder if she's afraid Dessa will disappear, too, or if she thinks she needs to take care of her."

The breeze blew Freya's hair back off her face. *She looked older*, I thought, *no longer a girl*.

"Probably a bit of both," I suggested, steering with my knee against the tiller, feeling the currents of wind and water against the boat.

"What will happen to us, Lena?"

"What do you mean?"

"Tirvan. All the villages. Can we go back to the same rules, the same way of living?"

I adjusted the tiller to slow a bit. "Do you want to? I guess I haven't thought about it too much. I've been thinking about finding Maya."

"But that's part of it. The old rules say three years must pass before she can return. Do you think that's right?"

I had considered this. If the Emperor could change the rules for deserters, why could not the village council change the rules for exiles? If—when—I found Maya, I planned to bring her back to Tirvan to make this argument at council.

"No," I admitted.

"What does your mother say?"

"We haven't talked about it. But I'm leaving to find Maya, as soon as I can."

"You really are going, then?"

"Yes. Do you think Dessa would lease *Dovekie* from me for a year?"

"As I said, all she does is work," Freya answered. "She got those hulls started before anyone else had even begun to think about it. I think she'll do it."

"Good," I said. "I'll talk to her in the morning."

Freya started to answer, but an unexpected gust of wind caught the sail, and her attention went to the lines. I looked up to see if her arm constrained her, if she needed my help, but that thought vanished. Far out on the ocean, beyond the calmer waters of the coastal coves, I saw the triple sails of a large boat. *Skua*.

We turned *Dovekie* around, running her back to the harbour on the strong off-shore breeze. *Skua* could not be seen yet around the southern headland. We docked and tied *Dovekie* quickly. Freya ran to find the council leaders. I went to find Garth.

He had saddled the smallest of our hill ponies for Pel and Sarr. They rode on leading reins in a circle around him on the common, learning to balance with only knees and thighs. The riding lessons had begun a week ago. Garth needed something to do, and the boys shadowed him constantly. Dian had suggested it. Both boys, in the normal course of events, should have gone with their fathers, or their father's proxy, after autumn Festival this year, but Festival would not happen now.

He saw me coming and said something to the boys. He gathered in the leading reins to bring the ponies to him. I reached the common and stood waiting while he unclipped the long reins from the head collars and slipped on the bridles.

"Ride up to and around the hill fields," he said to the boys, "then return the ponies to the barn. Rub them down well. Check their hooves and clean the tack. I will inspect both ponies and tack later, and I expect to find both spotless. Understood?"

"Yes, sir," they chorused, and rode away.

"*Skua* is coming." I said. "She'll be here in a couple of hours at the most."

His dark eyes widened slightly. He took a deep breath. "So, I will learn my fate."

"It can't be bad," I argued, as I had more than once before. "Gille will speak for you, and Tali. All of us will. Pel would have died without you. You have done what Dern asked of you."

"I hope you are right."

I wanted to put my arms around him, but I couldn't, not here in the sight of the village. He slept at his mother's house, as did I. Only Tali and my mother truly knew that the second bed in Pel's room went mostly unused. What others assumed, seeing the time we spent together, I did not know, nor did I care.

"You will tell them about Valle?"

He sighed. "I will, when the time is right," he said, glancing up at the hills. "I need to see that Pel and Sarr have got the ponies back safely, and return this harness. Will you walk up to the barn with me?"

I glanced at the sun. "I can't. I'm on guard duty soon, and my blades and leathers are at the house. Perhaps at supper?"

"Perhaps," he said. "We'll see what the tide brings." We separated; I walked across the common to Tali's house, where I put on my leather boots and jerkin and strapped on my sword. The secca I slipped into its boot sheath. In the days since their capture, the prisoners had given us no trouble. They remained chained inside the meeting hall, loosely enough to allow them to stretch out on their pallets and sit in some comfort to eat. We guarded them around the clock, eight women, one always a Cohort-Leader, six hours in the watch, escorting them to and from the privies, bringing food and water. Mostly, we fought off boredom. *Skua*'s arrival meant the end of this duty. The prisoners would become the soldiers' responsibility.

Walking up the hill to the meeting hall, I stopped to look westward out over the sea. I could just see *Skua* now, her sails catching the afternoon light. I wondered who else had seen her. I met Tali on the path, bringing two men back from the privies.

"Ah, Lena, good," she said. "I wanted to talk to you, and you're late."

"Am I? I'm sorry, Tali. There is news."

She raised her eyebrows. We shackled the men on the porch, then walked a distance away. "Look," I said, indicating where with a tilt of my head.

Tali looked. "*Skua*! Does Garth know?"

"That's why I'm late. I went to find him. Freya and I saw her when we were out sailing. Freya went to tell the council leaders."

A shout came from the porch, followed by a babble of Lestian voices. "You had best tell Kolmas," Tali advised. "Send for help if the prisoners are too restive. I'll see if Grainne or Dian can send another couple of horsewomen over."

I found Kolmas inside, standing at the full length of his chains. "What is happening?" he demanded.

I held up a hand. "A minute." I said. To the other guards in the room, I said "*Skua*'s back. She should make the cove in an hour or so. I've told Tali. We'll have help if we need it."

"Will Casyn be on her?" Aline asked from across the room.

"I don't know." I turned to the catboat's captain. "Tell your men to be quiet."

When the hall no longer rang with voices, I spoke.

"*Skua* will make our cove within the hour. She and her men were here for many weeks in the summer, helping us prepare to defend Tirvan. Her captain is called Dern. We have been waiting for them to return, to hand you and your men over. You will be their prisoners, now."

Kolmas licked his lips. "I have heard of this boat and captain," he said. "But I heard the general Casyn's name, too."

"He may be on board. He sailed away from here on *Skua* and planned to return. Tell your men."

He pitched his voice to be heard throughout the hall and onto the porch. The hall once again filled with voices, their tones questioning and sharp. Kolmas answered firmly. Slowly, the men quieted, dropping into conversation with their neighbours.

"What do you know of Casyn?"

"He is great general, they say," Kolmas replied cautiously, "who won many battles."

I nodded. "He is a fair man. We will tell him that when you saw the battle was lost, you surrendered, and that you have helped as much as you can. I do not think you need to worry if you accept the Empire's victory."

"If the Empire can feed us, many will accept," he replied, so quietly I had to strain to hear. "Some men said, ask the Emperor to lead us, not fight, but our king said no, fight. So we fought. But to say our king is wrong is treason, so I do not say that. What I think, I keep here." He touched his chest.

"Say that to Casyn."

Skua sailed into the cove to drop anchor an hour later. So many prisoners requested the privy once she had anchored that we set up a rotation, taking them out in pairs to see the ship. When the small boat launched, even from our height, I thought I could recognize Casyn and Dern.

The hours passed. We brought all the men inside to feed them. We gave them tea, adding the spices they liked. Their little shows of bravado had given way to a subdued acceptance, and mostly they sat, blankets around their shoulders against the chill of evening, sipping their tea. Kolmas watched them. I had grown to respect him.

I heard the footsteps on the path outside and straightened. The west door opened, and Casyn came in. Dern followed him, and behind him, Gille. Dern's eyes searched the room. He smiled when they found me. I grinned back, all restraint gone in the relief of seeing them safe. Casyn saw me, too, just a hint of smile touching his eyes.

"Lena," he said. "You lead the guard, tonight."

"I do," I said, hoping I could keep my face suitably schooled.

"I have spoken with the other Cohort-Leaders already," he said. "Well done. I know there has been sorrow for you, and for the village, but across the Empire the women's villages prevailed, and the Empire stands. Be proud, Cohort-Leader."

"Thank you," I said, unexpected tears pricking at my eyes, all levity gone from me. Casyn's eyes moved to Kolmas.

"Do you lead these men?" Casyn asked.

"I am Kolmas. I was captain," he answered. "These men were mine, yes. Some were my crew before. Some came to my boat only to fight. Some were sent to me, soldiers, but they are dead. I did not lead them. But these, yes." He spoke evenly, with neither pride nor humility. Casyn, nodded in his grave manner.

"I am Casyn, General of the Empire. Leste has fallen. Your king is our prisoner. Your women and children are unhurt. Your men have two choices. Swear fealty to the Emperor and the laws of the Empire, and we will take them home to freedom. Refuse, and they become slaves. Death awaits a rebellious slave."

"Freedom?" Kolmas said. "To farm and trade, as we have always lived, or to be soldiers of the Empire?"

"You must swear to the laws of the Empire," Casyn replied. "The Empire requires all men to be soldiers."

"And our women?" Kolmas asked.

"Will learn to farm and fish, and work metal and wood, as all women of the Empire do," Casyn said patiently.

"Only this, or slavery?"

"Why should there be choice?" Casyn asked, reason in his voice. "Leste was the aggressor. You invaded. We fought back, and not only kept our own lands but conquered yours. Enslaving you all would have been fair. But instead we offer you freedom for fealty."

"Freedom? This is not freedom, but I will swear, Casyn General, and I will advise my men to do the same. I do not see choice. Our woman and children are hungry. Do I bend my knee to you?"

"No," Casyn said. "Speak to your men, first. Tomorrow, we will hear your oaths." Kolmas nodded, sinking onto his haunches, his eyes shadowed. Casyn turned to me.

"Cohort-Leader," he said, "you and your guard are relieved. *Skua*'s men will stand watch tonight." He stepped aside to let the soldiers who had waited outside enter. As they filed in, Danel flashed me a quick grin.

"Anwyl leads this watch," Dern said. "Lena, will you explain your routines?"

As succinctly as possible, I told Anwyl, who greeted me with a quick grin, how we managed the guard. Five minutes later, I stepped out onto the porch of the hall where Casyn and Dern had waited.

Casyn stepped forward to grip my shoulder, a military gesture. "I am glad to see you safe," he said, his smile broader now.

"And I you," I said. Dern swept me up in a hard, brief hug, which I returned fiercely.

"I heard how Tice died," he murmured. "I am sorry, Lena."

I looked from one to the other. "Have you seen Garth?"

"We have," Casyn said, "but only briefly. We have much to talk about. You need not worry for him."

"Will he be chained again?" I asked.

"No," Casyn said. "He will face some hard questions, but no more."

"Tali," Dern said, "was most persuasive." He grinned, his teeth flashing white in the night. Tension drained from my shoulders and neck. I looked down toward the harbour. On the common, bonfires blazed, and I could hear music and laughter. Sudden joy bubbled up in me. *It's over.*

"Shall we join the celebrations?" I suggested, grinning. "I think I need some wine."

I pulled myself out of bed the next morning well after the sun had risen. Garth had slept in Pel's room last night. He had been quiet at the bonfires, leaving early but bidding me to stay.

Downstairs, I drank two mugs of water then set the kettle to boil. I stretched, considering food. I heard footsteps on the porch, and Tali came in, bringing cold air and the tang of woodsmoke with her.

"Good morning," she said. She had a mug in her hand. "Are you making more tea?"

"Yes, do you want some?"

"I could use another cup." She put her mug on the table.

"Have you had breakfast?"

"No," she said. "I don't want much. What about you?"

"I thought maybe some bread and jam."

"That would be good." She took the bread from the bin and sliced it. The kettle sang. I made the tea, setting the table with butter and blackberry jam. Tali brought the plates and knives, and we pulled up chairs.

I spread butter and a spoonful of blackberry jam on the bread and took a bite. The sweet-and-sour of the jam burst against my tongue. I had helped pick the blackberries only a few weeks before. "Lena," Tali said, when she had eaten her slice of bread and jam, "there is something I want to say to you before you leave."

"Yes?" I sipped my tea.

"Do you remember how upset Maya was when I had Pel?"

"She thought you should have been loyal to her father, even though he was dead. We had a big fight about it. I told her she was being stupid." I remembered the shouting and the tears, the extreme passions of twelve-year-olds. We hadn't spoken for days. In the hugs and kisses of reconciliation, we had taken our first tentative steps towards becoming lovers.

"We had similar arguments," Tali said. "I would be careful, Lena, of ever letting her know about your relationship with Garth."

"But we talked about liaisons," I protested. "We both accepted it. It won't change things between Maya and me."

"If this were truly a Festival liaison, I would believe that. But what is between you and Garth seems like more."

"No," I said, shaking my head.

She held up a hand. "Let me finish. Only you can know what's between you and my son. But can't you see that Maya would have difficulty accepting it for many reasons? For you to take another lover might be hard enough, but for that lover to be Garth, her beloved and lost brother? She will feel that you have both betrayed her."

I sat silent. The truth of Tali's words hurt. "Tali," I said finally, "it is only because he is Maya's brother that I could be with him. I said no to Dern. But I won't tell her. And he too will keep the secret."

"I think that is wise."

I sighed. "Perhaps I should have said yes to Dern and not turned to Garth. But I couldn't keep being strong alone, Tali, in those days after the killings, and he reminded me so much of Maya."

"I am not blaming you. We all need comfort and love, and memories are rarely enough. I waited twelve years to have Pel, but his father was neither the first nor the last man I held in my arms during Festival, regardless of my love for Mar. Perhaps Maya will have learned this, too, on the road."

"Maybe," I said. The thought had occurred to me in the night hours when sleep would not come. "I hope so. I'd be happier if I knew she was not alone."

Tali stood. "Come here," she said. I went into her arms, and she held me tightly for some moments. "Go safely, and be strong. And come back. We need you here."

"I will," I said, fighting tears. "I will."

When she released me, I saw tears glinting in her eyes as well. She smiled. "And now I had best get to work."

"I need to see Dessa," I said. "If she won't lease *Dovekie*, I'm not sure how I'll pay for this journey."

"Oh, I imagine she will," Tali said. She drained her mug and put it down, turning to leave the room. "I'll see you tonight."

"Tali?"

"Yes?" she said from the door.

"Thanks."

She nodded continuing on her way. I rinsed plates and mugs, put the remaining food away, then went down the hill to speak to Dessa.

"Aye, I'll take her," Dessa said. "But you'll need to clean her up. I don't have the hands to do that with building two new boats." We agreed on a price. I borrowed Freya again and we paddled *Dovekie* around to a small shingle beach where we could haul her out of the water. Using roller logs, we dragged the little boat well up onto the beach, gently laying her to one side. Barnacles encrusted her bottom. I would need to scrape them off and check the boards and caulking for damage.

"Thanks, Freya."

"Any time," she said. "I hope Dessa lets me sail her." We walked together back to the village before I left her to return to the workshop. Climbing up the hill to the field where the Han horses grazed, I saw Dian and Rasa working in the open door of the barn, Grainne with them.

"Lena!" Dian greeted me. "Have you come to bargain?"

"I have. Good morning, Rasa, Grainne."

"Good morning," they answered. Packs and harness lay scattered on the floor of the barn, and two of the horses stood tethered. The mare I wanted grazed in the field.

"It's Clio you want, am I right?" Dian said. I nodded. She went out into the field to catch the little mare, clipping a rope to her head collar. She walked her over. I put out my hand for her to smell me, then rubbed her neck. I liked the look of her, her compact body and calm eye.

"She's seven," Dian said, "well-schooled and gentle, for all she's trained to war. Let's get her saddled, so you can try her out." Rasa brought over a saddlecloth and saddle, quickly tacking up the mare. I swung up into the saddle, riding her out into the fields. She obeyed my hands and legs without protest.

After a few minutes, I turned her head to bring her back to the barn. "She's an easy ride," I said, dismounting.

"And built for travel," Rasa said, patting the mare.

"How much do you want for her?" I asked. Dian looked at Rasa.

"You'll need the tack, too, right?" Rasa asked.

"Yes."

Rasa named a price. "The Empire would take her for more," she said, "but they have more money. If you ever want, bring her back to Han, and we'll take her back."

"Or Tirvan could keep her as a broodmare here," Grainne said, "to improve the stock."

Rasa laughed. "We've given you ideas," she said. She slipped an arm around Grainne for a quick hug. Grainne leaned into her.

"Lena," she said, her voice diffident. "You should know. I'm going with Rasa and Dian to Han. I want to learn more about breeding horses and training them. You won't be the only one leaving Tirvan."

Surprise made me speechless for a moment. "Does the council know?"

"I told Gille yesterday."

"Well," I said, "I wish you luck and safe journey, Grainne. Will you send word, somehow, if you learn anything of Maya?"

"Of course," she said. "I wish you luck on your journey, too. I hope you find her."

I walked back to *Dovekie* without seeing the path. *The changes have started already. How strange to think of Grainne leaving.* Before this summer, she would have kept on working her hill ponies and talking to the men, spring and fall, about their mounts. If Spring Festival and her ponies' seasons coincided, she might even breed one or two to a small stallion, if the chance arose. But she never would have talked of leaving, or even thought it possible.

My steps brought me to *Dovekie*. I surveyed my boat. *Not too bad*, I thought, assessing the barnacles. I found a comfortable bit of driftwood to use as a stool and took up the scraper. Gulls screamed overhead, and waves lapped the shore rhythmically. I bent to the task.

An hour later, I heard the crunch of footsteps on the shingle. I looked up to see Dern approaching. He wore a leather jacket with the fleece turned inward. I sat up, and he smiled down at me.

"Don't let me keep you from your work."

"If I had a second scraper, you could help," I answered.

"I've scraped my share of boat's bottoms," he said, grinning. Then his voice changed, losing the levity. "How are you? Truly?"

"I'm...all right. I'm leaving Tirvan to find Maya."

He nodded. "Your mother told me. She also told me how Tice died. I'm sorry, Lena." He sat down on a piece of driftwood

"It was my fault. I shouldn't have sent her back on patrol when she was so angry."

He sighed. "I too have made bad decisions, as I told you once, decisions that cost friends their lives. So has Casyn. You bear some of the responsibility, Lena, but not all of it. Tice let her anger distract her. Or perhaps the man who killed her was simply better with a knife. You will never know. All you can do is accept the choice you made, grieve for Tice, and go on."

"I'm trying."

"It takes time. Going to Karst will help."

Was there anything my mother hadn't told him?

"I'm glad you will have company on the road," he went on. I looked up, startled.

"You gave Garth leave?" Hope leapt inside me.

"I did. He told us of his son. I have given him six weeks, plenty of time to ride to Karst. He is to meet us in Casilla after that."

I stood. "Thank you, Dern."

"He earned it. He's been on duty, in a dangerous situation, for three years. Much of our most valuable information came from him. He earned his pardon and his leave." He half smiled. "You care for him."

I nodded. "We both love Maya. It's a bond, and Tice is, too, in a way." I thought of the dreams I awoke from, dreams where the boy whose throat I had cut became Tice. Garth brought me back from those dreams, most nights. I straightened, looking down at him. "Dern...."

He shook his head. "There is no more you need to say." He stood to take me briefly in a soldier's embrace. "Take care, Lena." I watched him walk away along the shingle, the crunch of his boots on the pebbles fading as he neared the rocks on the headland. I felt tears in my eyes, for the small sorrow of what I could not be for Dern, and for the joy of what he had given Garth.

CHAPTER FOURTEEN

TWENTY MINUTES LATER, I saw Garth running toward me along the beach. I put the scraper down, standing to meet him. He flung his arms around me and swung me, radiant with relief. "Dern told me," I said, wrapped in his arms. "I'm so pleased, Garth."

He kissed my hair. "Did he tell you I will be Watch-Commander on *Skua* when I join her at Casilla?"

I pulled back so I could look at him. "No," I said, "He didn't. I don't know what that means, Garth."

"I'll command a watch, six men. It's a junior position, but not too junior for my age."

"An officer's rank, then?"

"Yes," he said. "It's so hard to believe, Lena. I never thought I would have a second chance." He looked suddenly younger. The wind caught his hair, and he laughed. "I never thought I would be so happy to be a soldier, either," he said. "But I've learned where my allegiance lies. I will serve the Empire honourably."

"You will." I took his hand. "I bought the mare this morning. We need to practice riding."

"Dern offered me Tasque for the journey. Casyn is going to check his shoes. You should ask him to check your mare's, too." He spoke rapidly, the words bubbling out of him. Like Pel.

"I will. She's called Clio." I looked back at *Dovekie*. "If I don't finish these repairs, we won't be able leave when we planned. I need few more hours here, at least."

He grinned. "I will see to the horses. See you tonight." He kissed me again, a long kiss. I felt my legs soften.

"Go," I said, but called after him as he started off the beach. "Garth!"

"What?"

"Have you told your mother?"

"She's next!" he called back, breaking into a run.

That night, Casyn came to Tali's house. We sat in the kitchen near the fire, Tali mending Pel's jacket. She hated sewing and scowled over the work. Garth and Pel played *xache*. Garth had chosen to teach him the game of war, in part to mollify Pel's disappointment over having to wait until spring for his father to come for him. I sat watching the two brothers moving the game pieces. The tortoiseshell cat, dozing on my lap, purred as I rubbed her ears. She had adopted Tali, not me, but I had the only free lap. I felt as lazy as the cat.

Tali welcomed Casyn, glad of an excuse to stop her mending. He accepted wine, pulling a chair up to the table. We talked casually of the village's food supply, the health of the prisoners, strategies in *xache*. When Garth and Pel finished their game, Tali sent Pel to bed over his protests.

"I'll take him up," Garth offered, swinging Pel up out of the chair to carry him up the stairs. Casyn watched them go.

"He is good with the boy," he said. "When he has served some time on *Skua*, he would make a cadet-master."

"You were Dern's cadet-master, were you not?" I asked. The fire and the wine had made me sleepy. Had Casyn not been there, I would have followed Pel to bed.

"I was," he said, with his slow smile. "He was nine. He had a good mind, even then. His class was my last before I moved on to other roles." He took a sip of his wine. "I must ride south, now, Lena. The Emperor's winter camp lies in that direction, and I must report to him within the month. If you would be willing, I would ride with you and Garth until our paths diverge."

"I would be honoured," I said, sitting up in my chair. The cat, disturbed, jumped down to wash her face in front of the fire. "And glad of your company and your guidance on the road. But I can't speak for Garth."

Garth came back down the stairs. "Speak for me on what?" Casyn explained. "Of course you are welcome, sir," Garth said, "but we'll be slower than you. Neither of us are accustomed to long hours in the saddle."

"No matter," Casyn said. "I can make up time after our ways part, and I should not push Siannon too hard for the first while anyhow. How long do you need, Lena, to finish your work on your boat and prepare?"

I thought. "Five days? Is that too long?"

"Not at all," Casyn said. "Five days it is."

Later that night, I woke wondering whether Gille had asked Casyn to accompany us. The thought disturbed me in a way I could not quite define. Garth, always a light sleeper, stirred beside me. "What is it, Lena?" he asked. I told him my thought. "If so, what of it? We're both glad to have Casyn with us, just as much for his company and as for his knowledge of the road. I doubt Gille thinks either of us need protection. Go back to sleep," he said gently. He rolled over. I fitted myself along the warmth of his back and drifted into a dreamless sleep.

†††††

The track widened, allowing Garth and me to ride abreast, behind Casyn. Looking back, I could no longer see even the smoke from Tirvan's chimneys. *Stop that,* I told myself. *Look around you. This is new.* The plateau we rode on was rocky, heathland and bog, without trees. A raven croaked from a boulder.

We came to the road. I had expected a cobbled track, but the builders had made it wide enough for two wagons to pass. Paved with squared stone, it spoke of permanence and age. Casyn signalled a stop. We rode up beside him.

"North," he said, pointing, "the road goes to Serra and Delle, and beyond it to Berge where it turns east again to run below the Emperor's Wall on the northern border. South, it meets the sea near Karst, and then again turns east to Casilla. The closest inns are an easy day's ride in either direction."

A map nestled in my saddlebag, drawn by Casyn, showing the villages and inns on the road. If no one at the first southward inn had news of Maya, I would accompany Garth to Karst, riding northward again as spring approached. The northern road, Casyn had counselled, would be treacherous for a lone traveller in a matter of weeks.

"Is there an eastern road?" I asked. When Casyn had brought me the map, I had focused on the inns, knowing that I was most likely to find Maya—or at least hear word of her—at one of them.

"No," he said, "or, at least, not a true road. A beaten track runs at the edge of the plain from the eastern end of the Wall to where the mountains meet the sea. There is a fort there, and the paved road runs out from Casilla to the fort, but the route north from there is used only by patrols, or messengers with urgent business. It is a lonely ride and dangerous. I have done it once or twice. Wolves and bears roam the mountains." He looked up at the sky. "It is going to snow. Shall we ride?"

We turned south, riding side by side on the hard surface as Casyn talked, telling us stories of other journeys on this road, in other seasons. The snow began, large flakes that melted on the ground. No wind blew, and I heard little sound beyond the horses' hooves on the cobbles and our voices.

After two hours, we stopped where a spring bubbled up into a pool. Someone had dug it out, modifying the flow so that the water rose into a clay-lined basin to run down into a broader pond. "Let the horses drink from the lower pool," Casyn directed. "We can take water from the upper." The water was cold, tasting of iron. I stretched, flexing the stiffness out of my upper thighs and stamping my numb feet.

When the horses finished drinking, we returned to the road. The land had changed from the flatness of the plateau to a series of gentle hills. The road rose and fell as we steadily lost altitude. Trees grew in small clumps. The snow stopped.

At the bottom of one hill, the road bridged a fast-flowing river. Beside the river, on the northern bank, a path wound into the hills to the west of us. "Where does that go?" Garth asked.

"There is a valley, about three hours ride from here, where the hunting is reliable," Casyn replied. "A hunt party comes most autumns to take venison, and sometimes boar." I felt as I had the night Tice told me about the south, ashamed of my ignorance about the world beyond Tirvan. The men knew a wider world, but women rarely left their home villages except to take up work in another. Tonight's inn lay only a day's ride from Tirvan, but I could think of no one who had ridden out to it. *Our safe harbour will become a prison*, I had said to Maya, long months before. Perhaps it already had.

We stopped again at noon near a small stream in open woodland that bordered the road. Casyn removed the horses' tack, leaving on rope head collars that allowed them to graze unimpeded. The clouds had thinned a bit under a weak sun. I gathered twigs and, in a blackened ring of stones, built a small fire to boil water for tea. Garth shared out dried meat and cheese and apples.

We ate without hurry. The heat from the tea in the tin mug felt good against my hands. "Where is the Emperor's winter camp?" Garth asked.

"At the southern edge of the grasslands," Casyn answered, "there is an area of rolling hills and small lakes before the land changes again to the fertile fields of the south. His camp is there. It's reasonably warm, and there is good hunting and fishing."

"What's he like?" I asked. The Emperor's name was Callan. He had been elected to the role some eight or nine years back by the senior officers of the Empire. Beyond that, I knew nothing of the man.

Casyn considered. "He's a bit taller than me, with dark hair, although it is mostly grey, now. He has great tactical knowledge, and sound and considered judgment, but he does not let himself be bound by tradition. He approved the recruiting of spies and asking the women's villages to defend Tirvan was his idea."

"You seem to know him well," Garth said.

Casyn smiled. "I suppose I do. He's my brother."

I laughed. "I said to Dern, once, that I did not think you were quite the average soldier. I'm glad to have been proven right."

Casyn leaned forward to pour himself more tea from the pot in the coals of the fire. "Being the Emperor's brother does not confer much status, except that I am also one of his advisors. And I have known him since I was seven and he was eight, which may give me a bit more knowledge of how he thinks, and why. We were in the same regiment until our early twenties."

We finished the tea. Garth brought water from the stream to cool the ashes of the fire. We re-saddled the horses, mounted, and returned to the road.

We kept the horses to an easy pace, but after another hour of riding, my legs and back ached. I shifted in the saddle, trying to find a more comfortable position. The mare slowed, tossing her head, not understanding my unintentional signals. I tightened my thighs, ignoring the pain, and took a tighter hold of the reins. The day grew dark, the clouds bringing an early dusk. My thighs and shoulders burned with soreness. Just when I thought I could stand it no longer, we came to the inn. It sat to the right of the road, a long, plain, two-storey building, with an archway at the midpoint leading into an interior courtyard. I had expected a smaller building, built of wood as Tirvan's houses were, with maybe a paddock and a stable, but the inn was built of stone and slate. It looked as if it had stood here a long, long time, growing over the years to house many men and horses. The sense of age disturbed me, somehow.

We rode through the archway into a cobbled yard. A woman came out from one of the buildings that enclosed the courtyard. "General," she said, "we haven't seen you since the spring."

"Mari," Casyn said. "Is all well here?"

"Aye," she said. Casyn dismounted easily. We followed his lead, Garth steadying me when my numb feet threatened not to take my weight. Mari stepped forward to take the reins.

"These are my companions: Lena of Tirvan, and Garth, Watch-Commander of the Empire's ship *Skua*." Casyn said, giving Garth the courtesy of the rank he would soon hold. "We've ridden from Tirvan today, at an easy pace, so the horses need only the usual ration of grain and hay. We'll be staying only one night, weather allowing."

"Aye," Mari said again, and with a nod to us, led the horses into the stable. We walked across the cobbles toward the inn. My leg muscles quivered with exhaustion. Casyn opened a door. We stepped into a hallway that led into the main room of the inn. I blinked in the sudden dimness. A bit of light came from a fire burning in a massive fireplace at one end of the room, and a bit more from small windows near the low ceiling, its crossbeams darkened by years of smoke. Under my feet, huge flagstones lined the floor. Tables of equally darkened wood, with benches on either side, took up half the room, and some chairs stood near the fireplace. The room was empty.

"Livia," Casyn called. A door opened in the far wall, and a young woman came through. She was about my height, with close-cropped hair and broad shoulders.

"General," she said in a tone of surprise. "I didn't hear anyone ride in." Her eyes flicked to Garth and me. "You'll want some supper."

"And beds for the night," Casyn agreed. But right now, drinks for us all." He introduced us as he had before. I stood swaying slightly with exhaustion.

"Welcome," she said, disappearing back through the door. We took off our fleece coats and our gloves. Casyn motioned us to the chairs near the fire.

Livia returned with a tray bearing three pewter mugs. I took a deep draught: cider, cellar-cool. On a low table, Livia placed a plate with some cold sausage wrapped in pastry. "Supper will be a couple of hours," she said. "This will help tide you over."

Garth took a piece, handing it to me. "Eat."

"Thank you," Casyn said to Livia. "All is well here?"

"It's been quiet," Livia said, leaning against the back of a chair. "A group of women from Han rode through a week ago, but they only stopped long enough to water their horses and to give us the news of victory. A number of men left this morning, so you just missed them. Bren of the tenth was here two days back, coming down from Delle. He left a message for you. I'll get it." She left the room. I could hear her talking to someone. I took another mouthful of cider. After a minute or two, she came back, to give Casyn a folded and sealed note.

Casyn broke open the seal to read the note, nodding to himself. He slipped it into the pocket of his tunic. "Before we leave, I'll give you a message for Turlo," he said to Livia. "He was at Berge, so you should see him in the next few days."

"Bren left a message for him, too," Livia said. She turned to me. "There is a hot pool," she said, "if you would like to ease your muscles after the ride. Find me when you are ready." I considered, my mind working at half speed. The thought of a hot soak was appealing, if I could find the energy to walk anywhere. My feet tingled with cold inside my boots, even by the fire. Casyn had told me a day or two before that the inns maintained the same strict rules that the villages did for all but the two weeks of Festival. I would bathe and sleep separately from the men. I wondered if perhaps the rules had changed here, too, this autumn.

I ate another sausage roll and finished my drink. Sighing, I pushed myself up. "I'm going to the baths," I said. I walked across the stone floor, feeling the stiffness in my legs. The door opened into a kitchen where Livia sliced carrots with a small boy playing near her feet. She turned as I came in.

"Ready for the pool?" She bent to pick up the boy. "My son," she said, smiling. I followed her out into a low brick hallway with arched ceilings. A short way down this passage, she opened a door, releasing a waft of sulphur. The oval pool was four paces across. It bubbled up from its underground source into a brick-lined basin, spilling out at the far end of the room into a shallow, tiled channel before disappearing under the wall. Wooden benches lined two walls, and robes of undyed wool hung on pegs beside towels.

"This is the last inn to have a hot pool on the way south," Livia told me. I remembered the Han riders' appreciation of Tirvan's baths.

"I always took them for granted," I said, and "I'm glad of this one." I sat on a bench to pull of my riding boots.

"Is this your first time on the road?" Livia asked.

I looked up. "Yes. I seek my partner, Maya, who chose exile rather than fight. Did she come this way?"

Livia considered. "Dark haired, travelling on foot?"

"Yes. Long hair, halfway down her back?" I struggled to speak calmly.

"I remember her. But she wasn't alone. She was with a woman from Berge: Alis, I think her name was." The child in her arms fussed, and she stroked his hair.

"Do you know where she was headed?" I asked, suddenly not tired.

"South," Livia said. "The southern inns are busier. They would likely have found work once they were past the Grasslands road ten day's ride from here—three weeks on foot. You will find her," she said, unconcerned.

"Gan!" the boy said, struggling.

"Yes, all right," Livia said, putting him down. "Find your Gran. She is in the linen-room." He ran off down the corridor. "He does not like to be still. May I stay and talk to you while you soak?"

"Yes," I said. She sat on the bench. I finished undressing and stepped into the pool. Under the surface of the water, a step, or platform, ran around the circumference of the pool. When I sat, the water came to just below my chin. I cupped some water into my hands, washing my face, running my wet hands through my hair. "What is life like at the inns?"

Livia laughed. "I can only speak for this one. I was born here. Eight of us live here, and three children. We farm a bit and make cheese and cider. We keep horses for the post riders and hold and pass on messages. Spring and fall, in a usual year, it's busy. In between, there are always messengers, officers like the General about the Empire's business, and hunt parties. And a few women, moving from one village to another."

"What's a post rider?" I stretched my legs as the heat penetrated my muscles.

"A messenger on urgent duty. They ride from one post, or inn, to another, changing horses at each so that the animal is fresh. The Empire pays us to stable a few horses for them and keep them exercised and shod."

"Are all the inns a day's ride apart?"

"A day's easy ride. Two days walking. The post riders stop at three inns in one day, eighteen hours in the saddle, six hours to eat and sleep. They can ride from the Wall to the Eastern fort in about ten days if they must."

"I can barely ride at a gentle pace for a day," I said ruefully.

Livia laughed. "What did you do, in Tirvan?"

"I fished. Maya and I have a boat, called *Dovekie*."

"You fought?" I heard no judgment in her question.

"Yes," I said. "I killed two men with a knife. If I wake in the night, shouting, it's because I am dreaming of it." Not quite the truth, but it would do.

"I'm sorry," Livia said, flushing. "I shouldn't have asked."

"It happened. I'm trying to learn to live with it. What were you to do in the invasion?"

"Nothing directly. If you hadn't been victorious, if the first people on the road again had been men from Leste, I was to ride north to the

Wall. There are ways across the hills. I too learned how to kill with a knife, to protect myself. But I didn't have to do it." The water draining away gurgled in the silence of the room

Livia broke the silence. "The young officer—Garth?" I nodded. "He looks like your Maya, if I remember her rightly."

"He's her brother."

She stood. "I should get back to the kitchen. Mari will have taken your saddlebags to your room. I'll show you where it is when you want. You may use a robe and leave it in the room." She hesitated. "Your room adjoins the men's, and no one else will be on that floor to see who sleeps where. If there were other travellers, I wouldn't tell you this. I would rather not be woken by your bad dreams, if there is a cure." She smiled. "I can make you anash tea in the morning if you wish."

I looked away, embarrassed. "How did you know?"

She shrugged. "He's too solicitous, and you watch each other. Mari, who misses nothing, saw it first. With only us, it means nothing, but were there other men here, there would be consequences. I imagine," she went on, gently, "that the General has let him know, while they are alone."

"Casyn did caution us," I said. "I'm sorry."

"There's nothing to be sorry for. Stay in the pool as long as you like. Supper will be ready in an hour."

I soaked for another ten minutes, then dried off and put on one of the robes, enjoying its warmth and softness. I left the wet towel hanging near the door, picked up my clothes, and walked barefoot down to the kitchen. Livia stirred a stew while an older woman kneaded bread at the centre table. The kitchen smelled wonderfully of lamb, rosemary, and yeast.

"This is Lena, from Tirvan," Livia said. "My mother, Keavy." Keavy smiled a welcome and pummelled the dough. I followed Livia up a narrow stair to the next floor. "These are the back stairs. You don't want to go back out into the common room. It's cold." She showed me to a small room overlooking the courtyard. It held a wide bed, a washstand, and a woven rug on the floorboards. My saddlebags sat neatly on the floor beside the washstand. I could see a chamber pot tucked under the bed. "When you're dressed," Livia said, "turn left out of the room. You'll come to the main stairs. Call when you come down, or just put your head through the door, and someone will get you a drink." She left. I dressed in lighter, woven trousers and shirt, rather than the felted wool of my riding clothes. Those I hung from pegs on the back of the door. I found my comb and ran it through my hair.

A knock at the door surprised me. I opened it, expecting Livia, but instead Garth stood in front of me. He smiled. "I'm just going to the hot pool, but I wanted to talk to you first." He closed the door. "I've been paying you too much attention, Casyn tells me."

I flushed. "Livia said as much to me at the pool."

"I thought I was being careful. If I've embarrassed you, forgive me."

"I'd rather be embarrassed, here, than for you to have problems with other officers, later."

"In Leste, men are gentle with women in public, putting their needs first. I had forgotten how different it was, outside of Festival, in the Empire." He stroked my hair. "I suppose I need to learn again."

I leaned into his hand briefly. "Livia also gave us leave to sleep where we choose tonight as long as Casyn is not offended."

"Do you want me with you?" Garth asked, smiling.

"Yes," I said. "This first night, in a strange place, who knows what my dreams will be?"

He bent forward to kiss me lightly. "I'll speak with Casyn." He turned to go.

"Garth," I said. "Maya was here. She went south with a woman from Berge."

He turned again, his face alight, and stepped forward to hug me. "Good." He released me, smiling. "We'll find her, Lena. I promise."

We ate lamb stew and fresh bread for supper in the common room, with more cider. Afterwards, Keavy brought us a bowl of apples. I ate one, then took a second and walked, with Casyn and Garth, out to the stables to see the horses.

They stood in loose boxes, with a good bed of straw. I fed Clio her apple. Someone had curried her, and she had a rack of hay and a bucket of water in her stall. Four horses, other than ours, all in good condition, shared the stable. "Are these the horses kept for the post riders?" I asked Casyn.

"For the Empire," he said, "yes. If Siannon were to become lame, I could leave him and take one of these four. Mari would keep Siannon until I could claim him or send someone for him."

"And if it were Clio who was lame?"

He shook his head. "You could, perhaps, make a private arrangement with Livia. They have a few hill ponies of their own. These horses are the Empire's, and Keavy and Livia are paid well to house them and keep them in condition for the Empire's soldiers."

"But you pay for Siannon's feed and stall?" I asked, trying to sort this out.

"No, nor for my own room and board. The same is true for Garth, now he is attached to *Skua*. If I wanted, say, boar and mushrooms seethed in wine for dinner, then yes, I would pay for that, as it isn't the usual fare. If I am content to eat what Keavy puts in front of me, and drink the wine she offers, I pay nothing."

"But I do," I said. "How much?" He told me, and I thought about the coins I carried. I could travel for a long time.

I yawned, tired from the long ride and the good meal. "Bedtime," I said.

Casyn fed Siannon the last piece of apple. "Keavy distils a brandy from their apples that is worthy of a glass," he said to Garth. "Will you join me?"

We walked back across the cobbled courtyard to the inn. Stars gleamed above us. I said goodnight to the men and walked up the stairs. I stopped at the top, disoriented. Left or right? I pictured Livia leading me up here earlier, and turned left.

In my room, I studied the window. I wanted to open it to the night breeze, but I couldn't see how it worked. I pulled at it. Nothing happened. Frustrated, I pushed against the frame, and it moved slightly. I took a step back to examine the window again. Thin cords ran upward from the lower frame. I pushed up, and the lower window rose smoothly.

I undressed, leaving my clothes on the floor, slipping under the covers. The mattress, stuffed with straw, made small rustling sounds as I moved. My hips and lower back ached, even after the baths. The sheets and pillowcase smelled of lavender. I fell asleep to the chirp of crickets and the murmur of voices from the room below.

I woke to Garth moaning in the throes of a nightmare, tossing his head on the pillow. I began rubbing his shoulder. "Garth," I whispered, "wake up." His restless movements calmed a bit. "Wake up," I repeated. He rolled towards me, opening his eyes. "You were dreaming." When he moved closer. I could smell the sharp sweat of fear on him. "The same dream again?"

"I don't remember all the images, but I was trapped somewhere again, tied up, I think, and I couldn't escape. I was so frightened and confused. I wish these dreams would stop."

I massaged his back. "They will," I murmured. Gradually, his breathing slowed and his muscles relaxed. His hands began to move gently on my skin. I slid my hands along his back to his hips and raised my mouth to his, offering and taking what I could against the memories and the night.

CHAPTER FIFTEEN

I WOKE AT DAWN. Outside, a cock crowed. Smells of fresh bread and frying sausages rose from the kitchen. Garth had gone. I got out of bed to wash at the basin before dressing again in my riding clothes. I packed my other clothes into the saddlebag.

Downstairs, Casyn stood, writing a note at the common room table. I put my saddlebags by the hall that led to the courtyard and went into the kitchen. Livia cooked sausages at the stove.

"Sleep well?" she asked.

"Thanks, yes."

She handed me a mug of anash tea. "There's honey on the table." She gestured with her head, her hands busy turning the sausages.

Casyn finished his writing and sealed the note with wax. I spooned honey into the tea, stirring it.

Garth came in from the courtyard. "It'll be sunny today," he said, "but not warmer."

Livia brought in bread and sausages and a bowl of scrambled eggs. After we ate our breakfast, I paid her.

"I hope you find your Maya," she said, smiling. "Good luck on the road."

In the courtyard, Mari had the horses ready. I slung my saddlebags behind the saddle and mounted. Livia brought her son out to wave goodbye to us. We clattered out through the archway, and onto the road.

For the next three days, we rode south through an unchanging landscape. The riding itself became easier as we and our horses became conditioned to the saddle and the long hours. On flat stretches, we could trot or sometimes canter. At about noon each day, we stopped to build a fire and eat. I brewed my anash then, drinking it bitter, without honey.

In the late afternoon each day, we came to an inn. They all seemed much the same. None had baths. I ate with the men, but slept alone, usually on a different floor. Each innkeeper remembered Maya, and

Alis of Berge, but none could tell me where they had gone. "South," they all said.

On the third day, we woke to heavy skies and a cold wind from the west. "Rain," Casyn said. An hour later, it started. The cold, stinging rain blew into our faces and across the open road. We pulled our hats down, tugged our collars up, riding into it. Clio dropped her head, and I let the reins lie loose on her neck. Water dripped off her mane, running down my coat to soak my legs.

In the early afternoon, we stopped in the shelter of some evergreens. The rain had not subsided, but the trees cut the wind. Casyn pulled a cloth bag of oats from his leather saddlebag. "Put the horses' head collars on," he said to me, "and then share this among them."

"We'll never get a fire lit," I said, unbuckling Tasque's bridle, my fingers clumsy with cold.

"Probably not," Casyn said. He sounded unconcerned. "Are you cold, either of you?"

I tossed Garth the end of the tether rope. He tied it around a branch. I poured a third of the oats onto the wet ground. Tasque bent his head, lipped the grain, and began to eat. "I'm fine out of the wind," I said. My felted wool trousers were soaked, but the leather coat and hat and my riding boots had kept me mostly dry. We finished feeding the horses.

Casyn gave me cheese and dried apple. "No point in trying to eat bread in the rain," he said.

We ate standing, half under the branches. Garth took a small flask from his pocket. "I bought some brandy from Keavy the first night. I think we could all use a mouthful." The brandy, resinous on my tongue, warmed my stomach and made my fingers tingle.

The rain fell all afternoon though the wind dropped. The horses plodded along the road, their hooves making small splashes with each step. Water ran along the stone channels at the edge of the road and stood in puddles in every dip of land. A buzzard sat miserably on a dead tree, its feathers striped by rain. By mid-afternoon, I began to shiver, and my teeth started to chatter.

"Dismount and walk," Casyn directed me, "until you are warm again."

I gave Clio the command to stop and swung off the saddle, my legs not wanting to obey me. Garth and Casyn dismounted as well. We began to walk. *This is what Maya did*, I reminded myself, feeling the stone through the soles of my riding boots. Rain dripped off my hat. Casyn set a brisk pace. Warmth soon spread, first under my coat, and then to my thighs, and finally to my feet and hands.

After about half an hour we remounted. At dusk, we came to the inn. We had walked for short stretches twice more, and Garth had given us another sip of brandy about an hour earlier, but now cold pervaded my body. Clio's dun coat looked almost black with water. We rode into the courtyard and dismounted, I leaned against the mare.

Casyn glanced over at me. "Go in. I want to look at Siannon's feet. I thought he was favouring his off hind this last while. Garth, find us a stable hand." The stable was connected to the inn by a roofed porch that ran the length of both buildings, widening at the stable to create a sheltered area for saddling and unsaddling. When we led the horses under the roof, their heads rose at the smell of grain. Tasque blew out a long breath, shaking himself like a dog.

Garth and I walked toward the inn door. "I can't remember ever being this cold," I said, wrapping my arms around me. I could not control the shivering.

"Get your coat and boots off and find the fire," Garth said. "Do you want more brandy?" I shook my head. Under the overhanging eaves we took off our hats and coats, my fingers clumsy on the buttons. Just inside the door were pegs and a brick floor with a drain. One leather coat hung there, dry. We hung our dripping coats beside it, leaving room for Casyn's, and went into the common room.

A man, middle-aged and bearded, wearing the dun-coloured travelling clothes of the Empire, sat by the fire studying a map. He looked up as we came in. Garth saluted. "Watch-Commander Garth, of *Skua*, sir."

The officer stood to return the salute. "Bren. Major of the Tenth. Come in by the fire. It's a wicked day for travel."

"Lena, of Tirvan," I said. I thought I saw a flicker of reaction, quickly controlled. We walked closer to the fire and its warmth.

As we came closer, Bren studied Garth's face. His hand found his belt knife. A muscle flicked in Garth's jaw as he endured the man's scrutiny. "I know that face," Bren finally said. "Son of Mar, of the Seventh?"

"I serve with Dern, on *Skua*, now."

"You deserted," Bren said coldly. "How can you claim you serve anywhere?" Garth said nothing. His papers, I knew, wrapped in oiled cloth, lay deep inside his saddlebags. "Answer me, man."

"We travel with Casyn. He is outside with the horses." I said, my voice wavering. "He will tell you." My voice sounded too high, too uncertain.

"Casyn?"

"Peace, Bren," Casyn said calmly from the door. He walked across the room to clap Bren companionably on the arm. "Garth has served the Empire honourably and well these past three years, providing us with information from Leste. He carries a letter of leave from his captain, and a pardon signed by me on the Emperor's behalf. Much of our most valuable information came from this man." Garth flushed at Casyn's words, but I could see him relax, almost imperceptibly

"So, he's one of yours, General," Bren said. He turned to Garth, hands out, palms up, in front of him. "My apologies, Watch-Commander. I should have realized, when you said you served with Dern. Casyn and Dern between them recruited the spies." He extended his right hand to grasp Garth's upper forearm. "Well done, soldier."

Garth nodded, grasping Bren's arm to return the formal greeting. "Thank you, sir," he managed.

The innkeeper came in with a tray of mugs. "Broth with wine," she said." She looked at me with a critical eye. I had sunk down onto a bench. "You're shivering," she said. "Sit by the fire and drink this. When you're done, I'll show you to your room, so you can change. Bring me back your wet clothes, and I'll dry them by the kitchen fire." The pottery mug was warm in my hands, and the broth smelled wonderful. I took a sip, then a larger swallow, feeling the heat coursing into my body. I drank it down as the fire warmed my legs.

The men spoke of war. I felt superfluous, and wet. When I finished my broth, I took the mug to the kitchen. The innkeeper stood at the sink, washing a pot. She looked up.

"Ready? I'm Aasta, by the way." She wiped her hands on her apron. "Follow me." She took me down a hall and up a flight of stairs to the women's bedrooms. The room, floored in wide planks, had a chair and table as well as the bed and washstand. A mug stood on the table, and a canister of tea. "I'll send Sari with some hot water, and she can bring back your wet things. Do you want the fire lit? This room's above the kitchen, so it's always warm."

I shook my head. "No, thank you. I'm warming up. The broth was wonderful." Aasta smiled, and with a nod of her head, left, closing the door behind her. I sat down to pull off my boots. I had just stripped off my damp socks when I heard a knock at the door. A girl of about twelve came in, carrying a pitcher of hot water.

"Hello," she said, a little shyly. "I'm Sari." She had long brown hair, braided back off her face. She put the water jug on the washstand.

"I'm Lena, from Tirvan." I took off my trousers, reaching for the towel that hung on the wall.

"Tirvan!" Sari said. "Do you know Maya?"

I stopped drying my legs. "She's my partner. I'm trying to find her. Do you know where she went?"

The girl shook her head. "No, not really. South. She was here for two days in the spring. If you find her, will you give her a message for me?"

"Surely," I said, curious.

"I'll write it out this evening, then," she said, smiling. She bent to pick up my wet trousers. "Your tunic?"

"It's dry. Is there nothing more you can tell me? Was she well? Was she alone?"

"She was well," Sari said, "save for a twisted ankle. That's why they stayed two days. She was with a woman named Alis, from Berge. There were two other women here, and they all left together."

With a wave, she left the room. I used some of the hot water she had brought to brew my tea, leaving it to steep while I washed, thinking of Maya. Four women together would be safer. I drank the tea, grimacing against the bitterness, and dressed in dry clothes.

"Lena," Casyn said, looking up. "Bren has a story I would like you to hear."

The room was warm. Casyn poured me a cup of wine from the jug in front of him. Bren seemed to be gathering his thoughts. I waited.

"The Empire's ship that came to Berge for provisioning had been in the south in midsummer," Bren said finally, glancing at me and then away, "at a retirement farm. One of the junior officers rode out to the nearest inn, to pick up messages. His horse cast a shoe on the journey and had to be reshod. It was a bad-tempered beast, so the woman who was doing the job asked him to hold its head. There were two stable-girls talking in the barn, apparently unaware that he could hear them.

"They were talking about a plan being made by some of the women who had chosen exile over fighting. They spoke of organizing themselves into a group, with chosen leaders. When the fighting was done, those leaders would go to the Emperor to ask him for a place where they could build a new village—a village true to the tenets of Partition and open only to those who chose exile. The girls also discussed who the leaders were likely to be." He paused.

"Maya was one of them?" I asked. He nodded. "That's—unexpected."

"Which part?" Bren asked.

"She wanted the rules of Partition to keep governing us, even though most of us voted the other way. In her mind, when we voted to fight, we betrayed tradition. But to lead a petition to the Emperor..." I shook my head. "Maya was never a leader."

"Perhaps," Casyn said gently, "exile has changed her."

Garth spoke. "When I was seven, Maya was my shadow, my playmate in everything. I did not want to leave Tirvan or her. I promised her that I would run away from the soldiers and come back for her. We would go beyond the Wall, or into the mountains, and live there secretly. It was a child's plan, but neither of us ever forgot it. When I did run," he went on, embarrassment shading his voice, "in the back of my mind I always thought I would go to Tirvan for Maya, someday, to take her away."

I turned to Casyn. "Can she petition the Emperor?" I could not remember ever hearing of a woman doing so.

"Yes," Casyn said thoughtfully, "but it is irregular. A woman's village, or an inn, or a trade guild, may petition, but not an individual. The women's councils, not the Emperor, deal with women's individual grievances. If Maya's band of exiles form a guild, and duly register that guild, then, yes, they can petition."

"A guild?" Garth said.

"Guilds," I explained, "are our governing bodies."

He frowned. "I thought that was the council?"

"Well, yes and no. The council is elected to make sure the rules of the guild are followed. At Partition, the group of women who founded Tirvan decided what village's rules would be and how we would live. They formed the guild that is Tirvan."

"So village rules are different from one place to another?" Garth asked.

"Some of them," I said. "But some were set once by larger guilds that operated over many villages. There used to be a fishing guild, and in theory I—and Maya—belong to it."

"What did it do?"

I thought back, trying to remember what Dessa had taught me all those years ago.

"It set the term of our apprenticeships, so they would be the same in all villages. Dessa told us that at one time, a small part of what we earned would have gone to the fishing guild. If we had needed money to buy *Dovekie*, or had a disagreement over fishing grounds that could not be settled by the village council, we would have sent word to Casilla, and representatives would have come to settle the issue. But that stopped a long time ago."

"Are guilds described in the Partition agreement?" Garth asked.

"Yes," Casyn said.

"Could a new village guild be formed?"

"Would the Emperor grant such a request?" I asked Casyn.

"To answer you both," Casyn said, "there is nothing to stop a group of women from requesting permission to start a new guild and a new village. As far as whether Callan would grant such a request," he went on, "I don't know." He leaned back in his chair. "Callan does not see himself as bound by tradition, which could lead him to reject a claim made on the basis of the rules of Partition. On the other hand, he might see it as fair recompense. The problem for this new guild would be twofold: where to find land for such a village and what the Empire's responsibility towards it would be."

We fell silent. I sipped my wine, trying to imagine a village open only to those who had chosen exile. Would chance have given them the right mix of skills? What would Maya, whose trade was the boats and the nets, do in a land-locked village? What would I do?

Nothing. I had not chosen exile. Maya was planning a future that did not, could not, include me.

The men resumed talking, but their words swirled and eddied around me, unheard. Aasta brought dinner: rabbit stew and dark bread. My stomach growled, reminding me that I needed food. I took the bowl Aasta offered me and a slice of bread from the basket.

The men talked of inconsequential things at dinner, Bren and Casyn telling stories of their younger days on the Wall. They had all of Garth's attention, and I found myself drawn in by the tales. Bren rarely looked my way, speaking only to Garth and Casyn. The rain fell steadily, and even through the thick walls of the inn, we could hear water running in the gutters and splashing on the cobblestones.

Sari came to clear the plates, bringing us dried fruit and biscuits, and, at Casyn's request, another jug of wine. "We'll stay here tomorrow," he said. "One day of riding in the rain is enough, and the horses could use the rest. Siannon has a bruised frog. He'll benefit from a day on straw."

I accepted another cup of wine. Without it, I reasoned, I doubted I would sleep tonight. My initial shock had passed; now anger crept in to replace it. *Perhaps I should just go to Karst with Garth, and then—what? Go home? Ride to the Wall up the eastern track, braving mountain storms and bears?* I looked up to see Garth observing me. Casyn and Bren spoke quietly together. I took a mouthful of wine, avoiding his questioning eyes.

CHAPTER SIXTEEN

I WOKE LATE THE NEXT MORNING, with a dull headache and heaviness in my muscles. I lay in the bed until the need for the chamber pot forced me up. Downstairs, Aasta gave me tea. After the third cup, heavily sweetened, I began to feel better. I ate a piece of dry toast. In the common room, Bren and Garth played xache. Outside, the rain continued.

I wandered around the room. Like the other inns, this one had low ceilings and a flagged floor. The walls were whitewashed between the timbers. Small windows under the eaves on either side looked out on the courtyard and the road. I had no idea how to pass the time. At home, we spent wet days in the repair of nets and traps or other chores. A long wet spell in winter usually meant a few days of games and stories. I played *xache* fairly well, I thought, but I had no one to play with. In any case, I suspected Bren and Garth had the only set the inn owned.

After some thought, I went out through the kitchen and along the corridor that connected the inn with the outbuildings. In the stable, I asked the ostler, Dorys, where to find Clio's tack. Dorys showed me the harness room where I found the saddle soap and the necessary brushes and rags. I sat down on an upturned bucket in an empty stall to set to work.

The saddle had started to gleam under my ministrations when I heard Casyn calling my name. "In here!" I called back.

He came to the stall.

"How is Siannon?"

"Better," he said. "He'll be fine for tomorrow, if the rain stops. May I talk with you while you work?"

"If you like," I said. He left in search of another bucket. I sat down to re-soap the cloth. I had started on the bridle when Casyn returned. He sat, hands resting on his knees, watching me in silence for a little while.

"I sat by the fire for a long time last night, thinking about Maya and what she and the other exiles want. I thought about what we asked of all of you, and how that has changed what the Empire is. Two hundred and thirty-three years have passed since the last assembly of men and women in the Empire. I think it is time for another."

I stopped rubbing soap into leather to look up, frowning "Another assembly?" I said. "With all of us? Where?"

"Probably the winter camp site," Casyn said in an amused tone. "And no, not quite all of us. The entire population of the Empire was not at the Partition assembly. Men and women were chosen to represent the views of larger groups." He leaned forward, intent on his vision. "Maya has a point. Both men and women have consciously chosen to change the precepts of the Partition agreement. Surely, we must forge a new contract, and what better time than now? For the first time in ten generations, men and women have lived together, worked together, and trained together. Dern, Bren, and I, and for that matter Callan, all think differently of women than our fathers did. Lena, can you say that you see us, men and the Empire itself, in the same way as you did in the spring?"

I shook my head. "No," I said slowly. "I have been thinking about this, a bit, while we have been riding. It seems to me that we—women, I mean—are schooled not to think beyond our village, its needs and customs. There's so much I do not know about the Empire, or even about the next village. Some of it is my own fault. I should have listened more at lessons, but some of it I was never taught."

"I am not much of a scholar," Casyn said, "but I have read what histories there are. The women's villages have become more inward-looking in the past few generations. There used to be, according to the records, more travel between villages, and the guilds met once a year. A trader's guild moved from village to village, bringing goods and news and ideas, and there were travelling musicians."

"What happened?"

"You know what happened. This lesson you did learn, Lena."

The tunnels, I thought. *Late springs, early winters, little food, not even enough to provision the men. Only a few children born, because the village could not afford more.* "The heavy snows. Of course." He nodded.

"I always thought it was just the north. But the histories say otherwise. That was when the Wall was built to keep the northern people penned in. They were starving and beginning to raid southward."

"How long did the cold last?"

"Maybe thirty years," he said. "Long enough to change how the villages functioned, to make self-sufficiency their first concern. When the weather warmed again, the village councils needed every woman to farm and fish. Travel would have been discouraged as well as, consciously or not, much teaching about the world beyond the village." He stood. "Please keep this to yourself, for now, Lena. We will talk again before our ways part." He smiled down at me as he left, his grave, slow smile. *His hair is greyer than it was in the spring. Does Gille miss him?* They had partnered only briefly, a month or two, but much longer than the Festival liaisons. 'We live apart and die apart,' Casyn had said in the spring, in a voice shaded with regret. I wondered, for the first time, if we had to.

When the bell rang for the noon meal, I had not finished cleaning the tack. After Casyn left I had sat, bridle in hand, trying to make sense of what I had heard in the past day. How could we give Maya and the other exiled women what they wanted, and at the same time shape a new contract between the villages and the military, and maybe even between women and men? Maya's group wanted the old ways. Casyn was thinking of something new.

The rain had stopped. The clouds moved east, and the day brightened. I walked across the wet courtyard. Sari came out of another building. *The laundry*, I thought, from the smells that came from the opened door, falling into step beside me.

"I have the message for Maya. May I give it to you at the meal?"

"Wait till the end, so as not to have it food-stained." A thought struck me. "Sari, does this have anything to do with Maya's plans for a new village?"

"You know about it! I wasn't sure. Yes, of course it is. The note is just to say that I would like to join them when I am adult and can choose."

"And this would be allowed?"

"Yes, of course," she said impatiently. "I couldn't choose exile because I'm too young. But I would have. I did not want to fight, and I'm glad I did not have to. Fighting is for men."

"I fought."

"Then why are you looking for Maya?" she demanded. "You won't be welcome. I better go," she said in a different tone. "Aasta will need me." She veered off towards the kitchen. I watched her run, trying not to resent the doubts her comment had surfaced. *Would Maya even want to see me?* I had fought. And killed.

We ate barley soup with goat cheese and bread at the long table. "We can ride tomorrow," Bren announced cheerfully. He had beaten Garth twice at *xache*.

"Will you play with me, this afternoon?" I asked Casyn. I had things I wanted to ask him. He looked surprised but agreed.

When Sari came to clear the table, she brought me the sealed note. I slipped it into the pocket of my trousers and went to the kitchen. "May I have a mug of hot water?" I asked Aasta. "I have a headache and would take some willow bark. I have some in my pack." She poured water from the kettle, giving me the mug without comment. I went down the hall to my room to make my *anash*. The bitterness, without honey, no longer bothered me. I wondered if I still needed to drink it, and if the irregularity of the hour each day I did drink it would have consequences. I would know in a few days. Beyond that, I refused to think. I took the note from my pocket and put it inside my pack.

I won the toss. We sat alone in the common room. Bren and Garth had gone to see their horses. I made my opening move. Casyn countered. We worked through a standard opening. Casyn knew his game and would beat me, I realized, but no matter.

"Casyn," I said quietly, "At the Partition assembly, what happened to those who did not vote for Partition?"

He slid a piece along the squares. "Some accepted the choice and lived out their lives under the new order."

"And others?"

"Exile from the Empire," he said. "Slavery, for some."

"Where did they go?" Exile from the Empire meant leaving the bounds of the Empire forever. I moved a piece; a bad choice. Casyn took it. "North, or over the mountains. They were given six weeks to get beyond the borders. After that, they would be captured and killed, or enslaved."

"And the men castrated, as Garth would have been?" I asked. I could not help myself.

Casyn put down the taken rider. "Garth was being trained as a medic," he said calmly. "Medics serve in the field and are part of the army. He would not have been castrated. How do you know of this, Lena?" I reddened.

"Dern told you," he surmised.

"We were talking one night about killing, about sending others to kill or be killed," I said. "It was very late, and we had drunk more wine than was wise."

"It is a barbaric practice," Casyn said, with an edge to his voice. I looked up, surprised. "The forces of the Empire accept change very slowly, and with much resistance. The threat of castration overcomes most boys' fears about fighting. That is the argument and the justification. But if one studies the records, for the generations we have kept them, the number of boys who cannot bring themselves to serve in the field has not changed. There are always a few. The refusal to fight has not been bred out of them, which is the real thinking behind the practice."

I moved a *xache* piece almost randomly, not thinking about the game. "Are you speaking for yourself, or as the Emperor's advisor?"

"Both," he said after a moment. "Callan feels as I do, but that cannot be said to anyone, Lena, not even Garth, or Dern, were you to meet up with him again. Our father, who was a brave man and a good soldier, fathered a third son, Colm. It was clear from the earliest days that he would never make a soldier. He is a scholar and a historian. He taught Callan and me what we know of the Empire's history, but he paid a high price." I could hear the bitterness in his voice.

He looked at the board. "We aren't really playing, are we?" he asked. I shook my head. He leaned back in his chair. "Perhaps this invasion by Leste was a blessing," he said. "Perhaps now we have a reason to talk of change."

"Did you talk of this, with Gille?"

"A bit," he said. "It was her idea for me to ride with you, so that we could talk. If you were to choose maybe half-a-dozen women to represent Tirvan at an assembly, Lena, who would you choose? Beyond yourself, and the council, of course."

I considered. "Tali," I said after a moment, "and Dessa. Maybe Kyan. And Casse, for her long experience." I thought a while more. "I would have chosen Siane, too. Her views were shared by only a few others in the village, but they should be heard."

Casyn nodded. "You will be a fine council leader one day, Lena."

"But never a general," I said lightly. He looked at me appraisingly.

"Would you be, if you could?"

I thought of the blood spilling over my hands, and of Tice's body in the willow. I shook my head. "No."

"I would have said the same at eighteen," he said. I wanted to ask him to explain, but he continued on. "When you stop at the inns, after we part, you might plant the thought of an assembly, just a hint, a suggestion made over wine and talk, nothing more. My brother needs to be seen to be serving the wishes of his people, not calling for a new order from the chair of the Emperor." He reached out to move a piece one square forward.

We played out the game, Casyn winning in five moves. I could not find a way to ask him to explain what he had meant about not wanting to be a general. It seemed too private a thing for me to probe. When we had finished playing, I went back to the stable to finish cleaning my tack, and to think. I thought I understood, a little, how Maya had felt in the spring, her world shifting toward an unrecognizable future. The familiar task provided comfort, and I gave myself up to it.

In the late afternoon, the rattle of hooves on the cobblestones broke the stillness. A lone rider came through the archway and dismounted, handing his reins to Dorys. She led the horse, a bay gelding, wet with sweat, into the stable. I went to help her. "Who is it?" I asked, unbuckling the bridle.

"Major Turlo," she said. "He's ridden hard today." She called to her apprentice. "Walk this horse till he cools, then curry him down well. I'll make up a bran mash for him. Keep him away from that water trough," she warned. The girl grinned at her, taking the horse by his bridle.

Turlo, I remembered, had been the soldier sent to Berge. I put my tack away and washed the smell of saddle soap off my hands. Then I crossed the yard.

The day had brightened considerably through the afternoon, and the common room seemed dark. The men stood near the fireplace. As my eyes adjusted to the dimness, I saw that the newcomer had the reddest hair and beard I had ever seen. I stopped, uncertain. Red hair belonged north of the wall. I remembered what Casse had said about the raids, and the rapes. I stepped forward.

"Lena," Casyn said, "this is Major Turlo. Lena was a Cohort-Leader and instrumental in winning the battle at Tirvan."

Turlo shook my hand. Younger than Bren and Casyn, he had bright blue eyes. "Good for you, lass," he said. "I wouldn't have wanted to be on the wrong side of the women of Berge. They fought well—only lost four, and the whole thing was over in a few hours."

"We lost four, too, but it took nearly three days to finish it. And without Garth, I am not sure what we would have done."

Turlo looked from me to Garth. "There's a story here. Let's have some wine and hear it." He strode over to the kitchen door. "Aasta," he called, "some wine, if you will, and five cups. And something to tide us over till supper. I've been riding since before dawn, and you don't want me keeling over on your hearth." I laughed. I liked this man. He seemed genuinely interested in what had happened at Tirvan, unlike Bren.

We arranged ourselves in chairs near the fireplace. "The invaders came at dawn," I started, "although we'd seen the sails the day before and were ready. All our cohorts lay in wait, hidden, and when the Lestians landed we let them move up into the village before we began the defence." Aasta came out with a tray bearing wine and small savouries. She put the tray down on the table, but she did not leave again, seating herself on a stool to the left of the hearth. I continued. Turlo listened without comment until I described recognizing Garth. He whistled, low and long.

"Luck was with you, Garth," he said, reaching for the wine flask. "Go on," he said to me. I took a sip of my wine before continuing on. I did not look at the men, but stared into the flames, trying to remember the order and the details of those hours and days. I told of the search for the Lestians, of Tice's death, of the raid at the burying.

"When Pel was taken, we decided we had no choice but to ask Garth to rescue him. Only he could get close to Cael, so we cut his chains to make it look as if he had escaped. He brought Pel home safely. And that is all the story I have to tell." Without thinking, I finished with the words Xani or Gille used when they told the stories of our history.

Aasta stirred. "A fine story," she said. "Brave women, brave men, and brave deeds. You're a rare storyteller. I'd hear that again, given a chance. Now I'd best look at the stew." She pushed herself up, to disappear into the kitchen.

Turlo looked at me thoughtfully. "It is a good story, and you did tell it well. Someone should write it down, though. Casyn, tell it to Colm when you get to the winter camp. He'll do it properly."

Casyn stretched. "I will. But Lena, you should find ink and paper to record it, too. Whatever I tell Colm will be my version of your story, and not the same. To be accurate, history needs many voices. Or so my brother would tell me."

Could history ever be accurate? I wondered, raising my wine to my lips. All the talking had dried my throat. *Who decided which stories were told?*

In the morning, Turlo announced he would ride with us. Dorys had come in at first light to tell him his bay needed to rest. "Two, three days, at least," she had said.

"Well, he'll get more than that," Turlo said, unperturbed. "I'll leave him here for you to doctor, Dorys, and take another. He's not mine, as it happens. My poor old fellow was a casualty at Berge, took an arrow in the throat. The bay's a post horse from the northern inn, so it's fair exchange."

The thought of his company pleased me, but Bren also rode with us, and that made me uncomfortable. He remained distant and humourless, and I could not forget his challenge to Garth that first night. We said our farewells to the inn-folk and mounted in the cobbled courtyard. Clio whickered at the post horse, a sturdy chestnut.

"Is yon a Han pony?" Dorys asked, pointing her chin towards Clio. I nodded. "So is this one," she said. "Seems they know each other." The two horses blew gently at each other. We rode out of the courtyard and back onto the road.

A fair day had dawned, and the clear sky was dotted with a few small clouds. The officers rode abreast, with Garth and me following. Turlo wore a quiver and carried a short bow, a hunting bow, for small game or birds. *Odd,* I thought, *for an officer.*

As the sun rose higher, the air warmed. We stopped at a stream to let the horses drink, stripping off outer tunics and cloaks. I stretched. "Why do you carry a bird bow?" I asked Turlo.

"To hunt," he said simply. "I've a taste for wild meat, and if I can get a brace of hare, or grouse, well, that's a fine meal."

"Turlo," Bren said, surprising me, "is barely civilized. Were he not riding with us, he would probably forgo the inns entirely, except to check for messages and buy wine, to spend his nights camped under a tree, roasting rabbit over a fire and singing barbaric northern ballads to the moon."

Turlo grinned. "Aye, I would," he agreed. "And glad you've both been, a time or two, of my prowess with bow and arrow. Shall I tell the young folk?"

For the next hour he told us detailed, and, I suspected, highly exaggerated, stories of hunt parties that would have failed and Wall garrisons that would have starved, without his hunting skills. He must have spent much of his service on the Wall. His stories made me laugh, and I welcomed the distraction.

We halted at noon at a rocky hillside scattered with pines and the scrubby oak of the highlands, to eat cold meat and apples before stretching out in the shade. The horses grazed the sparse grass between the trees. A jay called, then another, a harsh sound. Turlo raised himself on one elbow, raising a hand for silence. The jay called again. Turlo pointed, slowly. On the rocks above us, a wildcat sat, gazing down at us with its deep golden, unblinking eyes. The tip of its tail moved slightly. "A young one," Turlo whispered, "this spring's kitten. Smelt our meat, most likely." He sat up suddenly, and the cat vanished. "Don't want it thinking man and food go together."

"I've never seen one before."

"Nor I," murmured Bren.

"I have," Garth said, "before my father came for me. I was climbing in the hills above Tirvan, and I came across a litter. Their eyes were barely opened. The female must have brought them out for some sun. She snarled at me, and the kittens fled, but, oh, I wanted one. I planned to go back to capture one, but then it was Festival and the end of Tirvan for me."

"Just as well," Turlo said. "They're not to be tamed, and the female would have gone for your face. But I know how you felt. I had the same plans until my mother caught me dragging a fishing net into the hills and gave me a scolding I've never forgotten. 'Wild things are meant to be wild,' she said. 'You can't change their nature. If you want a pet, there's plenty of barn kittens.' She said a wild thing taken as a babe is never truly tame but can never be truly wild again either. It will only be a shadow of what it should be. I never tried to tame anything again."

"It would do a lot of men good to learn that lesson," Casyn said. He looked at the sun. "We should ride."

In the afternoon, the men's talk turned to war. I lagged behind. The land had changed again. Elm and ash stood among the oak, their leaves fading from green to yellow and brown. My hands rested on Clio's withers, the reins loose between them. Clio followed the horses ahead of her, needing no guidance from me. I thought about what Turlo had said, about not trying to tame something wild. *The Empire had forced Garth to go against his nature. Turlo too might have been meant to roam the bogs and hills of the borderlands, unconstrained by the uniform of the Empire. Yet he seems content, even happy. How can that be?*

We rode south, bypassing inns except to water the horses and have a meal for ourselves, making camp instead. Turlo proved as adept with his hunting bow as he had claimed, so we ate well those nights, roasting rabbit or partridge over the fire. On the road, I often rode slightly apart while the men talked of war, strategies and mistakes. Strategy had interested me only when it concerned Tirvan and its defence.

I thought often of Maya. I envisioned her rapturous at our reunion, begging my forgiveness. I saw her on the other side of the Empire, writing letters that reached me twice a year, and always six months late. I saw myself working at the closest inn or fishing port, riding up occasionally to meet her outside the village. I thought of many ways we could wait out the three years of her exile from Tirvan. Very occasionally, I let myself think about what life might be like, without her, forever.

Whenever that thought intruded, I purposely began to think of Casyn's proposal for a new assembly. I thought again about whom I would choose to represent Tirvan, weighing the strengths of Tirvan's women in my mind. *Casse would speak her mind, calling on long experience, but could she make such a journey? Would Dessa consider coming now, if it meant leaving Lara? The assembly would have to be in the summer, so the village delegations could camp on the way because the inns could not cope with large numbers.* In this way, the miles passed.

About mid-morning of the next day, Casyn dropped back to ride with me. He reined Siannon in until we rode at a slow walk. The others pulled ahead.

"What is it?"

"Bren makes you uncomfortable."

"Yes," I said. "I don't think he likes me being here."

"Bren is never easy among women," Casyn said. "His life is soldiery, as is true of all of us, but for him it is everything. He simply does not know how to talk to you."

"I don't fit."

"Exactly," Casyn said. "Bren is more rigid in his thinking than your Maya, Lena, but he is a good soldier and a fine strategist. His campaigns are planned meticulously, down to the last horseshoe nail needed. He has taught us all how important details can be."

"And I am not one of those details."

"Not one he has ever had to consider before," Casyn said with a chuckle. "He helped plan the invasion of Leste and then went north to manage the Wall garrisons. Their numbers were down, and he was the best man to organize the defence there. He opposed the involvement of the women's villages because he could not understand how it might work."

"Does he now?"

"I think he is beginning to," Casyn said. "But there is something more."

I eyed him curiously.

"His discomfort with women extends to Festival," Casyn said. "He cannot make himself understood or attractive to women. Twenty years ago, I convinced him to go to Tirvan for Festival. He met a woman he wanted to know better, but it didn't work out. Her attention was given already to another man."

"Because I am from Tirvan, he is even more uncomfortable."

"Yes."

"Do you know who she was?"

"No," Casyn answered. "He never told me."

I looked forward to where Garth rode between Turlo and Bren. "I wish you'd told me this days ago."

"I should have," Casyn said. "I thought you both might relax just by riding together."

"We've barely spoken, and I've been riding behind."

"That's why I told you," he said.

I nodded. "I'll try to join in."

At our mid-day break, Turlo offered to teach Garth to use the hunting bow. The day had turned glorious, the sky a clear blue with a light breeze. Garth accepted with alacrity.

"I'll come to watch," Bren said, standing. Garth nodded a welcome. He clearly liked Bren. After my talk with Casyn, I could see his distant manner in a new light. I no longer felt rejected by him, but I remained ambivalent.

"And you, Lena?" Turlo offered. I shook my head. My monthly bleeding had begun, and a general lassitude had settled over me. I stretched out in the warmth, drowsing as the hunters went off over a ridge. After a while, I stirred to see Casyn sitting on a nearby rock, a mug of tea in his hands. I rolled over, sitting up.

"I thought you had gone hunting," I said.

"Four is too many."

"May I ask something? About Turlo?"

"Bren this morning, Turlo now?" he teased.

"It seems to me that Turlo is much like Garth. He is happier hunting, or wandering the wilds, than anything else, yet he holds a commission and serves the Empire." I stopped, not sure how to continue.

"You are wondering why Turlo became an officer while Garth chose to desert," he said gently. "There is no easy answer to that. Turlo, for all his love of the wild, came willingly. His father was on Wall duty, a scout, and his tales of that life probably had the boy enthralled. Also, the Wall is a place where Turlo's skills and interests are needed and encouraged. By the time he came to the cadet camps, he was already a talented borders scout. But Turlo is also a born leader. He understands men much as he understands animals, instinctively, and we fostered that in him. Garth is a different man, and his opportunities were different. If Mar had been in a borders regiment, then, yes, perhaps he would have reconciled to the army, but perhaps not. I doubt that Garth will ever be truly happy leading men, but I think he will teach boys with care and discipline and with a greater sensitivity than he received." He sighed. "I am not sure I have answered your question, Lena, but it is difficult to talk about what might have been when we are speaking of men. I prefer analysing tactics."

"I've noticed," I said dryly. "Although you're not quite as bad as Bren." He laughed. "I still wish things had been different for Garth."

"And for yourself, and for Maya," he said gently. "As I do. But we cannot shape the circumstances to fit our lives, only our lives to fit the circumstances. What defines us, as men and women, is how we respond to those circumstances. Courage comes in many forms, Lena, and I think perhaps Garth, in trying to reconcile his nature to the expectations of the Empire—and ultimately his own expectations of himself—is more courageous than Turlo."

A gentle breeze rattled the dry leaves. I could hear the horses cropping grass. Casyn sipped his tea. I lay back again in the sun. "When do our roads part?" I asked.

"Two days from now. About midmorning on the second day, we'll come to a track that runs south-easterly, while this road swings to the west. We'll say our farewells there. The easterly track will bring us to the winter camp more quickly than the southern. Your errand takes you south, and neither should be delayed."

I nodded. I would miss him, but part of me wanted to be alone with Garth again, to talk to him of Maya and the future, and to camp under the trees and moon. I heard voices; looking up, I saw the men climbing over the ridge, rabbits swinging from their hands. Garth was grinning. A light breeze blew, his hair back across his forehead as he held up his brace. "Dinner tonight," he said. He looked relaxed, his eyes lit up with pride in this new skill.

"If we can buy some root vegetables, pot herbs, and perhaps a loaf of bread at the next inn," I said, "I'll stew those rabbits tonight, as a change from roasting them." This brought appreciative noises from Turlo, but then, anything to do with food usually did. We doused and scattered the fire, re-bridled the horses and tightened the girths before mounting, turning south again into the red-gold afternoon.

Two days later, in mid-morning, we rode up from the bowl of a grassy valley between two ridges of land. We urged the horses up to the crest. As Clio came abreast of the larger horses, I reined her to a stop to look out. I gasped.

Beyond this final ridge, the land fell away quickly in a series of declining hills. A sea of grass extended far beyond sight toward the horizon. From this height, we could see the roll of the land and the sweep and ripple of the pale, sere grasses. The sky soared above us, and the boundary between land and air looked like a hazy blur on the distant edge of vision. As I gazed at the space and enormity of the grasslands, an unrealized tension eased. I felt an inner expansion, the loosening of constraint. *I could live down there*, I thought, suddenly, fiercely, wanting it. *I could lose myself in that land, below that sky, in all that emptiness.*

"I had no idea," I said. "Rasa and Dian tried to describe it, but I didn't understand the immensity. It looks as if the grasslands go on forever."

"Not forever," Bren said. "Eventually, the land begins to change again, sloping down to the fertile fields of the south."

We sat our horses, looking down at the rippling grasses. A long-winged hawk hunted over the plain. I began to sort out features—clumps of trees in valleys, the occasional glint of a stream. The road itself stood out clearly, winding over hills and into valleys until it disappeared into the haze on the horizon. Another track branched off from it toward the east.

"The eastern road," Casyn said, following my gaze. "Let's ride."

A series of switchbacks led us gently down into the grasslands. We wound back and forth at a walk, reins loose, letting the horses choose the pace. The sun rose higher in the sky. Turlo and Garth talked about the game to be found on the grasslands and the best places and times to hunt. The sea of grass grew closer until we rode into it, the wave and ripple of the grasses in the breeze creating a constant susurration like waves on a beach. Small birds trilled among the grasses, darting rapidly from one clump to another or flashing high into the sky. When the sun had nearly reached its zenith, we came to the place where the roads diverged.

Just to the north and east of the fork, a small stream running out of the hills had been channelled into drinking basins. A rough ring of small boulders and logs marked the common resting point. We dismounted, removed bridles, let the horses drink from the lower pool, then hobbled them for grazing. Turlo built a fire. We made tea and ate cheese and bread.

Casyn stood, brushing the crumbs from his legs. After looking to me for permission, he pulled the map from my saddlebag to spread it on a flat piece of ground, weighing the corners with small stones. He beckoned us over. "We are here," he said, pointing. He traced the line of the southerly road. "There's an inn here, at the river. You could reach it by nightfall. Or there is a good camp some miles before that, in a stand of trees by a stream, just here." He pulled a blackened twig from the fire, making a mark on the map. "In another seven or eight days of easy riding, you'll reach Karst. Try not to push the horses. They—and you—will need to drink more often through the grasslands. The air is dry here. Groom them well at night." He stood, refolding the map before handing it to me. "It's time."

We smothered the fire and prepared the horses. I filled water skins. We had divided the food and camp gear that morning. When I handed the skins to the men, Turlo grinned at me.

"You'll do fine, lassie," he said. His mood buoyed me, and I grinned back.

"The evenings will be quieter," I said. "Don't drive the others mad with your stories."

Turlo laughed. "They've heard them all, and told them all, so many times, they can't tell my lies from theirs." He held out a hand, suddenly serious. "Go safely, Lena," I clasped it in the soldier's grip. He turned to Garth while I shook hands with Bren. I held out my hand to Casyn. He took it, holding it between both of his.

"Go safely. I will see you again."

"Go safely, Casyn." I had too much to say, and to ask, and time had run out. I turned away, willing my eyes dry, and mounted. Garth saluted Turlo and Bren, then Casyn, before mounting Tasque. I turned Clio's head to the south, raising a hand in farewell.

Clio's ears pricked and her stride lengthened as we rode south. I reined her in, waiting for Garth to come abreast of me on the road. "Clio wants to run."

"She must have memories of running free in the grasslands," Garth replied. "Still, why not?" We gave the horses their heads, pounding along the road. I bent low over my mare's neck, urging her on, feeling my own spirit rise with hers. I laughed with the sheer joy of life and sunshine and freedom.

We rode through the afternoon, watering the horses frequently. The sky soared above us, the blue unbroken save for a few small clouds in the west. We scared up grouse and hare, and once, cresting a small rise, we saw a herd of deer far in the distance. Garth sat his horse easily, relaxed and confident. He turned to say something and caught my eyes on him. He smiled.

"Camp tonight or the inn?"

I smiled back. "Camp."

We reached the campsite an hour before sunset. A stream ran beside a stand of trees under a rocky outcropping, providing a windbreak. We unsaddled and groomed the horses thoroughly, washing the dust from their eyes and nostrils. The western sky glowed red and orange and pink by the time we finished. I ran a hand through my hair. "I need a wash," I said. The shallow stream did not allow for swimming, but I stripped to wade in. Cold water came up to my knees. I dug my toes into the sandy bottom. Kneeling, I used my hands to cup water up and over my head, washing the dust from my hair and body. I felt Garth behind me. He poured water from his hands along my back. I gasped at the cold. As his hands left my back, the gasp became a moan. I turned to him. We kissed with increasing need until Garth broke away, taking my hand.

"I built a fire and spread the blankets. Let's get warm." He led me to the fire, and we made love with urgency and passion under the cobalt sky.

Later we ate more cheese and dried fruits and bread. The horses rested at the edge of the trees, standing head to tail and slouching on three legs. Stars fogged the sky. I lay back, looking for the constellations I knew. I found the hunter with his dogs, and the bears, and from there the north star. *I could follow it home to Tirvan,* I thought, *if Tirvan is still home.*

I propped myself up on one elbow. "Did Casyn say anything more to you about what will happen now?"

"I know my orders. Casyn is going to rejoin the Emperor in a little while, and there will a meeting of the senior officers. Why?" He reached forward to add a log to the fire. "Did he say something to you?"

"In a way. Garth, what if there were another, honourable, thing for you to do, other than the army? What if you could build roads or buildings, or trade, not as part of the army but as a free man, sanctioned by the Empire. Would you do it?"

He considered. "Not now," he answered finally. "I think I see a place for me, a way I can serve that I can live with, perhaps even be proud of. But if another way had been possible, and had been offered, yes, I'd have taken it. What are you thinking of?"

I hesitated. *If Casyn had not told him of my task, to incite the women of the Empire to demand a new assembly, should I?* "If Maya and her group can become a new guild, petition for a new village, with different rules from the rest of Tirvan, then why can't there be an equivalent guild of men, bound by different rules but still legitimate under the Empire? At twelve, you choose—land or sea. Why isn't there a choice to leave honourably and openly, to serve the Empire in a different way? You ran, Garth. You risked your life rather than submit to that choice. Others submit to worse."

He looked away. "I didn't know you knew about that," he said eventually. "But that is the law. The Empire won't change it because they need to breed men who will fight."

I shook my head impatiently. "This Emperor has already changed the rules. You are proof of that. We aren't horses, bred for the cart or the saddle, for strength or speed. We are human and capable of thought and choice and change. The rules of Partition, determining the fate of deserters, or at least some deserters, have been overturned. Surely this is the time to change other rules, too?" I took a breath. "What choices do you want for your son?"

The firelight shadowed his eyes. "More than I had," he said quietly. "I never planned to father sons for the Empire's army. I was to marry a trader's daughter, on Leste, and father sons for the boats and the trade."

"Maya swore she would give no sons to the regiments, either. But Valle is alive, and he's nearly three. Today you ride to claim him. In four years, you will ride to Karst again to take him to his place as a cadet."

He made an impatient gesture with his hand. "That's the way of our world." He stood, looking down at me. "Would you bear my child, knowing, if it were a son, that his future was pre-ordained?"

I had thought about this, riding the southward road. I shook my head. "Not if there are no choices for the child beyond what is circumscribed." In the flicker of the firelight, he smiled bitterly. He touched my hair.

"I need to think. I'll be by the stream." I watched him walk into the darkness, toward the sound of the running water. An owl called. In the clear, cold sky above me, the hunter followed his course, fixed, unchanging, with his dogs at heel.

CHAPTER SEVENTEEN

CLOUDS HAD BLOWN IN OVERNIGHT. They were not yet threatening rain, but by evening I guessed we would be glad of an inn's roof above us. Garth looked tired. I wondered when he had returned to the fire to sleep. We ate without referring to last night's conversation. I doused the fire and rolled up the bedding while Garth tacked up the horses. When our eyes met, he did not look away, but he did not smile.

We rode at a walk, letting the horses warm their muscles. The grasslands stretched ahead of us, undulating in broad swells of land bisected occasionally by small streams. Grouse foraged at the side of the road, sometimes taking to wing at our approach but more often scuttling into the longer grasses, which moved constantly, a soft background rustle.

"I thought about what you said, last night," Garth said, after we had ridden for half an hour. "Maybe I should leave Valle where he is. Perhaps the life of slave is better. He would be safe and fed, and if he's capable, he could rise high. Why should I give him to the Empire?"

"Leave him in slavery?" I said, shocked. "That gives him no choice at all."

"He has none now! Neither of us do. I go to Karst and say, 'This is my son. I acknowledge him. In four years, I will come back to take him away to learn to be a soldier.' Why isn't that slavery, too?"

I recalled Kolmas's words in response to Casyn's offer: *This is only another sort of slavery.*

"It would disrupt nothing to leave him alone. No one has prepared him for me. His life will just go on as it is now."

"He will be named fatherless, unwanted. You can't do that to him, Garth. Like it or not, he is your responsibility. Or are you running away again?"

Garth's face blanched, and I wished the words unsaid. He reined his horse in. I swung Clio around to look at him.

"Go away," he said, his jaw clenched. A chasm opened inside me.

"Garth—"

"Go!"

I closed my eyes for a moment then turned Clio south. I dared not look back, but after a few minutes, I could hear Tasque's hooves on the road behind us. *How could I have said that? Garth had no inkling that the Emperor might change the laws.* I had to tell him. He had risked his life for the Empire, in secrecy and silence, these last years. Gradually, I slowed Clio. When I could hear Tasque close behind me, I stopped.

"Garth," I said quietly. "I was wrong to say what I did. I have something to tell you. Will you listen?"

He looked grim, but he nodded.

"I have a task on this road, beyond seeking Maya. Casyn charged me with speaking privately to the girls and women of the inns to plant the thought of a new assembly, one at which a new set of laws, for all the Empire's men and women, would be written."

His eyes narrowed. "The Emperor wants this?" he demanded. "Casyn told you this?"

"Not exactly," I admitted. Clio shifted under me, feeling my tension and wanting to move. "But he did say the Emperor wants a new assembly, to make a new agreement between women and men. I have been instructed to plant the idea at each inn we pass, so that it arises from the villages and the inns, and not from Callan." A corn bunting called, clear and sharp, from atop a swaying stem. Tasque snorted.

Garth stared at the horizon. "He must have his own agenda. Did Casyn say what it is?"

I hesitated. "He alluded to it," I said finally. "But he made me swear I would tell no one." I met his eyes. The anger had vanished, but wariness lingered. "I will tell you, if you want." I felt my heart beat.

"No," he said after a moment's pause. "Keep your word, Lena. I have trusted this Emperor, or his proxies, for some years now. I'll trust you, too."

"I don't know the Emperor, but I trust Casyn."

"As do I," Garth said. He half-smiled. "They say that the Emperor can hold a battlefield in his mind, each dip of land, each outcrop, each copse, and see how the battle will go, before it is fought. He chooses his strategy and deployment based on this picture in his mind, a picture that changes with season and weather, or time of day, and yet he always knows what will happen."

"I would like to meet him, some day."

"Perhaps you will," Garth said, glancing at the sun. "We should ride. Karst is still some days ahead."

We rode on. Garth's reaction, his instant suspicion of the Emperor's motives, surprised me. His years of keeping secrets, of twisting the truth, had influenced how he saw the world. Something about our conversation niggled at me, a vague disquiet.

The sun rose higher, a pale disc behind the clouds bright and warm enough to burn the mist away from stream valleys and bring the first of the hawks up into the sky, hunting effortlessly over the plain. The clop of our horses' hooves accompanied the ripple of the wind and the faint, high scream of the hawk. At mid-morning, I heard the clink of metal and the murmur of women's voices from the inn.

Unlike the others we had passed, this inn was a wooden structure, long and low, with outbuildings roofed with turf. Stone formed the foundation, but above that, broad wooden planks, overlapping, comprised the unpainted and weathered walls. Behind the inn and its outbuildings, the post horses and some smaller horses, like my Clio, grazed, sharing the grass with a herd of goats.

One of the inn's horses caught our scent and whinnied a greeting or a challenge, wheeling to crowd against the fence closest to the road. Tasque returned the call. A woman stepped from an outbuilding, raising a hand in greeting. We rode into the yard. Chickens pecked in the dust. "Welcome," she said.

We dismounted. "Lena of Tirvan,' I said. Her eyes narrowed, but she said nothing.

"Garth, Watch-Commander of *Skua*."

The woman was in early middle age and stocky, with short hair and fine wrinkles around her eyes. She nodded. "I'm Zilde, the inn-keeper. There's feed and water in the stables for your horses, or a spare paddock if you want to turn them out. I'm afraid there's no one to take them for you. My girls have gone, leaving only myself, my mother, and my aunt, and they are too old to handle horses. Are you staying?"

I shook my head. "No. But the horses could use grain, if you have it, and if you have bread to spare, I'll buy some."

"There's bread," she said, "fresh-baked, and grain in the bin. Come in when you're ready." With a lift of her chin, she indicated the door into the common room of the inn. We led the horses over the yard and into the dim, cool stable where we stripped off their harnesses and found grain and water. As we worked, I considered Zilde's reaction when I mentioned Tirvan.

"I wonder if her girls chose exile." I said, half to myself.

"We can't exactly ask," Garth answered. "Will you do what Casyn asked of you?"

"I'm not sure," I said.

When we had seen to the horses, we crossed the yard to the common room door. We took seats at a table, and Zilde brought a jug of steaming liquid and mugs on a tray. She put the tray down on the table, pouring a dark, malty drink into the mugs. An older woman carried in a plate of bread rolls with hands twisted and swollen with the joint-ill. *No wonder we had to see to our horses ourselves,* I thought. A second woman came out with butter and a fruit preserve. "My mother, and my aunt," Zilde said. We introduced ourselves. Again, I saw a fleeting reaction to the mention of Tirvan.

We ate. The bread was still slightly warm, melting the butter and softening the tangy fruit preserve. *Quince,* I thought. The drink had a grain base, and Zilde, pouring herself a mug too, added a chunk of butter to it. "Where are you headed?" she asked.

"Karst," I said. "Garth goes to see his son before rejoining his regiment, and I have news to bear to the village." Zilde visibly relaxed at my answer.

"I thought, as you are from Tirvan, you might be going to join that Maya," she said. "She a friend of yours?"

"Yes," I said neutrally. "But I haven't heard much of her since she left, just some stories at other inns about a group of exiles."

Zilde snorted. "Stories is right. Stories about petitioning the Emperor for a new village for those what didn't fight. Or who wouldn't have if they'd been old enough to choose. My own daughters have gone off to find her, to join this group. They slipped off one night with their ponies, and me with no one to send after them. As if a bunch of stripling girls can build a new village, supposing the Emperor was foolish enough to grant the petition."

"Do you think he might?" Garth asked.

"How should I know?" Zilde retorted. "What do I know of the Emperor? You'd know more than me." She eyed him. "Well?"

Garth shook his head. "I've been on frontier duty for many years."

Zilde sipped her drink. "An Emperor who would ask women to fight could do anything," she stated finally. The two older women nodded in agreement.

"Maybe Maya's right to ask for change. Maybe we all should. The old rules have been broken. Maybe it's time to make new ones." I tried to keep my voice level, almost disinterested, a tired traveller just passing the time in an inn. Zilde shook her head.

"I always heard those long winters bred strange talk in the north," she said. She looked at me appraisingly. Suddenly her face softened slightly. "Did you fight?" I nodded. "Kill anyone?" I nodded again. She held my gaze. "Then I shouldn't be judging." She stood up. "I'll get that bread for you."

One of the older women bent to pick up the tray. "I liked the old rules," she said.

They left us to finish the meal. Garth looked at me quizzically. I shrugged. I had done what Casyn had asked.

We let the horses rest for another half hour while we drank second mugs of the grain drink. Garth wandered around the common room. I sat, watching him. His hair had grown out a bit, and he needed a shave. I no longer saw Maya as easily in his features. Finally, he swallowed the last of his drink. "Ready?" In answer, I put my own mug down, and we went back out into the day.

As we saddled the horses in the yard, Zilde came out, blinking in the light. "Will you take a message for me to the inns and villages? Tell them I've a place for an apprentice or two."

"Of course," I said, paying her for my meal.

She nodded her thanks. "Good luck on the road." She lifted a hand in farewell as we swung into the saddles and turned the horses. We scattered chickens and dust as we trotted through the gates and onto the road. The horses, rested and grain fed, wanted to run, but I held Clio back.

"Garth," I said, as soon as we had ridden out of earshot of the inn, "do you think Maya encouraged her girls to leave?"

He reined Tasque in to walk beside me. "No," he said, after some consideration. "She wouldn't. The girls were too young."

We rode on in silence, but the thought nagged at me. Garth had told me what he thought I needed to hear. *He didn't know Maya. But did I?*

The road ran straight south. From the tops of the undulating rises in the land, we could see it gleaming in the winter sun. The days grew steadily shorter until we had a brief eight hours of light in which to ride each day. We stopped at the inns to buy bread or cheese or just to pass on Zilde's request. This made it easier to bring the talk around to Maya and her dreams, and from there to the suggestion of change for us all, since someone always asked what had happened to Zilde's daughters. On the road, and sometimes in the middle of the night, my thoughts returned to the question I had asked Garth. *Had Maya encouraged the girls to leave?*

Late on the afternoon of the sixth day, the clouds that had been building all day released a cold, slicing rain with ice in it. From the last small rise in the land, we saw the smoke of an inn, two miles or so distant. We reined the horses off the icy stones of the road into the grass, riding into the teeth of the wind. By the time we reached the inn, ice coated the horses' manes and our hats, and our bodies shook with cold.

In the yard, I slid off Clio, leading her, on numb feet, through the wide door into the barn, not waiting for the innkeeper or the ostler. Garth followed behind me. I stripped off my sodden gloves and stuffed them into the pockets of my coat, and with stiff fingers worked at the girth. The leather had tightened with the damp, and my fingers stung. I felt helpless, frustrated, and suddenly tired of the road and strange inns and strange people. I missed Casyn. I felt the hot sting of tears behind my eyes. I took a deep breath, leaning my head against Clio's warm neck, ignoring the wet, rubbing my hands together.

"I'll take her," a voice said behind me, "and the gelding. You two get into the inn." I turned to face a woman of about my age. "Go," she said. "I'll take good care of them,"

I handed her the reins. "Thanks," I tried to say, but it came out as a croak. "She's Clio," I managed. The woman nodded.

"Tasque," I heard Garth say behind me. I saw surprise cross her face, and she looked at the grey more closely in the dim light.

"So he is," she said softly. She looked at Garth. "And why you have Captain Dern's horse is a story for the hearthside, when you're warm and have food and drink inside you. Go. I want to hear this story sooner rather than later!"

We stepped out of the doorway into a covered walk. The stable block attached at right angles to another block, which in turn ran at a right angle into the inn itself, creating a three-sided structure surrounding the yard. The covered walk ran along the fronts of all three buildings, the angled roof attached directly to the structure and supported by beams every eight feet or so. I walked gratefully along the dry cobbles, sheltered from the wind.

Inside, apprentices showed us to rooms, bringing hot water and hot drinks. I collapsed on the bed, not caring that I made the quilt wet. I held the mug of tea in my hands letting the warmth seep through. *I want to go home*, I thought. *I want the baths, and the sea, and to be alone.*

Some time later, washed and warmed and in dry clothes, I came down to the common room where a fire burned in the hearth. Rain slashed at the windows.

Two women playing a game—not xache—at the fireside looked up as I came towards the fire. "A nasty day," one said. "I'm Karlii, and this is Sherron. We're from Ballin." Karlii looked about my age, dark and not tall. Sherron bore her a strong resemblance: a sister, or cousin.

"Lena from Tirvan, heading for Karst." I included my destination to try to head off the now-usual reaction to the mention of my village. I didn't want to talk about Maya. Sherron's face lit up.

"I have a sister in Karst. She went to learn to be a wine-maker. Will you pass my greetings on to Hilar of Ballin, and tell her that I am well, and Karlii, and that we ride to Han?"

"I will," I said, "if you will take my greetings to Han, to Grainne of Tirvan, who travelled there after the fighting, and to Rasa and Dian. Tell them I am well, and that Clio is as good a horse as they promised. What takes you there?"

"Sad news. The women who rode to assist us were both killed in the fighting."

I nodded, feeling a pang of grief for Rasa and Dian. "I ride for the same reason," I said. "Our potter was from Karst. She was killed under my command." No one spoke.

Finally, Sherron shook her head. "There must be many of us on the roads, riding to bring sorrow."

"Or reassurance," Karlii said. "We've met one or two women who were going home to see how their families fared, and to show that they were unharmed. We carry messages of safety, too, to send north. We should resurrect the old messenger's guild," she said, smiling, but not, I thought, entirely in jest.

"You like the road?"

"I like not herding cows," Karlii said, making a face.

Sherron laughed. "And I like not making cheese, at least for a while," she said. "That's what we do in Ballin: herd cows, breed cows, milk cows, and make cheese and butter to send to Casilla. I'm a cheese-maker, and generally I like doing so. Karlii chose to be with the animals. The dairy was too confining for her." She smiled at Karlii.

"I thought about apprenticing to the herds and hunt," I said, "but for us it's mostly sheep, and days up on the hills watching for foxes and eagles after the lambs. I liked that part, but I hate sheep, so I apprenticed to the boats instead and learned to fish."

"Boats!" Karlii said. "On the sea?"

I nodded.

"I've never seen the sea," she said longingly.

"I had never seen the grasslands, nor the grape fields, nor Casilla. But I will."

Sherron pushed the draughts board to one side, pointing to the wooden settle. "Shall we sit?" She took a pewter mug from the mantle behind her, pouring me a drink from the jug on the table. I sipped: ale, rich and smooth.

"Thank you." I sat on the bench with one leg tucked under me.

"I have been to Casilla," Sherron said, "to sell cheeses. It's a day's travel from Ballin in the cart. I'm not a good trader, so I only went the once. It was an adventure for a young apprentice, I tell you, travelling the roads, staying at an inn, going to the market. I'd never seen so many people, women and men, in one place."

"Women and men?" I asked. "Was it Festival?"

Sherron shook her head. "No. Casilla is divided into two parts: the women's town and the Empire's quays and barracks and training grounds. The market is in the women's town, but the quartermasters and cooks from the barracks come to buy provisions and supplies. They purchased most of our hard cheeses."

"In Tirvan, we saw men only at Festival, but I remember, Tice—our potter from Karst—saying that they traded regularly with the retirement farms."

"You had men living with you in your village all this past summer, didn't you?"

"Yes. And I travelled south with men. But once the messages have been carried, we will return home. The men are even now returning to their regiments and companies. I have wondered whether life would return to normal."

"I don't want it to," Karlii said passionately. "No one asks each generation if they want to live by the rules of Partition. We must abide by the rules or leave. But even in leaving, we're only trading one village for another, and the rules stay the same. What if I want only to live with one man and bear his children and keep both sons and daughters by my side to raise?" In the firelight, I could see the glint of tears in her eyes. From behind the kitchen door, I heard Garth's voice, and then a woman's sudden laugh.

"My partner chose exile," I said, suddenly irritated, "because she did not want change. To her, the rules were sacred, and in choosing to fight, our village betrayed her. How can we make a world where both you and she are satisfied?"

"I doubt we can," Sherron said. Karlii said nothing. I looked from one to the other.

"But we must try." I took a deep swallow of the ale. "Perhaps," I said quietly, "it's time for a new assembly." Karlii's eyes glinted again in the firelight, but now it was with challenge and interest. "Take that thought north with you," I said, "to Han, and the inns along the way. Speak it quietly and only to women. If enough of us want it, the Emperor must listen."

"Do you really think it's possible?" Karlii asked, hope flickering in her eyes.

"I do," I said, realizing I meant it. "But be subtle, Karlii. Not all women agree."

She nodded thoughtfully. "I believe that."

The next morning dawned sunny, and the ice and snow melted before we had finished breakfast. Sherrin gave me a letter for her sister. I tucked it into my saddlebag then we walked out to the stable together. I introduced them to Garth, who had brought Tasque out onto the cobble to saddle. I tacked up Clio while Sherrin and Karlii did the same with their ponies. The four of us rode out of the courtyard together before taking our leave.

Sherrin turned her pony's head north. "Good luck," she said. "Don't forget that letter."

"I won't. Be careful on the road."

Garth raised a hand in salute, and we turned south.

"Good company?" Garth asked. He had not joined us in the common room.

"They ride to Han, with the same sort of news as I carry to Karst—two dead."

"A difficult duty," he acknowledged. We rode slowly, letting the horses' muscles warm.

"They will speak of a new assembly on their ride north."

"I left you alone last night, in part, because your conversation looked fruitful. My presence would have ended any discussion along those lines."

"What were the other reasons?"

"I thought it would look wrong. I need to behave with propriety, now. There are many officers on the road."

He spoke the truth, yet it rankled. *The world had changed. Why couldn't we all change with it?*

"I suppose," I said, urging Clio forward into a trot.

A few hours later, we came to the end of the grasslands. Soon after leaving the inn, we had seen the land change: outcrops of rocks and patches of marsh became more common, and the grasses grew thinner and shorter. The large rolls of land broke into small hills with shrubby growth in their folds. Broad-leaved plants appeared beside the road. We saw our first trees—oaks, but different from the ones at home. Their pointed leaves hung brown and desiccated. Intermixed with the oaks, we saw other trees, leafless. Under the trees, among the dried leaves, sparse grasses grew.

We came to a track leading east. It had rained recently, and hoof prints pocked the mud of the unpaved road: shod horses, and large. I remembered what Casyn had said on our first day out from Tirvan, of the Emperor's camp at the transition between grasslands and grape fields.

"A hunting party, perhaps," Garth speculated. "Or riders bearing provisions from Karst or Casilla. Those horses were heavily laden and walking. I wouldn't be surprised to meet the like in the miles between here and Karst, and I think the inn tonight will be busy." He caught my look. We had stayed away from inns when the weather was good. "We are done with camping, Lena. The inn we will reach tonight is the last on the road south. After that, farms and villages provide for travellers. Tomorrow, we ride to Karst."

I nodded silently. Our time together, as more than companions on the road, had run out. Tomorrow, we would pick up the threads of our separate lives: he to claim Valle, I to pass my sad tidings to Tice's family and council. From there, Garth would ride to Casilla and *Skua*, and I would go—*where?* I had spoken privately to the innkeeper the previous night. Maya had not stopped there. Nor had Karlii and Sherron seen her at Ballin. If no one at Karst knew of her, I would ride on with Garth to Casilla, but we would be no more than companions on the road. I thought of Karlii and her fierce love for her soldier. Sherron had told me later that he had been one of the men sent to Ballin to train the women. He had left under orders immediately after the battle, but reluctantly. His attachment to Karlii was as strong as hers to him.

I held out my hand to him. He took it.

"I'll miss you," I said. We had become lovers out of grief and loneliness, for comfort, but for me, at least, it had become more. Tali had been right. "I love you, Garth."

"And I you," he said, smiling. "I will never forget our time together." He tightened his grip on my hand, briefly, before releasing it. He leaned forward in his saddle to kiss me. I returned the kiss.

"You have no doubts about Maya?"

"Of course I have doubts," I said, impatiently. "She's planned a whole future in this village of hers, one that I can't be part of. I don't know what she's thinking, but I have to find her."

"And if she says, 'Go away'?"

"Then at least I will know." I did not voice the thought that slid unbidden into my mind: *Then I can go home.*

An hour later, we met a hunting party riding north. The packhorses carried deer carcasses, gutted and bled. We reined to a halt. As Garth rode forward to speak with the leader, I waited, letting Clio relax. Garth pulled his papers from his saddlebags, offering them to the other man, who shook his head. He gestured to me, and I rode forward. The older man's tunic bore the insignia of a captain.

"Captain," I said. "I am Lena, from Tirvan."

"Martin," he said, offering his hand, "from the twelfth. That's a good Han pony you're riding—a good choice for a long ride. I know who you are. I was in Casilla a week past, and Captain Dern asked me to look out for you on the road. You've taken good care of his horse, Watch-Commander."

"Did Dern have news for us?" I asked.

"No, just asked me to look out for you. He told me you both acquitted yourselves very well in the fighting. Did you meet anyone else on the road?"

"We rode with General Casyn," Garth answered, "and met the Majors Bren and Turlo. They joined us, but left us at the grasslands road."

"They hadn't arrived when I left for Casilla two weeks back," Martin said. "I'll be glad to see Turlo. He always brightens up a camp." He glanced up at the sun. "We must ride. I'll let General Casyn know I've seen you. Good luck to you both."

"Sir," Garth said, formally, saluting.

We allowed the laden pack animals and the rest of the hunting party to pass. Garth watched them for a minute.

"I wonder what Dern told him."

"About you?"

"Yes." He urged Tasque back to the road, and I fell in beside him.

"Well," I said, trying to be practical, "he must have said something of what you did. Otherwise, where have you been for the last five years?"

"Turlo told me to look men in the eye, answer civilly, and never lose my temper. There have been rumours about him all his life. His red hair tells of his northern blood, and he probably has been sent to spy north of the wall because of it, which makes his loyalties suspect to some."

"Turlo is well-loved," I said. "You heard what Martin said just then."

"Yes, but Turlo is known. I'm an unknown young officer with a questionable past."

"As Turlo was once, too," I argued. "It will be all right, Garth. You have the trust of Casyn, and by extension the Emperor. That must count for something."

"I suppose," he said, falling silent. He looked troubled. I too felt uneasy, disturbed by our earlier conversation and the thoughts it had engendered. I craved solitude, not the crowds and conversations tonight's inn promised.

The inn was indeed bustling. Our horses shared a box stall, and the apprentice showed me to a room in which two people had already stowed their coats and saddlebags. The beds, a washstand, and some hooks on the wall comprised all the furnishings, save the rush matting on the floor. The apprentice brought hot water so I could wash. I was drying my hands when the door opened and two women came in. We smiled hello. After retrieving something from a saddlebag, they left again. I ran a comb through my hair. It needed cutting. I put the comb away to go down to the common room.

Only women occupied the tables and benches. The men had a separate room. Here in the south, where villages and farms crowded closer together, and with regular traffic on the road between Casilla and the Emperor's camp, custom kept men and women apart. Voices and bodies filled the room. I went to the serving bar to order ale and food. When it came, I paid, then made my way to an empty place at the far end of a table. My roommates sat at the opposite end. They each raised a hand in greeting but made no effort to include me in the conversation. I ate my stew, listening.

I heard talk of crops and herds, of a good year for wine, of births and deaths. Women bet on a dice game at a table behind me, and someone played a stringed instrument of some kind in the far corner, quietly and without accompaniment. I thought of the map Casyn had drawn for me, trying to picture this inn. As far as I could remember, it sat at the hub of several roads, leading out to a semi-circle of villages—Ballin, Karst, two or three others. When I finished my food, I turned slightly to watch the dice game behind me. It seemed friendly, with much laughter and joking. One of the women looked up. "D'you want to join us?"

I shook my head. "I've never played. May I just watch?"

"Sure," she answered. "But where are you from, that you've never thrown the dice?"

"Tirvan."

"Well, isn't that something. I go my whole life without meeting anyone from Tirvan, and then I meet two women in a month. It's a long trip south. What brings you here?"

"I have business in Karst. This other woman from Tirvan, was her name Maya?" My voice sounded odd to my ears.

"That sounds right. What's your business in Karst, if you don't mind me asking? That's where I live. I'm Daria," she added, extending her hand to me. She was middle aged, dark-skinned like Tice, with greying, cropped hair. As we shook, I tried to order my thoughts.

"I must take my message to the head of the council."

"That's Anya," she said. She gave me a long look. "It'll be bad news, then." She closed her eyes, briefly. "I hadn't heard of any of us going so far north. I won't press you, child. I'll know soon enough."

"Please, when did you see Maya? And where?"

Daria stood, handing the dice to another player. "Keep my spot warm," she said, sliding onto the bench across from me. "A couple of weeks back, in Torrey. It's a village to the west where the river broadens out into marshland." I remembered that Danel, Freya's love, had come from Torrey. "They weave baskets there, and we buy them to hold the grapes at harvest. I'd ridden over to place an order for next year."

"Do you think she's still there?"

She shook her head. "I know she's not. We travelled a bit together the next day, but it's hard to ride to the pace of a group walking, so I left them after a while. She was going to see the Emperor. She said she wants her own village, she and her friends. Did you know?"

"Yes," I said. *Going to see the Emperor*. I realized Daria had asked me a question. "Sorry. What did you say?"

"D'you agree with her? About the village?"

"I don't know."

"Can't see what harm it would do, myself," Daria said. She stood up. "You ride to Karst tomorrow?" I nodded. "I've another day's business here, but I'll be there the following day. It's about four hours in the saddle if you're easy on the horse. Look for the bell tower and the hall. That's where most will be around mid-day, sharing a meal. Now," she called to her fellow dicer, "hand them over." She returned to her game.

I sat, feeling tears prick my eyes. Gradually, my thoughts cleared. *Tomorrow, I would ride to Karst to deliver my news. I would stay one night, then ride north again.* If the weather held, and I pushed Clio, I could be there in two days, three nights. I had to tell Garth.

"Daria," I said, urgency in my voice. She looked up. "I need to speak to one of the men. I don't know what is done here."

She gestured toward the serving bar with her head. "Tell Fryth who you need to speak to, and she'll get him. There's a room between the two common rooms where you can talk,"

"Thanks," I said. I crossed the room and caught Fryth's eye. "I need to speak with Watch-Commander Garth. Could you fetch him?"

"Aye, that I will. Wait in there." She pointed to a space opening from the servery. The door that adjoined the men's common room was closed. A bench stood against one wall, but I could not sit. I paced the small space until Garth entered.

"Maya has gone to the Emperor's camp," I said without preamble. "Two weeks ago. "

"Then she'll still be there." A mix of emotions crossed his face. "And I won't see her," he said quietly. I looked at him, shocked. I had not thought of this.

"Oh, Garth."

He shook his head. "But you will, and you'll know what to say to her, of me." He hesitated. "Do you want me to take word of Tice to Karst, so you can leave for the camp tomorrow?"

"No," I said, reluctantly. "Tice's death is my responsibility, and the news is mine to bear. But I won't linger in Karst, though I will be with you, if you want, when you claim Valle. I would like to meet him." I saw him relax, infinitesimally.

"I'd hoped you would be there," he said. In the half-light, I could not read his eyes. I wanted to put my arms around him. A burst of laughter came from the soldier's side. "I better go," he said.

I went back to my table, picking up my half-full mug of ale. I remembered a bench, outside, and found my way there in the cold night. No clouds obscured the sky. The stars glittered. I sat on the bench, drawing my knees up for warmth. I found the bear and then the north star. I could follow them home. So could any who had apprenticed to the boats. I had heard fireside tales about the different stars in distant lands. *If you travelled far enough, how did you find your way home?*

I shivered as the night's chill seeped into me. I went back inside to mount the stairs to my room. Stowing my saddlebags under my bed, I stripped down to my shirt and pulled back the covers. The blankets, woven of good wool, warmed me, and I gave myself to their comfort and to the oblivion of sleep.

CHAPTER EIGHTEEN

I SLEPT DEEPLY, NOT STIRRING even when my roommates came to bed. I woke when the first hint of light showed in the eastern sky. The morning star shone above the horizon. I dressed quietly and picked up my saddlebags.

Downstairs, Fryth was already at work at the servery. "The Watch-Commander is up, too," she said. "There's bread and cheese for you here and a mug of tea. Drink that, at least. It'll be cold on the road this early."

I thanked her, giving her the coins for the night's lodging and my breakfast. I sipped the hot, sweet tea carefully, feeling its warmth spreading inside me. I folded the bread around the cheese and took a bite, then stuffed it in my tunic pocket. I could eat on the road. I drank down the remaining tea, ignoring the heat.

"Good luck to you," Fryth said, turning back to her cooking fire.

I picked up the saddlebags, going out to the stables where the horses, saddled and waiting, snorted in the cold air. I pulled on my riding coat and gloves, then swung the saddlebags up and secured them. Garth emerged from the stable.

"Ready?" Awakening sparrows chirped in the eaves of the stable.

"Ready," I answered, though my mind shied from what the day would bring. We mounted and clattered out of the stable yard. The wide, paved road ran south from the inn to where two narrower roads branched off.

We took the westerly road at an easy pace until the sun rose high enough to melt the frost off the paving stones. I nibbled at my bread and cheese. Here and there, I could see the work of woodcutters. The road began to slope downward, snaking into a series of switchbacks. We turned a corner and stopped.

Below us, the forest gave way to fields, each planted with precise, parallel rows of trellised vines. Dirt tracks ran between the fields, houses, and outbuildings scattered among them. Smoke rose from the houses, and in the far distance, I spotted a larger building with a tower: the central meeting hall. Beyond that were more fields, and then a shimmer at the horizon: the sea. The sea. I looked away, back to the neatly ordered land, and the memory came to me of the grace and precision of Tice dancing.

We urged the horses to a canter as we passed the rows of grapes. A few were neatly pruned and tied, but the majority grew thick, hanging loosely over the trellises. Winter work, I remembered Tice telling me. We came to a house with a workshop beside it. The air smelled of freshly cut wood from a row of newly-manufactured barrels lined up outside the building.

A woman came out, her clothes powdered with sawdust. "Strangers!" she said. "I thought you might be Daria, although I couldn't think who the second horse would be. What can I do for you?"

I introduced us. "We have business in Karst. What is the way to the meeting hall? I must speak with your council leader—Anya."

She nodded. "Keep on this road until it forks then go right. At a canter, you'll be there before noon. Anya will be there." She looked at us both. "I'll expect to hear the meeting bell this afternoon. Would you like water before you ride on?"

We let the horses drink and accepted water ourselves without dismounting. The cooper handed us mugs with the same economy of movement that Tice had had. I drank the cold water and handed the mug back. We reined the horses back to the road.

The sun was high when we reached the hall—a low building, built of silvered wood on a stone foundation, with a bell tower rising high from the centre. A porch ran around the front and sides, covered with twining grapevines. Trees I did not recognize, gnarled and bent, grew to one side.

We dismounted. The horses sidestepped nervously, reacting to our tension. I stroked Clio's neck, damping down my jitters to calm my horse. A girl of nine or ten came running from inside the hall, stopping when she saw us.

"Is Anya within?" I asked her. She nodded. "Can you hold our horses while we go to speak with her?" She nodded again and came forward, holding out her hand for the horses to sniff. She stroked their muzzles. When I believed them to be calm, I handed her the reins. "This is Clio, and this is Tasque. They will stand for you, or you can walk them up and down, if you like." She took the reins, leading the horses towards the back of the hall. We went inside.

I had been expecting dark, but the hall swam with light from a series of windows high in the walls above the porch roof. Long tables ran across the room, and fireplaces took up most of the walls. Several women readied food at the far end. They looked up as we walked across the hall. One woman, grey-haired and tall, walked forward.

"I am Anya, Council Leader. Are you looking for me?"

"Yes," I said, meeting her brown eyes. "I am Lena, from Tirvan in the north. This is Garth, of *Skua*, who fought with us there. May we speak with you?"

"Privately?" I nodded. I saw her face tighten. "There is an office through here," she said, indicating a door to our right. "Please come."

Inside was a long table, covered with papers, two chairs, and a bench. Anya closed the door behind us. "Please sit," she said. She took the chair behind the table. Garth sat on the bench, leaning forward, tension in every line of his body. I sat on the edge of the other chair, my heart pounding. Anya looked at me. "This is not good news you bring."

"No," I said. I thought of my mother, instructing Kira on how to deliver bad news. *Be direct,* she had said. *Be honest.* "Our village potter died in the fighting. She was from Karst, and her name was Tice." Anya closed her eyes and was silent for a long moment.

"How did she die?"

"I was her Cohort-Leader," I said. "She was my cohort-second. After the main battle, some invaders were unaccounted for. I sent her to patrol alone, and she was stabbed." I swallowed hard. "I made a mistake, and it cost Tice her life. She was my friend." I waited. Anya's expression did not change.

"I am glad she found a village to take her in and a friend," she said. "Were you friend enough to know her story?"

I nodded. Garth looked extraordinarily calm.

"I am part of that story," he said. "I am Valle's father, and I come to formally acknowledge him."

Anya looked startled. "Tice told us the father was Lestian trader."

"She knew me as Kirthan. I was a spy for the Empire. I have a letter from my captain in my saddlebags to confirm this if you wish to see it. That afternoon, I thought Tice was going to uncover a message I had left, a message of significant import to the safety of the Empire. I offered her wine, instead, and myself. I didn't think of the possibility of a child."

Anya bowed her head for a moment and sighed. Then she looked up. "I will see that letter. I don't doubt you, but others will, so it's best that I have read it. I ask that you speak of this to no one until I have met with the rest of the council. You too, Lena," she added. "I'll tell Tice's mother and sisters myself this afternoon. The others will have guessed there is bad news, but Tice is not the only woman from this village to have sought a different life in the last years. I will call meeting tonight, so all may know. I'll ask you to speak then, if you will."

Garth cleared his throat then spoke in a firm voice. "I swore to make redress for my wrongs, where I could. Tice died before I knew of Valle. She tried to kill me."

"Was she trying to kill you or an invader?"

"Tice recognized him and called him by his Lestian name. I stopped her because I also recognized him." Anya raised an eyebrow. *Like Tice.* "His sister is my partner, and they look enough alike to be twins."

Anya returned her gaze to Garth. "Valle has your eyes. What redress would you make, soldier?"

"Whatever I can," he said, "beyond simply claiming the child. What would you have me do, council leader?" I heard the thread of anger in his voice, remembering that first night, so many weeks ago, when he had responded to his mother's insinuation of treason with the same controlled fire. *Maya has the same steel within her.*

Anya nodded, once. "Go now," she said, "and see to your horses. There is a paddock on the far side of the hall. Come back into the hall through the stables, and you'll find yourself in the kitchens. I'll find you a place to eat and wait. I think it's best if you do not mix with the village yet."

We did as she asked, walking silently back through the bright hall with the eyes of the women upon us. The horses, already unsaddled, cropped grass in the paddock, their tack hanging neatly on the fence. The child had disappeared.

"You seemed very calm," I said.

"As did you. But we still have Tice's family to face and the meeting tonight." He looked around. "It's so ordered. Tamed. It reminds me of Leste. No land is wasted."

He had never spoken of Leste before. I did not know how to respond, but he did not seem to expect a reply. He took his saddle and bridle off the fence. "Let's find the stables." I picked up my tack to follow him.

We found our way to a tack room, and then through the dark stable, down a hall to the kitchen where Anya waited for us. She took us to another room, with a table and chairs, bringing us food: wine, fish stew, bread, soft cheese, and small, wizened fruit I did not recognize. Then she left us. I took a mouthful of the stew. It was rich with chunks of a white-fleshed fish and shellfish and onion.

I could taste a spice I couldn't name. I ate hungrily, wiping the bowl clean with crusty bread to get the last drops. I put the bowl to one side and reached for the fruit. I bit into one, tentatively: sweet, and chewy. "What is this?"

"A fig. There were trees outside."

"It's sweet," I said. I spread some cheese on the bread. Sherron had said the hard cheeses went to the army, mostly. Garth stood to look out the small window. He had eaten his stew but nothing else. I could see the tension in his shoulders. "Have some wine."

He shook his head without turning. I poured some for myself. It was a pale golden colour, the colour of the winter grasslands. Above us, a bell tolled, three deep rings, then a pause, then three more.

Garth moved away from the window. "I feel helpless. All those weeks of riding and now to sit here in this little room, waiting."

"There's nothing else we can do," I said, looking around. I spotted a box sitting on a shelf and reached for it. "I'm wrong. We can play *xache*." Garth shrugged.

"Why not? It will pass the time." Garth poured himself some wine, and we tossed. He won, and we began the ritualized game, designed,

Casyn had told me, to teach men to think of war in terms of tactics and consequences, and of acceptable loss.

I had conceded one game and was winning the second when Anya returned. "Tice's mother and sisters are here. Before you see them, it is only fair I tell you a few things." She sighed. "Tamar, Tice's mother, is a woman of strong views and considerable pride. She was Council Leader for many years before the illness in her joints made it too difficult for her. When she learned Tice was pregnant, she became very angry. She forbade communication between Tice and her two sisters, and she would not see the child, nor Tice, even to say goodbye."

"How could she be so cruel?" I said, shocked.

"As I said, she is a woman of considerable pride. She saw Tice's pregnancy as a source of shame." Anya spoke with studied neutrality.

"Then who will raise Valle?" Garth said suddenly. "Is that not a sister's role, or a grandmother's?"

"Usually," Anya admitted. "Would you take him, Lena?"

"Me?" I tried to think. "How could I? I am going back on the road to find my partner. I can't take a small child with me."

"But once you find her?" Anya asked.

"I don't know." I took a breath, willing myself to calm. "If I am needed, I will come back for him as soon as I can and take him home with me to Tirvan."

"I am sure," Anya said, "that we can make arrangements for him here for a while if we need to. You might also take him to Casilla. Tevra, who was Tice's partner, might have him."

"Are we to pass him around, like a wineskin?" Garth said angrily. "This is ridiculous. Better he stays where he is than shove him from one place to another, never knowing where he belongs. I will not acknowledge him unless I know he will be taken care of."

"I will take him," I said firmly, "and keep him with me until he is seven if there is no one in Tice's family who will." I would think later about how I could do this, and what it might mean, for Maya and me.

We followed Anya out into the hall. At the fireplace at the far end, two women stood beside an older, seated woman with a cane across her knees. I judged Tice's sisters to be both older and younger than Tice. The older looked nearly thirty and the younger more or less my age. Tice had never spoken of them.

Tamar had a face that spoke of pain. Deep lines ran from her nose to the edges of her mouth. She regarded us levelly but made no gesture of greeting. Her daughters nodded slightly. The younger of the two had reddened eyes.

"Tamar, Joce, Ianthe" Anya began, "this is Lena, of Tirvan, who was Cohort-Leader and friend to Tice. And this is Garth, Watch-Commander of *Skua*." She turned to us. "Tamar is Tice's mother, Joce and Ianthe her sisters. Shall we sit?" It was not a request. We sat.

"Tell me how my daughter died," Tamar said, her voice cold.

"With respect," I said, hesitating, "I think you need to hear Garth first. Ours are not separate stories, and it begins here, with the begetting of Valle."

Tamar made a small pinched movement of her mouth. Her eyes flicked to Anya, and then to her daughters. Ianthe—the younger sister—made a small gesture with her hands.

Garth told them the bare facts, unadorned with reason or excuse. The women listened without interrupting until he told them of the meeting at Jedd's farm, and his need to keep Tice from the intelligence hidden in the rafters of the barn.

"Watch-Commander," Tamar said, "I knew my daughter's anger and wilfulness all too well. She made a choice, too, with the knowledge that a child could well be conceived. I cannot condone your actions, but I understand why you acted as you did. Why Tice did, I will never know." Her voice remained expressionless. Garth did not respond.

I wished I did not have to tell this cold woman anything. I glanced at the sisters. Ianthe fought tears, so I looked at her as I spoke. "I didn't know why Tice had come to Tirvan, except that we needed a potter. I didn't know her well until this past summer. She kept herself apart. When I was chosen Cohort-Leader, I chose her as my cohort-second, so that she could teach us to move the way she did. She handled a knife as if she had held one all her life." Ianthe smiled, slightly.

"We became friends. She told me of Valle, and how he was fathered. She told me she had acted out of jealousy and anger towards her lover who had had a child the year before." At that, Ianthe sobbed audibly, and Joce put her hand on her arm. Tamar did not move. I steeled myself for the next part.

"After the fighting, all but a few of the invaders were captured or had surrendered. Tice and I were patrolling for the few who still roamed the village when we saw Garth. She named him as Kirthan, and threw her knife to kill him. I had also recognized him, so I deflected the knife. He looks very much like his sister, my partner, Maya, who had left Tirvan in the spring. We took him captive," I stopped, swallowed. "And then I made a terrible mistake. Rather than argue with her about whether to kill Garth, I sent her back on patrol. She was angry and upset, and I should not have done so. She was stabbed in the back, distracted, no doubt, by her anger. I take responsibility. I am so very sorry."

Only the muffled sobbing of Ianthe broke the silence. Garth shifted beside me. Finally, Tamar spoke. "You have done your duty," she said. "For that, I thank you." She started to stand, Joce immediately supporting her.

"Wait!" Garth said. "My son, Valle. What of him?"

"He is nothing to me. Come, Joce, Ianthe. I wish to rest." She began to move away, Joce at her elbow. Ianthe turned to follow, and then stopped.

She stepped away from her sister and mother. "I will raise him," she said. "I will raise Valle if you acknowledge him, Watch-Commander." I felt a wave of relief, followed by an odd pang of disappointment.

"Not in my house, Ianthe," Tamar said. "I forbid it." Then she turned, to walk slowly away. Her footsteps, and those of Joce, and the slow tap of Tamar's cane echoed in the hall.

We stood silently until the doors had closed behind them. Anya spoke first.

"Are you sure, Ianthe?"

"Yes." Her voice wavered, but she swallowed, straightening her shoulders. "I am. I won't let my mother's pride sacrifice a child's future." She smiled. "He is a lovely child, Watch-Commander. I see him occasionally, when I have a reason to be at Jedd's farm. He doesn't know I am his aunt, of course."

"You are welcome at my cottage, Ianthe, you and Valle." She made a face. "Tamar won't approve, but I am Council Leader. It's my decision."

"How can I help?" Garth asked.

"Come to us at Festival, if you can, to be with him," Anya said. "Anything else would set him apart even more. There will be whispers and gossip, but we'll do our best to counter that. And we'll talk to him of you, so that he can brag of his brave father, as all the small boys do."

Garth smiled. "For all I did not want to be a soldier, I remember telling the others what a great fighter my father was." He sobered. "What will you tell him of his mother?"

"That she was my sister, and I loved her, and that she died in the fighting," Ianthe said. "And I'll show him her pots."

"Tell him she danced," I said. "To music, and with a sword, and both were beautiful."

"I believe that," Ianthe said.

"I had best send a message to the farm," Anya said, briskly. "We'll need Valle here, tomorrow morning, for the claiming ceremony. Ianthe, will you go?"

"Yes, of course," she said eagerly.

"Wait just a moment, and I'll write it. Lena, I was going to have you lodge with me tonight, but now I think Ianthe will need the bed. Old Ione keeps beds for men who come on business and for messengers. I'd already arranged for Garth to stay with her, and she will find a bed for you, too. Let me get this note written, and I'll take you there." She disappeared into the office.

"Ianthe," I said, before Garth could speak. "You don't have to do this and estrange yourself from your family. I will raise Valle, either here, or back in my home village."

"No," she said firmly. "Thank you, Lena, but no. He is my sister's child. I loved her, and I owe this to her. I'm used to my mother's ways, and Joce isn't as distant as she seems. She'll find ways to see me and Valle." She smiled. "You'll always be welcome if you wish to visit, to tell Valle of his mother's time in the north."

"I'd like that."

Anya reappeared with a sealed note in her hand, which she gave to Ianthe before turning to us. "Follow me."

Old described Ione well. I judged her to be eighty, at least. Our rooms—on different floors—were sparsely furnished, but the sheets smelled of lavender and sunshine, and the scrubbed floors shone. We fetched our own water from the well for washing, at Anya's quiet suggestion.

I shook out my cleanest clothes and washed in the cool water. The soap smelled of lavender too. I realized I would have no opportunity to talk to Garth before dinner, and that thought did not altogether displease me. I needed time to think about how I had felt when Ianthe said she would raise Valle. I understood why I was relieved, but why was I also disappointed?

I let the thought sit in my mind, not trying to find an answer. I dried myself with a towel that was old but neatly mended, and dressed. I brushed my hair and hung up my riding clothes. I would need them again tomorrow. *If I had stayed for Valle, then I would not be leaving tomorrow. I might never have seen Maya again. Maybe that would have been best.*

"Why?" I said out loud. I sat on the bed for a while, waiting, but no answer came. I lay down, drifting into sleep and jumbled snatches of dreams until the meeting bell rang across the fields.

Nearly a hundred women crowded the meeting hall, sitting in rows of benches arranged along the long axis of the room, facing east. Anya and two other women—both also olive-skinned, with grey in their hair—stood under the windows, conferring. Tamar sat in a high armchair to one side, a concession to her illness, I guessed, with Joce beside her. I did not see Ianthe.

When Anya saw us enter, she motioned us to a bench against the wall. "Sit here," she said as we approached. "Mikelle, Roxine, this is Lena of Tirvan, and Garth, Watch-Commander of *Skua*. Mikelle and Roxine are council leaders." Each woman took our hands in both of theirs, smiling a greeting. Their hands felt dry and cool; mine were damp with sweat and nervousness.

We sat with a hundred pairs of eyes on us. I tried not to look at the floor. Garth scanned the room then turned his attention to the council leaders. I did the same.

"Women of Karst," Anya called. Voices stilled.

"Women of Karst," Anya said again, her voice quieter. "Our guests have brought news." She turned to us. "Please stand, so all may see you." We complied. I looked out over the rows of women, but the brightness of the western windows made it hard to see faces. "Lena, of Tirvan village, and Garth, Watch-Commander of *Skua*, have ridden south with news of one of our women." Anya said levelly. "It is sad news they bring, although not entirely. You may sit," she said to us.

"Tice, daughter of Tamar and sister to Joce and Ianthe, was killed during the invasion of Tirvan," Anya said. A wave of voices spread across the room. One woman slipped off the bench to go to Joce and Tamar, kneeling to take Tamar's hands. Tamar shook her head. The woman rose to speak to Joce, reaching out to her. Joce stepped away from the embrace.

Anya continued. "She was stabbed, on night patrol. I am told she died quickly."

"Has word been sent to my sister, in Casilla?" The woman who had gone to Tamar and Joce asked.

"Not yet, Tevian," Anya answered. "The Watch-Commander rides there to join his ship in a few days. I had hoped he would take the letter, although I had not yet asked him. Unless you wish to go to Tevra yourself?"

"I wish I could," Tevian said, "but as you know my babe still needs the breast, and she's too sickly to withstand the ride to Casilla." She turned to Garth. "Will you take the letter, Watch-Commander?"

"Of course," Garth said. He sounded older, as if in the last days he had grown into his new roles: officer of the Empire, father.

"The Watch-Commander," Anya said to the room, "supported the defence of Tirvan. The ship on which he serves has sailed from there with the Lestian prisoners, but he sought his captain's permission to ride south with Lena. He, too, brings a message. While disguised as a man of Leste, and on the Emperor's service, he fathered Tice's child, Valle." Faces reflected surprise, disbelief, shock. Voices rose.

"What?'

"No!"

Anya raised a hand for silence. The room obeyed. Like Gille, she commanded respect. "The webs the goddess weaves brought them together again at Tirvan, long enough for this to be confirmed. He has come to acknowledge his son."

Chatter broke out again. Eventually Anya raised a hand again, asking for quiet.

"Who will raise him?" Tevian asked.

"I will," Ianthe said. She had been standing at one end of the hall, beside the fireplace, hidden in the shadows. "I have told the Watch-Commander—Garth—and my mother and sister. I will take Valle. The claiming ceremony will be tomorrow morning. We will live with Anya." As she spoke, she walked into the light of the room. I could see her trembling even from my distance. *Brave,* I thought. *So brave.*

"Bring him to me when you need to," Tevian said. "He's nearly of an age with my Kinley. They can play together." She strode over to Ianthe to hug her, murmuring something too quietly for anyone but Ianthe to hear.

"Women of Karst!" Anya called, pulling attention away from Ianthe and Tevian. "You have heard the news. Meeting is over. There is tea, of course, but please respect that Lena and Garth have ridden a very long way and are tired. For those who wish to witness, the claiming ceremony will be two hours after dawn."

We all rose. Mikelle and Roxine walked over to us, smiling.

"Thank you," Roxine said, "sounds quite inadequate, for what you have both done."

"What have we done?" Garth asked quietly. "Valle will have a different life, yes, and a father, but what of Ianthe? She's lost both her mother and her sister."

"I think," Mikelle said, "that perhaps Valle has provided the reason for Ianthe to leave her mother's house." She spoke slowly, choosing her words with care. "Do not worry for her, Watch-Commander, not on that front, at least. She and your son will be safe with Anya, and most of the village, even Joce, in her way, will support them, as we do with all our children."

"All your legitimate children," Garth said. Mikelle inclined her head, accepting the statement.

"Yes," she said. "But that isn't our choice. Had the child been a girl, Tice could have kept her. What does a village do with a fatherless boy who has no place in the Empire's armies?"

"I do not know," Garth said heavily. "Forgive me, Mikelle. I didn't mean to give offense."

"I took none," she said. She laughed. "Council leaders are thicker-skinned than that, Watch-Commander. Now, would you both like tea?"

A few minutes later, I had a mug of tea in my hand and a group of women about my age around me. I expected questions about Tice, but these women had other interests.

"Would you tell us of Tirvan?" one of them asked shyly.

"With pleasure," I said, relieved. I could handle this. "Not that there's a lot to tell. We are a northern village, but I suppose you know that. There is Berge, close to the Wall, and then Skeld, and Delle, and Tirvan. All are coastal villages, so we fish. I had a boat," I said, "with my partner. Many women fish, but others tend the herds—sheep, and some cows—weave, or work in wood or metal. We're isolated, so we must be masters of all trades."

"How big is your village?"

"About forty houses," I said. "And the barns and stables and workshops, and the docks and fish sheds. The village fans out from the harbour up into the hills." I thought of the sea I had glimpsed today, and a sharp pang of homesickness assailed me. "It's very beautiful in the spring when the meadows are in flower, and in the autumn, when the heather blooms."

"Who came to you, to ask you to fight?" a slightly older woman asked.

"Casyn," I said. "He is a general, but he was born in Tirvan. I think that was the way of things."

"Yes," the older woman said. "The man who came to us, Rolan, was born here. He is Anya's brother. I wondered if that had been the case everywhere."

"We were lucky," the older woman went on. "We lost no one. The defence was easier than you might think. We're bordered on the south, where the land meets the sea, by sheer cliffs of chalk, nearly impossible to climb. We concentrated our defences at the harbours, with riders moving between. Other cohorts guarded the roads to Casilla and to the Four-Ways Inn. We attacked from above, with arrows and spears, and burned their boats. They surrendered quickly." The older woman spoke with calm precision, and, I thought, deep passion.

"Were you a Cohort-Leader?" I asked.

"Yes," she said. "As you were, from what I have heard."

There is talk, I thought. *Of course there is.* "Yes. Our tactics were very similar, but we lost four women."

"Would you do it again?"

"Oh, Halle," someone said impatiently, "Do you have to bring this up now? I want to hear about the north. I want to hear about snow."

"If you mean, would I defend my village again, and in a leader's role," I said slowly, "then, yes. But I have no love for fighting and less for killing."

"But now we know we can, if we must," she said quietly, "and we can wield weapons and think tactically. Can we forget this, to go quietly back to what our lives were before?"

"Most of us will," I said. The younger women listened, their eyes flicking between us.

"But not all," she said. "I'm Halle," the older woman said. "May we speak in the morning, before you leave? Anya will tell you where to find me."

"If you like." She unsettled me. In truth, I did not want to speak with her again, but could think of no way to refuse her. I crossed over to where Garth sat with Tevian and Ianthe.

Together, we walked out into the starry night. A warm wind blew from the south. I could smell the hint of salt from the ocean. Bats flew and chattered overhead, hunting insects.

"The *siraca*," Tevian said. "The wind from the south. It's never winter here, or not for long. Tomorrow will be glorious."

CHAPTER NINETEEN

THE DAY WAS GLORIOUS, INDEED. Two hours past dawn, I walked outside without my coat, marvelling at the warmth of the breeze against my skin. At home, the peaks above the village would have been white for weeks now, the ponds frozen. Snow might even be forcing us to spread ashes on the pathways and resort to brooms to keep porches and doorsteps clean. Fires would burn day and night in the houses. Here, it smelled like spring, with the winter solstice still more than a week away.

I had awoken early after a night of deep and exhausted sleep. I crept out to the pump, hoping I would not disturb Ione, to wash my hair under the cold stream. By the time I took a bucket back to my room, bathed, and dressed, the sun had risen.

I stood at my window, letting my hair dry, watching the sun light the rows of vines, dyeing them pink, creating long shadows. I heard Ione rise and go out to the kitchen; I heard Garth come downstairs and then go back up. A while later he came down again. A bird called, a squeaky mix of notes. I watched a hare lope along the edge of the field. The breeze carried the faint smell of the sea.

I found my comb, tidied my now-dry hair, and went out to the kitchen. Ione drank tea at the table.

"Th' wa'ch commander's gone," she said. She had no upper teeth in front, so she slurred some words. "A' th' hall."

"I'm going there as well, but I'll come back later to change and pack. Should I pay you now or later?"

She shook her head. "No char'e. Tice was my gran'-niece. No charge, for ei'er of you."

I nodded, my heart in my throat. "I'll give the coins to Ianthe, then, for Valle." I offered. She smiled, showing her gapped teeth.

"Tha's good."

At the hall, Garth stood speaking to Ianthe and Anya. A dozen or so women sat on the benches, Tevian among them. Mikelle and Roxine came in just after me.

"Lena, good morning," Anya said. "Will you stand as witness this morning?"

"Yes." A claiming ceremony needed three witnesses. I wondered who the other two were.

"Do you know the words?"

"I think so. I've attended claiming ceremonies before, but never stood as witness. In Tirvan, after the mother states the father's name, the witnesses state their names and that they have witnessed. Is it different here?"

"No," Anya said. "Ianthe will speak in Tice's stead, and I'll leave your witnessing to last, so you can hear the others speak. Is that all right?"

"Yes," I said. "We always do the father's witness last in Tirvan."

Outside, hooves clopped on the path. Anya went to the door to open it. A tall man, not heavy, but soft-looking, came in carrying a small boy. I heard a soft gasp from Ianthe. The child did not cry, but he had one thumb firmly clamped in his mouth. The man handed the boy to Anya before bending to kiss the child's forehead.

"You are his father?" he addressed Garth with an undercurrent of challenge.

"I am," Garth said mildly.

"I am Alister," the man said, "under-steward at the farm owned by the General Jedd."

"You have helped to raise my son till now?"

"We all have. He's a good boy, and clever." He glanced over at Valle, but the child had burrowed his head into Anya's shoulder. She rocked him, murmuring.

"Then I owe you my deepest thanks," Garth said. "I am Garth, Watch-Commander of *Skua*, and if there is ever anything I can do for you, I will, if it is in my power." He extended a hand to Alister, who took it, looking mildly surprised. They shook. Alister took one last look at Valle, inclined his head to us, and left.

Anya came forward, carrying the boy. Valle raised his head, looking at us doubtfully, still sucking his thumb. His skin glowed olive, and his hair curled tightly around his scalp like his mother's, but Anya had spoken truly: his eyes were Garth's.

"That was well done," Anya said to Garth. "Valle, this is your father. Can you say hello?"

He shook his head, turning his face back to Anya's shoulder. He said something.

"Valle?" Anya said. "Tell me again?"

He looked up at her. "No father," he said. He looked ready to cry.

"Is that what they told you? They were wrong, Valle, but only because they didn't know. This man is your father. His name is Garth. He's been away a long time, but now he's come to see you. Say hello."

Valle looked at Garth. "Tholdier?"

"Yes," Garth said, smiling. "I'm a soldier. Would you like to ride on my shoulders?"

"Yeth," Valle said, holding out his arms. Garth took him, swinging him up on his shoulders. I remembered him picking Pel up the same way. Valle laughed, putting his hands in Garth's hair. Garth looked up at his son and grinned, his face suddenly alight.

You are not, I told myself sternly, *going to be jealous of a child.*

"Are we ready?" Anya asked.

"Yes," he said.

We arranged ourselves in a half-circle, facing Anya.

"We are here this morning," Anya began, "to witness the claiming of this child, Valle, by his father, Garth of *Skua*, soldier of the Empire." She smiled. "While it is usual for the child to be present, and often for the father to hold him, it is not usually on his shoulders. But no matter. We will continue." She handed Garth a piece of paper. "Garth of *Skua*, please read the words written here, and, if you agree, speak them to us all." Garth unfolded the paper awkwardly, balancing Valle with one hand and skimmed it. Then he nodded.

"I, Garth of *Skua*, son of Mar of the Seventh and Tali of Tirvan," he said clearly, "acknowledge this child, Valle, to be mine, borne by Tice of Karst. He will be raised by his aunt, Ianthe of Karst, until he is seven, and then I or my proxies will send for him, to serve the Empire."

Ianthe stepped forward, smiling up at Valle. "I, Ianthe of Karst, in proxy for my deceased sister Tice, daughter to Tamar of Karst and to Theron of *Petrel*, recognize that Garth of *Skua* is father to this child and has acknowledged him. I will raise him to know his father, and his duty to the Empire, and prepare him to serve it." Her voice caught slightly at Tice's name, but her words rang clearly in the hall.

"I, Tevian of Karst, witness this."

"I, Roxine of Karst, Council Leader, witness this."

"I, Lena of Tirvan, witness this."

Valle sat on his father's shoulders, his hands in his hair, looking up at the rafters. I wondered what they had done with him in the slave quarters. He seemed resilient and cheerful. Very likely, they had made a pet of him. *What would he make of a world of women for the next four years?*

Garth swung him down, keeping a hold of one hand. Ianthe took the other. He looked up at her.

"Hello, Valle. I'm Ianthe. Let's go eat. Are you hungry?"

We walked to breakfast at Valle's pace. I walked beside Tevian, trying not to feel left out.

We ate sausages and eggs, and warm biscuits, and figs in honey, as the sun shone through the windows of Anya's house. Ianthe fed Valle biscuit pieces drenched in honey and gave him a spoon for his scrambled eggs. I watched, smiling. I spoke with the others, feeling myself growing hollower inside, a space the meal could not fill. Finally, I pushed my plate away and stood up.

I had no reason to linger. Garth would stay for a few days. Twice a year, for a week, many sons saw their fathers. Fathers and daughters were almost never united, unless like Maya they had a brother in the same village. Between visits, the boys heard stories of their fathers, of soldiering and the Empire, to prepare them. Garth would come back, if he could, for the next four years, spring and fall. And Ianthe would be here, with his son.

Garth turned my way. "You're not leaving yet?"

"Not quite. I need to change and pack. I'll say goodbye before I go."

I walked the short distance between Anya's house and Ione's. In my room, I changed into my riding clothes, found my coat, and packed my saddlebag. In doing so, I found Sherron's letter to her sister. I had forgotten it. I looked around the house and yard for Ione but could not find her. I would ask Anya to say goodbye for me.

I carried the saddlebag and my coat to the hall, draping them over the paddock fence. Clio trotted over. I rubbed her neck and led her into the stable to tack her up. I worked methodically, focusing only on what I had to do, and not what came next.

The girth tightened, I swung my saddlebag up and secured it, then strapped my coat behind the saddle. I picked up each of Clio's feet to check for stones. When I could find no more reason to delay, I opened the paddock gate to lead Clio out. Tasque whickered at her.

"I'm sorry, Tasque," I said to Dern's horse with tears pricking my eyes. *I will not cry over a horse,* I thought. Clio walked obediently behind me as I led her over to Anya's house. I tied her reins to the porch and went back in, the letter in my hand. Everyone still sat around the table, but Valle now lay stretched across Ianthe's lap, sleeping. Garth stood up.

"Anya," I said, "I nearly forgot this. Would you give it to Hilar, who came from Ballin? It's from her sister."

"Of course," Anya said. "Must you go?"

"I must. I, too, have someone to find." She put out her arms, and I hugged her. I said my goodbyes to the other women, taking one last look at Valle. Then I turned to Garth.

"I'll come out with you," he said. We walked out into the sunshine. Clio whickered at him. He held out his arms, and I stepped into them. He wore only a light shirt, and I could feel his muscles and his warmth. He smelled of lavender soap, and his own, so-familiar scent.

We stood like that for several heartbeats before I pulled back. "He's beautiful, Garth."

He smiled. "His eyes are like Maya's. Did you notice?"

"Like yours, too. Take care of yourself." I hoped he could hear beyond the words.

"And you," he said. "Tell Maya I've never forgotten her,"

"I will."

"I'll see you again," he said, putting out a hand to caress my face. "Perhaps not for a few years, but I will. That's a promise, Lena."

I smiled. "If you don't, I'll come to find you. Farewell, Garth."

"Farewell." He watched as I mounted Clio and turned her head north. We each raised a hand in goodbye.

I pushed my little horse harder than I ever had. We galloped until we reached the end of the grape fields, which forced me to focus on the road, my balance, and nothing else. The cooper called out to me as we galloped past, but I only raised a hand.

At the climb back up into the forest, we slowed. Even then, feeling my urgency, Clio broke into a trot wherever she could. At one switchback, I paused to give her a breather, looking for the first time back down through the trees to the fields below. Beyond the vines, I could see the glint of the sea. Suddenly, I remembered I had told Halle I would speak with her this morning. There was nothing I could do about it now.

When the land flattened again, I kicked Clio back to a canter. We ate up the miles steadily, and gradually I calmed. I forced myself to think of Maya. Jays called at us as we rode through the trees. In the distance, I could see the glimmer of a stream. I slowed Clio. She needed to be cool before she could drink.

When we reached the stream, I allowed Clio a few mouthfuls before I tethered her away from the water. The altitude made it cooler here. I unstrapped my coat from behind the saddle, shrugging it on. I ran my hands up and down Clio's legs, but found no heat or swelling. Clio pricked her ears and whickered. I looked down the road to see a horse and rider approaching.

"Ho, Lena," Daria called, dismounting. "I did not expect to see you on the road again so soon. Where's your companion?" She led her horse to the stream to let him drink.

"He stayed in Karst," I said. "He'll ride to Casilla from there in a few days." I told her briefly what had passed. She said nothing, only raising an eyebrow when I told her Garth was Valle's father.

"I am sorry," she said, when I finished. "Both for Tice—I liked her—and for Tamar. She has driven another daughter away with her pride. But the child will do well with Ianthe. I always thought she'd find a reason to break free some day. What about you? You'll have a cold and dangerous ride to Tirvan, this time of year."

"I ride to the Emperor's camp, to find Maya."

"Why?"

"I left Tirvan to find her."

She regarded me steadily. "Did you?" she said finally. "But you've known about her new village idea for a while. There will be no place there for you, you know."

I looked away. Daria pulled her horse's head up, away from the grass he cropped. "Don't mind me," she said. "I speak my mind. I'd best be on my way."

"Will you take a message for me? I was supposed to speak with Halle this morning before I left, and I forgot. Would you tell her that I'm sorry, and it wasn't intentional?"

"Halle the fisherwoman?" She mounted her horse. "There are two Halles at Karst."

"I don't know. Maybe a bit younger than you? She asked about the fighting at Tirvan."

"That's her." Daria snorted. "What did she want? To talk about how to change our lives, now we know how to fight? She's like your Maya, wants something new, only completely opposite. Halle wants to live among men and be a soldier. She spent too much time with Rolan." She looked down at me. "I'll give her your message. Good luck to you." She raised a hand in farewell and clattered onto the road.

I watched her go, wishing obscurely that she had stayed longer. I had craved solitude, but now that I had it, I wished I didn't. I took Clio over to the stream. As she drank deeply, I thought about what Daria had said. *Maya has made her choice. She wants a life without me.*

As clearly as if she stood beside me, I heard Tali's voice, speaking to my mother all those months ago when Maya had chosen exile: *She said that she would go to look for Garth.*

Garth had unknowingly given Maya the idea—and the courage—to choose exile, but she had not found him. I had. I felt suddenly lighter. I laughed, startling Clio, who snorted and sidestepped. I made soothing sounds at her, and she bent her head back to the stream. *I would go to the winter camp and ask to see her. I would tell her about Garth, and Valle, and I would say goodbye. And then? Then I would go home.*

Riding under the bare limbs of trees, Clio broke into her rolling trot. I let her pick the pace, no longer feeling the urgency of this morning, glad again to be alone. I wondered if I would have a chance to speak with Casyn at the winter camp. I wanted to tell him I had done as he had asked.

From what Daria had said, Halle wanted something even more radical. *Had she formed her ideas on her own, or had they been suggested to her?* I could not be the only one charged with spreading the idea of change, I realized. Casyn had no way of knowing how far south I would reach in my search for Maya, or what villages I would visit.

The sun had not quite begun its downward arc. I would reach the Four-Ways inn in another hour, I thought, if we maintained our steady pace. I could buy food there and grain for Clio, enough for the ride to the Emperor's Camp, where I would stay a day or two, let Clio rest, make my reports. The thought of seeing Maya no longer made me anxious now that I knew I did not come to plead with her.

I felt Clio's shoulder drop and shifted my weight to compensate for the stumble. She slid a bit on the stones of the road, then stopped. I dismounted. She held her near forefoot off the ground.

I ran my hands down her leg, but it seemed sound. Her hoof appeared undamaged, but the shoe hung loosely, and I could see where a nail had worked free. I had checked for stones with half my mind trying not to think of Garth. I could easily have not seen one missing nail.

Cursing, I pulled at the shoe, but I could not remove it. I led Clio a few paces down the road. She showed no sign of injury. I couldn't ride her, but we could walk. I loosened her girth, swapped the bridle for the head collar, and led her on.

We limped into the courtyard of the inn about two hours later, the loose shoe making an odd rhythm to Clio's steps. I took her into the stable yard where a very young apprentice came out to meet us.

"Your horse has a loose shoe."

"I know. Where is your stable-master? I'd like her reshod as quickly as possible."

"Bad luck," the girl said. "She's gone to Casilla to trade for nails and such. She won't be back for a day or two." She bent to pick up Clio's hoof, examining the shoe.

"Is there no one else?" I asked. My boots pinched, and my stomach growled. I had hoped for an hour's rest and refreshment, while Clio's shoes were seen to.

"The other apprentice went with her. She could do it, but I can't. I'm not big enough. Sorry."

I sighed. "Can you stable her, then, and give her some grain and water? She's cool enough. We've been walking for two hours." The girl nodded leading Clio away. I turned toward the inn.

I found Fryth at the servery, and the inn busy. She greeted me by name. I asked for food and ale, and for a word with her when the custom slowed. She nodded. I took the meat pie and mug of ale over to a table. I had eaten little at breakfast, and hunger had gnawed at me for the last hour. I wolfed the pie. About half an hour later, Fryth came over.

"You weren't long at Karst," she said, sitting opposite me. "How can I help you?"

"How far to the Emperor's camp, from here?"

"On horse? About ten hours. You'll not get there today. Better to stay here and start early tomorrow."

I explained about Clio.

"Ah, I see," she said. "I expect Alda back the day after tomorrow, but it will likely be late. I've beds and stalls enough for you to stay here, though. If you're short of money, I can always use another pair of hands."

"It's not that. I just don't want to delay. My obligations at the Emperor's camp will only take a day or two, and then I can ride north. There's an inn in the grasslands, the first after the highlands, where I can work this winter and be that much closer to home when spring comes." I had thought this out, walking Clio along the road. Zilde would give me a bed and work, I hoped.

"I see," Fryth said. "Then you won't want to dally. The grasslands are no place to be in winter. We've had post riders in here who've lost fingers and toes to frostbite riding through them."

"Do you have a horse you would trade me for Clio? She's a good horse, bred in Han." I did not want to give up my little mare, but I saw no other choice.

Fryth considered. "I'd rather not. There's another solution, maybe. I learned my trade at a smaller inn a bit north of here, and I can turn my hand to most things. I can't shoe your mare, but I think I can take her shoes off. At least the loose one," she amended. "Then I'll lend you a horse. You can lead your mare behind you and get her reshod at the Emperor's Camp. Someone will be riding this way, and they can bring my horse back then. Will that serve?"

"Very much." I wanted to hug her.

She stood up. "Let's give it a try."

Pulling off the loose shoe turned out to be simple. With something to give me leverage, I could have done it myself, on the road. Removing the three others took more skill. The apprentice walked Clio around the stable yard a few times while Fryth and I watched.

"She'll do, I think," Fryth said. "You've not far to go on stone, as the track out to the camp isn't paved." I remembered the hoof prints in the mud. She turned to the apprentice. "Which of our horses will Lena's tack fit best?"

The girl considered. "Plover. He's freshly shod. He was going to be ridden to Casilla, but then Alda decided to take Sparrow instead because he can carry more weight. He's in the paddock. I'll get him ready." She handed Clio over to me, running out of the stable yard.

"Chatterbox, that one," Fryth said, watching her fondly. "She's my granddaughter. I wanted her to learn to cook, like her mother, but it was horses from when she could walk. Do you need food for the road?"

"Yes. And a bit of grain, if you have it."

"Grain's in the bin," she said. "Take what you need, then we'll settle up for that and the food."

Piebald Plover stood half a hand shorter than Clio, with feathering around his hocks. Endurance, not speed, was what this one would give me, but if I had to lead Clio, then it didn't matter. The apprentice had put my saddle on him, but a different bridle. "He likes this bit better," she explained.

I thanked her, giving her an extra coin. I swung up onto Plover's back, and she handed me Clio's lead rope. I wanted to tie it to the saddle, but she would not let me. "You need to be able to let go of her if something happens. What if a bear attacks you?" I thought it unlikely, but I saw her point. Plover stood calmly. "He won't kick your mare," Inge assured me. She patted his neck. "Be good," she said to the pony. "He likes to be scratched between his ears."

"I'll take care of him," I promised, signalling him to walk. He moved away obediently, Clio following. She had come to Tirvan on a lead rein, I remembered.

We rode north through the afternoon. I discovered Plover had a gentle mouth and an uncomfortable trot. Mostly we walked, though, for Clio, and because I felt suddenly battered with exhaustion. I rode in an almost trance-like state, feeling as if I had left pieces of me behind, in Tirvan, in Karst, on the road, and only a shell straddled the pony beneath me.

I reached the wide track to the camp at dusk. The sun had set about half an hour before, and the western sky still glowed a deep pink. The evening star hung over the horizon. I guessed I still had a bit of time to ride until it was too dark to see, and the track looked dry and level. I turned Plover's head to ride eastward among the trees.

Half an hour later, I had to stop. I could see almost nothing now, and I still had camp to make. I heard water to the left of the track. I dismounted, tying the horses to the nearest tree, then walked in the direction of the sound until I found the stream. A level patch near the stream would do for the tent. I led the horses to the stream; while they drank, I unsaddled Plover and found the bag of grain, pouring half of it out on the ground in two piles. I led Clio to hers and tethered her, then returned to Plover. I took his bridle off, and put on his head-collar, knotted the rope around a branch and left him to eat.

By starlight, I gathered fallen wood and chose a place for a fire. Once it was burning steadily, I found my bread and cheese and ate. Then I sat by the fire, wondering what to do. I still felt this odd sense of being split into many pieces. Despite my exhaustion, I did not think I would sleep. I made tea, sipping it slowly.

Pitching the tent seemed like too much effort. I spread the saddle blanket on the ground, curling up on it with my blanket wrapped around me. The darkness pressed down on me. I had never slept outside alone before. I could hear the stream and the horses' breathing, and from far off the call of an owl. The wind rustled the dry leaves of the oaks. I drifted into sleep.

I awoke a few hours later, needing to empty my bladder. When I opened my eyes, I could see each tree clearly. The moon had risen, full and bright. I unrolled myself from the blanket, moving a short distance away from my bedding to relieve myself. I could see the horses standing head to tail. Plover raised his head. I thought my movement had awoken him, but he swung his head left and snorted. Clio too looked left. *What was out there?* I had no weapon. I stayed crouched with my heart beating in my chest, watching the horses. They continued to stare into the night, ears pricked. *Whatever they sensed interested them*, I decided, *but either they did not think it dangerous, or its scent came from some distance away.*

I straightened, considering. The sense of dislocation had left me somewhat while I slept, and I could think a bit more clearly. The sound could simply be another horse, or even a person on foot, but that seemed unlikely. Suddenly, a long, wavering wail broke the night. I gasped, and then laughed in relief. A rabbit had just lost its life to a hunting owl or a fox.

I considered building up the fire and trying to go back to sleep, but I doubted I could. *You are being scared by the words of a twelve-year old*, I told myself. *If there were bears, or wolves, Casyn—or more likely Turlo—would have told you.*

"Enough," I said out loud. I doused the embers of the fire, rolled up my blanket, and prepared the horses. I led them back out to the track before mounting Plover. He swung his head towards the west and home, but when I asked him to walk east he did so without balking.

After a while, Plover's easy pace let me doze in the saddle. The moon rose high in the sky and began her descent. The night grew colder, and the wind picked up slightly. My fingers on the reins, even inside my gloves, grew stiff. I was thinking about dismounting and walking when the next gust of wind brought the scent of wood smoke. Plover pricked his ears, picking up his pace. Through the trees, I could see the faint glow of banked night-time fires. Clio whinnied.

I heard a male voice, and an answering whinny from the darkness ahead of me. The fires brightened, as if newly fed with dry fuel.

"Name yourself," a voice commanded. In the sudden brightness of the replenished fire, I could see nothing. A good defensive move.

"Lena of Tirvan. I seek the Emperor's camp."

I heard footsteps, and then a young soldier holding a torch approached me. Plover shied at the proximity of the torch, and I gentled him.

"We were told to expect you," he said. "Have you ridden all night?"

I shook my head. "I slept a while. What time is it?"

"About four hours to dawn. Come. I cannot leave guard duty, but there is a place you can rest, and food and water for you and your horses."

"Can I not ride on?"

"No," he said. "Such are our orders for anyone not of this company. And there would be no point at this time of night. Better to sleep."

Disappointment washed over me, but knew I could not argue. I dismounted, stiff with cold, and followed the young soldier. He showed me a tent.

"There is a camp bed in there on which you may rest. The latrine," he said, and I heard a shading of embarrassment in his voice, "is just over there." He seemed very young. He pointed north. "I'll picket your horses and feed and water them. I am relieved an hour before dawn and will wake you then."

"Thank you. And your name?"

"Darel. Of the third."

"The piebald is Plover, and the dun Clio." I went inside the tent to the promised camp bed and a small brazier, not lit. I pulled off my boots and stretched out. The bed cradled my aching body. *In a few hours, I would see Maya.* I closed my eyes and slept.

CHAPTER TWENTY

WHEN DAREL WAKENED ME, the sun had not yet risen. I found my boots in the dark, pulling them on. Darel had Plover tacked up and Clio on her leading rein. His own mount, a bay with the look of a Han-bred horse, stood ready to go. He did not introduce me to the soldier now on guard duty. I raised a hand to the man from across the camp, and he acknowledged me with a nod.

"It's about a quarter of an hour to the Emperor's camp," Darel volunteered once we had started out. "The woman's camp is another bit beyond that. I am to take you to General Casyn, though. Those were the orders."

"How long has the General been here?" I asked to make conversation. "I rode south with him to the grasslands road where we parted eight or nine days ago."

"He arrived three days ago, he and Major Turlo." Something in his voice as he said Turlo's name caught my attention. I looked at him more closely. In the dawn light, I could see his fox-red hair.

"And the women," I asked. "How long have they been here?"

"About two weeks. The Emperor gave them tents and food. They're camped in a small valley east of our camp. We're not allowed to go there."

"How many women are there?" Ahead I could see the shape of tents and fires, and figures moving. Voices carried in the still air. I heard a laugh, boisterous and familiar: Turlo.

"Perhaps three dozen," Darel said.

We rode into the camp: a village of tents, set up in orderly lines. Men moved outside the tents, getting ready for the day. I saw them looking up at me. Darel sat his horse with a straight back and a serious look on his face, riding directly for a group of larger tents on a slope some yards ahead. I looked around, curious, to see a figure striding towards me. I reined Plover in, grinning.

"Lena!" Turlo shouted. I dismounted. He lifted me off my feet in a hug. I wondered, breathless, what the watching soldiers made of this. Turlo put me down and stepped back. "Cohort-Leader, welcome to the winter camp," he said. "Let me take you to Casyn." He looked up at Darel. "Well done, cadet," he said, smiling. Darel flushed. "Take care of the Cohort-Leader's horses, please." He turned to me. "What happened to your Han mare?" I explained. "Cadet!" he called to Darel, who had begun to lead horses away. Darel turned in the saddle.

"Sir?"

"Get the mare reshod, please. Come," he said to me, striding ahead. I followed him into one of the large tents. "Casyn, look who I've found!"

"I think the whole camp heard," Casyn said, rising. He too stepped forward to embrace me, in the formal soldier's manner. "Welcome, Lena. I am very glad to see you." He smiled at me, and I smiled back. "Have you breakfasted?"

"No."

"Turlo?"

"I'll not say no to food."

"Why does that not surprise me," Casyn said dryly. I laughed, feeling ridiculously glad to see them both. Casyn called to someone for food and drink, bidding me sit while we waited. "No debriefing until you've eaten, Cohort-Leader." I sat on the stool he indicated, looking around. Unlike the small sleeping tents we had used on the road, this tent was tall enough to stand in, and not just in the centre. A screen blocked part of the space, but the rest of the room held a desk and chair, several stools, and a couple of chests. A lit brazier provided warmth. This was not luxury, but certainly comfort, more than I had envisioned.

In short order, tea, bacon, and bread fried in the bacon fat arrived. The soldier who brought it unfolded a small table, placing it in front of me, and another for Turlo. I ate hungrily, Turlo leisurely. Casyn drank tea.

When I had finished and held a mug of tea, Casyn spoke. "You know Maya is here?"

"Yes. I had news at the Four-Ways Inn."

"But you went to Karst first."

"Garth offered to take the news of Tice's death, to let me come straight here, but it was my duty. And I wanted to be there for Garth, to witness his claiming of Valle. I'm glad I did." I told them, as concisely as I could, of what had transpired at Karst.

Turlo muttered "Stupid woman!" when I told them what Tamar had done, but Casyn simply listened.

"Karst breeds proud women," he said when I had finished. "And men. But it sounds as if the boy will be safe and properly raised."

"Yes," I said.

"And what of your task for me?" Casyn asked. Startled, I glanced at Turlo. Then I relaxed. Of course, he knew.

"I did as you asked. The suggestions that we could ask for a new assembly proved of great interest to some, laughable to others, and I think one or two women thought me mad. One woman I spoke to wanted even more, to be a soldier, living and fighting beside the men."

Casyn raised an eyebrow. "An idea fraught with difficulties. But your sense, overall, is that there is support for change?"

I wanted to answer him accurately. I sorted through all the impressions I had gathered. "There are certainly those who just want life to go back to what it was, but most women seem to realize that it can't, or won't, and many don't want it to."

"And then there is Maya and her compatriots," he said. "How do we resolve these divergent wishes?" I sensed this question was rhetorical and did not reply. I swallowed the last of my tea.

"May I go to her now? If you have more questions for me, I will be glad to answer them later."

Casyn looked up. "She will not see you," he said gently. "She has told me so." I started to speak, but he held up a hand. "I won't stop you from trying. Indeed, I have no authority to do so, but I wanted you to know that she will have you turned away. You should also know that her first question to me was to ask about your safety."

"I am not surprised that she has said she won't see me. I heard enough on the road to expect that." Even so, I had held on to a vestige of hope. "Did you tell her about Garth?"

"No," Casyn said. "I felt that was yours to tell, and perhaps a reason for her to see you after all."

"Thank you for that. It was, in the end, why I came."

Casyn studied me. I needed to say these words to someone, to make them real before I said them to Maya.

"I realize there can be no future for us," I said steadily, "but her last words to Tali were that she was going to look for Garth. She's missed him all these years. I have to tell her he is safe."

Casyn nodded gravely.

"I have a note to give her from a girl at one of the inns," I said. "I'll write my own note, saying I have news of Garth, and deliver them both. Do you have pen and paper I could use?"

"Of course." Casyn showed me his writing box, and I sat beside the brazier in the tent to write a short note.

Maya, I am at the Emperor's Camp. I would like to see you, if only for this: I have news of Garth. He is safe and well, and I have a message from him. I read it over. It sounded cold to me, but what more could I say? I signed my name, folded the paper, and sealed it.

"I'll take her," Turlo said, unfolding himself from his stool. We walked out of the camp between rows of tents, along a path that ran up to the top a small rise. Below, in a small valley beside a stream, stood a dozen or so tents. I could see several women working around the tents, but not Maya. Turlo put his hand on my shoulder. The gesture almost made me cry. I wanted to lean into him, to be comforted.

"Come back to the General's tent when you're ready." I nodded my thanks, and walked down towards the tents, my body tense with apprehension.

I saw someone notice me at the encampment. Hands pointed, and women conferred. Two began to walk towards me. They met me on the path, still a good distance from the camp.

"Hello," the older of the two said. She had short hair and kind eyes.

"I am Lena of Tirvan."

She held out her hand. I took it. "I'm Alis, originally from Berge," she said, "and this is Kirthe, from Torrey. Will you talk with us a minute?"

I decided to take the lead. "I don't expect Maya to see me." I saw the flicker of surprise in Alis's eyes. "I've heard enough of your plans, on the road, to understand why." I hoped my voice sounded calm. "But I have two notes for her. One is from a girl at one of the inns on the grasslands. One is from me." I handed them to Alis. I saw her glance at Kirthe. "Please tell Maya that the note from me concerns her brother."

"I'll tell her," Alis said. "I'll give her these when she wakes. She and some of the others were planning late into the night."

"Thank you." I hesitated. "She is well?"

Alis smiled, fine lines fanning out around her eyes. "She is well."

Walking back up the hill, I remembered Garth saying how helpless he felt, waiting at Karst for Tamar to react to our news. But I didn't feel helpless. I felt like I did late in the summer, ready to face what was coming, but still apprehensive. Part of the way up, I turned to watch Alis and Kirthe. I hoped to see which tent they would enter, but they joined a group of women washing clothes at the edge of the camp. I realized they could see me watching.

I thought about crouching at the top of the hill, to watch the camp for a glimpse of Maya, but the idea seemed childish. I walked back between the rows of smaller tents. Men looked at me curiously, but no one spoke to me. The air smelled of wood smoke and horse dung and rang with the clang of metal and shouted commands.

Casyn sat writing outside his tent, the brazier beside him. He looked up as I approached.

"I've left the messages with one of the women," I said. "They saw me coming and walked up to meet me on the path."

"Be patient. I think she will see you."

"For news of Garth."

"That will be what she tells the others," he agreed. "Now, I have been thinking of what to do with you. You need a place to stay, and you are neither of this camp nor the women's. I think it would be best for you to camp just slightly apart from us. I'll have a tent issued to you, and a camp bed and brazier, and my aide will show you where to raise it. Following Turlo's lead, wise man that he is, you will be called by your rank of Cohort-Leader in public. As you should call us by rank, outside of private conversation. The men will follow our lead."

He stood, and almost immediately a middle-aged soldier appeared. I recognized him as the man who had brought breakfast. "This is Sergeant Birel, my aide. Sergeant, this is Cohort-Leader Lena, from Tirvan. She needs a tent and the usual fittings."

"Yes, sir. If you would come with me, Cohort-Leader?"

I followed Birel through the camp. We stopped at a large tent, with wagons covered in canvas behind it. He went inside, to come back out with a folded tent. I took it, surprised at its weight. Blankets came next. "I'll show you your campsite and then we'll come back for the rest of the things."

We walked beyond the periphery of the tents to a small grove of trees. I looked around. The trees gave me some privacy as well as protection from wind and rain. After we put up the tent, I followed Birel back to the stores for the brazier and charcoal, and then for the camp bed. He showed me how to put the bed together. Wooden pegs held the frame, and a rope strung through holes in the frame supported the sleeper. More trips gained me water jugs and other necessities. My little camp came together quickly.

"I'll detail some soldiers to dig you a latrine pit and put up wattling around it."

"I can do that."

He shook his head slightly. "Best not. No officer would, in camp. The General would like you to join him for the midday meal after you refresh yourself."

I looked down at myself. I had ridden hard and long yesterday, and slept rough, and it showed. I had not even considered this when I had gone to the women's encampment. Briefly, I wondered what Alis and Kirthe had thought, but then dismissed the thought. *What of it?* "I'll be there. Thank you for all of this," I added, gesturing to the camp.

"Not at all," he said briskly. "Shall I give you some time before I send the team over?"

I could stand in my tent, but only near the centre. I moved the washstand, filled the bowl, and stripped. I realized I should have lit the brazier when I felt the water. I washed and dressed quickly. As I combed my hair, I wondered if the camp's barber would cut it for me.

As I stepped out of my tent, a team of two soldiers approached, one with a spade over his shoulder, the other carrying wattle panels.

"Cohort-Leader," the one with the spade addressed me. "Sergeant Birel sent us to dig your necessary. Do you want to say where?"

"I'll leave that to your judgment." Did you thank soldiery for such work? Then I remembered Casyn's unfailing politeness to his subordinates. "Thank you."

I walked back up the short path into the main camp. I hoped I could remember how to find Casyn's tent. A few men nodded to me, and a young officer, passing, greeted me by rank.

"Lieutenant," I said, glad that I could recognize his insignia. "Can you direct me to the General Casyn's tent?" He pointed. "Thank you."

Birel was waiting for me there. "Please come with me," he said, without further explanation. We ascended a slope to where a large tent stood, somewhat apart. Birel pulled open the flap.

"Cohort-Leader Lena, sir," he said, gesturing me to go in. I stepped under the flap into the interior. Three men rose to greet me: Casyn, and two others I did not recognize, both roughly Casyn's age. One wore unrelieved black, and the other, the brown uniform of the Empire. I glanced uncertainly at Casyn. He turned slightly toward the man in uniform.

"Callan, may I introduce Cohort-Leader Lena, of Tirvan. Lena, this is Callan, our elected Emperor."

I had absolutely no idea what I was supposed to do. Callan smiled.

"Welcome, Cohort-Leader." I had expected him to look like Casyn, and around the eyes I could see a resemblance. But he stood half a head taller than Casyn and carried less weight on his lean frame.

"Thank you, sir," I said, just audibly, through very dry lips.

"And this is my advisor, Colm," he said, indicating the other man. The third brother, I remembered, the historian and castrate. He looked quite a bit like the Emperor, but less defined, with watchful eyes. He returned my greeting with only a hint of a smile.

"Shall we sit?" Casyn said. I waited for Callan to sit first. *Casyn, I thought, you could have warned me. Young officers are trained in protocol. I am not.*

"Casyn has told me what happened at Tirvan, both at his arrival and during the fighting," Callan said. "I will not ask you to elaborate on that unless there is something you particularly want to tell me." He paused.

"No, sir," I said. "Except that without Garth, now Watch-Commander of *Skua*, more lives would have been lost, a child's among them."

"His acts are known to me," he said, nodding. "Tell me, if you will, what you heard on the road from other women at the inns."

I repeated what I had told Casyn. Colm took notes, and Callan listened intently. When I spoke of Halle, and her desire to be a soldier, he smiled.

"She would envy you, then," he said lightly.

When I finished speaking, he glanced at his brothers before turning back to me.

"What do you know of the Partition agreement?"

"What all women know," I said. "Two hundred years past, an assembly was called to resolve the differences between what the men of the Empire and the women of the Empire wanted. They talked and argued for nearly two weeks, and in the end, voted for what we have today: the women's villages and the Empire's army, and all the rules and the customs that have grown up around those."

"Do you know how many women and men voted for Partition?"

"No," I said, surprised. "I don't." I had never thought to ask.

"It was a majority of both men and women, but not quite six in ten were in favour. Nearly half the Empire's people did not want Partition, but preferred a free choice in how to live."

"And they had to abide by Partition or choose to be exiled." He looked surprised. "I asked Casyn: I wasn't taught it."

The Emperor shook his head. "None of us were. Until Colm found the records in a storeroom at the eastern fort, it had been completely forgotten. Very likely, the actual result of the vote was never widely known. But I have known now for nearly a decade, and over those years, I have found myself wanting to know if we—all of us, the Empire—still want to live this way."

He chooses his strategy and deployment based on a picture in his mind, a picture that changes with season and weather, or time of day, and yet he always knows what will happen, Garth had said. It had niggled at me, then.

"May I ask you something, sir? If this is presumptuous, please forgive me. I am not schooled in the correct protocols."

He grinned. "In this private conference, you may speak freely."

"Someone told me, once," I said, choosing my words carefully, "that in planning a battle, or a campaign, you always seem to know what will happen. When you planned the campaign against Leste, did you see in asking the women's villages to fight, that when it was done, we would have little choice but ask for a new assembly, either to affirm Partition or create something new?" I took a breath, suddenly, deeply angry. "Were we pieces in your game, Emperor?"

He took it calmly, with a brief glance at Casyn. "Yes," he said simply, "and no. The need to have the women's villages defend the Empire against Leste was real. The reasons Casyn gave to you at Tirvan were the truth. But did I see the outcome you spoke of? Yes. But I did not, and I swear this on my honour as the Emperor, I did not manipulate the threat to us from Leste. The Lestian invasion was not of my making."

"And if it hadn't happened? How would you have brought about a new assembly?" I could feel Casyn watching me. I wondered if Colm was still recording our conversation.

"I do not know," he said. "Perhaps I would have just asked if it was wanted."

"I think we would have said no."

"Probably," Callan agreed, "but the seed would have been planted. If the question was asked again, two or three years later, the answer might have been different."

I heard a cough at the door. Colm got up to open the flap, revealing Birel and another man bearing trays of food and wine. They came in, to arrange the food on low tables, add coals to the brazier, and silently leave. Colm poured wine for us all. My anger had gone, vanquished by the Emperor's calm reason.

Bread and cheese, apples, walnuts were handed around. Callan, it seemed, ate much as his men did, although I doubted they drank wine of this quality. I felt uncomfortable.

"Sir," I said suddenly, "please forgive me. I overstepped."

He took a drink of his wine. "Not at all," he replied, easily. "Those who advise emperors should be able to challenge them as well. It would concern me if you did not want to know the mind of the man whose ideas you were spreading. Casyn told me to expect no less."

We ate. Our conversation, it seemed, was over. Afterward, Casyn stood. "I will walk with you, Lena." We emerged into the midday sunshine.

"You could have warned me."

"I could have," he agreed mildly, "but then you would have thought about what you wanted to say. I preferred the conversation to be unrehearsed. You did well."

"I challenge the Emperor, and you call that doing well?"

He stopped. "Yes, Lena, I do," he said. "You are not under his command, for all that we will treat you as a soldier while you are here. You owe him courtesy, which you have given, and honesty, which is what he heard from you. If there is to be a new assembly, women must be prepared to speak their minds and not defer to the title."

I could see Casyn's logic, but it still made me a bit uncomfortable.

"Casyn…General," I amended, as we were in public. "What am I to do, here? You've said you will treat me as a soldier, but where and how should I spend my days? I can't always eat with you. Should I spend my time alone?"

"There is no reason you cannot mix with the younger officers when they are off-duty. Darel, for one, would be glad of your company. Your ponies will need exercise, of course, and I thought you might like to spend some time with Colm, when his duties allow. You might find it interesting to learn more of the Empire's past."

"I would," I said slowly, "but has he the time?"

"He will find a few hours, I think."

After we parted, I walked back to my tent to change into my riding clothes. I found the horse-lines, and Plover, but no Clio. I asked the soldier on duty.

"Gone to be reshod, Cohort-Leader. A nice little Han mare, if I may say so."

"She is," I agreed. "I'd like to curry the piebald. Is there a brush I could use?" He brought me one, seeming unsurprised by the request. I thought of Casyn with Siannon, and Dern with Tasque. Officers, it appeared, frequently took care of their own horses. I gave Plover a good currying while he stamped and snorted with pleasure, rippling his skin under his coat. I remembered what Inge had said, and rubbed him between his ears, breathing in the warm smell of horse. The grooming soothed us both.

The day was sunny and cool, with a light breeze. Back at my tent, I built a fire pit, and from the firewood someone had stacked by my tent, I made a fire, heating water to wash my clothes. The sun had dropped well down in the western sky, and I had just hung the last shirt over the line I had strung between two trees when I heard footsteps.

"Cohort-Leader," Colm greeted me. "Are you busy?"

"I'm just finished." I hesitated. "I don't know how to address you."

"The men call me Advisor, but in private my name will be fine. My brother tells me you would like to learn some of the Empire's history."

"I would," I said, marvelling once again at Casyn's generosity. *With everything he must have to do, he still found time to talk to Colm about me?* "I'm beginning to realize how little I know. Casyn has told me a few things, and of course I was taught a little as a child, but much seems to have been missed."

"Where would you like to begin?"

"Let me build up this fire, first" I said. "I have wine, if you like?" He assented, and after I had put a few more logs on the fire, I ducked inside my tent to find the bottle and two cups I had received earlier from the stores tent. He pulled two rounds of wood close to the fire to make rough seating. I poured the wine, handing him a cup.

"Thank you," he said, sipping. If he noticed the rougher quality compared to what he drank with Callan, he made no sign.

"What was life like, before the Partition agreement?"

"That is a difficult question," he said. "There is nothing written to tell us exactly how people lived. But I've made a study of old records, from before Partition—tax rolls and tally sheets, the court records. Such things tell a story, if you know how to hear it. It would seem that men and women, for the most part, lived their lives together in the villages that now belong to women. They owned land, separately or together, and learned and practiced trades. The army was then a trade like any other: a choice for men, not an obligation."

"Only for men?"

"I think so. I find women's names mentioned rarely in the army's records, and even then, it's not clear what their role is. I think perhaps some of the cooks and launderers may have been women, and even perhaps the horse-masters. But I don't think they fought."

I watched Colm as he spoke. In the sunlight, I could see more resemblance to Callan, but his features lacked Callan's definition and strength. He reminded me of Siane, after her leg was smashed, and she could no longer farm; softer, a blurred copy of her previous self.

"What happened to bring about Partition? I was taught only that it came about because the men wanted to invade north, and the women didn't." I had accepted that, all my life, but no longer.

"There's some truth in that. The Emperor of the day, Lucian, offered free land in the north to any man who joined him in the conquest of those lands. Many chose to join him. The Empire at that time had grown crowded, as unlikely as that seems now, and arable land was in short supply. But then Lucian had to tax the villages more to feed his larger army, and the villages, depleted of much of their workforce, had difficulty providing the food. The headwomen of all the villages—for women have always run the village councils—objected. They banded together and approached Lucian to demand an assembly. From that assembly came Partition and our lives as we know them today."

"But we didn't take the north," I said, frowning.

"Many who would not live under the rules of Partition fled north, so when Lucian marched beyond what is now the Wall, he found an organized resistance and a larger fighting force than he had expected. Some of them had been trained in his army and knew his tactics. His invasion failed, and the border was set. We patrol it to this day."

"When word of the planned invasion by Leste came, did you remind the Emperor of Lucian's failed invasion?"

He smiled. "You are quick. I did not need to. Callan forgets nothing."

We talked for some time. Colm told me of Lucian's successor, Mathon, who had built the road, and expanded the eastern fort. He described the small forts that predated the Wall and then the building of the Wall, when the increasing cold led to more border raids. "Some accounts indicate that before the Wall was finished, women and children slipped through the border patrols and begged for refuge at

Berge where they were taken in. The red hair of their Northern fathers remains not uncommon in Berge to this day, as you have seen in Turlo." He glanced at the setting sun. "I must go. Casyn and my twin will be looking for me."

"Your twin?"

"Callan and I are twins. He is the older, by six minutes, something he never let me forget when we were children."

It explained so much—not only Colm's apparent acceptance in the camp (although who could argue with the Emperor about whom he chose to be his advisors?) but also Casyn's conviction that parentage alone did not make a soldier. I wondered if Garth knew.

"If you like," Colm said, "I'll introduce you to some of the junior officers. It would be good for you to have some companions in camp."

We walked together to a large tent set among smaller sleeping tents. "This is the common area for the junior officers when they are off duty," he explained. The door flaps were tied back, and inside I could see three men playing dice.

"Advisor," one man said, standing.

"Lieutenant," Colm said. "May I introduce Cohort-Leader Lena, from Tirvan. She will be in camp with us for some days and needs to learn our routines. Cohort-Leader, this is Finn, Lieutenant of the Fourth." With that, he was gone. Finn looked to be in his early twenties, stocky and pleasant-faced.

"If you would rather I did not join you, Lieutenant, I'll go back to my tent."

"Not at all. We would be glad of your company. Our own gets a bit stale after a while." He introduced me to the others. They seemed genuinely pleased to have me there. I accepted a cup of ale and found a chair.

"Tirvan," Finn said. "That's quite far north. How fared you, in the fighting?"

"I'll tell you, if you like, but would you answer something for me, first?"

"Certainly, if I can."

"How is it decided who comes to the Emperor's camp? You're from the Fourth, Lieutenant. The young soldier on guard duty the night I arrived was from the Third. And you, "I gestured to the others, "are all from different regiments."

"We're seconded to the Emperor's Regiment for a year," Finn explained. "It's part of every officer's training. Cadets like Darel are sent if they are considered to have potential as officers. I was here as a cadet. I think most of us were. If a senior officer comes to serve with the Emperor, he may also bring some men along."

"How big is the camp?"

"There are one hundred and sixty men, and ten officers, not including the Emperor. And various officers who come and go, like Major Turlo, and General Casyn, although he will stay, now, I think." He paused. "You know the General, I believe?"

"He came to Tirvan in the spring to ask us to learn to fight, and then stayed, to help train us, and be our blacksmith for a time. I had no idea he was a general for the longest time."

"Almost all the men who went to the villages were senior officers, but they did not want that known. I imagine the council leaders knew, in each village, but otherwise it was felt that the villages would rely too much on their expertise and not develop their own. Tell me of your defence plan, and how the fighting unfolded."

I explained, painting them a picture of how Tirvan sat on its hillsides, and the harbour and coves, and how we had planned to use the tunnels and hiding places in the village. I told them of the waterfall, of learning to climb up it, and of burning the forge. I told them of the caves in the hill fields, and how they had almost been our undoing.

"When Pel was taken, we weren't sure what to do." I paused. "But one man we had captured during the fighting was not truly of Leste. He was a spy for the Empire."

"A spy!" one of the other officers, Gulian, exclaimed. "I heard rumours of this. How did you know he was telling you the truth when he claimed to be such?"

"I recognized him. We were children together in Tirvan. He agreed to try to rescue the child, and did so, killing the invader in the process. And that was the end of it."

"Casualties?" Gulian asked.

"Four dead," I said. "And some wounded. One was seriously burned when we set fire to the forge."

"It sounds a fine campaign."

"Did you go to Leste?" I asked. Dern had told me a bit about that part of the fighting. As in the villages, it had been quick and fairly bloodless, except for some of the King's Guard.

Finn shook his head. "Not I. I was here as part of the Emperor's Guard. But Gulian and Galdor went."

They spoke of the island. They described the long and low terrain, terraced with grapes and other fruits and spices, and they spoke of the fear of the women and children in the towns and villages. Only old men and boys remained in Leste to defend the island. When it became clear that the Empire's soldiers had orders not to kill, but to subdue—"Hard, that was, learning to wound rather than kill," Galdor said—most surrendered quickly. Only the King's Guard fought with conviction, and they were outnumbered five to one.

"Of course, we have garrisons there now," Gulian said. "I hope to serve on Leste after my time here. I'd like to be warm again," he added, with a mock shiver.

"But it is warm," I protested.

"Perhaps to a northerner," he grumbled. "I was born in Casilla."

A steward came in with food, spreading it out on the long table. If my presence surprised him, he did not show it. He lit more lamps, placed them on the table, and set four places. We ate roast fowl, and potatoes, and nutty, spiced parsnips with a good wine. Afterwards the steward brought tea, and tiny squares of honey-soaked pastries stuffed with walnuts. I had rarely eaten so well.

"Is the food always this good?" I asked, refusing another pastry.

"Here at the camp, yes," Finn said. He took the pastry I had turned down. "But not on campaign."

"Or up at the Wall," Galdor added.

After dinner, they offered to teach me to dice. Forbidden real gambling, they played for points, "and glory," Finn said. Four dice were tossed from a cup, and the one who came closest to twenty-one, but not over, won. The game involved no skill, just pure chance, and we played as if the future of the Empire hung on the outcome.

Galdor won. Hugely pleased, he laughed a deep, rumbling laugh. Finn stood. He seemed to be the leader, whether by length of commission or by natural leadership, I didn't know. "We're on duty an hour before dawn, so it's time to retire. If you're up that early, Cohort-Leader, please join us for breakfast. Otherwise, we would be pleased to have you join us again, tomorrow afternoon."

"I've enjoyed this evening," I said truthfully. They had demanded nothing of me, the conversation remaining on military matters, food and drink and the dice game. *When had I last simply had fun?* I said goodnight, walking through the dark camp to my tent.

I stretched out on my camp bed, not yet ready to sleep. Someone had lit the brazier in my absence, and the tent was comfortably warm. I chuckled, remembering Gulian's complaints of the cold.

I thought about what he had said of garrisons on Leste. Was Leste now subject to the Partition agreement? How could I not have asked Casyn this, or Dern? If not, could the Empire have two provinces, with different ways of life? Surely that would breed discontent. I would have to remember to ask.

CHAPTER TWENTY-ONE

I AWOKE TO THE TRUMPET announcing watch change, an hour before dawn. The sides of my tent flapped, and I heard water dripping. I swore, remembering my washing.

I put my head out of the tent. The air had turned colder, and a fine, light rain fell. I pulled on my heavy pants and found my jacket. After visiting the latrine, I made my way to the junior officers' commons. None of the officers were present, but a steward appeared almost immediately.

"Would you like breakfast, Cohort-Leader?" he asked. Not by a flicker of an eye or expression did he indicate that he found my presence unusual or inappropriate.

"Please. And may I have tea?"

"Right away."

He brought me tea, a mint-based infusion, and shortly afterwards eggs and toasted bread, butter and honey, and a dish of apples and figs. By the time I finished eating, several other young officers had come in, but none I knew. To a man they greeted me politely, and by rank, but they ate together at the other side of the tent.

I walked back to my tent. The rain had stopped, and the wind whipped the clouds along. With luck, it would clear, so my washing would dry. I needed to move. I had slept well, and sitting about had never appealed to me.

At the horse-line, I found my tack neatly stowed in a brush shelter nearby. I saddled Clio, who idly browsed on a biscuit of hay, and mounted. We headed for the hills above the camp. I had noticed other riders there yesterday, not in formation but out for exercise. A clear trail, pocked with hoof prints, showed the way. On the hilltops, the wind blew fiercely, making me glad of my fleece coat. I set Clio to a gentle canter. She needed little urging, after two days not under saddle. We followed the trail that ran below the ridge-line away from the camp.

The camp sat in a natural bowl, shallow-sided and sheltered. If it were in danger of attack, the hillsides would have to be patrolled at all times. I wondered if that had happened during the invasion.

Below me, the hillside flattened into fields cleared of brush. Training grounds, I decided: places for drill and practice. Hearing voices ahead, I followed the trail around a pinnacle, and saw, in the field below, men practicing archery with bows nearly as tall as themselves. In the wind, many arrows went wide of the butts. I assumed shooting in the wind was the purpose of the exercise. I watched for a while, my hands itching to hold a bow again.

I turned Clio to head back. The wind made my eyes tear. Back at the horse-line, I unsaddled and brushed Clio before returning her to her place on the picket. The exercise had settled me. If my clothes had dried—*if they haven't blown halfway to Casilla*, I thought—I would do some mending. I would need to light the brazier, though, and warm the tent, or my fingers would be too cold to hold a needle.

A cadet met me on the path. "Advisor Colm asks if you would meet him at the Emperor's compound, Cohort-Leader. Do you know the way?"

"I do. Thank you, cadet." I turned up the slope, wondering what Colm might want.

The Advisor waited for me outside the tent. "Good morning, Lena. You have a visitor." He gestured to the tent.

"Maya?" My gut churned.

"Yes," he confirmed calmly, "and a companion." He opened the flap, and I stepped inside.

Maya's hair was short, as short as mine. She looked even more like Garth. "Your hair…" I said, through dry lips. She looked thin and tired.

She put a hand up to it, shrugging. "It was more practical for travelling." Alis stood behind her, near the corner of the tent. She caught my eye, smiling slightly.

"Lena, why are you here?" Her voice held the steel she shared with her mother and her brother.

I took a breath to steady myself. "To bring you news of Garth." My throat felt tight.

"Truly?" she said, with a thread of hope in her voice. "That wasn't just a ruse, to make me see you?"

"Maya!" Alis whispered. Maya ignored her, her eyes on me, challenging.

"Have I ever lied to you, Maya?"

Her face softened. "Forgive me. I couldn't let myself believe it."

"We should sit," I said. "I have a lot to tell you." We found chairs, and I sat facing the two women. Maya and Alis sat close together. Alis took Maya's hand for a moment, giving it a squeeze. Once, that would have elicited anger from me, or at least jealousy. Now, I felt nothing but a numb acceptance.

I took a deep breath. She would not like all of what she would hear, but I would speak the truth. "I was leader of one of the cohorts at Tirvan," I began. I could see her recoil slightly. That hurt, even now. Alis took Maya's hand again. "Tice, the potter, was my cohort-second. We captured Garth on the night of the invasion. He had been serving aboard the Lestian catboat as a spy to the Empire." I heard her gasp, but went on. "He had long hair, braided in the Lestian style, and I recognized him because he looked so much like you."

"He serves, then," she said. I could hear the undercurrent of disappointment in her voice.

"He does," I said. "His current rank is Watch-Commander, aboard the ship *Skua*. But this wasn't always the case. Before he became a spy, he deserted."

"The punishment for desertion is death!" Her voice rose with panic. "How is he alive and serving?"

"He found passage away from the Empire on a Lestian trader, and lived and worked on Leste for some time. Eventually he was captured by the Empire and offered an alternative to the usual punishment: to serve the Empire by gathering information on the Lestian plan. To be a spy. He agreed and did so for three years. We may owe our success this autumn to Garth, Maya. You should be proud of him." I hoped she would not hear the struggle for control in my voice. I heard myself defending—no, praising—Garth to his sister. It told me where my allegiance lay.

I looked into Maya's hazel eyes, so much like Garth's. They glittered with unshed tears.

"Did he speak of me?" She sounded so very young.

Part of me wanted to say no, to hurt her, to dash her hopes. But I had loved her. In some way, I still did. I loved them both, and I could not be cruel. Garth had trusted me.

"He said to tell you he had never forgotten you." Her face blazed with happiness. "One night, he told me that in the back of his mind, when he ran, he always hoped to come back to Tirvan for you, forgetting you would be an adult, with a life of your own."

"I wish he had."

Suddenly, I grew angry. "You can't have it both ways. If you want tradition, Garth should be dead, executed for desertion. The only reason he isn't is that the Emperor Callan recognizes that tradition has its place, but people must move forward."

"Maya and I, all of us, had the right to say no and choose exile," Alis said, her voice edged with anger.

"At Partition, those who would not live by the agreement were exiled beyond the boundaries of the Empire. Would you accept that, if an assembly so ruled?"

"Yes," Maya said, raising her chin. "If a full assembly so rules. But as you said, this Emperor sees that tradition is not all, and the villages have made their feelings towards the Partition agreement clear. Why shouldn't we be allowed to stay within the Empire?"

My anger fled, replaced by a wave of tenderness. "I hope you are," I said gently.

"Truly?" She sounded surprised.

"Oh, Maya, our lives may have separated, but I want you to be safe."

She did not meet my eyes, but simply nodded. After a moment, she looked up. "And I you, Lena. What will you do?"

"I don't know," I admitted. "Go home, I think, but not until spring. Perhaps go to Casilla, so that I can say I have spent a season in the city. Or work the winter at an inn."

She stood. "Thank you for the news of Garth. I won't see you again unless the Emperor commands it."

"Wait," I said hurriedly. "I have more to tell you, about Garth."

"More!" She sat down again.

"We rode south together. In fact, I left him only three days ago, in Karst. We've been together since the invasion."

"Why?" She frowned.

"We both had business in Karst. Dern, his captain on *Skua*, gave him permission to ride down and meet the ship at Casilla, at midwinter. It made sense for us to ride together. Casyn rode part of the way with us, too."

"You went to tell them about Tice?"

"That was my mission. And Garth went to acknowledge a son he did not know until now he had fathered. I bore witness for him. He's there now, getting to know the child."

"Oh," Maya said. She seemed confused, as if she could not assimilate this. *Perhaps she can't,* I thought. *Garth is an ideal to her, not quite real.* Alis studied Maya, looking just a bit worried. I took a breath to steady myself and gave her the last gift I had to give.

"Garth will likely be at Karst, spring and fall, for the next few years, duty allowing. His son is three. You have four years."

Hope bloomed in her face. "Oh," she breathed. "Yes. Yes. Thank you, Lena."

I stood. "There's one more thing."

"What?"

"We never said good-bye."

She looked at me for a moment, then stood. I stepped forward and put my arms around her, lightly. She felt as unsubstantial as a bird. "Farewell, Maya," I whispered, and let her go.

I had known, at some level, what would happen at this meeting since the night at Aasta's inn. I had wept for Maya, the night she left, and many times since. I did not weep now. I walked out of the tent into the wind and clear air, feeling whole for the first time in many weeks.

Back at my camp, I took my lighter clothes off the line and went into the tent. I lit the brazier, and did my mending, then folded and packed away shirts and underclothes, readying myself to leave. The sense of calm, of something completed and concluded, remained with me. I realized I needed a drink. I sat on the bed and was reaching for the jug of water when I noticed a book beside it with a note tucked inside. I opened the note.

"This is my own history of the Empire," the note read. "I thought you might like to read it." It was signed "Colm."

I picked up the book and turned to the first page. In neat, upright script, I read. "In the third year of the reign of the Emperor Lucian..."

I read, or thought about what I was reading, until mid-afternoon. Like learning knife-play, it was an exercise in attention. If I kept my attention on what I read, I did not have to think of my future. When the slant and colour of light told me that evening fast approached, I put the book down to walk to the commons.

Galdor and Finn welcomed me. With a mug of ale in hand, I threw dice, laughing, and nibbled on olives and bread. The evening had become night when suddenly both Galdor and Finn shot to attention.

"General," Finn said. "Please come in."

"At ease," Casyn said. "I won't disturb you, but I would like to speak with the Cohort-Leader. Can you spare her from your game?"

I excused myself and followed Casyn out into the night. He did not speak until we had walked a few yards away from the commons.

"You have seen Maya," he said gently.

"She wanted news of Garth, and I gave it. I won't see her again."

"That is her choice?" Casyn said.

"It's not mine," I said sharply.

"Forgive me," Casyn said. "Are you all right?"

I swallowed and nodded. "I am. I was prepared for this."

"Have you thought what you will do now?" he asked.

"A bit," I said. "I could go back to one of the inns, Zilde's, near the end of the grasslands. She needs help. I could winter there and ride home in the spring. I haven't really made a decision."

"The Emperor asks that you stay until Midwinter's Day. He would like your counsel, and your presence, for some proclamations he will make that day."

"My counsel?"

"Think about the number of women you would want to attend an assembly from each village, and about how they should be chosen. We spoke of this on the road, if you remember." I nodded. The request reminded me of what I had meant to ask.

"Is Leste bound now by the Partition agreement? And if so, will they have a voice in this assembly? Or are there different rules for Leste?"

He smiled. "If you are not council leader at Tirvan by the time you are thirty, I am no judge of young officers," he said. "That exact question has taken up much of my brothers' time, and mine, in the last days. We have a plan, but," he said, "it is for no one's ears, until Midwinter's Day. By then, the governor of Leste will have arrived with his advisors to hear the future of his province."

Leste's former king now governed in name only. All the decisions came from his advisors, senior officers of the Empire. Galdor and Finn had explained it all to me over dice. "When will he come?"

"Soon. The wind yesterday would have made for good sailing from Leste. If they land tonight, as I think they will, they will arrive the day after tomorrow."

"I'll stay." I wanted to see this once-king of Leste. I wanted even more to know what Callan would say, to Maya and the others, in response to their petition. Even with the delay, I should be able to reach Zilde's inn before the worst of the winter set in. Staying would give me a bit more time to think, too.

"I'll tell the Emperor. Will you go back to the dice?"

I considered. I felt oddly light-hearted. "Yes, I was winning."

The odd euphoria lasted through the night, only seeping away when I returned to my camp for the night. Lying on the bed, in the light of the brazier, I tried, unsuccessfully, not to think of Maya. I could see that she and Alis had become more than just travelling companions. As I had with Garth, she would have looked for warmth and comfort in a changed and frightening world. I could not find fault, there. *I wish she had not cut her hair.* I wanted Garth. I began to cry, then—not the racking sobs of new bereavement, but the slow, trickling tears of old grief. I curled up, hugged the thin pillow, and let the tears come.

Several days passed. Garth, I calculated, would have left Karst to meet *Skua* at Casilla. I wondered if Tali had done this, tracking in her mind what she could imagine or guess of Mar's movements. The

Governor of Leste did not arrive. I rode most mornings, spent the afternoons reading, or talking to Colm when his duties allowed. I met some of the other junior officers, and, with permission, went with them one morning to practice archery at the butts. To my pleasure, I outshot half of them.

Turlo came to my camp one afternoon. I was sitting outside my tent, reading in the hazy sunshine and cool air. I had a small fire burning to counter the chill.

"Hello, Cohort-Leader," Turlo called, from several strides away. I looked up, smiling, happy as always to see him. "What are you reading?" he asked, sitting beside me.

I showed him. "Colm's history," he said, surprised. "You're honoured. He doesn't usually let that out of his sight. How are you, Lena?"

"I'm fine. Really," I added, to his quizzical look. I spoke the truth. I felt peaceful, accepting.

We talked of inconsequential things for some minutes. After I laughed at something he said, he looked at me thoughtfully.

"Who's your father, Lena?" he asked then laughed at my startled reaction. "I have a reason to ask. Beyond the usual, I mean. I am far too old to ask you for that reason, more's the pity."

I flushed. "Galen, of the Third." A thought struck me. "Your regiment."

He grinned. "I thought so. You laugh exactly like him. I know Galen well. He's on borders duty. Do you want to send him greetings? I'll see him when I ride north again."

"I wouldn't know what to say. I've never met him."

"Pity," Turlo said. "He's a good man. May I tell him of you?"

"If you like," I grinned. "But try to tell the truth, Turlo."

He laughed, deeply. "I only lie about hunting."

Turlo had left, and I had returned to reading when Colm arrived. I had begged pen and ink, and paper from him yesterday, wanting to write down thoughts, or questions that occurred to me while reading. I greeted Colm.

"I haven't written much," I said.

"That isn't why I have come. The Emperor would like to see you."

"Now?"

"If it's convenient," he said, smiling. I had grown to like him very much in the last days. Grave and thoughtful, like Casyn, he tempered his considerable knowledge with an undercurrent of humour and endless patience with my questions.

After carefully placing my book on the table inside, I accompanied him to the council tent. Callan had a document in his hand, reading, but he put it down as we entered.

"Cohort-Leader," he said. "Thank you for coming,"

"How may I assist you, Emperor?"

He gestured me to sit. He looked tired. Colm found his writing materials.

"If we were to hold a new assembly, perhaps next summer, how many women from each village should attend?"

"Three," I replied. "From most villages, these would likely be the council leaders. But I also think that there should be a way for those women whose views might not be that of their leaders to have their voices heard."

"Go on," he said.

"In my village, there was one woman, Siane, whose views were not those of the majority. She found the taking of life, any life, abhorrent, to the extent that she ate no meat or fish. She died in the fighting, but if she hadn't, I think her opinion should have been heard. Perhaps letters could be written, to be presented at the assembly?"

Callan nodded. "That could be done. Why did not this Siane join the other women who chose exile?"

"She voted against fighting, but she came to realize that she would fight and kill to protect her daughter. She refused refuge with the children during the fighting."

"Bravery comes in so many faces," Callan said. I heard an echo of something someone else had said to me, once. "What else, Lena?"

"What about the inn-keepers?"

"We had thought of that. There is an inn-keepers' guild though, like most guilds, it is inactive. It could be revived and three women chosen from within it to represent them."

"Will there be time?" I asked.

"It will be difficult," he admitted. "I had originally thought to hold the assembly at mid-summer, but I think it will have to be a few weeks later to give the inns and villages time to prepare."

"May I suggest one more thing?"

"Of course."

"When you send word of the assembly, if you can find a way to do so, send a copy of Colm's history to each village. In Tirvan, we have forgotten—if we ever knew—much of what is written there. To make informed decisions, everyone should have the chance to learn what you and your advisors know."

He raised his eyebrows. "An interesting idea," he said. He turned to his brother. "Could we do so?"

Colm considered. "Not the full history," he said finally. "But if it was summarized, leaving out some of the details, then, yes, I think we could. There is a copy at the cadet school. I could send a messenger, asking them to condense the last chapters while I begin on the early ones."

"Write the order, and I will sign it."

"Do you need your book?" I asked Colm.

"No," he said, "I have another copy."

"Thank you, Cohort-Leader," the Emperor said. I took my leave. Outside, in the thin sunshine, the flag of the Empire—a white horse before a wall outlined in grey and black, against a green background—snapped in the breeze. From my reading, I now knew the flag had once had only the horse as insignia. I wondered when the Wall had been added. I walked back to my tent. I wanted to be at this new assembly. I had helped to shape it, and I wanted to see the outcome.

CHAPTER TWENTY-TWO

ELON, THE DEPOSED KING OF LESTE, arrived the next day. I stood among the officers as he and the soldiers guarding him entered the camp under grey, afternoon skies. Elon had a thick cloak wrapped tightly around him against the biting wind. A hood covered his head, and he wore fur gloves. I could hear him coughing. Finn snorted. "He doesn't look much of a king."

"Have you even seen a king before?" I asked.

"No," he admitted. "But I expected a soldier, like the emperor. Not a sick old man."

I shook my head. "Leste barely had an army. Why would he be a soldier?"

Finn shrugged. "I just expected it, that's all."

They rode to the council tent. We watched as the effort of dismounting brought on a bout of coughing that nearly bent him double. One of his escorts took him by the upper arm, helping him into the tent.

I walked with Finn back towards the junior officer's common.

"Who are the officers guarding him?" I asked Finn.

"Majors Blaine and Nevin," he replied. "I don't know them, really. I spoke to Nevin once when I was delivering weapons to his section of the Wall. They both held Wall posts until a year or so back when the Emperor brought them south. Blaine commanded the troops that took the palace on Leste."

"And they've been there ever since?"

"Yes. There's a lot of work to be done there, and Elon had to be well-guarded. My guess is they'll go back with him to be the Empire's force behind the king's nominal governorship." He grinned. "That should suit them after years and years on the cold Wall. Although maybe not," he added, "they were born up there, somewhere. They have the same mother, but different fathers, I think. Nevin's son now holds the garrison that his father used to. Maybe they like the cold. Like you," he said, giving me a gentle poke.

I twisted away from his teasing fingers, smiling. It felt good to be treated casually. I liked Finn. The somewhat staid and formal character he had presented when we first met hid a well-developed sense of humour and a keen understanding of men. I guessed that senior officers were always the topic of much gossip and speculation among cadets and junior officers. I wondered what they said about Callan and his brothers, Colm especially.

"Quite a job they'll have," he said, "bringing the Empire's ways to Leste."

"Will they have to abide by the Partition agreement?"

Finn nodded. "There can only be one set of rules. Anything else would breed discontent, both here and there."

"But men who have never fought and women who have never learned the trades—surely it can't happen all at once."

"Probably not," Finn agreed. "But we can't leave the men to start plotting rebellion. They'll have to be brought into the army somehow."

"What happens to the trading ships?"

"We have traders," Finn argued. "Soldiers who serve on boats often buy a trader at retirement. They live by the agreement. Leste can, too." A burst of laughter from a row of tents caught his attention. "I'd best get those men working. See you tonight?"

I nodded, continuing to the commons. I wanted some tea, and I had nothing particular to do this morning. When the steward brought my tea, I settled down at one of the tables. Finn did not even consider that the women of Leste could start a rebellion. Nor had I, I reminded myself, until this year.

Midwinter's Eve dawned cloudy and cold, the coldest day of the winter so far. Light snow fell. Today, the leaders from the women's camp made their formal petition to the Emperor, and Callan had asked me to be present.

"Maya won't like that," I said to Colm, when he came to tell me.

"But the Emperor will. Callan has the right to choose his advisors, and his audience," Colm reminded me. "You won't be asked to speak, but your presence is requested."

The meeting began an hour after mid-day. I had slept badly, lying awake in the small hours, wondering if Garth had reached *Skua*. I spent a restless morning, grooming Plover and Clio, attending to small chores. At mid-day, I washed and combed my hair, before walking down to the junior commons. Finn's orders required his presence at the petition hearing as part of his education, and we had agreed to meet beforehand.

"This could be long," he said. "Better have something to eat." I helped myself to bread and cheese, and an apple.

"What's the protocol?"

"Follow the lead of the senior officers. Stand if they stand, and sit when they do. We'll be seated by rank with junior officers at the back, so just do what I do."

"That's assuming I'll be sitting with you," I said.

"Where else do you think you'd be?" He grinned. "As long as you're here, Cohort-Leader, you're one of us, even if we don't make you drill troops and ride guard."

"I'd be happy to ride guard. I wish you'd suggested that earlier. It would have given me something to do."

"You still could. I can speak to the officer in charge."

I shook my head. "No point, now. I'm leaving after the Midwinter ceremonies."

"Going home? That's too bad. I'll miss you." He pushed his chair back. "We'd best go. Doesn't do to be late."

At the council tent, the women had not yet arrived. The Emperor's chair of state stood centred against the long wall, flanked by chairs for Colm and Casyn. Three rows of seats extended out from and behind them. As Finn had predicted, we sat at the back behind the senior officers, facing a half-circle of chairs.

I heard voices outside then several men entered. I recognized Elon and two of his guards. "Why is he here?" I whispered to Finn.

"To witness the Emperor's judgment," Finn whispered back.

They sat in one of the front rows. From behind, I could see the governor's greying hair, curly and close-cropped. He wore a shimmering blue-green robe. When he turned to speak to his guard, I saw a thin, lined face. He coughed, but not as badly as he had on his arrival.

Other officers came in, Turlo among them, to take the other chairs, until only the Emperor's chair and the two flanking it remained empty. It no longer felt appropriate to whisper to Finn, so I sat quietly, watching.

Six women entered, Maya, Alis, and Kirthe; the others I did not know. They had dressed in their cleanest clothes, but they looked worn, and their boots were covered with scuffs and patches. The women sat in the half circle of chairs facing us. I hoped they could not see me. We waited.

Finally, the tent flap opened one more time, and Callan entered, followed by his brothers. Callan wore dark grey, with a robe of the same colour, trimmed with white fur. His head was bare. We all stood. The women glanced at each other, unsure, and followed our example.

Callan sat in the chair of state, resting his hands on the carved arms. Casyn and Colm took the chairs flanking him, and the rest of us sat. When the room quieted, Callan spoke.

"We are here today to hear a petition for the founding of a new village." At the side of the tent, I noticed someone writing, keeping the record. "Who speaks to this petition?"

Three women stood.

"Name yourselves," Callan said.

"Alis, formerly of Berge." She sounded calm.

"Maya, formerly of Tirvan." Her voice did not waver, but she spoke quietly.

"Kirthe, formerly of Torrey." All three met the Emperor's gaze.

"Have you the guild document?" Callan asked.

"We have." Alis came forward, and Colm rose to accept it. He unrolled it, read it through, then handed it to Callan, who did the same.

Callan nodded. "These are in order." He looked up at the women. "Who will speak?"

Alis stood. "I will begin." She took a moment. "In the spring of this year, messengers were sent from the Empire to ask the women's villages to break with the Partition agreement and learn to fight, to defend the Empire. I, the other five women here, and the thirty waiting at the camp, said no, choosing exile.

"Those who are here today chose to go south, hoping to find a village to take us in, one that had voted against the Empire's request. We found no such village, but as more women joined us, we began to talk of forming a new village that would be true to the tenets of Partition.

"As we travelled, our numbers continued to grow. We went to Casilla, thinking we might find a corner of the city where like-minded women had gathered, but we could not find one." She paused as Elon broke into a bout of coughing. Then she continued. "We travelled east to the edges of the Empire, and then north again, on the track that runs along the mountains. Eventually, we found a valley where we thought we could camp and be safe. We spent the rest of the summer there, hunting for game and fishing. We survived." She stopped. "I will let Kirthe speak, now."

From my seat at the back, I could not see the reactions of the officers. I glanced at Finn, trying to read the expression on his face. He looked thoughtful.

Kirthe, short and square, looked to be in her late twenties. She spoke clearly: "In the autumn, after we had been in the valley perhaps eight weeks, an Empire's Messenger stopped to tell us the invasion had been thwarted, and the Empire was safe. He was riding north to the Wall, but took the time to deliver this message to us. We thank the Empire for this courtesy." Callan inclined his head, and Hedda continued. "We decided then that the time had come to petition for the right to form a new village. We debated sending only the three of us, but in the end, we wanted our numbers seen, so we are all here."

The Emperor held up a hand. "You are exiled only from your home villages. Why do you not seek work and a home in another village now that the fighting is done? To build a new village—plough unbroken land, clear forest—is an enormous task."

"For two reasons. First, we have been together now since late spring," Hedda said, "bonded by our shared beliefs. And we are mostly young, strong, and skilled in many trades. We would prefer to stay together."

"Why did you not all arrive together?" Callan asked.

Maya stood. "I will answer that," she said. I watched her closely but could see no sign of apprehension. "One of our number, Willa, from Ballin, died of a fever in the late summer. Three of us went to Ballin first to bear news of her death. Two others were late arriving because they had gone north to take two girls home. The girls were too young to choose to join us, and we would not let them stay." Zilde's daughters, I guessed.

"Why did you not send them home immediately?"

"They came to us late in the summer. With the invasion imminent, we felt they would be safer with us."

"Your plan is to keep this village true to the Partition agreement," Callan said. "But what if a new assembly changes the law of the land, and the Partition agreement is obsolete? Will you abide by the law, or choose to be exiled beyond our borders?"

"That will depend," Maya said, "on what the law is. If we cannot live by it, I suppose at least some of us will look for another land where we can live in peace."

"Exiled," the Emperor said again. My heart clenched at the word.

"Perhaps," Maya said evenly. I could see the resolve in her face and hear the iron in her voice. *Like Garth,* I thought.

Callan nodded. "I would hear the second reason you wish to build a new village."

Maya glanced at Alis, and then over at me. Alis started to stand, but Maya shook her head, once.

"No one village could take us all, and wherever we were, our beliefs would once again place us in the minority. We would always be waiting for the next time an Emperor's Messenger arrived, always waiting for the next time we would have to choose exile. We are not prepared to do that. If our petition is refused, many, if not most of us will choose to leave the Empire, sir." Now I could see the signs of strain in her tight jaw, and the tiniest tremble of her muscles.

"If your petition is granted, and the Partition agreement stands," Callan said, his voice breaking into my thoughts, "your village will follow it. You would provide food and other goods to the Empire's armies and bear children by her soldiers?"

"As a village, we would," Maya said. "Whether or not a woman chooses to bear a child would remain her decision, as it is now."

An evasive answer, but not one Callan could dispute. I wondered how much of this he knew already from his previous meetings with these women. He bent to Colm, asking him a question. He listened, nodding. Then the Emperor straightened.

"One last question," he said. "If I choose to grant this petition, I also must decide what land to grant with it. Did you raise buildings at the eastern valley?"

"A few," Maya replied, "but none of any permanence. Brush and log shelters, for the most part."

"I will consider your petition, and tomorrow I will give my ruling. Please return here at mid-morning." He stood. We followed suit. He saluted his officers, inclined his head to Elon, and walked out of the tent, his brothers just behind. Elon followed them, flanked by his two guards. The women left last.

Outside, a weak sun had broken through the clouds. I asked Finn to excuse me, following the path the women had taken away from the council tent. On the far side of the camp, I called to Alis. All six women stopped and turned.

"May I speak with you?" She looked at Maya, who shrugged. They conferred in low voices, then the other women continued on while Alis waited.

I took a leather purse from my pocket as I approached. I held it out to her. "Maya and I held a boat in joint ownership in Tirvan. I leased the boat out for a year when I left. By law, I can't give her half the lease money, but nothing prevents me from giving it to you."

She looked at the purse, and then at me. "I'd be foolish to say no. We'll need money, whatever happens." She took the purse, began to leave, then turned back. "Thank you."

The petition hearing had not taken very long, after all. I wondered what to do now. Tonight, there would be some merriment at the junior commons, Midwinter's Eve being a traditional time of fun and feasting. I thought about the games and song and food I would miss tonight in the meeting hall at Tirvan. Even the littlest babies came, and toddlers fell asleep on benches or the floor as the night progressed.

Traditionally we stayed awake long into the night, sleeping late the next day.

Finally, I went back to my tent to nap. I slept fitfully and lightly, disturbed by dreams. When I awoke, it was dark. I washed my face and brushed my hair, then walked through the rows of tents. Already the camp seemed noisier than usual with voices raised in song and laughter. Inside, the junior commons smelled wonderfully of food. Gulian, seeing me come in, poured a cup of something and handed it to me. It steamed, smelling of spices. I sipped carefully, tasting cider.

We ate roast pig and goose with winter vegetables, followed by nuts and dried fruits. Spirits ran high. "I'd rather be me than the Emperor, tonight," Finn shouted in my ear at one point. "He has to entertain the governor of Leste. It'll be all protocol and politeness, there."

After we had eaten, the stewards and some of the officers moved the tables back, leaving a clear space in the centre of the tent. Instruments—an elbow pipe among them—squeaked and moaned in discord while their players tuned them, and then a lively, irresistible jig began.

I let myself be pulled onto the dance floor. The dance had steps, and I worked them out after a minute or two—a pattern of back and forth, meetings and partings. No one minded my missteps, and when that dance ended and another began, I kept dancing.

Later, hot and sweaty and thirsty, I stood beside Finn when the pipes changed their tone to something low and mournful. The tent fell silent. One man stood alone on the floor. When the drummer began a low, slow beat, he began to dance, slowly and formally, his hands raised, his fingers gesturing. I did not understand what I saw, but my throat tightened.

"What is it?" I whispered to Finn.

"The Breccaith," he whispered back. "It is always danced this night, and at Midsummer, to remember those who will never feast with us again."

I watched the dance, and the faces of the men I could see in the firelight. Some shed unabashed tears. The stewards moved silently among us with trays bearing filled cups. Finn handed me one, indicating with his fingers not to drink. The music slowed, and the drumbeats ended. On a last wail of the pipes, the dancer sank to the ground.

In the silence that followed, Finn raised his cup. "To our fallen brothers."

"To our brothers," the tent echoed.

"And sisters," I said quietly, drinking the toast. The dancer stood to join his friends, and the music began again, now softer, less insistent. The men danced in pairs or small groups. Finn touched my shoulder.

"Will you dance with me?"

We moved onto the dance floor. He took my hands, showing me the steps.

"You dance well."

"I was taught by a woman from Karst," I said, remembering the lessons on the playing field at Tirvan, all those long months ago.

"The one who was killed?"

"You remembered."

"We're trained to," he said simply. "Every man, every officer. And not just to send the messages back to the women's villages or to brothers or sons in other regiments, but so their lives and deaths are not without meaning. It is what an officer must do. We live our lives to honour those who died."

I wanted to point out that I wasn't an officer, but I stopped myself. I had been one when Tice died, and Finn thought of me as such.

The dance ended and another began. Finn guided me through the first steps again, his hands warm around mine. We had just repeated the steps again when another man, one I did not know, came up behind Finn.

"Don't keep her all to yourself. My turn, now."

"Josan, you're drunk," Finn said shortly.

"No matter. She's the only woman here. You don't get her all night."

"I am not dancing with you," I said. "I don't know you, and I don't want to. I'm dancing with Finn."

"More'n dancing, too, I'll bet." Josan said. He lunged forward, grabbing at my breasts. I took a step back. Finn took Josan by the arm.

"Leave us be." Others had stopped dancing now to watch.

"I outrank you," Josan growled, pulling free of Finn's grip. He lunged at me again. Without thinking, I pivoted, ducked, and came up under his outstretched arm to punch him hard in the stomach. He doubled over. I shoved him hard. He fell and lay groaning.

A round of applause made me look up. "Well done!" Galdor called. I stood panting a minute. Josan moaned again, pushing himself up. Suddenly he vomited, to the groans of the men nearest.

"Come," Finn said, pulling me away, back to the tables. He found me wine, and I sat on the bench.

"I think," Finn said, looking at me with respect, "Josan is lucky you did not have a knife."

I took a mouthful of the wine. "He is lucky. I didn't even stop to think."

Finn nodded. "He isn't a bad officer except when he's been drinking, and then, well, you saw what he's like. Are you all right?"

I nodded. "I am. But, Finn, do others think that you and I—?"

He shrugged. "I doubt it." He hesitated. "I'm not a man for women, Lena, and most here know that. Even Josan knows that when he's sober enough to think."

"Oh," I said. "I didn't realize—"

"Why would you?" The music had started again, but this time without the elbow pipes, just the drum and stringed instruments. Someone began to sing. "Shall we join the singing? It's good fun."

"Yes," I said, "let's."

The commons still rang with song—somewhat off-key—when I excused myself and left. The watch had changed an hour ago. The newly off-duty junior officers had appeared at the commons, wanting food and drink, determined to make up for the four hours they had missed. We had all eaten again and joined them in more toasts. I was beyond satiated, and more than somewhat drunk. At my tent, I stripped off my outer clothes, falling onto my camp bed, my head spinning. I heard a voice coming from the camp, young and true, raised in solo song:

The swallows gather, summer passes,

The grapes hang dark and sweet;
Heavy are the vines
Heavy is my heart
Endless is the road beneath my feet.

Maybe Tice's song was mine, now, too.

I slept through the watch-change bugle in the morning, waking only when the sun rose high enough to brighten my tent. I had a raging headache and felt more than slightly sick. I wondered how long the revels had gone on.

I drank some water and prepared myself for the day. At the council tent, people had already gathered. Last night, before the merriment had completely taken over, Finn had told me to get here early.

"By custom," he said, "any off-duty soldier can come to hear the Emperor's proclamations, and they will. It's something to talk about, to tell their sons and their lovers, so expect crowds."

The entire front of the council tent had been opened to allow a standing crowd to hear, if not see, the proceedings. I wondered if I would have to stand, too, but Birel saw me, showing me to a chair inside. Today, only the chair of state and the two advisor's chairs stood at the far end of the space. Rows of chairs for the audience faced them, with two tables for secretaries at the far edges. Some of the junior officers from the second watch joined me. One of them yawned. His blond hair looked uncombed.

"What time did you get to bed?" I asked.

"Maybe an hour before dawn. We broke up when the first watch left to prepare for duty. You left earlier, didn't you?" I nodded. "I should have, too." He groaned. "Maybe I can sleep a bit after this." He brightened. "I heard you really laid into Josan last night," he said, grinning. "Good for you. He's a pain when he's drunk."

The space filled quickly, but the front row remained empty, reserved for the petitioners and for the governor of Leste. Maya came in with Alis and Hedda. The other women would listen from outside today. I guessed, turning in my seat to try to see, (and then wishing I hadn't moved) that most of their camp had come to hear the Emperor's decision.

The governor wore the same sea-coloured robe over his tunic and leggings. When he coughed, he reached inside his robe for a handkerchief. He did not sound well. The same two senior officers walked slightly behind him: Blaine and Nevis, I remembered.

Canvas rustled behind the chair of state, and Callan entered through a door I hadn't seen before, followed by his brothers. We all stood. He too wore the same robes as yesterday, with the addition of a pendant of silver. Casyn wore his uniform, and Colm had dressed in his usual black. He held papers in his hand. They took their seats. We sat, and the tent and the crowd outside settled into silence.

Callan relaxed into his chair. I thought he might stand to speak, but he did not. I wondered if the crowd outside could hear.

"We gather this Midwinter's Day, the eleventh year of my election to Emperor, to hear my ruling on a petition as well as other decisions of mine that affect the Empire. These rulings are being recorded, and copies will be sent to all regiments and villages. I will speak first to the petition, then on several other issues that pertain to the Empire as a whole, and, finally," he inclined his head, slightly, to the governor, "on the future of our newest province, the island of Leste."

"To the petition, then." The three women stood. As he looked at them, I thought I saw the barest hint of a smile around his eyes. My head pounded. "In the matter of the petition for a new village, I grant the petition." I heard a gasp from the women and cheering from outside. *Thank you, Callan,* I thought, watching Maya's face. She did not smile, but I saw the look of strain replaced by one of quiet acceptance. She had reached for Alis's hand, before Callan spoke, and she held it still. I saw Alis squeeze her fingers.

When the crowed had quieted again, Callan continued. "I grant the petitioners the land in the eastern valley where they camped this past summer." He shifted his gaze to address the women direction. "You are charged with following the Partition agreement, or any other agreement that becomes the law of the Empire. If you refuse, you will be cast out. You will be exempt from providing food and other goods to the Empire for a period of five years while you establish your village, but are expected to honour the twice-yearly Festivals beginning in the autumn of this year. I offer you the choice of returning to your village lands now or remaining where you are camped until the spring. If you choose the latter, I will also make available to you the forge and carpentry of this camp, when my men do not need them, to begin to prepare for the construction of a new village. You need not decide this now," he continued. "Is there any reply you would like to make?"

"Thank you, Emperor," Alis said. "May we divide our women, send some back to the valley to clear trees and hunt while others remain here?"

"You may," he said. "You are now the women of your village, whatever you choose to name it, and your decisions on how you order your village business are your own."

"We are grateful for your ruling," Alis said simply. She smiled, looking from side to side at her companions. They sat.

Callan looked over to Colm.

"I now turn to the other matters. It has long been my intent to build a permanent road from the eastern fort to the Wall, at the foot of the eastern mountains. Construction will begin in the spring and will take many years." A new road, and Maya's village would stand right beside it. I wondered who had suggested to them that they look for a place to camp on the eastern track.

Alis frowned. The three women conferred with whispered words and gestures, until Colm cleared his throat.

"In the beginning," Callan continued, "the work will be done by those men of Leste who would not submit to my authority and are now slaves." At the mention of Leste, I glanced at the former king. Elon's eyes narrowed. "But in the future, it will not be so. Already, we teach boys to design and build those structures needed by the Empire— roads, bridges, canals, but they learn this trade as soldiers. Now, this trade will be one of the choices cadets can make at twelve years of age. It will be considered an equal choice to the others, in service to the Empire, and will carry with it all the rights of those in Empire's service. Like the choice of becoming a medic, it will be without the requirement to learn the arts of warfare beyond self-defence."

Now Valle has a choice, I thought. Watching the men, I saw surprise, even astonishment, in the quick glances to each other. Several eyes went straight to Colm. Did they think him the architect of this? Outside, I heard murmuring. I wondered what the senior officers thought.

The Emperor waited, watching us. When he had our attention again, he spoke once more.

"There is one more proclamation," he said, "addressing the Partition agreement. When I asked, in the spring, that the women's villages be active in the defence of Tirvan against the threat from Leste, I was also asking them to break with the agreement made at the Partition assembly. They did so. Therefore, it is my belief, and, I understand, the belief of many women in the villages and at the inns, that a new assembly is required, either to reaffirm the Partition agreement or to create a new agreement. The assembly will take place three weeks after Midsummer. Three women will be chosen from each village, three will represent the inns, and we will have an equal number of men. This will," he said, with a nod to Alis, "include the newly-formed village. The new assembly will be held here."

This proclamation drew more glances, but less surprise, among the men. The women again conferred in whispers. The officer beside me leaned over. "By the god," he whispered, "there'll be lots of talk in the commons and the tents tonight. These are enormous changes, Lena, more than any Emperor has decreed in decades, centuries, maybe. And not popular with all, I think." His brow furrowed as he spoke.

Colm rose to speak to the secretaries. I saw them find new paper and check their nibs. When Colm returned to his seat, Callan spoke again. "Now I will speak to the future of Leste. This fair island is now a province of the Empire. The former king, Elon," he inclined his head to him, "governs there, assisted by a council chosen by me. But if Leste is a province of the Empire, then its laws must reflect those of the Empire. To this end, all Lestian men and boys between the ages of twelve and fifty-five will enter military service in the spring. Next year, we will take boys at eleven, and the following year, ten, until boys leave their home villages at seven to be prepared for service. Men beyond the age of service will be charged in teaching women the skills and trades that will be required of them. Of changes in taxation, and the laws of marriage and inheritance, I will speak privately with the governor and his council." He looked to Elon. "Do you wish to speak?" Elon stood, the effort making him cough.

Suddenly, I heard commotion and shouting, the jangle of harness. Callan raised a hand for silence. The tent flaps parted, and a soldier came in, dressed for riding, and splattered with mud. In his hand, he held a folded piece of paper.

"Emperor," he said, without hesitation, his eyes on Callan. "The Wall has been breached, and the north is attacked. Here is the report." Officers stood at the words, blocking my view. I slid along the seats, ignoring the nausea the motion caused to move to the side of the tent, where I could see. The messenger strode forward, handing the paper to Callan.

Callan broke the seal, scanned the paper quickly, then handed it to Casyn. "Our thanks, soldier," he said. "Senior officers, Advisor, attend me. This audience is over."

Casyn looked down at the paper. He said something, one word, I thought. *A name?* I saw Callan hesitate, a moment of indecision. He glanced at his brothers before all three turned.

The conquered king of Leste stood, coughing, slightly bowed, a handkerchief at his mouth, with Nevin and Blaine at his side.

"Nevin," Callan said, his voice oddly gentle, shaded, I thought, with grief. "Your son, so recently commander in your stead, opened the gates to the northerners. Why?" I looked from the Emperor to his officers, trying to understand.

Elon straightened. His hand dropped from his mouth, returning the handkerchief to a pocket of his robe.

"No!" Casyn roared. He grabbed Callan by the shoulders, pushing, turning him away. The Emperor twisted desperately, hampered by his heavy robes. A knife flashed, turning end to end across the small space. Soldiers moved quickly, pulling out weapons. A body leapt, blocking Callan from the blade. I heard a gasp, a truncated scream. Chairs fell around me, and men shouted. Frozen, I stared at the man dying in his brother's arms. The blood soaked, unseen, into the black fabric of his tunic.

Callan's face contorted as he looked down at his brother. "Colm," he said, the sorrow and love in his voice palpable, "Oh, Colm. I saw the meaning too late. I am so sorry, my twin, my little brother." Gently he lowered his brother's body to the floor and stood to embrace Casyn. They stood with bowed heads for a moment. I looked away. Nausea threatened to overwhelm me.

The Emperor turned to the room. A second dead man lay on the floor: Elon, his throat cut. Callan looked down at him coldly.

"I would like to leave him on the hills for the carrion birds," he said, anger in every syllable. "But his body must go home to Leste. Otherwise, they will say he is not dead, and he will become a hero waiting to free them from bondage." He glanced at the two men who had guarded Elon, standing defiantly beside the dead king. Blood gleamed on the blade in Blaine's hand. Callan turned to his soldiers. "Take them," he said. Nevin shifted, as if to run, but he had no chance.

"As for those who plotted with the king of Leste," he said, pitching his voice to clear steel, "death is their reward. Major," he said, looking to Turlo. "See to it at once. Then join us for a council of war." His eyes dropped to Colm's body.

"My brother will be buried here, with the full honours given to those who die in service to the Empire," he said, his voice gentle now, but still commanding. "Two hours from now, on the hill. Then we ride north." Callan and Casyn lifted Colm's body together to carry him out of the council tent.

I pushed forward through the jumble of chairs and people, ignoring my headache. Officers hurried from the tent, shouting orders. The three women huddled together. A spray of blood stained Alis's tunic. She had been closest to Elon when Blaine had cut his throat. Maya and Hedda seemed shocked. "Come outside." I shepherded them through the confusion of the crowd outside. Maya clung to Alis and would not look at me.

I found the rest of the women standing together, confused. One woman, seeing the blood, turned Alis toward her, searching for injury.

"Are you a healer?" I asked.

"A midwife," she said. "Is Alis hurt?"

"No, just shocked. The blood isn't hers. Take them back to the camp and give them hot tea with lots of sugar. They just saw two men killed."

"Dear goddess," the midwife whispered. "We don't belong here." She began to shepherd the others away.

I called after her. She turned. "There is war coming again. From the north, across the Wall. This camp, these men, will be riding north in a few hours. Look to your safety."

She looked frightened. "Where should we go?"

I shook my head. "I don't know." I saw other women turn to look at me. "I don't know where you might be safe. I don't know what these invaders, and those of the Empire who helped them, want. You must make your own choices." I knew my words sounded cruel, but I had nothing else to give them, not right now. "If I learn more, I'll try to bring word," I added, to soften the message.

Later, I walked down to where the junior officer's tents had stood. Finn and Galdor were overseeing the collapse of the camp. They greeted me, but their orders occupied them, and they made no attempt at conversation. I stood for moment, undecided, before speaking.

"How did the Emperor know, Finn? About Nevin and Blaine?"

"The paper the rider brought," he said slowly, "must have said exactly where the Wall was breached. Nevin's son commands a section of the Wall. And Blaine..." He stopped.

"Was Nevin's brother."

He nodded.

"Why?" I said softly. "And why did Blaine kill Elon?"

Finn shook his head. Galdor shrugged. "The second question is easier," he said. "Elon was their co-conspirator. With Elon dead, there would be no one to bear witness against them. As to why, I don't know," he admitted. "But this is older than the Emperor's proclamations today, older than the battle with Leste this year. I've heard it said Blaine wanted to be Emperor, but realized he stood no chance against Callan in the vote."

"They'll have to increase the garrisons on Leste, now," Finn said. "There will be uprising because of this. Gulian may have his wish for warm weather granted."

I watched them directing their men, and the rapid, disciplined way in which the camp came down. These men knew their work.

"I didn't know him well," I said, after a while, "but I liked Colm."

"We all did," Finn said.

"Not all," Galdor said quietly.

Finn frowned. "What do you mean?"

"I've overheard talk, once or twice. Some of the men thought it unnatural that the Emperor had a castrate as his advisor, brother or no."

"But he taught most of the officers," Finn said dismissively. "And every one of them at camp will be at the burying."

"True," Galdor said. "And many of the men as well."

"I wonder who the Emperor will appoint to govern Leste," Galdor said.

"Casyn," I said, without really thinking.

"The General?" Finn considered. "You might be right. But that would deprive the Emperor of both his advisors, so perhaps not. Bren, maybe." He turned to me.

"Will you be leaving us now, Lena?"

"Yes," I said, "but I'll stay for the burying. I pray you prevail, again, in the battles."

Finn shook his head. "A winter war," he said, "and against our own men. There is no easy victory, this time."

"This is Lucian's war all over again," Galdor said. My heart contracted. The comparison fit. Could we win this war? I needed to go home, I thought, right away. Would I be in time to defend Tirvan? And what would happen to Maya? I shuddered. I felt helpless, tiny. I wanted, more than anything, for someone older and wiser to tell me what to do.

We stood at the burying ground on the windy hillside. The day had turned grey, but no snow or rain fell. I shivered in my fleece coat. As Finn had predicted, many of the officers and not a few of the men had come to witness the brief ceremony. I looked around.

"Where is Turlo?" I whispered to Finn, standing beside me.

"Gone north to scout out the invaders."

I nodded. Who else, for that task?

A piper played a sad descent of notes. We turned to watch four officers, one of them Casyn, bearing Colm's body to the grave. The bearers walked slowly under a double line of crossed swords. They laid the covered pallet by the dug grave, turning the sheet back to reveal Colm's face. As a man, they turned east and bowed. Callan stepped forward. Bareheaded, he raised his voice against the wind. "Colm had no rank, no position in the Empire's service, beyond being my advisor," he said. "But he died a hero. He gave his life for me, and therefore for the Empire. We honour that today." He knelt to place a hand on Colm's brow. "The god of soldiers receive you, my brother, or I will know the reason why when I stand before him myself." He, too, turned to the east, but did not bow, although he inclined his head. The bearers stepped forward again, carefully lowering Colm's body into the grave. The piper played the same sad notes. Callan bent to take a handful of earth. "Farewell," he said, throwing the earth into the grave. Casyn followed suit. Then they turned and walked down the hill. They had a war to plan.

I packed my saddlebags, leaving out only my heavy riding clothes. Outside my tent, I could hear the creak of leather and the clang of metal as the troops rode out. In my hand, I held the history Colm had given me. I walked out of the tent to go in search of Birel. I found him supervising the loading of boxes at the council tent.

"Wait here, please," he said, after I explained what I wanted. He ducked inside the council tent, emerging a minute later. "Go in."

The tent, stripped of Callan's things, seemed even larger. More boxes waited for the supply wagons. Casyn stood, a map in his hand. He looked up. I could see the lines of fatigue and grief around his eyes.

"Casyn. I am so very sorry."

"I will miss him all the days of my life," he said simply. "It should have been me, protecting Callan. But for once, Colm was faster than I."

I handed him the book. "Colm lent it to me." He opened it, reading a few words. Then he closed it and handed it back.

"Keep it. Colm meant you to. He told me he wished all his pupils had your mind."

"He taught me so much." My voice caught, and I looked away.

"And me," Casyn said. He straightened. "What will you do?" I heard an odd hesitation in the question. I looked up at him. His brother had died violently this afternoon, and yet he went on, defending his Empire, putting his grief behind him. How we respond to circumstance is what defines us, he had told me once. I owed him so much. I realized I loved him, as I supposed I might have loved a father. I took a deep breath. There were too many choices, or only one.

"What would you have me do, General?" I said. I glimpsed a brief smile in his eyes.

"Look at this map with me, Cohort-Leader," he said. He spread it out on the big table still standing against one wall. "We are here," he said, pointing, "and here is where the hills of the north give way to the central grasslands. You remember?" I nodded, remembering how my heart had lightened at the sight of the sea of grass below me, so many days and weeks before. "We need to engage the rebels well north of this escarpment. If we are on the grasslands and they are in the hills, they will have the advantage of ambush and retreat into the valleys and rocks, and we will be open to them, to be picked off like deer at the autumn cull. We may already be too late, but we must try, and that means a fast ride north. At the same time, we must send more men to Leste. Insurrection there is a certainty." He smiled, grimly. "We are again where we were when I first came to Tirvan, but this time we have an enemy both within and without and not the strength of men to meet both. The planned response to an invasion from the north, a breaching of the Wall, was made years ago, but that plan was known to Blaine and Nevin, and has doubtless been passed on to Nevin's son, who opened the gates to the northerners. We must use another plan, but there is no certainty of success."

"You need every man."

"And every woman. But this is harder than asking you to fight against Leste. Now we fight, in part, against our own people. I cannot compel anyone, and I would not try. But every woman who would choose to come, whether to battle or to serve as messengers and medics, grooms and cooks, everyone is needed, if we are to hold our Empire."

And if we don't, Tice and Siane and Colm have all died for nothing. Live your life to honour those who died, Finn had said. I thought of Halle, in the council hall at Karst. She would come. How many others?

"There is no one to protect Maya and her women," I said slowly.

He shook his head. "We cannot spare anyone. I sent a cadet to tell them, to advise them to try for Casilla. The city will be safer, I think."

"Thank you," I said. That would have to do, for now.

"I am sending cadets east to Casilla and the eastern fort with messages, but we would not send even those, if there was another way. Will you ride west, Lena? Ride to the Four-Ways Inn, and back to Karst, as Emperor's Messenger?"

"Where do women go, who would join you?"

He pointed down at the map. "Here," he said. "Where the hunting trail meets the river. Tell them to bring provisions, extra horses, heavy clothes, tents if they can."

I nodded. "I need an hour to break camp and to pack."

He looked at me steadily for a minute. "Make it half that. I will have Birel bring you the letter naming you as Emperor's Messenger. He can help you pack. Ride your mare. The pony will keep up if led behind unburdened. You can leave him at the Four-Ways Inn and ride even faster. Go now, Lena."

I swallowed and nodded, turning to leave. Tears burned hot behind my eyes. I had just ducked through the tent flaps when Casyn called to me.

"Cohort-Leader," he said. "Will you come north?"

I turned to face him: a dark figure against the canvas of the tent. I could see the motion of his hands as he rolled the map.

"I don't know," I said. "If.... if I can, General."

The wind moved the tent flaps behind me. I saw him nod.

"Go," he said. "And thank you."

In my camp, I packed Colm's book, and with it the paper and writing instruments he had given me, into my saddlebag. I had begun to write an account of these last months, beginning with the day Casyn had arrived. I had thought I would have time to work on it at the inn or in the grape fields.

Birel arrived, bringing the letter with the Emperor's seal. I stowed it in my saddlebag as well. We collapsed the tent, rolling and tying it.

A soldier led Clio up, with Plover on a leading rein. She carried my tack, and my travelling gear. Clio whickered at me. I rubbed her nose. Birel threw my bags over the back of the saddle. I mounted and took the reins, glancing east, towards the women's camp. Already the sky grew dark. The winter sun was low on the horizon.

"Go with the god, Cohort-Leader," the sergeant said. The soldier's benediction. He saluted me. I returned the salute. Then I turned Clio's head west, toward the setting sun, and rode.

Lightning Source UK Ltd.
Milton Keynes UK
UKHW010836251120
374071UK00003B/188